Town Hall

A Novel

By
Clay Hutto

Published by HARBINGER PRESS
5390 NE 35th Place
Portland, Oregon 97211

Library of Congress Control Number:
2015944125

Hutto, H. Clay, 1957 –
Town Hall / Clay Hutto
ISBN 978-0-9799088-1-1
Satire – Newspapers – Politics – Oklahoma –
Mortuaries – 20th Century – Fiction.

For Grant,
the talented young journalist
and
Tammy Wynette
for her musical inspiration

Prologue

Buffalo City is a town of 9,569 souls in Beckham County, Oklahoma. It is located on Interstate 40 and Historic U.S. Route 66 in western Oklahoma near the Texas border, approximately 120 west of Oklahoma City and 130 miles east of Amarillo, Texas. Founded in 1901, Buffalo City has endured the Dust Bowl, tornadoes, flash floods, wind storms, prairie fires, blizzards, droughts, Comanche raids, various forms of pestilence, economic upheavals such as the Great Depression, and sundry other tribulations, both natural and man-made. In contrast to all the ills it has experienced, nothing much of consequence has ever happened in Buffalo City. The townspeople, a hardy and resilient lot, have persevered but none have accomplished anything of historical significance. In fact, for all of its existence Buffalo City has been an obscure, politically insignificant town.

That is, until the spring of 1979, when the President of the United States, one James Earl Carter, Jr., commonly known as Jimmy, made good on a campaign promise to return to the small and colorless city. This is the story of that monumental event.

Chapter One
Monday, March 19, 1979

"It's been confirmed!" exclaimed Millard Greeley, publisher and editor of the *Buffalo City Stampede* (and also mayor of the town) as he burst into the newsroom. Dale Smith and the three other newsroom employees looked up from their typewriters, not with alarmed expressions because Millard Greeley occasionally burst into the newsroom exhorting them to cover a particular story or to pronounce a new policy or to offer a penetrating political insight. They did, however, stop typing their respective stories.

Millard Greeley, a man of average height but above average girth, stood before them wearing dark slacks, a white shirt, a paisley tie, but without his suit jacket because he always took that off while working in the editor's office although the nature of his work was something of a mystery since the only tangible fruit of his labor was the weekly editorial that was published in the Sunday edition.

"I say it's been confirmed," he repeated, which Millard Greeley often did. In fact, Dale Smith had once joked with Dwight Willard that the newspaper ought to be called the *Buffalo City Repeat*.

The four newsroom employees, Dale Smith, sports editor; Dwight Willard, managing editor; Floyd Byrd, roving reporter and photographer; and Rosemary Rogers, the features editor, waited to hear more.

Millard Greeley, as if performing in a play, paused dramatically. He waited until his four employees had focused all their attention upon him then he said a simple declaration: "President Carter is coming to Buffalo City."

Rosemary Rogers stood up from her desk and began clapping. Even the dour Floyd Byrd duplicated her ovation. Dale Smith and Dwight Willard, however, remained seated but they did look at one another with impressed expressions.

The applause brought George Sinclair, the business manager, and Mrs. Milford, the elderly officer manager, out of their offices. When they were told the historical news, they began clapping, too. Down the hallway, peering in through the doorway that lead to the composing room, were the two middle-aged women who worked there along with the older man who typed the hard copy into the Compugraphic machine.

"Congratulations," shouted George Sinclair, a tall, graying man of sixty. He extended his large hand to the publisher, the editor, the mayor, the man who had now put Buffalo City on the map.

Millard Greeley shook hands with his business manager and nodded at the rest of the employees and allowed the applause to subside before he spoke.

"Congratulations to us all," Greeley pronounced. "I received the phone call just minutes ago from the President's travel secretary in the White House. President Carter will arrive this Saturday for a town hall meeting. He'll stay the night, attend church Sunday morning, and then depart. That means we don't have much time to prepare. I want the *Buffalo City Stampede* to be functioning at the highest possible level. After all, our coverage will be not only for our readers but also for posterity itself! Now, there's more to discuss and more plans to be made but that's enough at present. So, let's get back to work. We have a paper to get out!"

With that final exclamation, Millard Greeley turned and bustled off. George Sinclair and Mrs. Milford retreated to their offices, and the four newsroom employees returned to their work. Dale Smith, the youngest at twenty-one, didn't quite understand what was going on. Why would the President of the United States come to Buffalo City? He knew the President had recently started a campaign of visiting towns and cities in the country to defend and advance his political objectives. The President's popularity had been in decline for several months and much of the country blamed his lackluster leadership for the feeble economy, the growing unemployment and high inflation in particular. But why would the President come to a town as small and insignificant as Buffalo City?

Deadline was approaching, so Dale had to get busy. His questions would have to wait.

-II-

Millard Greeley left the newspaper, crossed Main Street, turned left, passed the Carnegie Library with its rather ornate façade, and proceeded to the Buffalo City Municipal Building one block away. As he hustled down the sidewalk, nodding at the citizens (and voters!) he passed, he remembered the wonderful sensation of the applause he'd generated just a few minutes before with the announcement of the President's visit. He liked hearing applause, especially as an acknowledgment of one of his noble deeds. As a boy, he'd never been praised for anything. Poor at sports, romantically awkward, not an especially bright student, Millard Greeley the boy had never heard that delightful sound of approval. No one had ever cheered his athletic exploits; in fact, after embarrassing debacles in little league baseball and junior high football and basketball (he was big for his age but utterly uncoordinated and, truth be told, something of a sissy), he retired from competitive sports and since then had never touched a bat, a club, or a ball of any kind.

All through school he had been a mediocre student. Science and math in particular had bored and puzzled him. He'd never won any academic prizes. He'd never made any academic honor societies. He did believe he had talent with words, both written and spoken. He had particularly enjoyed speech classes and considered himself something of an expert debater. As a teenager he'd even tried his hand at composing verse. But when he submitted poems to his high school and college literary magazines (under a pseudonym because he felt embarrassed revealing his innermost thoughts and feelings even in the sonnet form) and his creative work had been rejected he had stopped writing poetry. In fact, he banished his dreams of becoming an author from his mind and instead focused on writing journalism. At Oklahoma University he had majored in journalism, a practical choice considering his father published the *Buffalo City Stampede* and upon graduation Greeley would return to help his father run the newspaper. But even his practical experience working for his father as a youth didn't help him in the college studies. He consistently received B's and C's, even in his journalism courses. One journalism professor had the temerity to tell him that his rather ornate writing style would be better suited for churning out potboiler novels than writing concise newspaper articles.

His social accomplishments were just as dismal. What few dates he had in high school and college were painfully pointless since the girls he'd escorted to musical concerts or plays invariably shirked from any romantic contact when the date concluded. In less intimate social situations, Greeley acquitted himself better. He considered himself an accomplished raconteur and even acquired a reputation for being something of a wag in his fraternity (although a few of his frat mates had given him the disagreeable nickname "Bladder"). But it wasn't until he returned home to Buffalo City that he clearly saw Possibilities in his life. Knowing that one day he would inherit the *Stampede* gave him confidence. He discovered that he had a knack, a gift really, for superficial social interaction. His facility for small talk and his rather unctuous good manners made favorable impressions on ordinary townsfolk, older women in particular, and Greeley began to realize that he could parlay these underestimated skills into something quite useful: a career in politics.

When he announced his ambitions to his father, Millard Greeley, Sr., the rather imperious old man was unimpressed, unconvinced, and unpersuaded. Part of the problem was that the junior Millard Greeley was so utterly different in bearing, appearance, and temperament than the senior Millard Greeley. A casual observer, in fact, would never make the genetic connection between father and son. Where the son was roly-poly and boyish, the father was tall and authoritative. Where the son was talkative and flamboyant, the father was laconic and austere. Where the son was hyperbolic, the father was understated. In fact, the differences were so pronounced that Greeley junior long suspected that his father not only disapproved of him but occasionally had doubts about his filial authenticity.

In fact, had not Mrs. Greeley been a woman above reproach, had not been a woman of exquisite sensibility and genuine religious fervor, Millard Greeley senior might have been justified in having some parental doubt. Of course, his wife, sweet-tempered and gentle, could never deceive him so the senior Greeley had to reluctantly accept the biological fact that Millard junior was indeed a product of his seed.

Eventually, Millard Greeley senior reluctantly assented to his son's political ambitions. If nothing else, getting involved in small town politics would keep the boy out of the newspaper office to some degree and that would improve the paper's efficiency.

Greeley junior's first campaign was for a city council seat. An indefatigable campaigner, he actually knocked on every Buffalo City resident's door during the contest, and easily won against an irascible old rancher who more than once had said he didn't "give a good damn" if he won or not.

Four years later, at the age of thirty, Millard junior set his sights on being mayor. He employed the same energetic campaign strategy and enjoyed the full support of the *Stampede* for his quest and he narrowly won the fiercely contested election. Of course, under the Buffalo City governmental structure the mayor didn't wield much power but that didn't faze Millard junior. He actually preferred the ceremonial aspects of his position to the practical use of power.

Unfortunately, a week after his son won the office, Millard Greeley senior passed away. He'd married rather late in life, had sired only one child, but he seemed to be such a hale and hearty man of seventy that when he collapsed in his office from a massive coronary it came as a shock to everyone.

And no one was more shocked than Millard Greeley, no longer a junior. He'd always felt something like awe (or was it simply fear?) for his father, a man who lived a rugged and individualistic life, who'd worked a variety of tough jobs from oil roughneck to cowboy to soldier (he'd enlisted after the bombing of Pearl Harbor at the age of 34 and had been wounded at Sicily) and had also educated himself in literature, arts, political philosophy, and the sciences. He was the kind of man who could go to a bar, down three whiskeys in a row and not get drunk, get into a brawl, and while engaged in fisticuffs quote Kipling.

Millard's father, after his medical discharge from the army, had accompanied an army buddy back to his hometown of Buffalo City where Millard senior bought the struggling weekly newspaper. He secured a loan from his buddy's banker father (Mr. Quigley), upgraded the facilities and equipment, turned the paper into a daily, and within a few years had made the *Stampede* the best run and most prosperous newspaper in western Oklahoma.

With the death of Millard senior the son became the sole publisher and editor of the *Stampede*. That alone would be enough to daunt a lesser man. But added to Millard Greeley's responsibilities was the leadership position of mayor. Could Millard Greeley succeed at both demanding positions? Greeley suspected that many people had private doubts, but he had indeed succeeded as evidence by his latest coup, the pending arrival of the President of the United States.

Oh, how Greeley wished his father was still alive to see this amazing accomplishment! Perhaps that would have impressed the demanding old man. But if his father was gazing down from heaven (and Greeley was certain of that) then the old man was no doubt beaming with pride while at the same time shaking his hoary head at the unexpected turn of events.

Millard Greeley opened the glass door to the city municipal building and strode inside. He saw the receptionist sitting at the desk, but when his eyes scanned the lobby he didn't see anyone present. Then he remembered it was just after noon.

"Oh, *hello*, Mr. Mayor!" greeted the attractive young woman.

"Greetings, Susan," said Greeley.

He paused a moment to take in the young lady's comeliness. Long blonde hair, big green eyes, a pouting mouth, and a tantalizing figure clearly discernible under the clinging forest green garment she wore. Susan, the youngest daughter of the city's lone psychiatrist, Dr. Arnold Smith, was going to be one of the contestants for the title of Miss Buffalo City to be held Friday night. What a weekend this would be! Miss Buffalo City on Friday followed by a visit of the President on Saturday.

"Apparently, everyone's out for lunch," Greeley said, trying to mask his disappointment. He'd been looking forward to making the announcement of the President's visit to a full assembly.

"Oh, yes, they *are*, Mr. Mayor," Susan said in a soothing, supplicating voice. "I think several of the council went over to *The Beefeater*."

Greeley pursed his lips but not wanting to appear disturbed – for he thought it important for leaders to always project confidence and good cheer, especially in front of young people – he tried to beam a smile at the sympathetic receptionist. Unfortunately, Greeley had a rather small mouth with unimpressive teeth. At that moment, he wished he had that famous Carter full-mouthed grin.

But the effect worked on Susan as her smile broadened in response to his.

"Well, I'll amble off to my office for a little while. Any messages?"

"No, I'm *sorry*, Mr. Mayor, nothing at present."

Feeling a little piqued (no messages for him! Didn't the oblivious denizens of Buffalo City know what political genius they had for a mayor?), Greeley gave Susan a curt nod but with a smile and proceeded through the lobby to his office. Walking down the hallway he happened to glance into the city council chambers and spied the tall figure of man whose back was turned to him. Greeley brightened. At least there was one fellow present who would appreciate the significance of his accomplishment.

Greeley turned to enter through the doorway, getting ready to smile his broadest smile, when the figure, clad in an expensive black suit, turned to him and Greeley saw, to his disappointment and even distaste, that the man was Byron Mors.

"Oh, hello, Millard."

"Greetings Byron."

An awkward pause followed. Neither man particularly liked the other. They had grown up together in Buffalo City. They had attended the same grade school, same junior high, same high school, had even attended OU at the same time but fortunately pledged to different fraternities and therefore hadn't traveled in the same social circles. They had one more thing in common. Both were sons of successful fathers. Otherwise, they were opposites. Byron, tall and lean, quiet and observant, possessed a reassuring kind of charm that was quite useful in his necessary but rather distasteful occupation. Unlike Greeley, Byron had been a popular boy in school. He made honor societies. He excelled at sports, quarterbacking the football team, starring as the shooting guard on the basketball squad, and pitching for the baseball team. Of course, he'd been something of a Romeo as a youth, dating all the attractive girls in high school. Greeley had expected that Byron would attain similar success at college and Byron certainly seemed headed in that direction, Phi Beta Kappa and BMOC and all that sort of rot, but something had mysteriously happened to him during his junior year at OU. He left school, even left the state, and spent almost two years in California before returning home and eventually finishing his studies at OU as a mortuary science major. And why that major? Because his family owned and operated the largest and most successful funeral home not only in Buffalo City but all of western Oklahoma. When Byron Mors returned to Buffalo City to eventually assume leadership of Mors Funeral Home and Peaceful Prairie Chapel, Greeley had been secretly pleased that his nemesis had failed to be something more impressive but he still resented Byron's presence in Buffalo City. Because no matter how lofty Greeley's accomplishments, he knew Byron would never be impressed.

In fact, that was the reason for Greeley's sudden reluctance to break the news.

"Something up, Millard?"

That was a characteristic of Byron's that Greeley particularly disliked. A certain kind of intuition. Perhaps Greeley disliked it because he sensed he lacked it.

"You could say that, Byron."

Byron Mors waited. Greeley avoided looking at his eyes. They were arresting blue eyes, rather dark of hue, which made an interesting contrast to his black hair. The expression in those blue orbs could be penetrating in a kind of icy incisiveness or they could convey a dignified sympathy that Greeley imagined was especially effective in dealing with his bereaved customers.

"Well, actually, Byron, I just had some wonderful news. The President is coming to Buffalo City."

"President Carter is coming here? When?"

Greeley noted how Byron asked that question in

a completely even if not unimpressed way. No undue emotion. He wasn't impressed or astonished.

"This Saturday. And he's going to stay overnight in Buffalo City. In fact, he's going to stay the night at my mother's house."

Byron Mors lifted one of his dark, rather thick eyebrows.

"Yes, it's quite an honor for the town," continued Greeley. "The President is going to convene a town hall meeting Saturday night soon upon his arrival. I think I can say without question that this event will be the most monumental occasion in Buffalo City history!"

"And quite an honor for you," said Byron in his uninflected voice.

"I'm just pleased to be of service to the citizens of Buffalo City."

"And when are going to announce this historic occasion?"

"There will be a story in today's *Stampede.* I will also request some airtime at KBUF. And I intend to inform the members of the city council soon."

"You've informed one already."

"Yes, so I have."

Byron had been elected to the city council just last year. A Republican, just like his father, his election made it three Republicans and two Democrats on the city council. Occasionally, an impasse occurred during city council business because Greeley, a Democrat, made the vote a tie. And the most recalcitrant Republican was always Byron Mors.

"Well, I must be off," Greeley said with feigned good cheer. "There's much to prepare for. And so little time."

Byron nodded and Greeley promptly left the chamber and headed for his office at the end of the hall. He opened the door, appreciated the patriotic splendor of the red, white, and blue color scheme (rug white, curtains blue, chairs red), and seated himself behind his mahogany desk. He picked up the telephone in preparation for one of many phone calls. Perhaps the first person to call would be his wife, Carol. She should be home with little Millard, age three. There were several other people to notify as well, a dozen details to attend to, a schedule to be arranged, and most importantly, deciding where the President's town hall would take place.

But Greeley didn't make the call. Instead he hung up the telephone and stared at the large map of Oklahoma and the Texas panhandle affixed to the opposite wall. He tried to summon the enthusiasm and optimism and good will that he'd felt after he'd received the telephone call from the White House. It was like a dream come true and he had been buoyed in a state of bliss. How he had looked forward to notifying everyone, especially the VIPs of Buffalo City, some of those movers and shakers who still regarded him with condescension! But now his mood had changed. It was that unpleasant encounter with Byron Mors. Instead of feeling pride for his accomplishment, he felt peevish. Even worse, he felt a strange sensation of dread seep into his mind. Greeley tried to shake the evil feeling. It was absurd to feel such anxiety. Everything was going fantastic! History was about to be made! And yet a nameless kind of fear, a nagging foreboding, a dark doubt remained inside his mind and he attributed all of that to the unfortunate meeting with that damned undertaker!

-III-

Dale Smith joined Dwight Willard in the press-room as they watched the two pressmen, Percy Pollack and Harley Dee Grubbs, strap on the metal plates. Five minutes later, Pollack pushed the green go button and the press began rolling. The eight cylinders churned, the stream of newsprint rolled from the first to the eighth cylinder, and a loud, whirring sound of moving machine parts and a softer whizzing sound of paper ripping through the air filled the press-room.

Dale and Dwight Willard walked over to the last station of the press where the printed paper was being cut and folded and Dwight reached down for an issue. He scrutinized the front page; still thinking the 72-point headline *President Carter to Arrive in Buffalo City Saturday* was too large. After all, a war hadn't been declared. But Greeley had insisted on the largest headline size possible. Dwight then opened the paper and scanned the rest of the eight pages to spot any glaring errors. Not seeing any, Dwight signaled Pollard to pick up the speed. The press pulled the paper through its rollers at an even greater speed and furiously spat the newspapers out at the other end. Dale and Dwight watched for a few minutes. Monday was a light news day. There would be only two eight-page sections.

The press made such a din that it was difficult talking in the press-room so Dale motioned Dwight to come outside. They walked through the side door that led to the loading dock and walked down the steps. The delivery truck was already present, parked next to the dock, waiting for the steel garage door to open so the newspaper bundles could be hefted onto the truck's bay. Dale and Dwight walked past a small group of men waiting for the press run to conclude and turned the corner. Dale paused and Dwight, a man of average height and build who had a mostly ordinary face except for a droopy light brown mustache, leaned against the brick wall.

"So why is the President coming to Buffalo City?" Dale asked.

Dwight grinned underneath his droopy mustache. "He's been here before."

"He has? When?"

"Back in '76. When he was running for president the first time."

Dale didn't remember that. He'd been a sophomore in college and he hadn't paid much attention to politics.

"Yep, he stopped in Buffalo City early in his campaign and appreciated his reception so much that he promised, if elected, he'd return. So, I guess he's keeping his promise."

"That sounds unusual."

"Coming to Buffalo City or a politician keeping his promise?"

Dale grinned. "Both I guess."

"It was big news back in '76, although he only made a campaign stop for a few hours. I'd just started working here at the paper. It'll even be bigger news this time."

"I'll say. Didn't Greeley say Carter's going to stay overnight?"

"That's what he said."

"Sounds like a lot of time to spend in such a little – " Dale was about to say "crummy town" but he caught himself in time.

Dwight smiled his melancholy smile with his droopy mustache. "You don't seem to have a very high opinion of our fair town."

"It's not that exactly," Dale said, although in his ten months of living in Buffalo City he did find the town rather boring. "I mean, the President of the United States is coming to Buffalo City. And he's going to stay the night here. You'd think he'd have more important things to do."

"Carter's been doing these town halls for several months now. I guess there must be some kind of political benefit to it. Makes him look more like a man of the people or something."

"But has he ever been to a town as small as Buffalo City?"

"Not to my knowledge. But whatever his reasons for coming here, it's certainly big news for us. You should like that. I've heard you complain before that nothing ever happens here. Well, now it has."

"Yeah, I guess so."

"That means more work," Dwight said without any enthusiasm.

With a publisher and editor who also served as mayor, Dwight often felt overworked. Millard Greeley preferred practicing politics rather than running the paper so Dwight performed many of the editorial duties normally done by the editor. He didn't get any additional pay, however.

"And that means you'll have to help out some on the news side," added Dwight.

"What do you mean? I'm the sports editor."

"We're going to be running bigger papers this week. And by the way, Greeley told me that he's bringing in another reporter. Just for the week."

"Another reporter? Who?"

"Some guy named Whitaker. He's a graduate student in journalism at OU. He's going to spend his spring break here in Buffalo City. Now that's some fun vacation."

"A graduate student?"

"You should like that, Dale. You'll finally have someone around who's not much older than you."

Dale didn't remember complaining to Dwight about that. But it was true. Everyone on the newspaper was older. Some employees were almost elderly. It was one of the reasons why he found Buffalo City so boring. There didn't seem to be many people his age and with his interests around. The town had a new junior college with low enrollment, but the few young people he'd encountered who went there didn't interest him. They seemed as dull and practical as their elders. The people in their early twenties who didn't go to the junior college or hadn't left town for one of the state universities were married and thus seemed older by their jobs and family responsibilities.

"When's this new guy arriving?"

"Greeley said tomorrow evening."

"Good."

"Better get back to the news room," said Dwight. "I got a lot to do."

"That's right," Dale said. "News for posterity!"

Unlike the managing editor, there wasn't a lot for Dale to do after making the day's deadline. He went back to his desk anyway and tried to look busy. He flipped through the freshly printed Monday paper but only scanned the news and sports stories. He didn't bother reading with any depth his sports articles since he'd just worked on that page a few hours ago. He did notice, however, a couple of typos but he didn't mention those mistakes to anyone.

While going through the motions of being busy, he thought about President Carter's upcoming visit and how that event would certainly enliven the dull routine of the newspaper and might even bring some zest to the usual prosaic proceedings in Buffalo City. Dale had been working at the *Stampede* for ten months now and during that time nothing of significance had happened. Even the sports teams he'd covered we thoroughly mediocre.

Dale decided that he'd pretended to be busy long enough, so he got up and walked over to Dwight's desk. The managing editor was checking his notebook, perhaps scrutinizing quotes from one of his sources. Dale liked Dwight. The managing editor was an amiable sort, easy-going and calm, never ruffled even when the deadline got tight, but at times he seemed a little glum. Dwight was married, the father of female toddler and an infant son, and Dale thought perhaps that was partly the reason for his occasional melancholia.

Dale didn't know how much Dwight got paid, but he imagined it wasn't a lot. Millard Greeley wasn't known for his generosity. Working long hours at a small town daily for modest income with a wife and two kids to support didn't sound like a reason for good cheer.

Nevertheless, Dwight had always been friendly and supportive although so busy that Dale rarely received much advice. In fact, Dwight didn't even have enough time to proof Dale's copy. Consequently, almost every day the sports pages had an error or two in it. Seeing the typos after the press run always embarrassed him, but strangely enough neither Dwight nor Millard Greeley had ever reprimanded him for his sloppiness. In fact, Dale got the impression that the publisher and editor didn't scrutinize the sports pages much at all except to read stories about his alma mater, the University of Oklahoma.

Dale stood at Dwight's desk and waited for the managing editor to pause in his work. When he did, Dale said the usual words before taking his leave: "If you don't need anything, I think I'll be going."

Dwight, his pale blue eyes looking paler than usual and a little bloodshot, perhaps from lack of sleep because of the infant, smiled faintly. "Okay, Dale. See you tomorrow."

Dale left the building of the *Stampede* and walked across the street to his car, a 1967 blue Chevy Impala. He glanced back at the newspaper building. It was a sturdy new structure, made of white brick, with a long, horizontal tinted window five feet high that a passerby could peer into and vaguely see the workings of the newsroom. The paper had re-located to this building just a few years ago. Millard Greeley had invested in a new, modern press, and the paper needed more room. Dale had seen the ramshackle building that had once housed the paper. It was located two blocks to the south, not far from the big grain elevator that towered above the town.

Dale got in his car, started it, and drove one block north and turned west onto the town's main drag, Broadway Boulevard, where most of the town's businesses were located. The four-lane, divided road ran east to west and was part of old historic Highway 66. Motorists would sometimes detour from off nearby Interstate 40 and drive west on this road just for the kicks.

As he drove, Dale thought of when he came to Buffalo City to interview for the newspaper job ten months ago. He remembered exiting off Interstate 40 and driving into town and being surprised by how dun and dusty everything was. It was early June, but the grass had shriveled into brown tundra and even the few trees looked overwhelmed by the heat with their dull leaves and slumping posture. It was a windy day and he could feel the hot breath of the wind as it howled in the side window of his un-air conditioned car. Driving through the outskirts of town he saw a large tumbleweed bounding across the street, the dead weed looking like a giant gray-brown spider with its spiny legs curled up in death. It was not an auspicious sight.

The interview, however, went well. Just the day before, Dale had seen an ad in the *Daily Oklahoman*. Instead of writing an application letter to the P.O. Box, Dale, out of college and back from a month long trek across Europe and eager for a job, called the newspaper. He had a concise conversation with Millard Greeley. Dale gave the publisher and editor a quick rundown of his qualifications, which wasn't much: He had graduated magna cum laude in English and journalism from his hometown college, edited the school newspaper his senior year, had never missed a deadline as newspaper editor or as editor of his high school yearbook, and was a dependable, hard worker.

Millard Greeley seemed impressed with Dale's initiative and forthrightness. He asked if Dale could drive out for an interview. Dale said sure. Greeley asked if tomorrow was too soon and Dale said no. Greeley gave him directions and said he'd see him at 3 p.m. the next day.

During the interview, Greeley did most of the talking. He spoke with great enthusiasm about the town of Buffalo City and its only newspaper. Greeley said the *Buffalo City Stampede* not only served the town but also several surrounding counties. It had the largest circulation of any newspaper in western Oklahoma except for the paper in Clinton, which was published in a larger city, and besides Clinton was forty miles to the east.

Greeley said Buffalo City was steadily growing, that it was a town on the move, that it was poised for great things, that in addition to the wheat farming and cattle ranching, the oil industry was perking up and the town was at the start of another oil boom, especially with gas prices going up, and that Buffalo City would be right in the middle. That meant more ad revenue, bigger papers, more news, and the paper needed an energetic, young sports editor to help cover the plethora of athletic events. Mostly that would mean covering high school and city amateur sports. The junior college didn't have any intercollegiate sporting teams yet. And the town didn't have any professional teams, not even a Class C minor league baseball team, although some enterprising townsfolk were making inquiries about luring a team here from the Texas panhandle.

While Millard Greeley sang the praises of Buffalo City, Dale discreetly glanced about his rather handsome office. Greeley's office even had walnut wood paneling and a large, old-fashioned oak office desk. Greeley's appearance surprised Dale. He didn't look that old, perhaps in his late twenties, but later when Dale asked him a few questions he found out that Greeley had graduated from Oklahoma University with a journalism degree in 1968, which was ten years ago, so that made Greeley around thirty-two years old. Greeley's deceptively youthful appearance was due to his shiny, pudgy face and his brown button eyes. His short brown hair was neatly styled and also gave him a boyish appearance, like a kid fresh from a haircut. His blue pin-stripped suit didn't disguise his portly physique. His large belly strained the buttons of his white dress shirt and hung over the black leather belt. Dale also noticed that Greeley had rather small, white hands that he frequently gesticulated with. The fingers, though rather thick, had a finesse to them that seemed almost feminine.

Greeley spoke rapidly in a clear tenor voice that often rose in pitch when his enthusiasm got the better of him. Even sitting at his large desk, Greeley seemed to vibrate with energy. Later, when Greeley showed him around the *Stampede*, Dale noticed how the editor and publisher bustled about, his rotund body moving with alacrity in spite of its girth.

As the interview came to a close, Greeley asked him a few questions. Dale repeated the qualifications that he had given over the phone the previous day. He emphasized that he was a hard worker. Greeley seemed to appreciate that and then leaned forward.

"Are you a smoker?" he asked.

"No, I don't smoke."

"Very good. Very good, indeed. This is a non-smoking shop."

Dale, sensing the interview was about over, brought out a notebook with clippings from his college newspaper work. He showed them to Greeley. The editor and publisher looked at them more than read them, although he did so with a thoughtful expression on his chubby face. After a few minutes of quick perusal, Greeley nodded and leaned back in his leather chair.

"I'm impressed with your clips, Dale Smith. More importantly, I'm taken with your earnest manner. It reminds me of when I was a young man. So, how would you like to work for the *Stampede*?"

Dale, surprised to be offered the job so quickly, nevertheless said okay.

"Excellent! I think you've made a wise choice. Now when can you start?"

"Any time."

"How about Monday? That'll give you the weekend to get your affairs in order."

"Okay."

"Excellent! Now let me show you around the news-room and introduce you to your co-workers."

Millard Greeley rose from his chair and offered his small, pudgy hand and Dale shook it and then the editor started to exit his office when he suddenly stopped.

"Oh, my. We didn't discuss your remuneration."

Since Dale looked a little confused, Greeley added, "Your salary."

"Right."

Greeley smiled, not a large smile because his mouth was rather small but Dale saw a couple of unimpressive teeth flash into view. "We usually start off our new reporters at two hundred."

"Two hundred?"

"Two hundred dollars a week. We also provide health insurance and contribute five percent to a retirement program."

Dale could hardly imagine working at the *Stampede* until he retired. Also, the salary didn't sound that great. He'd made almost half that amount working his part time job during college as a campus policeman.

"After a probationary period of a month you'll get a modest raise. Perhaps to two twenty." Since Dale still didn't look impressed, Greeley added, "And I think I can find inexpensive lodging for you. Because of the oil boom, it's difficult finding anything moderate in price. Some of the oil roughnecks have to stay in motels in the less reputable parts of town, but I think I can find you a comfortable but not too dear accommodation. After all, as mayor of the town, I have many contacts."

"You're mayor of the town?"

"Yes, I've been mayor for three years."

"And you're also the editor of the newspaper?"

"Editor and publisher. As you can see, I am a busy man."

Dale had never heard of a newspaperman who was also a politician. From what little he knew, mostly from old movies, newspapermen should be wary of politicians. But Greeley the mayor probably could help him find a decent but cheap place to stay. And he needed a job. He'd spent nearly all his savings on his trip to Europe.

"What do you say, Dale Smith? Is it a deal?"

"Okay."

Now, ten months later, Dale drove past several businesses, gas stations, motels, and restaurants, most with highway 66 inspired names: 66 Sunset Motel, 66 Bar and Grill, 66 Pump N Go, 66 Diner, and so on. He then turned north on McKinley Avenue and drove two blocks until he came to a sturdy stone and brick house on the corner of Third Street where he rented a room. He turned his old Chevy into the driveway and parked it underneath an awning. Then he got out, climbed the two steps of the porch, glanced at the porch swing that he liked and sometimes lounged on while reading, and opened the front door and entered the house.

Even though he only rented a room, Dale had the whole house to himself. His landlady, Mrs. Kennicott, was an old widow and had been living in a nursing home for almost a year. After Dale had accepted the newspaper job, Millard Greeley remembered the old woman had a room for rent. So Greeley drove Dale to the nursing home, a two-story red brick building on the west end of town not too far from the Great Plains

Regional Medical Center, and they went inside and spoke with Mrs. Kennicott. The old lady asked Dale a few questions. Dale politely answered them and she seemed taken with his good manners. In addition, she liked the mayor. She'd known him all his life. She'd watched him grow up. She trusted his opinion.

Everything was soon arranged. Mrs. Kennicott told him he could have the back bedroom. She reached her thin fingers to her purse on the nightstand and fished out a house key. With a quavering hand, she gave it to him.

Dale took the key and nodded at her. She was very old. Older than his grandparents even. The skin on her pale face looked thin and almost translucent and clung to her bony features. She'd tussled her light colored hair into a bun, but the hair on top of her head was so sparse that some of her pink scalp showed. Her light blue eyes had a milky quality to them. Her nose had a long, hooked appearance. Her lips had thinned with age and they were almost as white as her skin but when she smiled she showed large, strong looking teeth.

As with the salary, Dale had forgot to ask about the rent. "Oh, yeah," he said, a little embarrassed, "how much is the rent?"

Mrs. Kennicott acquired a shrewd look on her nearly emaciated face. "How about a hundred, young man?"

"Every week?"

She laughed a throaty, almost hoarse laugh that was nevertheless genuinely full of mirth. "Oh, no. Every month."

That sounded pretty good. Greeley was right. He

did know how to find a good "accommodation."

"Okay."

They finalized the arrangements. Dale would have kitchen privileges as long as he cleaned up after himself. Dale said he'd bring the rent to her in a couple of days. Dale and Greeley said good-bye to Mrs. Kennicott. The old lady smiled and said she'd look forward to his visit.

As the Dale and Greeley left the nursing home, Greeley said wasn't Mrs. Kennicott a dear. Dale said yes she seemed like a very nice old lady.

"She's one of the original settlers of Buffalo City," said Greeley. "She was ten years old when her family moved here in 1901."

"1901? That's before statehood."

"I like a young man who knows his state's history," said Greeley with a nod. "And Mrs. Kennicott is quite well off. She doesn't need the money. But she wanted someone to stay in her home while she's convalescing."

Dale nodded and wondered what would happen if the old lady returned home. She seemed to like him. Maybe she'd let him have the room anyway. Now his modest salary didn't sound too bad since he had such cheap rent.

That initial meeting with Mrs. Kennicott had been ten months ago. The old lady still remained in the nursing home and Dale still rented a room in her home for a hundred bucks a month.

As he now walked into the Kennicott house, he passed first through the living room. It was a tastefully decorated room, although a little dusty since it hadn't been thoroughly cleaned for almost a year. Since Dale rarely occupied the room, there wasn't much to clean but he did think that maybe he should vacuum the rug and wipe off the dust on the television screen.

He went into the kitchen and ignored the bowl and spoon in the sink. He'd wash them along with the dinner dishes after supper. He proceeded through the kitchen door to his room, the back bedroom, and first drew open the curtain to let in some sunshine. His bedroom was fairly comfortable. The reddish carpet was thick and felt good when he took off his boots and socks and rubbed his toes against it. He turned on the radio on the nightstand and only half listened to the broadcast. Buffalo City only had two radio stations in town. One, KGOD, a religious station that played mostly Christian contemporary music, and the second, KBUF, that played country and western music. Sometimes he could pick up one of the radio stations in Amarillo that played rock and pop music but often he didn't bother because he disliked the disco music that dominated the station's play-list.

He dropped into an old easy chair and pulled off his boots and socks. Even with the curtain parted, the room remained rather gloomy. That was one problem with being in the back. A large elm tree stood in the backyard and blocked out some of the sunlight. Across the room stood his bed. It was not a large bed, but it was thick and heavy, and it was built into the space next to the wall and elevated a foot from the floor by a wooden platform. The bed fit snugly against the wall and it reminded him of something you'd find in a bunkhouse. He liked sleeping in it and pretending he was a cowboy in the Old West.

Working at the Buffalo City newspaper wasn't so bad. He'd made his job easier by inventing his "system" so there wasn't as much deadline pressure as there had been at first. He had to cover the major high school sports so he rarely had a Friday night free. He had to work six days a week and he didn't have a Saturday off but on the light news days he worked less than eight hours. He liked living in Mrs. Kennicott's house and hadn't been bothered by anyone yet. The old lady had a daughter living in Amarillo and a son residing in Denver but neither had been to the house so far. The rent was cheap so even with his modest salary he was able to save a couple of hundred dollars a month because of his frugality. Also, there wasn't much for him to do in Buffalo City. The town had several bars on the more disreputable south side of town, past the railroad tracks, which catered to the cowhands and oil roughnecks, but Dale never frequented the bars because he didn't drink. The town had several churches. Millard Greeley had suggested to Dale that he was welcome to attend his church, the handsome Baptist church on the north side of town, not too far from the country club. But Dale had declined. He wasn't interested in attending church anymore. He used to go to the Nazarene church back in his home town, mostly because his girlfriend did, and he'd even graduated from the local Nazarene college, but he had no interest in attending the Buffalo City Nazarene church. He wasn't religious anymore, never had been really, at least not in any conventional sense, and besides Sunday was the only day he could sleep late.

Buffalo City had one movie theatre, The Prairie

Palace, but it showed mostly "popcorn" movies, those big-budget, mass audience features that he increasingly found simplistic and boring. So, on most Sunday afternoons, he'd make the two-hour drive to Amarillo and see a more interesting film. Sometimes one of the theatres would show an "art" film, a more serious film with a smaller budget, or on rare occasions a theatre would show an actual foreign language film and he'd go see that.

But his main complaint about living in Buffalo City was that he didn't really have any close friends. He'd met a girl named Helen Brown at the Carnegie Library last summer. He often went to the library to read magazines after work, especially news magazines. He thought he should since he was working at a newspaper and didn't really know much about politics or current events. Helen worked there as a student assistant and she noticed him coming into the library and one day, about a month after moving to Buffalo City, they struck up a conversation and he discovered they shared a similar sensibility. She was the first person he'd encountered who shared his interests in literature and film and art in general.

As the weeks passed, Dale grew to like her although his feelings were always platonic. In spite of her name, Helen didn't have a face that would launch a thousand ships. She was a little on the plain side with her smallish gray eyes and dull brown hair, and her rather slight figure didn't inspire any passion either. But she had a lively sense of humor, and an intellectual curiosity that Dale shared. Sometimes he'd take her for a Coke after he got off work and they'd have interesting conversations. They even went to one movie in Amarillo together.

With the coming of fall Helen had to leave Buffalo City for college. She was a sophomore at Galilee Nazarene College, the same college Dale had attended in his hometown of Galilee, a small town about ten miles west of Oklahoma City. When Dale found out she was going to GNC, he thought it was an example of a certain irony present in life and they both laughed at the coincidence.

She wrote a letter from GNC and Dale wrote back and they began a regular correspondence. When Helen returned to Buffalo City during Christmas break, they continued their non-romantic excursions. Dale, in fact, hadn't even met her parents. Mr. Brown worked as a foreman at the lumber mill and Mrs. Brown taught English at Buffalo City High School. Helen had two older siblings, a brother living in Oklahoma City and a sister living in Amarillo. Both of them were married with kids and whenever she talked about them Dale tried not to sound too interested because in the back of his mind he wondered if she was trying to make domestic life sound appealing.

Other than Helen, there had only been one other person that Dale considered a friend and that relationship was limited too because of his age. About a month after coming to Buffalo City, a tall man nattily dressed in a dark business suit came into the *Stampede* to talk to one of the ad salesmen. It was after deadline but before the press run and Dale sat at his desk reading a book. Everyday Dale brought a book with him to work, usually a novel, so he could read during his breaks. Dale glanced up from his book and noticed the man. There was a certain quality to him, perhaps it was the fine tailored suit or perhaps it was the way he carried himself with a certain kind of graceful fluidity, or maybe it was the slightly sardonic expression on his face, a subtle look that suggested he wasn't as conventional or proper as he appeared to be. After the man, who seemed to be in his early thirties, went into George Sinclair's office to discuss buying an ad, Dale forgot about him and returned to his book, *Man and Superman*. Dale had read the play by Shaw a few years before as part of his regular non-class readings. While looking for something to read from his stack of paperbacks he saw the play and remembering he liked reading it the first time and he decided to re-read it and see if he understood the play better now.

Dale was engrossed in the play so he didn't notice the man until he cleared his throat. Dale looked up, surprised to see the fellow standing before his desk. They were the only two people in the newsroom. Dwight, Floyd Byrd, and Rosemary Rogers were out to lunch.

"Interesting reading," said the man.

"You've read it?"

"Yes, I admire all the plays by George Bernard."

That reference produced a small smile from Dale. "Yeah, I've read quite a few. In fact, I read this play a few years ago but I didn't fully understand it."

The man smiled and he had a rather handsome face, which improved even more in appearance when he smiled. Then he leaned forward and spoke in a quieter, more confidential voice: "You better be careful reading such iconoclastic literature. You might get a reputation around here."

Dale played along. He immediately clapped the book shut and quickly hid it under his AP style-book.

"My name is Byron Mors." He reached out a hand and Dale shook it and gave his name. "You're the new sports editor, aren't you?"

"Yeah. Well, I've been here for a couple of months now."

"How do you like things?"

"Fine." Dale noticed that Byron Mors understood that his terse reply actually meant the opposite.

"Have you ever read anything by Ayn Rand?"

"I read a book of hers back in high school. *Anthem*."

"So you haven't read *The Fountainhead* or *Atlas Shrugged*? Those are her more mature works."

"No, I never have."

"If you like, I'll bring you a copy of *Atlas Shrugged*. It's a long novel but very rewarding reading. It gives the best distillation of her philosophy of Objectivism."

Dale wasn't sure what Byron Mors meant by Objectivism but he nodded his head to disguise his ignorance. "Sure, I'd be interested in reading something different."

"Very well, I'll bring you a copy. I have two. I better be going. Nice to have met you, Dale."

"Same here," Dale said, feeling a little silly since he didn't have the easy charm of Byron Mors.

Dale didn't see Byron Mors for several weeks, but when he did it was after work while Dale was walking over to the Carnegie Library. He heard someone calling his name, turned, and saw Byron smiling at him. He extended a thick paperback toward Dale, *At-*

las Shrugged, and they had a brief but pleasant conversation. A couple of weeks later, Dale returned the novel to Byron and they discussed it. Dale hadn't really liked the novel. He didn't think it was especially well written and the story seemed too much like a melodrama or even a soap opera and he wasn't impressed with the philosophy either but it was obvious that Byron Mors admired it so Dale didn't express any of his reservations. Dale did find Byron interesting. He had a sophistication that he hadn't encountered in any one else in Buffalo City and he seemed to have a genuinely curious mind.

From time to time, the two encountered each other and they would engage in a stimulating conversation usually centered on what they had been reading or about the dull social mores of Buffalo City. A couple of months passed like this, then one day Byron Mors came to the newspaper office and not seeing Dale in the newsroom waited until he reappeared. Dale apologized for not being around and said he'd been in the press-room playing chess with the assistant pressman.

"You play chess?" asked Byron.

"Not very well."

"I enjoy playing, too. But I have a hard time finding someone to play with. Would you like to play a match sometime?"

"Sure."

"My wife is going to be out of town next Monday. She and her sister are driving to Oklahoma City to visit their mother. How would you like to come over Monday night? We could get in a couple of matches."

Dale had found out some time ago that Byron Mors

owned a funeral home and chapel and that he lived on the second floor of his establishment.

"You mean come over to your place, where your business is?"

Byron smiled a gracious smile that Dale supposed he used for his customers. But it was a disarming smile just the same. "You're not squeamish?"

"No, not really."

"Well, that's interesting because I'm a little squeamish. But a game of chess will settle me down just fine. So, are you interested?"

Dale said he was and Byron told him when to arrive. That next Monday Dale came at the appointed time and the two had an enjoyable game of chess which Byron won rather handily but Dale had liked playing and conversing with him. They continued to encounter each other from time to time during the week and they discussed literature or art or politics and about once a month when his wife and child were out of town spending the night with his mother-in-law Byron invited Dale over to his home for a game of chess.

In fact, they had scheduled a game of chess that night. Dale looked forward to those nights. Of all the people he'd met in Buffalo City, Byron Mors was the most sophisticated and interesting. If Byron hadn't been twelve years older, married and a father, maybe the two of them could have developed a deeper friendship. But Dale was grateful to even have a part-time friend. So far, they rarely spoke about anything personal. They confined their conversations to mostly intellectual and cultural issues. That was fine with Dale. He'd never really had an intellectual friend.

Dale stood up and walked into the kitchen and glanced at the clock. He was supposed to be over at Byron's at 7:30. Dale still felt a little strange about going over to Mors' Funeral Home and Peaceful Prairie Chapel to play a game of chess. There was really nothing macabre about it. Dale arrived at the side door, not the front entrance of the business or the back area where the hearses were parked and where the corpses were carried into the morgue. Byron would be waiting for him. He opened the door, welcomed him, and the two would proceed down a hallway to his spacious office. The chessboard would already be set up. They sat on two comfortable leather chairs with a handsome oak table between them. The office itself seemed almost like a study. The spacious room had all the usual business items in it but also contained two large bookcases. One bookcase seemed to have mostly work related literature, books like Twentieth Century Funeral Home Practices or Advanced Embalming Techniques. But the other bookcase featured mostly books about literature and history and especially philosophy. Dale had scanned some of the titles on the book spines and noticed there were works by Plato, Aristotle, Descartes, Kant, Schopenhauer, Kierkegaard, and especially a number of titles by Nietzsche and existentialists like Sartre and Camus.

When Byron noticed Dale looking at the philosophy books he asked if he was interested in such work. Dale admitted that he'd taken a few courses in philosophy in college but he said he had never really understood it that well. That amused Byron and he said he had felt the same way although he had initially been a philosophy major in college. After the chess match, which so far Byron had always won, the two had drinks (Dale had a 7-Up and Byron a scotch) and talked about literature or philosophy and other intellectual topics. Dale enjoyed listening to Byron. He had a resonant tenor voice, always carefully modulated, and spoke with precision and without a trace of a southwestern twang.

On Dale's second visit, Byron gave him a tour of the funeral home, but only the public part of the business. He escorted him into the chapel, then the Display room where the deceased would be presented for public viewing, then to the Showroom where all the caskets were on display. Dale could hardly believe how many caskets the room held. Byron gave a quick dissertation on their different properties, the variations in price and quality and Dale thought he sounded rather like a car salesmen with all the jargon and the different kinds of "options" available.

On subsequent visits, Dale half expected that Byron would show him the behind-the-scenes workings of the funeral home: The morgue area, where the corpses were embalmed and treated or maybe the cosmetic area where the bodies were dressed and groomed. But so far, Byron had never offered and Dale hadn't the nerve to ask for a tour of that part of the necropolis.

The first visit had been a little eerie, but Dale was getting used to the funeral home. He still thought playing chess in a place of the dead was a bit strange, but he liked playing with Byron and enjoyed their discussions afterward.

Besides, he didn't have anything better to do.

In their previous five matches, Byron Mors had always won. But this time, Dale, employing an unconventional strategy, had gained an advantage.

Rather than attack from the middle, Dale had marshaled his forces to Byron's left. Perhaps Byron thought the attack a feint, because he was slow in recognizing the danger. He didn't make the prudent move and castle and now as Dale inexorably advanced his pawns and knights Byron's queen was trapped and the king vulnerable.

Dale glanced at Byron who was studying the board. His expression, normally placid, appeared to be mildly concerned. Three moves later, Dale knew, and he knew Byron knew, that he'd won the game.

Two moves later, Dale said, "Check and checkmate."

Byron surveyed the board then with the tip of his finger he toppled the king signaling defeat.

"You've certainly improved, Dale," Byron said, leaning back in the leather chair.

"I've been playing more of late."

"That was an interesting strategy that you took."

"It wasn't much of a strategy. I just did something I've never done before."

"Sometimes that is the most effective strategy."

Dale shrugged in response. He noticed that Byron, although dressed causally in dark slacks, a gray sweater, and a white shirt underneath, still looked almost elegant in a gentlemanly way. Dale had noticed another interesting detail during the match. Byron had immaculate nails. They were short and neatly trimmed, without a smidgen of dirt underneath them. Dale wondered if Byron got manicures.

In spite of the almost feminine neatness of his nails, Byron's hands were large and strong looking. They were graceful hands, nonetheless, and Dale had noticed how deftly he moved the chess pieces. But then everything about Byron Mors, from the way he spoke to the way he moved with a kind of fluid agility, to his tasteful attire and well-groomed person, conveyed a natural masculine grace that Dale supposed was quite advantageous in his sensitive business.

"Yes, that was an unconventional approach," Byron said, referring to the just concluded chess match. "You also seem to enjoy reading unconventional books. At least by the standards of Buffalo City."

"My hometown, too," said Dale.

He'd told Bryon a little about his hometown of Galilee, how religious most of the people were, how the Nazarene church exerted considerable influence on the schools and town. Dale had mentioned that very few people in his hometown were interested in literature or philosophy or art. He didn't think they were bad people; in fact, just the opposite. But most people in Galilee viewed life from a rather narrow perspective. Byron had nodded. He said it wasn't much different in Buffalo City.

"I wonder how unconventional you are in other matters," Byron now said with a half-smile.

For some reason that question embarrassed Dale but he answered anyway. "What other matters?"

"Have I told you that I was initially a philosophy major in college?"

Dale wondered why Byron had avoided answering his question but he played along. "I think you mentioned that once but I also noticed you have a lot of philosophy texts in your book case."

"I don't read them anymore. But at OU I was a philosophy major. During my junior year I went through something of an existential crisis, if I may call it that." Byron paused and picked up his glass that contained a small amount of bourbon. He swallowed it slowly as if considering its alcoholic properties but he was really thinking about his story. Byron nodded toward Dale's glass. "Would you like another?"

"No thanks." Dale's glass had contained nothing so intoxicating. He'd drunk his usual 7-Up.

"You've never been an imbiber?"

"I've tried alcohol, but I never liked it."

"Did you like the effects?"

"Not really. I like having a clear mind.'"

Byron nodded.

"Tell me more about your existential crisis," Dale said.

"Too much philosophy. Too much thinking. Unlike you, I don't always like having a clear mind."

"Why would that lead to a crisis?"

"During the winter of my junior year a thought appeared in my mind that I couldn't shake." Byron paused and looked at Dale with an odd expression, one almost of severity that he'd never seen before.

"Yes," Dale prompted.

"I became convinced that life is utterly meaningless. We live, but compared to Time it is for a very brief moment, and then we die." Byron gave a wry smile. "Yes, I know. A banal realization. But the point is that I genuinely believed it. I saw no point to anything.

Somehow I continued my studies and didn't lose my mind or commit suicide. But I was very depressed and I isolated myself from my friends for a while. I knew in order to save myself I had to give up philosophy. Give up the life of the mind.

"This was the beginning of 1967, an interesting year. But I had been so focused on my studies and reading Nietzsche and Heidegger and other philosophers that I hadn't even noticed that society was changing. Even in our backward state things were changing. I began to change, too. My depression lifted. I dedicated myself to the concept of carpe diem. After final exams instead of going home to Buffalo City I kept going west. I drove all the way to San Francisco."

"Really? You just took off?"

"Ended up at Haight-Ashbury. Became a hippie. Grew my hair long. Grew a beard. Wore love beads and sandals. I smoked dope, dropped acid, grooved to music, slept with as many chicks as I could. I forsook the life of the mind for the life of the senses."

Looking at Byron Mors now, with his natty attire and proper demeanor, Dale could hardly believe it.

"Did you like doing that?"

"At first, very much. You must have heard all the clichés about that time: the Summer of Love. But those clichés contain some truth. It was a magical, almost mystical summer. People really were wearing flowers in their hair and had a communal sense of love. But as with anything else, it didn't last. To use the lingo of that time, the trip went bad. The good vibrations turned unmelodious. I don't know why exactly. Maybe we simply lost our illusions or got too self-indulgent.

Maybe we got bored and then we grew malevolent. But summer turned into winter and '67 turned into '68. And 1968 was a very bad year."

"Is that when you came back home?"

"In October of '68. Like I said, the scene had changed. But something else happened, too. My younger brother, Blake, was killed in Vietnam."

"In the war?"

"The *conflict*. But he got killed anyway. The sap volunteered. He didn't get drafted. And he did it after his high school graduation in 1966 when everyone should have known how pointless the war was. Killed during the last stage of the Tet offensive."

"That's too bad."

"A waste. I had a student deferment while in college then I drew a high lottery number. But my younger brother volunteers for the Marines. So with Blake dead my parents wanted me home so I returned to Buffalo City. A few months later, I went back to OU. But this time as a mortuary science major. I was going to take over the family business.

"And in fact it was Blake's death that made me consider that maybe life isn't utterly meaningless after all. Rather ironic. A meaningless death revealed meaning in my own life. I stopped reading philosophy. I concentrated on more practical matters. I didn't swear off the life of the senses but I tried to be more balanced in my approach. I decided the life of the mind could co-exist with the life of the senses."

"Balance is good," Dale said, knowing he sounded silly but not knowing what else to say.

"And speaking of the life of the senses," Byron said

with sly smile, "have you ever seen a X-rated movie?"

"No."

"Would you like to see one?"

"You mean in theory?"

"I mean right now. I have a collection of X-rated films and a projector. If you'd like, we could view one."

This was certainly an unusual invitation, thought Dale. He had to admit he'd been curious about seeing such a movie. You couldn't see them in his hometown, although there was a seedy theatre that showed them in downtown Oklahoma City. He imagined a moving picture would be more stimulating than *Playboy* magazine. He'd bought a copy a few months ago and hid it under the bed in his room, although there wasn't anyone entering his room to make any inspections. He'd felt rather foolish buying the magazine but that evening he'd been so lonesome and lustful that he couldn't resist it.

"Okay."

Byron Mors smiled and stood up and Dale followed him out of the office. They walked through a short hallway that led to the interior of the building. They passed the Casket Selection room (Byron had taken Dale on a tour of that room in a previous visit and Dale had been bewildered by the multitudinous variations of the sleek, rather luxurious receptacles) then passed the Slumber Room, where the deceased in their caskets were patiently waiting to be viewed by the mourners. A dim light illuminated the room and Dale slowed just enough to glance into the room. He saw an open lavender casket with what looked like a middle-aged woman lying in it. The sight startled and disturbed him but he pushed the image out of his mind and quickened his pace as Byron led him to a circular stairway that led to the second floor. They climbed the stairs and Byron entered a dark room with Dale following. Byron turned on a lamp and Dale saw they were in a fairly large room with a maroon carpet, a large bookcase, two easy chairs, two folding chairs with a padded checkered seat, and a rather large desk that had a cabinet with two closed small doors. Near the back of the room was a table with a Super 8 movie projector perched on it. The largest wall was bare and standing before it was a stand with a white screen already stretched out.

Dale observed that the room had been prepared for a screening. He wondered if Byron had planned on him agreeing to a viewing or if Byron had enjoyed a sneak preview himself.

"This is our guest bedroom," said Byron, "without the bed."

He went over to desk with the cabinet and pulled apart the two small doors. Inside the shelves were two-dozen boxes of movies vertically lined up in a neat row.

"Any preferences?" Byron asked.

Dale walked over and peered inside the cabinet. He saw some pinkish images on the rather narrow spines of the movie boxes but he couldn't see any details. The displayed titles were hard to read from where he stood.

"No, whatever you want."

Byron pulled out three boxes and went over to the projector, took one film reel out of its box and began threading the film into the projector.

"You know, I belonged to the projectionist club in high school," Dale said, suddenly feeling the need for levity.

"I'll bet you never showed films like these."

The threading completed, Byron instructed Dale to turn off the lamp. Dale walked over to the table stand and pushed the off switch and as the room fell into darkness the projector began to whiz and whirl and a white rectangle of light first appeared on the screen.

Dale took a seat on one of the padded folding chairs and stared at the screen. A giant X appeared followed by vertical bars then more white then the film's title appeared: *Getting Plumbed*.

A not very attractive middle-aged man dressed as a plumber and a fairly attractive young woman dressed not as a normal American housewife but more provocatively with a mini-skirt and halter top appeared at the front door of some nondescript ranch-style house. They began talking but Dale couldn't quite make out the dialogue because of the poor audio quality of the film and because the projector's built in speakers weren't very powerful. But Dale guessed the woman had called the plumber because he came in and he followed her to the bathroom.

Dale felt an uneasy sensation in his stomach. Having sex in the bathroom didn't sound very appealing.

Once the couple got to the bathroom the woman started talking again and Dale made out enough of the dialogue by reading her lips to know she had said, "The darn shower drain is stuck up again," and then the woman bent over at the waist and gazed down at the supposed clogged drain. As she bent over, her mini skirt rode up above her hips and her amazingly round, white, plump buttocks appeared in view. Then the camera zoomed in on a close-up of her posterior and Dale, growing aroused, winced a little at seeing a small purplish bruise on the right cheek.

A reaction shot of the plumber: an exaggerated look of astonishment quickly followed by an almost comical leer.

The camera returned to her rump and the plumber sprang into action, so to speak. He grabbed her, caressed her, undressed her, undressed himself, and after two minutes of vigorous foreplay, he mounted her from behind in the bathtub while she writhed and screeched, her impressively large breasts flopping, as she flailed her arms until one of her hands grabbed a hold of the shower handle. She tugged on it and water spouted out of the shower-head at the precise moment the hairy plumber did some spouting himself.

"Hit the lights," Byron instructed, and Dale rose with a little difficulty, and turned on the lamp. The pressure in the groin of his pants subsided a little as Byron threaded another film into the projector.

"Was that illuminating?" Byron asked.

"I'll never think of plumbing in the same way again," Dale replied.

Byron laughed and requested that he douse the lights.

The next feature, entitled *Pandora's Box*, developed a classical Greek myth motif that Dale found sort of interesting. Pandora wore a Greek tunic (did women wear tunics back then?) that was so small her large breasts almost popped out of the top. She was the most desired maid in Athens but she refused all suitors. Even the Prince failed to win her heart. It looked like Pandora was destined to remain a virgin. But then Pandora confided to her girlfriend the real reason for her chastity: she had a very small vagina.

Pandora's secret got revealed and the King posed a solution: she will be penetrated first by the man with the smallest penis in the kingdom (a philosopher), then by a man with a somewhat larger one (a merchant), and so on until she is ready for the massive member of the Prince.

The Prince's and Pandora's final copulation was accompanied by an orgy with about a dozen couples doing it including one female couple. When they appeared on the screen, Byron said, "They're from the Isle of Lesbos," which Dale thought was rather funny although he didn't find the movie funny.

In fact, the movie sort of repulsed him while at the same time arousing him. There were too many shots of penises of different sizes. And too many close-ups of Pandora's box. But the lesbian couple had excited him, which sort of puzzled him.

The third film was entitled *Three Holes* and it started with a three couples playing golf on a very scruffy looking golf course. After the usual banal chatter that was required of these films, the couples began playing strip golf. The women lost, of course, and when all three females were naked, the men started having sex with them. The conventionality and repetitiousness of the movie began to bore Dale a little and he thought the title simply referred to three copulations, but near the end of the feature two of the men left their female partners and went over to the other couple. The two abandoned females proceeded to have wild lesbian sex, including using a golf club, while the three men started having sex with the woman, a full-figured red-head, but instead of taking turns the men had sex with her all at the same time. That is, they each occupied one hole: the mouth, the vagina, and the rectum.

Dale had never seen anything like that before and the sheer perversity of it shocked him to his core, especially when the tallest man sodomized the woman. Bent over, her butt high in the air, her distorted face close to hole number nine on the golf course, the camera moved in and showed a close-up of the woman's anus just before the man's penis penetrated it. But her anus was not an ordinary one. It was amazingly large and distended and it easily accommodated the man's phallus.

That sight stunned Dale. He'd never seen anything so obscene. The photos in *Playboy* and especially *Penthouse* were becoming increasingly graphic. The ones in *Penthouse*, in particular, showed every detail of a woman's body, but their posterior apertures were all of normal size and condition.

Two other factors contributed to Dale's feelings of shock and disorientation. Starting in the middle of *Three Holes*, Dale thought he heard a faint but persistent utterance, not from the film soundtrack, but from Byron Mors. Dale sat about five feet in front of Byron and he was tempted to turn and confirm his suspicion, but he resisted. The sounds weren't exactly moans of ecstasy, but they were disturbingly close.

The second factor was that he felt a strange, divided feeling inside him. While he watched the X-rated fare he felt a growing frustrated arousal, a persistent glow of lust that could not be fully gratified, but his mind felt fully self-conscious and aware. He felt almost as if he'd been split in two: a body full of powerful physical sensations with pulsing blood and rapid breathing and a mind divorced from those sensations and instead full of conflicted thoughts.

One of the thoughts rolling in his head was the realization that while he and Byron watched the film with its recorded display of the very much living naked bodies of the actresses (and actors) below them on the first floor lay some very dead bodies patiently waiting to be disposed of.

Perhaps there was another body lying in the morgue-like preparation room. That was weird enough to consider, but Dale began thinking about the corpse of the woman he'd seen when they had passed the viewing room. He'd only got a glimpse of her and he'd immediately thrust the image out of his mind, but while watching the porn films the image of that dead woman kept popping up in his brain, interfering with his lustful urges. He remembered how the dead woman looked: not young, but not old, decked out in her Sunday best lying in an opened lavender casket. Her silver hair was unconvincingly styled as a doll's, and her face, even from the distance of his perspective, revealed an elaborately made-up mask. Her hands, small and artificially smooth, were folded on her lower chest.

The weird contrast between the living and the dead resounded in his mind and he could never completely forget it as he watched the X-rated films.

On one level what made the obscene films so powerful and alluring was that these were real women (and men). They had been filmed performing these sexual acts, and even though Dale knew intellectually what they were engaging in was something of a fraud, in fact, a travesty of genuine sexual passion, the performers were nevertheless real people engaging in real sex. But as he watched the women perform (he avoided as much as possible looking at the men), the image of the dead woman downstairs forced itself into his mind and created a profoundly confused feeling.

"Like to see another one?" asked Byron Mors, his voice now sounding completely normal.

Dale didn't turn around in his seat. He heard the flapping sound of the film on the receiving reel as it came all the way out of the projector.

"Man, I don't think I can take another one."

Byron Mors gave a short laugh. "It's difficult seeing so much visual stimulation without relieving yourself of that tension."

Dale stood up and turned on the lamplight. He definitely wasn't interested in relieving himself of any tension in the presence of Bryon Mors.

"What is your reaction to what you just saw?"

Byron's voice sounded almost professorial, as if he were asking a class of aspiring pornographers to analyze the contents of a film in the academy's canon.

"I don't know. I feel sort of strange."

Byron rewound the *Three Holes* film. The machine whirred pleasantly. "I remember the first X-rated film I saw. At my fraternity. Back then, however, they were called stag films. Just a short black and white featuring a couple of harlots. I'd never seen anything remotely like it. My hometown, as with yours, was not privy to such spectacles."

Dale turned and saw Byron rewinding another film. He looked utterly calm as he stood there contemplating his projector as it performed its task.

"How did you react?"

"When I saw my first one?"

"Yeah."

"I was absolutely stunned. I'd seen a few *Playboy* magazines, of course, and I'd gotten some glimpses of bare breasts and thighs during my obligatory adolescent fumblings but I'd never seen anything so graphically carnal."

"Did you like it?"

"Yes, somewhat. More so after I got over my shock. And as with many sources of restricted pleasure, you grow to appreciate it with experience."

Dale wasn't sure what Byron was talking about. Sometimes Byron spoke with an almost academic obscurity. Then Dale wondered if that wasn't on purpose. Such language put distance between the raw experience and the mental understanding of what had just transpired. That is, it rationalized something that wasn't rational.

Finished with his rewinding task, Byron looked at Dale with a small, sly smile. "You weren't offended, were you?"

"Not offended."

"Did you think it was wrong?"

Dale considered that word. Wrong sounded rather

simplistic and judgmental, reactions that he thought Byron Mors would have disdain for.

"Yeah, I sort of did. Not just watching the films but the larger context of everything. These films are sort of exploitative, aren't they? Essentially they're the filmed actions of prostitutes."

"You think prostitution is wrong?"

"It's against the law."

"Officially, yes. But you'd be surprised by how accepted it is in certain locales. In many ways, it is tolerated and even protected. Not in towns like Buffalo City or your hometown, of course, but in certain communities that you'd never suspect."

"You mean frat houses?"

Byron laughed. "I think today's fraternity brothers don't need to employ professionals. No, I mean there has traditionally been acceptance of certain transgressive behavior among the elite in a society. It's accepted that certain men of stature, of high standing, have the ability to control their appetites and therefore, on certain occasions, can indulge themselves. These men have important responsibilities and they wield considerable power so they can't make their occasional indulgence public knowledge. But such men often have strong passions and since they have to exercise considerable control during the normal proceedings of the work-a-day world they sometime have to expunge these powerful passions."

"You mean like in Nietzsche and his Superman?"

"Similar notions are expressed in Shaw and other writers such as Ayn Rand."

"I'm not sure if I fully understand those ideas."

"Maybe you just don't approve?"

"I don't think I know enough about it yet."

"You do recognize that some men are superior."

"Superior in what way?"

"In intelligence, in strength, in talent, in will."

"So they should do what they want."

"It's not quite that simple, but essentially yes. And in spite of our moralistic public professing, there's always been recognition of that. Not to the point that the elite should be completely above the law. There has to be some conventionality for a society to function. There probably is a need for, as Shaw terms it, middle-class morality. But that's for the average man."

"What if someone thinks he's superior but he's not? What if he is really just average after all?"

"Then those men are simply egoists. But there are also those men who don't know they are superior."

Dale was getting the feeling that all this rather abstract talk was leading to something more concrete. He didn't know what. But Byron seemed to be subtly flattering him and even though Dale felt sort of gratified he didn't trust that emotion in himself.

"Take, for example, yourself. You're a reporter working on the local paper. But you obviously want more. You're trying to develop your intellect. There's no need for a journalist to be reading the kinds of books you read. If anything it will be counter-productive. The world of journalism is a superficial world. It doesn't and isn't able to probe beneath the surface of human experience. Only science and art can do that. You're not a scientist but maybe you wish to be an artist. If that is so, then I'd say don't limit your experiences. Embrace the world in all its variety. Explore it intellectually *and* physically."

"You mean embrace the life of the senses?"

"Don't deny that part of life." Byron paused and his demeanor changed. He acquired that suggestive, rather sly look that Dale had seen earlier in the evening. "Didn't you tell me that you used to have a steady girlfriend back in your hometown?"

"Yeah, but that ended almost a year ago."

"You're young and full of life and you're denying yourself potent life experiences."

"Not on purpose exactly."

"It's not easy finding the right kind of girl in a town like this. Even for a good looking kid like yourself."

Dale ignored the compliment. He thought Byron's definition of a right kind of girl was probably different than his. "I'm not sure what you mean."

"If you'd like to enjoy the company of an experienced woman then perhaps I can help you?"

"Here in Buffalo City?"

"Actually there is a whorehouse just outside the city limits on the south side. But that's for the cowhands and roughnecks to get their rocks off. I was thinking of something a little more sophisticated and it's not in Buffalo City."

Dale had never heard of any brothels in Buffalo City or in the surrounding area. He guessed he didn't have the necessary instincts to become an investigative reporter. "I don't know."

Byron Mors nodded. "It's something you have to think about."

"Do you make use of that particular service?"

"On occasion I do."

"But you have a wife."

"She doesn't know about it. I'm very careful."

"Does she know about your collection here?" Dale waved a hand over to the open cabinet doors with the two dozen X-rated films all neatly and snugly lined up inside.

"I'm afraid she did discover that."

"How did she react?"

"Not approvingly," Byron said with a subtle smile.

One thing Dale liked about Byron was his understated sense of humor.

"We've been married for seven years and we make allowances for each other. Marriage, as you may one day discover, is not as simple as in the movies."

"The unmarried life isn't so simple either," Dale said and that elicited a smile from Byron. After a somewhat awkward pause, Dale said he had better be going. Byron nodded and ushered him out of the room and they walked down the circular stairway.

"There's another option," Byron said as they walked down the hallway that lead to the side exit.

"What's that?"

"If you prefer the services of an amateur, I can perhaps suggest a receptive party."

Dale paused before opening the door. He wasn't sure if he wanted to know but he was curious so he asked whom.

"A young woman who works here. Her name is Louise Henderson. She worked late last Monday and she saw you come in. She later asked me about you. She's also seen you around town. Her younger brother plays on the high school teams."

Dale had no recollection of that name. "Louise?"

"You're memory might be jogged more by a description. Average height, blonde hair, dyed of course. Unremarkable face although she does wear copious amounts of make-up. Zaftig figure. In particular, rather large breasts."

Now Dale recollected her. He'd seen her sitting in the stands during the football and basketball games he'd covered. She had a loud voice and didn't mind drawing attention to herself.

"You said she might be receptive. You don't know that from personal experience, do you?"

Byron Mors' face took on an almost shocked expression since he was now the proper and rectitudinous funeral director rather than the leering, lustful porn viewer of minutes before. His exaggerated reaction almost made Dale laugh.

"Absolutely not. One thing a man in my position has to do is maintain a façade of complete respectability. This is a conservative town and gossip can quickly ruin you. I am very careful and I never approach any of my female employees or my wife's friends or any other women in this town. That's one reason to utilize the services of an out-of-town professional. But in your case, you don't have to worry so much about that."

"How do you know Louise would be receptive?"

"I have a sense about these things. I read people well. Some might say I have an uncanny sense of intuition."

Byron was being flippant now and Dale slipped into that mood as well. "Well, thanks for the info. I got to get home. I have a busy day tomorrow. Oh by the way, did you know that the President is visiting Buffalo City?"

"Really?"

"Yep. What do you think about that?"

"Not much. I'm a registered Republican."

Dale grinned and said goodnight and Byron returned the sentiment and Dale left, hearing the door shut behind him. He walked through the side parking lot to the next block where he'd parked his car. For some reason, Dale never parked his car at the Mors Funeral Home and the Peaceful Prairie Chapel. Maybe all along he suspected that something odd if not disreputable would happen there and he didn't want his car to be identified. Dale thought about the bizarre evening that had just ended. Chess, porn movies, proffers for prostitution service, all in a building concerned with the care of the dead. It was the strangest night he'd ever experienced.

And yet, it was sort of fun.

Chapter Two
Tuesday

Keeping to his usual routine, Dale got to the newspaper a few minutes after eight. He walked in through the main door to a small lobby then turned right and opened another glass door that led to the editorial part of the newspaper office. A long counter and a short, swinging twin-door separated the working area of the newsroom from the public part. Dale passed through the swinging twin-door, an act he enjoyed because he liked striding through and feeling the two small, wooden doors part then flap a little when he passed through. Walking over to his desk in the far corner of the room he glanced about the editorial area and didn't see any more commotion than usual. In fact, his two fellow co-workers, Dwight Willard and Floyd Byrd, sat at their respective desks looking over paperwork while drinking coffee. Both of them had the same pensive, rather glum demeanors. Dale had expected to see more enthusiasm and energy in the office since the President of the United States would be in town in just four days.

Dwight, from his slightly larger gray metallic desk that was positioned near the hallway that led to the publisher's office, glanced at Dale and said, "good morning" without any enthusiasm. Dale returned his greeting sat down at his desk that was furnished with a telephone, an index card roller, a double-layered paper holder, and a beat-up Underwood manual typewriter.

Dale glanced over to Floyd, whose desk, similar in its functionality, was pushed head-to-head with Dale's. This was an arrangement that Dale disliked because when sitting at his desk he faced the grumpy, middle-aged man and he didn't like looking at his dyspeptic face. To evade the face-off, Dale sat at a leftward angle and had pushed his typewriter to the far left corner of the desk.

Dale had the worst desk in the office, one without a "view." The long, rectangular tinted window was directly behind him so he had to turn around and stand up to get a gander of the outside. There wasn't much to look at anyway. Just a couple of stunted trees, a few scraggly bushes, ordinary sidewalks and the two-lane street. The buildings across the way were unremarkable, too: a drugstore, a five and dime, and a barbershop.

When he'd sat down at his desk, Floyd had nodded at him and Dale had returned the semi-friendly greeting. Since the beginning, Floyd had been uncommunicative with him and at times even projected a resentful aura. Dale didn't know why the older man had that attitude. He guessed Floyd was in his late thirties but he might have been a few years younger because Floyd had one of those plain country faces that seem to acquire a premature middle-aged meatiness. He was of average height and had a stocky build. He wore his brown hair short and his eyeglasses, the old-fashioned kind with thick black frames, diminished his small gray eyes. His thin-lipped mouth rarely smiled. His most dominant facial characteristic was his long, beaked nose. When introduced to him for the first time, Dale had thought

65

how appropriate his last name was.

The fourth member of the editorial office was the features and women's page editor, Rosemary Rogers. She usually didn't arrive until eight-thirty. But when she did appear, her exuberant arrival immediately increased the energy in the room. Rosemary, although in her early forties, was still rather attractive. She had silvery blonde hair, worn in an old fashioned, rather elaborate hair-do which reminded Dale of one of those country and western female singers of the '60s. All of her facial features were comparatively small, even her cobalt blue eyes weren't especially large, but her features were pleasingly symmetrical. But Rosemary's most appealing characteristic was her vivacious personality. Rather garrulous, she made conversation with just about everyone when she wasn't pounding out her "lifestyle" stories on her manual typewriter and when she spoke to her interviewees on the telephone she would often let out peals of laughter. She had a trilling laugh and an almost fruity voice and although Dale didn't ordinarily appreciate talkative people, he came to enjoy her banter, especially since Dwight was naturally quiet and Floyd had a sullen disposition.

Dale's first duty every morning was to run the AP wire. So, after checking his in-coming mail for anything important (there wasn't; just a couple of press releases), he walked over to Dwight's desk and took from him the list of wire stories that Dwight wanted. Then Dale walked into the back of the composing room where the AP ticker tape was rolled on a cylinder. The tape, narrow yellow paper with computerized codes punched into it, accumulated through the night and by early morning it had grown to a roll of about ten inches in diameter. Connected to the cylinder was a line gauge that led to a throttle. Dale took hold of the end of the tape, read the AP story number, usually ending in the low hundreds, then pressed his foot against the throttle, which sent the tape spinning out of the cylinder. He ran the throttle until he came to requested story number. For instance, if the first story needed for typesetting was number 87 then Dale would hit the gas, so to speak, until twenty inches of tape was spit out. He'd stop the cylinder, check the tape, and if it had stopped at story number 89, he'd press the throttle lightly until he came to story 87. Then he'd clip off the tape, run the 87 story out, then tear that part of the tape, roll it up, and set it aside. Then he'd find the other stories in the same manner until he came to the end of the tape.

It took a while for Dale to get the knack of running the AP wire. For the first couple of weeks, it was hit and miss. But as time passed, Dale became quite adept at running the tape. Now, he could usually come within a few inches of the marked stories and instead of taking an hour to run the tape, as it had when he first started doing the work, he now could accomplish the task in less than thirty minutes.

Working at the *Stampede* had been his first full-time newspaper job and the first month had been challenging and even a little exasperating. He had edited his college newspaper during his senior year but even so he wasn't quite prepared for the regimen of being sports editor at a real newspaper. His first day had especially been difficult. It took longer than expected to write his two stories, one a simple account of the previous night's men's league softball games and the other a short advance story about the Tuesday night American Legion baseball game. He also had to select several interesting wire stories to fill out the single sports page and he'd taken more time than he ought reading the dozens of wire stories and then selecting five of them to be printed in the sports section.

The other problem was that the sports stories were always typeset after the news and features. So Dale, after typing his stories on a roll of yellow paper, had to give that copy to the typesetter who then re-typed the stories on the Compugraphic typesetting machine. That machine produced paper tape with computerized coding that was then threaded through another Compugraphic machine that actually produced the photosensitive copy. As sports editor, Dale was responsible for pasting up the sports pages, so he had to wait until the photosensitive copy was produced. Since his hard copy was the last to be re-typed, the photosensitive copy was also the last to be delivered to the composing room. So on his first day at work Dale stood at the paste-up table waiting for his copy and headlines to arrive. He had watched nervously as the clock ticked closer to the 3 p.m. deadline. Finally, the materials arrived and he went to work. As editor of his college paper he had pasted-up copy on layout sheets but the student newspaper had been a tabloid and the *Stampede* was a broadsheet. The size difference confused him a little. Cutting and waxing and pasting the copy, the heads, and blocking out space for photos took more time than he had anticipated and he found himself racing against the approaching deadline.

About ten minutes before deadline Millard Greeley had strolled into the composing room, no doubt to check on the new hire, and Dale had seen a concerned look on the publisher's pudgy face. Dale, even as a tyro journalist, knew it was a cardinal sin to miss the deadline; he'd never missed one during his student editorship even if it meant staying up late into the night before the morning deadline. But now, the first day of his first real newspaper job, he was in danger of missing the deadline.

In the end, he made that first day's deadline. However, the fact that he'd come so close to missing the deadline – he'd finished his page with just a couple of minutes to spare – was a cause for concern.

With practice, Dale got more efficient doing all the tasks required to produce the sports pages. But during that first month every day had been a challenge making the day's deadline. The primary problem was that his hard copy was always the last to be typeset and therefore he only had thirty minutes for paste-up. Dale also thought the whole system was rather inefficient. First the reporters typed their stories with their typewriters then the typesetter typeset the hard copy. In effect, it was a double effort. Since there was only one typesetting machine and three editors that meant that Dale, whose hard copy was typeset last, had to wait the longest and then he had the shortest time to do paste-up.

Then one day, about a month after he'd been hired, Dale realized he could change the system. The typesetter, a heavy-set balding man nearing sixty, who, nevertheless, was an accomplished typist, took his lunch break at noon. Since the typesetting machine was free for half an hour, Dale decided to make use of it. He went into the composing room, sat down at the typesetting machine with his notes, and composed his sports stories directly on the machine. He also learned to run the computerized tape containing his sports stories through the Compugraphic machines where the coded tape was used to create the photosensitive paste-up copy. He had simply watched the two women who worked in the composing room to see how it was done. Now he could write his copy on the typesetting machine and then process his own tapes and thus get his paste-up copy ahead of everyone else. From that point on, he never came close to missing a deadline. In fact, he became so proficient at writing stories on the typesetting machine and calculating the right length and size for his headlines in his head (instead of using the rather cumbersome formula of basing the length and size of a headline on specific letters and fonts), that he often completed his pages an hour ahead of deadline. With his pages finished, he often ventured into the press-room to talk to the two pressmen. Dale asked them about their jobs, observed them in action, and he eventually learned about making negatives and plates and basically understood how the press worked.

Now finished with running the wire, Dale took the dozen rolled up tapes for news and features and placed them on the top of the first Compugraphic processing machine. The other three tapes were wire sports stories. He put two tapes on top of the second

Compugraphic processing machine then he threaded one tape into the machine's gears and hit the run button and watched the tape being processed. The two women who worked in the composing room would later run the news and feature tapes. By nine the news pages would arrive in the composing room from the ad department with the display ads already pasted in place. The advertising-to-news ratio in the *Stampede* was around 50/50 which was actually higher than the recommended 40-60 ratio that Dale had learned about in one of his journalism courses. When he'd discovered the higher advertising ratio, Dale had been a little surprised and disapproving, but as he continued to work at the *Stampede* he came to realize that the practice of journalism was often different than the theoretical principles he'd learned about from text books.

His first task completed, Dale returned to his desk. Rosemary had arrived. She greeted him with her usual friendly but not especially personal greeting while still maintaining a lively discussion on the telephone. On his way back to his desk, he'd noticed that Millard Greeley wasn't yet in. That meant the publisher had first checked-in at city hall, no doubt to supervise the elaborate plans for the presidential visit.

The rest of the morning Dale read press releases and made a couple of phone calls to get information and statistics from the track coach and girls softball coach. He organized his notes so he could quickly write his two sports stories that he'd do on the typesetting machine when it was free. Spring wasn't a particularly busy time for sports. The only sport he regularly covered in person was the high school baseball team and there was a late afternoon game that he would attend later that day.

At noon he wrote his stories, processed them, then assembled the photosensitive copy on the layout table. He completed the paste-up in twenty minutes, which he estimated was a new record. Deadline wasn't until three, so he had an hour and a half to kill.

He walked into the camera area of the press-room and encountered Percy Pollack, the head pressman, and his assistant Harley Dee Grubbs. Both were in their mid-twenties and neither was a candidate for friendship. Pollack, who had a pleasant, unassuming personality, was married with two small children and he didn't have any free time. Grubbs was single, but Dale had never thought of asking him what he did after work. There was something unappealing about Grubbs. He was a scruffy, lean fellow with an angular face and a spidery goatee. He was taciturn and watchful and Dale didn't trust him even though he didn't really know him. A few months after starting work, Dale found out that Grubbs played chess. After Dale developed his new more efficient system of producing his sports pages and therefore had more free time he'd sometimes go into the press-room during a lull and two of them would play a game.

Pollack said hello when he saw Dale enter. Grubbs nodded his head and Dale once again noticed a glint of some less agreeable emotion reflecting in Grubb's narrow yellowish-green eyes. Resentment perhaps; Dale had won their last chess match.

Pollack said he was going over to the drugstore for a snack and asked if anyone wanted him to bring anything back. Grubbs and Dale both said no. Pollack shoved off and Dale looked over to one of the work-tables and saw a chessboard with all the pieces positioned for play.

"Got time for a game?" Dale asked.

Grubbs frowned more than nodded but he got up and ambled over to the worktable. Dale followed.

"You're white this time," Dale said.

They sat down and both surveyed the board. The chessmen were just ordinary plastic pieces with the classic incarnations. Dale glanced at Grubbs. He didn't know much about him. Pollack had once told him that Grubbs had dropped out of high school near the end of his junior year. Pollack and Grubbs were cousins and had been in the same grade and had sort of been friends throughout their school days. During high school, Pollack had worked part-time as distribution driver and an inserter. He'd hung around and watched the pressman do their jobs and he was naturally me-chanically adept so when an opening for assistant pressman appeared Pollack was a natural choice. Five years later, the old head pressman retired and Pollack was promoted. Then when the assistant pressman's alcoholism resulted in his dismissal, Pollack recom-mended to Greeley that he hire his old friend Grubbs. That was two years ago.

One of the other tidbits that Pollack had told Dale about Grubbs was that Harley Dee had left Buffalo City when he'd dropped out of high school and had bummed around the country. Grubbs had spent some time in Chicago and once had bragged to Pollack that he'd got to know some political radicals.

Pollock thought it was just talk. But Dale, as he now studied Grubbs, thought it was possible. Grubbs had an underlying contemptuous attitude that he sometimes had a hard time concealing. Perhaps Harley Dee Grubbs had rubbed shoulders with some radical types back in Chicago. He wondered if that was where Grubbs learned to play chess. Dale thought it was unusual for someone like Harley Dee, a blue-collar kind of guy, a high school dropout, somewhat uneducated, to like chess. And he played it pretty well.

"Is the President really comin' here?" Grubbs suddenly asked. He stared at Dale with his odd slanted yellowish-green eyes. He turned his face at an angle and the dim overhead light shone on his eyes and made them look even more yellowish.

"Yeah, he is."

Grubbs' thin mouth twisted in a grimace, then he snorted.

"What? You don't like the President?"

"I don't give a damn about the President," Grubbs said. He peered at Dale in a challenging way as if inviting him to dispute that. Then Grubbs looked down at the chessboard with a more placid expression and tugged on his wispy goatee. "Just wonderin' if it was true."

"It's true. History in the making." Dale said the last sentence in a semi-satirical way. Already he was anticipating the silliness and pomposity that would spread through town.

Grubbs smiled thinly, showing his crooked teeth. "I guess anything happenin' to the President is history, too, ain't it?"

"I guess so," Dale said, not really getting his point. He was anticipating the chess game. He waited for Harley Dee Grubbs to make the first move.

As the chess match proceeded the game initially took on a rather familiar pattern. Dale and Grubbs traded several pawns and one bishop each. Then it appeared that Grubbs had an opportunity for a quick strike. He moved his queen into the middle of the board. Dale had noticed in the past games that Grubbs liked using his queen early. He and Grubbs had played a dozen matches by now. Early on, Harley Dee had won all of them. But with experience, Dale had improved. He was beginning to see the board with more perspective and plan his moves more in advance. Instead of merely reacting, he could now take the initiative. He and Grubbs had split the last six matches and Dale could tell that Harley Dee didn't like losing his edge.

Grubbs threatened with his queen. Dale thought his moves were too aggressive, almost reckless, so he employed a different kind of strategy. He basically lured Grubbs to move his queen farther into his territory by enticing him with a vulnerable rook. Grubbs took the bait. He attacked the rook not noticing the lurking knight.

As soon as Dale touched the knight, Grubbs realized his mistake. Dale heard him say, "*damn*" under his breath. Dale captured Grubbs' queen. The gambit had worked.

Dale had never tried a gambit before and he felt pleased with himself that it had worked. A queen for a rook. He now had the advantage and as long as he played the endgame cautiously he would win.

It took almost a dozen move but Dale prevailed. When he said, "check and check-mate" he tried to use as neutral of voice as possible. He didn't want to gloat although this had been the best game of chess he'd ever played.

Grubbs, slumped over, stared at the board, one hand tugging on his pathetic goatee. He grimly nodded and reached out a hand to topple his king. Then he suddenly took a big swipe with the back of his hand and knocked all the chess pieces hard against the near-by wall. He jumped up, knocking over the board, and stormed out of the camera room cursing under his breath.

"Hey, man," Dale called after him, "it's only a game."

-II-

But chess was much more than a game to Harley Dee Grubbs. It was one of the things he took pride in. All his life he'd been overlooked and under-appreciated. He knew he was homely looking; at times, he felt himself to be physically repulsive. Growing a goatee had given his angular face a little distinction but sometimes he thought it too scraggly and wished he could produce fierce, thick whiskers that would match his tough, wiry inner self.

Still fuming at his loss, Grubbs walked out of the back door of the press-room and turned the corner and leaned against the building's brick wall. He took out a pack of Lucky Strikes, gave it a jerk, popping up a quartet of unfiltered cigarettes. He nabbed the tallest one with his thin lips and with his other hand pulled out a lighter, flipped its lid with an equally practiced and deft twist of the wrist, then thumbed a flame. He lowered his face and puffed on the cigarette. Now ignited, he took in a long draught and felt the smoke diffuse through his lungs.

He'd always been a bad student. Not because he was stupid. He just hated the regimented way of school and especially liked defying the fussy female and weak-chinned male teachers. In and out of trouble, truant, habitually tardy, he lasted as long as eleventh grade when he realized, as he stood smoking in the alley behind the high school, that he didn't have to go back. So he didn't.

He'd never shown the slightest talent in anything except hunting. He quickly discovered in grade school that he couldn't draw, couldn't sing, and wasn't athletic. His suspicious and quick-to-take-offense personality didn't attract friends. He remained mostly a loner all through his childhood and adolescence although Percy Pollack, a cousin, had always been a reluctant friend. Really less a friend than a guy who took pity on him, like the kid who takes in a stray mutt that he really doesn't want.

But Grubbs had discovered he had a talent for one mental activity: chess. He taught himself to play the game by watching the older men in Hyde Park in Chicago when he'd stopped off in the city near the end of his travels, when he'd tramped all over the West and Midwest. The game had a special appeal for him that he really didn't understand. He enjoyed how the pieces looked and how they functioned. He especially became interested in the knight not only for its symbolic status but also because of its irregular way of moving. That's one reason why falling for a knight gambit had disgusted him so. He was the player who ordinarily wielded the knight's unconventional power to great effect.

He also despised losing to that Dale Smith. There was something about him that grated on his nerves. He had to admit that Smith had never been snooty or superior. He seemed interested in the work that he and Percy did and never lorded it over them. But Grubbs had enjoyed defeating him in chess. Beating a college grad. But Smith's skills were growing and the idea that he might develop into a better chess player than himself filled Grubbs with bitter resentment.

Not ordinarily reflective, Grubbs tried to understand why he felt such resentment for that Dale Smith guy. Maybe it was because he saw in Smith qualities that he himself lacked. Smith was educated, a college grad, and he read unusual, intellectual-kind of books. Grubbs knew he had a special kind of intelligence, too, but not that kind. Not the book kind.

Grubbs also felt jealous of Smith's physical attributes. Grubbs guessed most girls would find him attractive. Smith was a pretty good-looking guy with dark hair and dark eyes. He had a strong build with broad shoulders. He'd heard from Percy that Smith had been an athlete in high school although he didn't know if he'd been any good because Smith never talked about it. So he didn't brag about himself. Big deal. But at least Smith wasn't tall. In fact, Grubbs was an inch or two taller and that realization filled Harley Dee with a small sip of satisfaction.

Grubbs stopped thinking about his chess nemesis.

He didn't like comparing himself to other people, especially to guys who on the surface appeared more impressive. Grubbs knew most of them never achieved anything of importance. Most of them had it too easy. No, it was people like himself who did things. His kind did things because unlike so many other people they weren't afraid of failing. Grubbs had failed so much already (school, jobs, girls) that he was no longer afraid of failure and that in turn made him bold. But most importantly, he felt that inside him there was a kind of greatness lurking, a greatness born from daring to do what others fear to try.

Grubbs thought of what Smith had told him about the President's visit. So it was true. The President was coming to Buffalo City. What a joke! Why would he come to this dusty, windy, boring, asshole of a town?

Then Grubbs felt his heart leap and his pulse pound. A bold idea had exploded into his mind and he felt excited, a feeling he hadn't felt in a long time, but the feeling was even better than that, more like exhilaration. That feeling, a cross between fear and joy, excited him like no other feeling. The conventional part of him, what little of that there was, feared defying a norm, a rule, a law, but another part of him, his rebellious side, thrilled at the idea of violating that norm, rule, and law. He felt as if he were glowing inside with the anticipation of doing something wrong and sinful and that feeling reminded him of the time when he first visited the whorehouse and sat downstairs waiting for his turn.

He could do it. He had what it took. No one else did in this shithole of a town. All it would take was some planning and the guts to do it. And Grubbs had guts.

He'd smoked the cigarette almost to its end when out of the corner of his eye he saw Millard Greeley, that fat bastard, turn the corner of the building and come waddling his way toward him. Grubbs first instinct was to extinguish his cig; Greeley disapproved of smoking, wouldn't allow it in the newspaper offices or the back shop. Grubbs then felt disgusted with himself. He didn't give a good goddamn was Greeley thought.

Greeley stopped before Grubbs and looked disapprovingly at the smoldering stub of the cigarette.

"Are you on your break?" Greeley demanded.

"Yeah," Grubbs lied.

He saw the pudgy bastard give him a skeptical once over. Grubbs maintained the rather hostile expression on his face.

"Well, make sure you don't bring *that* in the newspaper," Greeley instructed, pointing to the dying cigarette as if it were an obscene appendage.

Grubbs dropped the cigarette to the sidewalk and crushed it with the heel of his work boot.

Greeley puffed out his chest in a pretense of belligerence but the act only made his paunch look more pronounced. Grubbs almost smiled. He knew Greeley was a little afraid of him. Then Greeley gave a dismissive glance and proceeded around the corner to enter the newspaper by the rear exit.

Grubbs' narrow, yellowish eyes watched the mayor disappear from view. Then he thought: maybe I ought to assassinate that fat bastard, too.

Millard Greeley walked through the press-room then the composing room then the newsroom with a peeved expression on his face. He glanced critically at his employees, not annoyed at anything they had done, but because he still felt insulted by his encounter with Grubbs. Perhaps he should fire the disagreeable Grubbs. A smoker! And such an insolent fellow to boot. And his shabby appearance. Did his grimy work clothes need to be so soiled and did his lupine face have to be so unkempt? And that disgusting growth of hair on his chin. Next time he interviewed a potential employee, even for a tech position, he'd make clear that facial hair was verboten.

Greeley tried to compose himself. If he fired Grubbs then he'd have to hire another assistant pressman. It was hard finding a skilled tech man who would work for the modest wages he paid. And the new fellow might turn out to be just as arrogant, although he doubted anyone could look as repellent as Grubbs.

Greeley, after parading through the newspaper office just to keep his employees on their toes, retired to his office. He settled himself into his leather chair and gazed appreciatively around his office, focusing in particular on the mounted plaques and framed citations of journalistic excellence that the *Stampede* had won during the past decades. Well, he had to admit, there weren't that many accolades festooning his office wall, but he anticipated that a new chapter of journalistic achievement was about to commence this week. Greeley leaned back in his chair and imagined for a moment the *Stampede* winning a Pulitzer Prize for community affairs or political commentary (from his own penned editorial) with the coming days coverage of President Carter's visit.

So far, everything was going superbly. All the community leaders had grown ecstatic by the news. Everyone was cooperating and demonstrating admirable *esprit de corps*. Even the Republicans were tantalized by the news and so far they had been amenable to all his suggestions. Plans were unfolding with the perfect precision of a crackerjack marching band. All of it led, of course, by a brilliant drum major.

Greeley, feeling a warm bath of self-approval wash over him, picked up the telephone and called the municipal government building, otherwise known as city hall. He asked the office manager, a middle-aged woman named Edith Swift, to confirm that the Western Oklahoma Community College fine arts auditorium had been reserved for the presidential visit. Greeley was certain it would be free since spring break recess would start Friday.

"I'm afraid there's been a snafu concerning that Mr. Mayor," said Mrs. Swift in her rather unpleasant nasal twang.

"What do you mean? I asked for it to be reserved yesterday."

"Yes, sir, I know that. But a snafu has appeared."

Greeley wondered why Mrs. Swift was so fond of that word. "Well, what is it?"

"According to Mr. Mors it is against the by-laws of the community college to host a partisan political event."

"What partisan political event?" sputtered Greeley.

"Well, President Carter's speech."

"It's not partisan! It's the President!"

"Well, according to Mr. Mors – "

"I don't give a hang what Mr. Mors thinks! What authority does he have in this matter anyway?"

"Well, he's on the community college board of directors and – "

"I don't care! He's wrong! The President is not coming to Buffalo City for a partisan event. He's not coming to campaign. He's not coming to fund-raise. He's coming for a town hall meeting."

"Well, Mr. Mors said – "

"All right, Mrs. Swift, I think I comprehend the problem." Greeley paused and threw open one of his desk drawers and fumbled for a WOCC handbook. He thought it contained the college's by-laws. That blasted Mors! Already interfering. "All right, Mrs. Swift, just as a precaution I want you to see about the reserving the high school gymnasium for Saturday evening. It won't be nearly as splendid as the fine arts auditorium but we need a back-up plan in case *Mr. Mors* is correct."

"Certainly, Mr. Mayor. I'll contact Superintendent Smiley right away."

"Very good. Call me back when you have the information. Also, put the fine arts auditorium issue on the agenda for a special city council meeting tonight."

Mrs. Swift said she would and Greeley hung up the telephone and searched his desk once again for the handbook. He didn't find it. He leaned back in his chair with a dissatisfied expression pursing his flabby cheeks. Actually, Greeley now remembered there was indeed such a prohibition in the by-laws. But it was absurd to consider the President's town hall meeting as a partisan political event. But leave it to Mors to advance that dishonest argument. And since the council had two other equally unreasonable Republicans, Greeley worried that he wouldn't be able to force the issue.

Blast! And everything was going so superbly! He'd have to notify the White House advance man (actually, it was a woman) that they might have to move the town hall meeting to another venue. What an embarrassment. Greeley had made such a favorable impression with the White House and now he'd be making an unfortunate change. And to think it was the community college that Mors was using to foil him. The existence of the community college was mostly due to Greeley. It was his idea and he'd enlisted the aid of prominent Democrats and the Democrat governor to push the plan through. Western Oklahoma was overwhelmingly Republican. All those ranchers and farmers and oilmen. But Greeley had argued that bringing in a new community college would alter the political balance a little. Greeley had already made in-roads with the Buffalo City school district employees, often reminding them which political party had their interests best in mind. The school district employed nearly 200 people and Greeley knew that almost all of them voted Democrat. The nursing home employees did likewise. Most of the workers at the Great Plains Regional Medical Center also voted for Democrats. Creating the community college and using the same political tactics would add hundreds of other Democrat votes. When Greeley pitched this idea two years ago, the state leaders had appreciated such a shrewd argument and the community college came into being. The college didn't have a large enrollment. It didn't employ a great many teachers or staff people. Some townspeople wondered why a town as moderately sized as Buffalo City even needed a community college. But Greeley was certain that as Buffalo City grew so would the demand for a junior college education. More importantly, the college would hire more workers and those state employees would vote for Democrats. Greeley knew he was right! Already the rather small number of instructors and administrators and staffers had added to the Democrat vote. Now, being a Democrat in Buffalo City wasn't so gauche. Even some of the town's merchants were voting Democrat.

Yes, things were changing for the better in Buffalo City. There was still a two to one Republican to Democrat ratio in the town but that was much better than ten years ago when the ratio was three to one. Who knows, maybe in another ten years it would all be even-Steven.

Yes, things were improving even in spite of that damned Byron Mors!

-IV-

Byron Mors hung up the telephone. He'd just received a phone call from the hospital. An elderly man had died an hour ago and his son-in-law, acting upon a suggestion by the attending physician, had requested that the Mors Funeral Home and Peaceful Prairie Chapel attend to the body. The son-in-law would ar-

85

rive in an hour. Byron, as he always did with prospective clients, had asked the woman on the other end of the line if she knew the son-in-law's occupation. She said he was a lawyer with a practice in Dalhart. Very good, thought Byron. The odds for the Deluxe Package were excellent.

Byron called down to the Preparation Room and instructed the delivery attendant to drive the hearse – rather the Funeral Coach – to the Great Plains Regional Medical Center and pick up the deceased.

Byron left his office and walked over to the spacious greeting room where his secretary and receptionist, Amy Comer, had her desk. He informed her that a new client would soon arrive. Amy, an attractive but not too attractive young woman (also not too young – customers didn't like them too young) smiled her becoming broad smile, not the subdued sympathetic one she employed for customers, and Byron, for a moment, took in her brunette hair and blue-eyed good looks. Amy was, by all accounts happily married, which was necessary requirement for working for Byron. He preferred married women because in theory they were less of a temptation. But lately, Byron had been visualizing Amy naked and although he tried to keep that alluring image out of his mind he found that he was having more difficulty doing that than he had before.

Byron quickly walked away before the effects of Amy's naked image transformed his facial expression from a avuncular grin into a satyr-like leer. To make matters worse, his mind suddenly conjured up a few images of last night's X-rated films. Ordinarily, he kept so busy during the day that his mind remained free of interfering erotic content. But lately graphic sexual images would materialize in his mind, even when offering his condolences to grieving family members as they discussed funeral arrangements. Perhaps he should cut back on his porn viewing. But the very thought of not indulging in his voyeuristic habit vexed him. Almost every night, after his wife went to bed, he watched his films for almost an hour. Increasingly, it was that prospect of sensual delight that carried him through the dreary day. But now the Night Byron was intruding into the realm of the Day Byron.

He checked his wristwatch. His wife, Kate, was supposed to be home by three. Kate and her younger sister, Bette, along with Joy, the Mors' three-year old daughter, were returning home after spending the night with Kate's mother in Oklahoma City. The two daughters visited their mother at least once a month. After the divorce and her ex-husband's remarriage, Kate's mother had departed Buffalo City for her old hometown.

Byron decided to wait for Kate outside the funeral home. He walked down the hallway that led to the west side of the building. This was the family's entrance. By using this entrance they could avoid the interior of the funeral home since a short hallway led directly to the circular stairway and the residential rooms upstairs.

He opened the door and scanned the street for her car, a new blue Buick Electra. No sign of her. He reclined against the brick wall and impatiently waited. While he did this he thought back to the delectable proceedings of last night. He smiled to himself. He hoped he hadn't scared the young man away.

87

Another concern momentarily popped into his mind. What if Dale Smith revealed any of their conversation or described the visual spectacle that had taken place last night to someone? That might prove problematic. But Byron discounted such a possibility. Dale seemed to be a discreet young man, and besides, he imagined that Dale would keep mum for no other reason than he probably felt embarrassed by their nocturnal cinematic activities.

Byron wondered if he'd been too candid about his past and his current illicit interests. He didn't think so. The young fellow seemed more impressed than shocked, although viewing the X-rated fare definitely stunned him.

Why was he even interested in this Dale Smith? Byron didn't quite know. He found the kid interesting, perhaps because he sensed potential in him. He was bright, although not especially well educated. Hadn't he graduated from some second-rate religious college? Every time Byron read the sports pages he'd spot one or two typos in the kid's copy. But he wrote well, with a certain style, especially in his columns. The topics he selected didn't interest Byron much; he wasn't very interested in sports any more although he had to keep abreast of the sporting world simply to engage in discussions with his friends and peers.

He, this Dale Smith, had a curious mind. Byron found that interesting. Imagine anyone in Buffalo City reading George Bernard Shaw and James Joyce and Dostoyevsky. Perhaps he could help direct Dale's reading, help guide his inquiring mind into a more enlightened direction. Maybe he could serve as a mentor and help shape the young man's sensibility.

It occurred to Byron that there was another reason for his interest in Dale Smith. And it wasn't intellectual. The young man reminded him of someone, a boy he'd grown up with and had become good friends with for a few years in mid-adolescence. This friend, Curtis Hartman, looked somewhat like Dale. Both had dark hair and eyes with an athletic build. Curtis had been one-quarter Indian, Comanche in fact, and his skin had an attractive bronze color. Dale had a similar kind of complexion.

Byron and Curtis had become good friends when they turned fifteen. They especially had a memorable summer before their sophomore year. Maybe their friendship would have continued but Curtis' family moved to the Texas panhandle and Byron lost touch with him. It wasn't until several years later, after Byron had graduated from college and returned home, that he discovered that Curtis had been killed in Vietnam. He'd been a marine and died in a battle at Quo Trang province, the same area where Blake had been killed. Curtis had been killed six months after Blake.

Even though it had been ten years since he last saw Curtis, the news of his death knocked Byron for a loop. He'd heard the news from one of Curt's cousins who lived in Buffalo City.

Kate's car appeared and Byron watched as she drove into the private parking area and parked next to Byron's Mercedes in the spaces reserved for the family vehicles.

"What is the occasion for this welcoming committee?" she asked as she exited the Buick. Kate was, as usual, tastefully dressed in an ivory satin blouse, a vermilion cashmere sweater, and a blue wool skirt of slightly less than moderate length that showed her long, shapely legs.

Byron went over and she offered her check for a welcome home kiss.

"Where's Joy?" he asked.

"Bette said she'd baby-sit her for a few hours." She noticed his frown. "She was just awful on the ride back. Cranky and temperamental and she wore me out. I wanted to take a nap when I got home so Bette agreed to take her for a few hours. What's the problem?"

Byron tried not to show his displeasure with Kate. Sometimes he didn't think she was the most doting of mothers.

"Oh!" Kate said, not waiting for Byron's response. "Guess what I heard on the radio while driving in?"

Byron thought Kate most attractive when she grew excited, then her fair complexion grew rosy and her green eyes widened in a becoming way, She was an attractive woman anyway. She wore her blonde hair fairly short now, the styled locks descending only to the nape of her neck. She had smallish but refined, symmetrical features and an oval-shaped face. Her figure, although not as trim as before she became a mother, still looked slender because of her above average height.

"Martians have landed in Grover's Corners."

Kate looked puzzled. "What?"

"I'm joking. What did you hear on the radio?"

Kate grew animated again. She grasped Byron's hand with both of hers. "The President is coming to

Buffalo City!"

"The president of what?"

"The President of – " Kate suddenly understood Byron's jest but she didn't think it was funny. "You know what I mean."

"Yes, I heard the news."

"You don't sound impressed. After all, the *President of the United States* is coming here. To Buffalo City!"

"I'm not impressed because he is not impressive."

"That doesn't matter. What does matter is that it's happening here. In our town."

Byron almost smiled because Kate, especially when returning from visiting her mother, complained how dull Buffalo City was. She wished they could move to a real city.

"Yes, who would have thought?"

"Just because you disapprove of him. I think he's a fine man. A decent man. He has a difficult job and I'm looking forward to having him come here and speak. This is going to be a memorable weekend. The Miss Buffalo City Pageant on Friday and then the President!"

This year Kate would be one of the judges for the Miss Buffalo City Pageant. She also served on the League of Women's Voters and participated with other civic committees and society groups. Her father, Arthur Anderson, was the chief administrator of the Great Plains Regional Medical Center. Byron actually got along well with his father-in-law. Not only did the old man prove useful in contributing to Byron's business but also Mr. Anderson was something of the town iconoclast. He didn't attend church, didn't engage in any boosterism, and didn't try to be one of the boys.

He'd even divorced his first wife so he could marry his much younger secretary. Byron had to officially disapprove of his father-in-law's behavior in his social circle, but he secretly admired the old man's independence. Kate, however, had been somewhat estranged from her father since his remarriage six months ago.

"Byron, you aren't listening."

He hadn't been. His wife had been gushing about the exciting, historically important events this coming weekend. Byron tried not to show his annoyance. In fact, he had a secret desire to ruin one of the historical events, namely the presidential visit. He wished he had the power to undermine the whole absurd spectacle. If he didn't have the power, then maybe Nature did. How about a nice tornado?

"I was listening," he told his wife. But she knew he hadn't and as he fetched the luggage from the car and walked with her into the building he had to listen to her berate him for his indifference.

They walked up the stairway to the residential area with Kate walking ahead. Byron watched her hips sway underneath her skirt. He thought about a scene from one of the porn movies he'd watched last night and that image, along with his wife's walk, which actually wasn't that seductive, put him in a lustful mood.

Once they got to their bedroom, he tossed the small suitcase and overnight bag on her bed and then went over to where Kate was standing before the dresser's mirror. He considered pinching her fanny but he knew she wouldn't like that so instead he put his arms around her waist.

"So how long is Bette going to baby-sit Joy?" he

asked in a suggestive voice.

In the mirror's reflection Kate gave him an exasperated look. "You can put that thought right out of your head. I've been driving for over two hours. I'm tired."

Byron took his hands from off her waist. "You're always tired."

Kate didn't respond. She walked away from him into the bathroom. He heard water gurgling from the faucet. He went over and sat on his bed.

He didn't have time anyway. A client would soon be arriving. Byron would use his best sales technique to convince the bereaved man (well, probably not so bereaved; he was the son-in-law) to splurge for the most expensive package.

He rose wearily from the bed. He was looking forward to tonight.

-V-

Dale crept closer to the on-deck circle and aimed his camera past the player practicing his swings and focused on the batter standing at the plate. Dale heard the ball skimming through the air and he pressed the shutter button. The click of the shutter opening and the batter's bat solidly connecting with the ball was perfectly synchronized. Dale looked up from his camera to see the baseball bounding into the alley between center and left. As the runner on second sprinted around third and headed for home and the batter raced past first and headed to second, Dale got ready for another shot. He timed this shot well, too, and captured the runner scoring the winning run standing up,

93

the throw from the outfield arriving one second too late.

Photography was sort of fun, thought Dale, as he took another photo of the Buffalo City Buffaloes bench members rushing into the diamond to congratulate the two guys who'd won the game in the bottom of the seventh.

He watched the celebration for a few moments, remembering with pleasure when he'd been in a similar celebrations playing high school baseball. In one game during his sophomore year he'd scored the winning run with he'd slid head first into home plate and in another game during his junior year he'd knocked in the winning run with a double. He remembered how wonderful those athletic exploits had felt and as he looked upon the baseball players still celebrating he suddenly felt a kinship with them. The feeling surprised him because he'd never felt any emotional connection or identification with the Buffaloes teams before.

That had proved to be a problem, his perceived lack of emotional involvement with Buffalo City teams, and he'd created the problem himself at the beginning of football season. Every Friday, the *Stampede* ran a sports feature about the upcoming football games and the newspaper staff made predictions. As sports editor Dale, of course, was required to make his prognostications, but Dwight, Floyd, George Sinclair, the business manager, and even Rosemary Rogers also made predictions. The five of them made predictions on ten games, five pro, four college (OU, OSU, Texas Tech, one at-large college game) and one high school game: the Buffalo City Buffaloes.

That first week of predictions, Dale, thinking he should approach his role in an objective, professional sort of way befitting a real sports editor, picked Buffalo City's opponent, Black Kettle, because that team had won the 3A football championship the previous year and were ranked second in pre-season. The Buffs, meanwhile, had recorded only a .500 record the year before and were ranked only number ten in the first poll.

The other four prognosticators, however, all picked Buffalo City to prevail but even then Dale didn't foresee any problem with his pick.

But when the Buffs won in an upset, 13-7, and Dale went into the locker room to get a few quotes, he noticed he was greeted without any warmth; in fact, a few players were outright hostile to him and made mention of his insulting prediction. One player, the team's linebacker, Larry Henderson, had muttered a threat. Even the head coach, Harmon Edwards, treated him with mild disdain for daring to go against the team.

So, he'd learned something that he should have remembered from his own football playing days: players and fans take things personally. From that point onward, Dale didn't go against the Buffs, not even when they tangled with Clinton, their undefeated arch-rival. Dale predicted Buffalo City would win even though he knew they wouldn't. The Buffs were having a good season but they weren't yet in the class of the Clinton Comets. So, when Buffalo City lost and he entered the locker room to get the obligatory quotes he expected a friendlier reception. But he didn't get it. He wasn't treated with rudeness or suspicion as before, but a mild resentment remained. He'd proved at the beginning he wasn't an ally. The players and coaches weren't fooled by his suspicious change of heart.

Dale, of course, didn't think a sports writer should be an ally but he didn't try to demonstrate his objectivity as candidly as before. His sports coverage was mostly written objectively but with some sympathy for the various Buffalo City teams. As the year progressed from football to basketball to now spring sports, no one, not a coach or a player or a fan, had again threatened to punch him in the nose like Larry Henderson had.

The baseball game now over, Dale went over to the dugout to get quotes from the baseball coach and to double-check some information with the official scorer. The problem with taking photos while covering the game was that he couldn't keep as detailed notes. In fact, Floyd Byrd, the staff photographer, was supposed to be taking photos of the baseball game. But Floyd, as he increasingly was doing, had claimed he had a conflict with another assignment and had asked Dale if he could shoot the game photos himself.

His duty now completed, Dale left the baseball diamond and headed out the field gate. As he walked toward his car, he noticed a trio of girls standing next to the concession stand talking. He glanced at them, noticing that they looked a little older than high school age, and proceeded to walk past. That's when one of them, a blonde with curls of hair piled on the top of her head like a poodle, said in a loud voice, "Would you like to take our picture?"

Dale stopped and looked at the blonde. She smiled

at him and he noticed she didn't have a pretty face but it was colorful due to her rather excessive make-up. She wore jeans and a long-sleeved red jersey that fit a little snugly. Her clothes emphasized her full figure (the word *zaftig* echoed in his mind), especially her large breasts. That last feature commanded his full attention for a moment then he glanced at her two friends. They were less colorful, less ample versions of the blonde. Both were brunette and both wore their hair with the same kind of precise wildness. That is, they piled a large, almost tangled mop of hair on top of their heads but in the back the hair hung long and straight.

"Okay, I'll take your picture," he said and as he aimed his camera at them, reading the aperture and adjusting the focus, the three girls giggled and huddled together with the blonde in particular striking a vampish pose, her lipstick red lips spread wide in an almost mock starlet smile.

Dale snapped the photo and the girls giggled again and the blonde one said that her brother played on the baseball team. "He's the catcher, Larry Henderson. Did you take a picture of him?"

"Didn't he strike out three times?"

"Oh, you're funny!"

Actually, he was just being accurate. He gave a vague wave of his hand signaling his departure. As he walked away, he heard Louise Henderson (he'd guessed who she was at first sight thanks to Byron Mors' description) say to her two girlfriends in a voice loud enough for him to hear, "oh, he's *cute*."

As Dale left Buffalo City Memorial Park to drive

back to the newsroom, he thought about Louise. She was not the type of girl he ordinarily found attractive. She was too ostentatious, both in her appearance and her manner. However, seeing her brought back to mind the words of Byron Mors. She'd asked about him? Well, she was obviously flirting with him just a minute before. He guessed she really was signaling her receptiveness. He didn't know if he'd take the bait. Even though at times he keenly felt like a lonesome stranger in town, and he certainly missed intimate contact with a female, he wasn't sure he wanted to embark on an affair that would simply be sensual in nature.

The fact is he still ached over the dissolution of his romance with his college girlfriend. They'd gone together for over a year and a half, although it wasn't the time span that mattered as much as the intensity of their romance. That's what it was, a romance, just not an affair or steady dating. He'd loved her and he doubted he'd ever love any woman as much as her. But it had been for the best that they parted. She was still in their hometown of Galilee attending the Nazarene college for her senior year and living her impeccable, sheltered, and beautiful life. In the end, he had rejected that world and she had rejected him, and he'd left his hometown of Galilee upon his graduation from college.

His mother and sister still lived in Galilee with his grandparents. His remarried father, and some of his other relatives, lived in near-by Oklahoma City. He still had friends in Galilee. Dale had visited both his mother and father a couple of time since coming to Buffalo City for the newspaper job. But when he was back home he felt out of sorts and on edge. He didn't like being in his hometown knowing his girlfriend was there, only a few blocks away in the college dormitory. Being in close proximity to her made the memories even harder to bear. Even after nearly a year he still felt her absence and he wondered when he'd get over his melancholy.

Thinking about her brought on that empty ache and he grew angry with himself for thinking about her. He knew it was over. Unlike some sappy movie, they'd never get back together and he knew it was absolutely necessary for both of them that they remained apart. Still, he hated the feeling of emptiness he felt when he thought of her.

Maybe what he needed was another girlfriend. Helen Brown, the girl he had conducted a platonic friendship with for the last few months, wasn't a likely candidate. He liked her and enjoyed her company but he felt no romantic or erotic feelings for her. She kept in touch while attending GNC by writing letters. She was supposed to be back in Buffalo City Friday for Spring Break. Her parents were going to their cabin for the week and she was supposed to be going with them. But she'd hinted in her last letter that she'd stay behind if he wanted her to.

He didn't think he'd like Louise the way he liked Helen but he did feel some strictly sensual interest in her. When walking to his car, he'd cast a quick glance back at the girls and Louise had her back turned to him and he liked how her blonde hair hung long and straight to the middle of her back, as if the tail end of her mane was pointing to her large but curvy jean-clad butt.

What depraved, lustful creatures we men are thought Dale. That observation brought back last night's celluloid orgy. Now, in the light of day, he could hardly believe that a man as outwardly respectable, intelligent, and cultured as Byron Mors spent his nights as a lascivious voyeur. What a bizarre evening. Then he visualized some of the scenes from the porno films he'd witnessed and became so engrossed in the mental spectacle he almost ran a red light. He hit the brakes and his Chevy's tires squealed. He was downtown and while waiting for the light to change he glanced out his side window and spied Byron Mors across the street walking out of Western Men's Hair Salon. Byron walked down the sidewalk nodding graciously at passersbys, attired in his usual dapper way in a dark business suit, somberly stylish, with every lock of his neatly groomed raven hair in place.

Dale smiled. No casual observer encountering Byron Mors would ever suspect the tall and dignified funeral director of secretly being a nocturnal porno fiend. Wasn't Byron the very epitome of a brazen hypocrite? If Dale hadn't earlier been recalling those same erotic films as well as Louise Henderson's enticing figure then maybe he would have readily made that accusation. Now he wasn't so sure. Maybe Byron Mors was just another common example of human imperfection.

Chapter Three
Wednesday

Dale had gotten to work earlier than usual so he could develop his film before The Bird (that's what he'd privately nicknamed Floyd) could commandeer the darkroom. Dale developed the film he'd shot yesterday and hung the negatives to dry then left the darkroom and instead of going back to his desk he went to the newspaper's morgue. Seeing no one in the rather small room, he examined last week's unbound volume. He was looking for an obituary.

He first looked at last Friday's issue and found two obits but neither matched the person he was looking for. He flipped to the Sunday issue (the *Stampede* didn't print a Saturday paper) but the three obits didn't fit the description. But Monday's single obituary seemed right. It read:

Virginia Johnson Yates, 49, of Buffalo City died Saturday. Born in 1930 in Batesville, ARK, she moved to Buffalo City in 1949 with her husband, Clint Yates, when he accepted a position with the Hennessey oil and natural gas firm. Mrs. Yates, a homemaker, was the mother of three children and was active in the PTA and a member of the Buffalo City Seventh Day Adventist church. She is survived by her husband, her son, Clint, Jr., 29, and daughters, Mary-Beth, 27, and Teresa, 23.

Flowers should be sent to Mors Funeral Home and Peaceful Prairie Chapel.

A small black and white photograph of Virginia

Yates when she was a young woman was printed next to the obit. Dale studied the photograph. She looked like a nice lady, not especially pretty, but with a pleasant smile and an attractive early '50s hair-do.

Dale felt fairly sure that this was the woman he'd seen in the casket Monday night. The deceased looked about that age. At least, the body didn't look a lot younger or older. If she died Sunday she probably would have been prepared for public viewing for early Tuesday.

Ever since that night the image of the dead woman in the casket would enter his mind at rather odd times. He even had a dream last night in which she made an unwelcome appearance. In the dream Dale had been watching X-rated movies when he glanced away from a scene in *Three Holes* to the side of the room where he saw the dead woman displayed in the casket. Then he sensed someone sitting beside him and he turned and saw Louise Henderson. He noticed she was quite naked. She smiled at him, that same kind of smile that she'd used in her pose for the photograph. To his right he heard Byron Mors whispering in a strange, almost moaning voice that Louise "was receptive."

A typical weird dream of his but when he woke he wondered who the dead woman was. Now he knew. She was Virginia Yates, mother of three. He wondered how she died. It didn't specify in the obituary.

Reading about her rather ordinary life and thinking again of seeing her corpse displayed in the funeral home created an odd feeling in Dale: more a feeling of melancholy than despondency. She died fairly young. As he thought of her, his melancholy feeling deepened into something like grief and he bowed his head and said a short prayer for her. He wasn't formally religious anymore but he still believed that people had souls so he said a prayer for her soul wherever it was.

Dale left the newspaper morgue and entered the newsroom. He noticed that an unfamiliar young man stood beside his desk. He looked too young to be a coach, besides Dale thought he knew all the town's coaches, so he wondered whom this guy was. Dale passed by Dwight's desk and the managing editor nodded his head in the direction of the stranger.

"That's the new guy."

"The new guy?"

"Yeah, the fellow who's going to help out this week. He got in last night. Come on, I'll introduce you to him."

Dale followed Dwight across the room and was introduced to the new guy, whose name was Will Whitaker. Dale and Will shook hands. Will smiled a small smile, not so much a shy one as an ironic one and that expression caught Dale's attention. While Dwight made the equivalent of newspaper small talk, Dale discreetly examined the new reporter. He was about average height, with a slim build, and was dressed in a semi-casual way: brown oxfords, chinos, a blue dress shirt, a tan corduroy jacket, and a navy blue tie. Dale liked the corduroy jacket and blue shirt because he was wearing those same articles of clothing, too, but unlike Will, Dale's brown jacket didn't have any elbow patches. Dale's manner of dress, in fact, was always on the rustic side. He wore boots and Levi's and usually didn't wear a tie.

Will's most noticeable features were his reddish

hair and his large spectacles. His hair was of moderate length, neatly combed. The eyeglasses had rather stylish large frames. Behind the lenses Will's light blue eyes peered out with an intelligent, candid expression, not at all like The Bird's beady resentfulness.

As on cue, The Bird appeared and Dwight introduced them. Dale watched Will's reaction to Floyd's flabby handshake and rather indifferent greeting. Will didn't show any umbrage, he simply took it in stride. Another characteristic that Dale found interesting.

Introductions now concluded, Dwight glanced around the newsroom in an apologetic way and said that unfortunately they didn't have an open desk. "I thought Will here could share your desk, Dale, if you don't mind."

Dale glanced at Will who tilted his head in a way that seemed to say, "sorry for the inconvenience."

"No, I don't mind," Dale said, appreciating Will's unprepossessing attitude.

"We'll bring in a table and chair and set it next to Dale's desk to provide a little more desk space. And we have an extra typewriter for you," Dwight told Will.

Will said that would be fine. He didn't need a lot of space. Dwight once again welcomed him to the *Stampede* and told him to feel free to ask questions and then returned to his desk.

"You're a grad student at OU, aren't you?" Dale asked.

"Yes."

"And during Spring Break you decide to come out here to help us."

Will nodded.

"I can understand that. After all, who wouldn't prefer coming to western Oklahoma rather than going to some sunny, sandy beach and enduring all those girls in their bikinis?"

"Well, I tend to sunburn easily."

Dale grinned. "It's sunny here, too, but there's not any beaches or bikinis."

"Not until now. I did bring my bikini."

"I hope you won't wear it in the newsroom."

This time Will grinned. "I suppose that's against the dress code."

"Not at all. Millard Greeley often wears his in his office."

Will laughed out loud.

"I take it that you've met our publisher," Dale said.

"Yes. Last night."

"He's also the mayor of Buffalo City."

"Yes, so I was told."

"I understand that's quite common in the newspaper world. Katherine Graham used to be mayor of D.C."

"Does she wear her bikini at the *Washington Post*?"

"No, only Ben Bradlee wears a bikini there."

"Not Woodward or Bernstein?"

"They wear only one-pieces," said Dale. Will grinned and Dale thought it was time to end to their repartee. "Didn't you edit the OU student newspaper?"

"Yes, during my senior year."

"I edited my college newspaper, too."

"Where was that?"

"At Galilee Nazarene College."

Will rubbed his chin in a thoughtful way. "I think I've heard of that before."

"Galilee is only about ten miles west of Oklahoma City."

Will Whitaker pointed his finger at Dale as if identifying him at a police line-up. He smiled slyly. "Now, I remember. You got in some trouble for an April Fool's spoof."

Dale could hardly believe that Will had heard of that. "Yeah, that's right."

"I read that spoof. It was called *Smoke and ...*"

"*Smoke and Mirrors.*"

"Right! A friend of mine showed me a copy. It was hilarious."

Dale was amazed that his notorious satire had circulated to Norman. "Well, the administration didn't share your amusement."

"Didn't they try and kick you out of school?"

"Not quite. But they probably would have if my mom's house hadn't been destroyed by a tornado."

Will studied Dale with amused look on his face, trying to determine if he was being droll or not. Dale was about to tell him that he was exaggerating but only by a little when Dwight interrupted their conversation. The managing editor signaled Dale with a wave of his hand.

"Oh, yeah, I have to run the AP wire," Dale said. "Look, go ahead and sit at my desk. I'll be gone for twenty minutes or so. You can plan all the scoops you'll dig up here in Buffalo City."

"Okay, thanks. I do need to think about those scoops."

Dale grinned and left as Will sat in his chair. As he walked over to Dwight's desk, Dale thought: At last, someone at work with wit and brains. These next few days might be fun.

-II-

Millard Greeley needed to relieve himself. Sitting at the head table at the weekly Kiwanis luncheon he tried to ignore the urge. After all, he was basking in the hearty bonhomie of his fellow Kiwanis. Even those members who were Republican were congratulating him and expressing their admiration for putting Buffalo City on the map. Greeley had nodded modestly throughout the their approbation. He enjoyed the slaps on his back, delighted in their warm and hearty handshakes, and grew even more affable than normal as he divulged the strategy that had brought this historical achievement to fruition. To help celebrate the occasion, Greeley had quaffed three glasses of iced tea and now he had to answer the call of nature. He excused himself and took leave of his admirers.

As he walked to the men's room of *The Lariat Inn and Restaurant*, he recalled his sage answers to the questions he'd been asked by his fellow citizens these past two days. The most prominent of which was: How did he do it? Greeley always gave a more complicated answer than was warranted. The truth of the matter was that he'd lobbied tirelessly. He had kept in touch with the Carter administration on a regular basis, mostly by post. Three years ago he first wrote an epistle to the Carter campaign thanking them for stopping in Buffalo City for those few hours back in April 1976. In a gracious and subtle way he reminded them of the hospitality they'd enjoyed in Buffalo City and how the denizens of this fine town would be proud to host the future president again. When Carter won the election, Greeley had sent a cable congratulating him on his historic and well-deserved victory. He'd kept the message short (cables aren't cheap) but he did praise the new President for his decency, honesty, and keen intelligence and stated that he knew he'd restore honor and integrity to the White House, two cardinal virtues that had been so ignominiously missing during the Nixon and Ford regimes. Greeley continued sending complimentary missives to the Carter administration every month for the next three years. He often closed his letters with a little reminder: that President Carter had declared to the grateful citizens of Buffalo City that if elected president he would one day return.

Then a few months ago Carter began attending town hall meetings around the country. Some political commentators saw this as a cynical political attempt to by-pass the unflattering media coverage he'd regularly been receiving. But Greeley saw it as a brilliant political *cri de coeur*: President Carter wanted to unburden his heart to his fellow citizens and in return sincerely wanted his people to speak to him. It was just the opposite of cynical. It was Carter being Carter, a genuine man of the people, who, now in a time of political extremity, longed to return to the bosom of the People and seek sustenance.

Greeley had said as much in a letter posted just two months ago. Other mayors of small (but progressive) cities probably were too jaded to expect anything in return. But Greeley believed.

108

And a week later, he received a reply.

The first communication came by mail and notified him that the President was considering Buffalo City as one of the sites for a town hall meeting. The letter contained several forms to be filled and Greeley promptly complied and mailed them back. The next communication was via telephone. The assistant to the Chief of Staff chatted with him and informed Greeley that Buffalo City was definitely in the running. Two agonizing weeks passed. Oh, how Greeley longed to tell someone of the wonderful possibility of the President's second coming. But the mayor was prudent. He didn't want to jinx the wondrous possibility by blabbing about it. Greeley didn't even tell his loyal wife, even though Carol was the very soul of discretion.

Just when he'd about given up hope, he received another telephone call a week ago. Turned out that the next town hall meeting was scheduled for a small Missouri city situated along the Mississippi River but heavy rains had produced a flood and that town couldn't host the town hall. The White House knew of Greeley's interest and had heard of his masterful organizational skills. Was it possible for Greeley to marshal the forces to host the town hall meeting on such short notice?

Greeley averred he could. Greeley could move mountains when it came to serving the President.

The White House would be back in touch soon. Two days passed and the call came: the President would be returning to Buffalo City. Would Saturday work out?

Of course, said Greeley.

He'd related this story to dozens of people over the

past few days, often embellishing his role and making the whole process much more complicated and mysterious than it actually was. But anyone would forgive Greeley of indulging in some exaggeration. After all, he'd accomplished a political feat than no one else could possibly have done here in Buffalo City.

Greeley slipped into the men's room and unzipped. He was rather enjoying his copious urination in this well-appointed lavatory when he heard the door open. He heard footsteps echo on the tile then he heard the sound of a zipper humming its song. Greeley, ordinarily not a man who peered at his fellow urinators, glanced to see who stood at the other urinal. When he saw whom it was Greeley's bladder almost entirely shut down. It was Byron Mors.

"We're going to have stop meeting like this, Millard."

That was one of Byron Mors' qualities that Greeley did not appreciate: his tasteless sense of humor.

"I assure you, Byron, if I knew I was going to encounter you here, I would have chosen a different rest room."

"The ladies room?"

Millard tried to get his urinary system to function again. It was as if a big foot had stepped on a water hose, impeding its flow. As soon as Greeley thought of that unpleasant analogy, he felt pressure building in his abdomen.

Making his discomfort more acute he could hear that Byron Mors was having no difficulty with his flow. He heard a steady hiss of fluid being expelled.

"Do you know, Millard, what the word *Kiwanis* means?"

"Of course, I know. I've been a member for seven years. It means, 'we build.'"

"That's the official motto. The original word is derived from the Ojibwa, the meaning of which is to "fool around." There's also a longer phrase: 'I make noise; I am foolish and wanton.'"

"I wish more people could hear such sacrilege. Then they wouldn't be fooled by your false image. But I've always known the real you."

"And I have always known the real you, too."

Just like Byron Mors to deflect a perceptive point with a rhetorical quip thinks Greeley. However, Greeley wondered if Byron knew more than he thought he knew. He put that notion out of his head and got to the real issue.

"I want to ask you a question, Byron, if I may."

"Shoot."

Greeley winced at that word. He still wasn't shooting. Instead he stood with his unresponsive pecker in his hand waiting for that someone to take his foot off the hose.

"Why did you so adamantly and unreasonably object to the community college's fine arts auditorium being used for the President's town hall meeting?"

Greeley had called an emergency session of the city council for yesterday evening and just as he would have predicted Byron Mors led the insurrection.

"It's against the by-laws for the college to host partisan political events."

Byron Mors, his task now completed, zipped up. He quickly washed his hands with professional skill.

"How is the town hall a partisan event? You never

answered that question last evening."

While drying his hands, Byron turned and made sure no one occupied the stalls. "Just between you and I, it probably isn't."

Greeley involuntarily jerked. The urine suddenly splashed out with such pent-up force that it sloshed against the back of the urinal and a few disagreeable drops landed on his trousers.

Byron Mors paused for a moment, his expression contemplative. "You better see a urologist, Millard. I think you have a problem." Then he promptly exited the restroom.

Greeley, his task also now completed, cursed under his breath: that damn undertaker!

-III-

After making deadline, Dale asked Will Whitaker if he'd like to take a tour of the *Stampede* with him. Will nodded his head with mock-eagerness and said he'd be "honored" see the inner workings of the newspaper.

Dale first led him over to the advertising and business side of the building. They quickly zipped around the offices and Dale introduced Will to George Sinclair and Mrs. Milford. Then they ambled down a hallway that connected the classified ad office with the composing room. There Dale acquainted Will with the two women who did paste-up then they proceeded to the camera room. The *Stampede*'s camera room had received an upgrade just a month ago; a new vertical camera had been bought and the darkroom had been completely refurbished. Instead of a regular door, the darkroom now had a revolving cylinder for entry. As they approached it, Dale paused and extended a hand as if introducing it: "And now for the orgasmatron." Will laughed, obviously getting the reference to *Sleeper*, a 1973 Woody Allen movie.

Dale entered, followed by Will, and they stood in the glow of the red safety lights. They examined the vertical stat camera. Dale had learned a few months ago to make PMTs using it and then they exited the same way they came in.

Once outside, Dale said, in a sated, almost weary voice, "Whew, two orgasms in one day," and he knew that would be a running gag between the two of them for days to come.

Dale then led Will to the press-room and they first encountered Percy Pollack. They briefly chatted and then Dale spied Harley Dee Grubbs standing near the back of the press with an oily rag in his hand. Dale started to go over and introduce the assistant press-man to Will when Grubbs, a strange expression on his face, something like a sneer, abruptly turned and swiftly walked out the rear door.

"What's his problem?" Will asked.

"Oh, Vlad is just shy."

"Is his real name Vlad?"

"No, it's just a nickname I have for him."

"Why? Is he Russian?"

"I don't think so. But he does resemble, with that goatee, Lenin."

Will nodded thoughtfully. "A revolutionary in the press-room. Sounds dangerous."

"I think his bark is worse than his bite. Although,

113

I don't really know. He's never bitten me. " Then Dale thought about Grubbs' violent reaction to his loss during yesterday's chess match. He told Will about the strange encounter.

"Revolutionaries can be sore losers," Will said.

"Or winners," said Dale.

Will nodded and then followed Dale into the distribution and circulation area of the newspaper, where there weren't any revolutionaries, just two members of the exploited proletariat.

-IV-

Harley Dee Grubbs rode in the passenger side of his brother's rusty green 1967 Ford pick-up as the junky truck rattled over the rutted dirt road on the way to the Grubbs' family farm. The radio, tuned to KBUF, the town's country and western station, blared the recent hit song, "Mamas Don't Let Your Babies Grow Up To Be Cowboys."

Grubbs glared at the radio. He hated most country songs; in fact, he loathed most music, whether pop, classical, jazz, or country. He especially detested romantic or sentimental lyrics. Such lyrics made him want to puke. The only music he really enjoyed was heavy metal music. He'd been a Led Zeppelin fan from the beginning. He had dozens of heavy metal albums by Black Sabbath, Judas Priest, Iron Maiden, Motorhead, and AC-DC. Back in his tiny apartment on the edge of town, he'd crank up the volume on his stereo and let the raucous rumblings fill his living room and wouldn't turn it down until the neighbor in the adjoining apartment threatened to call the cops.

Grubbs turned his glare to his older brother, Doug, who tapped a thick finger on the steering wheel and sang along with the tune. Doug's voice sounded like a squealing pig. Oblivious to the unmelodious sound, Doug continued to cheerfully bellow the song not pausing even when he got a lyric confused with another song's.

"Turn that shit off!" Grubbs shouted.

"Aw, Harley Dee, I like that song. It sounds real good."

Grubbs stared at his brother who grinned his goofy grin at him. Even though Doug was two years older and five inches taller and seventy pounds heavier, Grubbs had been the dominant brother as long as he could remember. Even when they were little boys observers would see the much smaller Harley Dee lambasting the hulking Doug for some minor transgression and the bigger brother hanging his head in shame and enduring the verbal and sometimes physical assaults. Doug obviously had the physical power to batter his younger brother but he had such a mild and docile temperament, coupled with a feeble intellect, that he never fought back.

Grubbs knew it was more than that. He knew Doug, for some strange reason, had genuine affection for him. He'd often proclaimed how "smart you is," when Harley Dee performed some uncomplicated mental task. Grubbs didn't think his older brother was an imbecile. Doug had been held back one grade, but he could read and write after a fashion. He knew a few facts and he had enough sense not to stand out in the rain. But there was no denying that Doug had never exercised his brain and as a consequence it had shriveled to the mental size of a peanut.

Doug didn't need much smarts doing the work he did. He helped out with the family farm and also had a job as a bin sweeper at the grain co-op.

But it was Doug's docility that drove Grubbs nuts. In spite of his size and strength, Doug could be bullied by a man half his size. Women, of course, manipulated him with ease. His older brother's meekness exasperated him. On more than one occasion Harley Dee had exploded: "You're as big as a bull but you're nothin' more than a cow!"

Thinking about Doug's deficiencies had taken the fire out of Grubbs' ire. He gave his brother a reluctant look of pity.

"Least turn it down a little."

"Sure thing, Harley Dee."

As Doug reached a huge mitt to the radio knob, a second song filled the cabin, "Take This Job And Shove It." Grubbs put a hand out to prevent Doug from executing the request. He sort of liked this song. Doug returned his big hand to the steering wheel and both brothers listened to the hit country tune. Grubbs thought about work earlier that day: How Dale Smith had brought some other young college grad into the press-room. That pissed him off! Smith just showing off. But Grubbs also knew that he still rankled over losing that chess match.

Grubbs savored the lyrics of the song. He'd like go into that fat bastard Greeley's office and tell him to shove it. He knew Greeley underpaid him. Greeley underpaid everybody except maybe the business manager. Grubbs didn't know much about the financial operation of the newspaper but he reckoned that Greeley and the business manager, George Sinclair, made off right well while the rest of them worked for peanuts.

While Grubbs nursed his resentments, the pick-up rambled down the dusty road until it got to the family farm. The truck passed through the opening of a rickety wood fence and headed for the barn when both brothers saw a dozen other vehicles, mostly trucks but also a few big American-made gas-guzzlers, parked before the red barn.

"Think there's another AAM meetin'," said Doug, a he parked the truck next to an old rusting Cadillac.

Grubbs nodded grimly. He wasn't in the mood to listen to a bunch of old farmers bitch about commodity prices. Like most everyone they just gabbed. Why didn't the bastards take action? Not just organizing tractorcades but doing somethin' that took balls.

The two brothers ambled over to the farmhouse, a big, ugly two-story dingy-white wooden structure that needed painting. The Grubbs farm, until recently, had been successful operation. They grew mostly wheat, but also alfalfa and corn. Harley Dee's father, Grover Grubbs, ran the place. His mother, a thin homely woman that Harley Dee favored in his looks, took care of the house and did all the myriad of chores from cooking, cleaning, washing, canning, mending, sewing, and nursing, that farmer's wives had been doing for centuries. Harley Dee had two older sisters, Bertha, thirty, and Gladys, two years older than Bertha, and both were homely young women. Bertha favored the mother, Gladys the father. In spite of their plain looks they both had gotten married. Their husbands worked on the Grubbs' farm and each family had its own small house on the far end of the farm.

Harley Dee had never been interested in the farm. Even when he lived at home he shirked his chores and preferred going out and shooting game. He'd developed into a crack shot and since he brought the family fresh game several times a week no one, except the family patriarch, complained about his laziness concerning his farm duties.

Grubbs and his brother now climbed the back porch and heard inside the house the rumble of men's voices. They opened the screen door and walked into the spacious kitchen. Bunched around the long dinner table were seven men, most wearing overalls, and five other men were standing around the stove, sink, and refrigerator. These were the core members of the American Agriculture Movement in these parts. Harley Dee's father, Grover, the ringleader of the local AAM, sat at one end of the kitchen table and looked with disapproval at the arrival of his two sons.

"Can't you see we're havin' a meetin'?" he said in his heavy, disdainful voice, about the only tone he used except on those rare occasions when playing cards and drinking whiskey. "So no need to come trampin' in here."

Grover Grubbs was a big man, although not quite as big as his oldest son, but with the same kind of massive, hulking shoulders and powerful arms. Nearing sixty, he now had a big paunch. He was balding with small, shrewd light blue eyes, a short plug of a nose, a thin, critical mouth, and a big jaw and jutting chin. Harley Dee thought his old man resembled that actor, Burl Ives. He didn't have the actor's piping tenor voice, though. Instead Grover had a thick, guttural voice. Otherwise, his father, as he grew older, increasingly reminded Harley Dee of Burl Ives, and not the Burl Ives who spoke the narration and sang friendly songs on the "Frosty the Snowman" show, a kid's Christmas special that Harley Dee had once seen and especially detested (Doug liked it a lot though), but the Burl Ives in an old western, *The Big Country*, that Harley Dee had seen on TV. In that movie, Burl plays a demanding, cantankerous rancher feuding with a neighbor over water rights. The old rancher is so disgusted by his son's cowardice that near the end of the movie he shoots him down.

Harley Dee could imagine his own father doing that. But it wouldn't be for cowardice.

"Oh, sorry, daddy," Doug said, already starting to back out of the kitchen.

"I'm just here to get some shootin' in," said Harley Dee.

"Dandy. Go do it then."

"First, I'm goin' to my old room to fetch my rifle."

Harley Dee loped across the kitchen, ignoring his father's disgruntled expression. He walked to his old bedroom, not bothering to say hello to his mother in the living room, and got his rifle from the gun rack all the while listening to the group of men discussing their next plan of action. Harley Dee didn't care about the group's plans. He didn't even know when the American Agricultural Movement started. Probably just

119

some farmer fed up with low prices and government agriculture policies and he fussed to another farmer who bitched to another and soon the "movement" started. His father got involved a year ago and began to take it mighty seriously. In fact, the old man actually drove his tractor along with three thousand other AAM members and their tractors all the way to Washington, D.C. in February to lobby for higher prices. Harley Dee had to admit that his father's participation in the tractorcade secretly impressed him. He knew his father was a sonuvabitch but he never thought Grover would turn into a protester.

Harley Dee weaved his way through the AAM members, holding the hunting rifle high above his head as if traversing a stream of water.

"That sonuvabitch Carter is supposed to get here Saturday," Grover Grubbs told his colleagues. "We got to get as many of our members out there and greet that bastard with a big-ass tractorcade."

"Can we protest the President?" asked one of the men. Tall, lean, grizzled, and middle-aged, he wore a baseball cap with the word *McKenzie's*, one of the local feed stores, emblazoned on the front.

"We shore as hell can," Grover Grubbs growled. "It's our constitutional right."

"Too bad we can't do more than tractorcade him," said another member, a hefty man with a cowboy hat perched on his head, as he watched Harley Dee negotiate his exit.

"I got two sons," Grover said disdainfully. "The eldest is as dumb as a post. The other one is not worth a damn at nuthin' but shootin' that rifle."

Harley Dee heard his father's comment and he smiled a thin, nasty smile. If only old Grover knew.

Outside Harley Dee signaled Doug to follow and they walked past the barn into the pasture where a couple of old nags nibbled the spring shoots of grass. They walked two hundred yards to a narrow creek where a scraggly cluster of cottonwoods stood.

"It's gettin' sort of dark out, Harley Dee," said Doug as he peered to his right at the orange-yellow sun squatting on the purplish horizon.

"It's light enough." Harley Dee realized he'd have to find out for certain when the President would be arriving in Buffalo City. He wasn't even certain where the event would take place. He needed to know the time of day, the location, how many people would be with him, and his itinerary. There were still a lot of loose ends to tie up and he only had three more days.

They walked to the stand of trees and Harley Dee picked out the tallest stump, perhaps two feet high, and told Doug to place one of the whiskey bottles on top. Harley Dee handed Doug his rifle, a 30-06 semi-automatic, then pulled out a .38 revolver from out of his belt. They paced thirty feet away. Harley Dee put the revolver back under his belt and the end of the fatigue jacket concealed the handle. He tried to look nonchalant, not really focusing on anything, then at the count of three he pulled the end of the jacket out of the way with his right hand and with his left hand he reached for the revolver. He held the butt of the revolver in his palm, his thumb cocked the hammer, and his first finger felt the trigger. He squeezed and a bullet exploded out of the muzzle and shattered the whiskey bottle.

Doug slapped his two big hands together in a clumsy clap. "That's wuz a really good shot, Harley Dee!"

Grubbs thought if he could get close enough and not attract the attention of the Secret Service then he'd almost certainly hit his target. But only four years ago two different women had tried to kill President Ford with handguns. Both missed. He wouldn't miss but he worried that the Secret Service would especially be on the lookout for a close proximity shooter with a handgun. The other concern was that he'd almost certainly be either shot or captured. No, the rifle would be a better option if he could find a good lair to shoot from.

Harley Dee stuffed his revolver back inside the waist of his pants then took his rifle from his brother and told Doug to put up another bottle. Harley Dee walked fifty yards away then turned and looked back at his brother standing a few feet away from the bottle on the stump. He could see it okay, but the bottle looked like it was only a foot high rather than two. Plus there would be several obstacles, including people milling in the crowd, blocking a clear shot. No, if he was going to use a rifle he needed some elevation.

Harley Dee scanned the pasture, then the wheat fields where medium-sized stalks of winter wheat were waving in the breeze. Everything around him was flat. Then he saw the red barn three hundred yards away.

He marched in its direction.

"Where you goin', Harley Dee?"

"Stay there and don't move. I'll be back in a few minutes."

Harley Dee made it to the barn in five minutes. He climbed up into the hayloft and went over to the small window that framed the trees at the creek. He peered across the field where his brother stood. He'd like to be higher up, but for now, for the dry run, this would do.

He shouldered his rifle and braced his left elbow on the windowsill. He gazed through the scope until he found the stump and the whiskey bottle on top of it. Even in the fading sunlight, the scope magnified the bottle so Harley Dee could read the label: Wild Turkey. He put his finger on the trigger and enjoyed the feeling of the rifle in his hands. He then slowly moved the barrel to the right about five feet and picked up Doug's hulking figure in the scope. He positioned the cross hairs at the middle of Doug's empty head. How easy it would be to squeeze the trigger and end the big dumb animal's pathetic life.

He moved the rifle barrel back five feet to the left, found the bottle, took aim, held his breath for a moment, then slowly exhaled as his finger pressed the trigger.

The Wild Turkey bottle exploded into dozens of shards and splinters a split second after the rifle's curt retort.

Doug jumped and started bellowing. He waved his arms and danced like a burly, clumsy marionette.

Harley Dee lowered the rifle and smiled thinly at his brother's near hysterical dance and comical shouts. Yeah, his plan was going to work.

Dale and Will walked out of the *Stampede* office, each holding a copy of that day's newspaper. They slowly ambled down the sidewalk both of them scanning the front page. Dale noticed that Will's story, a news feature about local politicians' reaction to the President's impending visit, was positioned just below Dwight's lead story. Dale also noted the name on the by-line: William F. Whitaker.

Dale read the lead paragraph. Clear, concise, cleanly written. He skimmed a few more paragraphs. Precisely written journalism, well organized. Will seemed to be an excellent newspaperman.

They stopped before a green '77 Volvo. Dust covered most of the car. It must be Will's.

"Nice car," Dale said.

Will shrugged. "It was a graduation present."

"So, where are you staying in town?"

"At the Washita Best Western."

"Is Greeley springing for it?"

"Oh, yeah."

"That's why you're not staying at the Hilton." Actually, Buffalo City didn't have a Hilton but there were a couple of fairly expensive hotels. "Do you have any plans for tonight?"

"Not tonight. Tomorrow I'm supposed to dine with the publisher-mayor. Friday and Saturday, of course, I'll be on assignment."

"Yeah, me too. The reason Greeley didn't invite you to dinner tonight is because it's Wednesday."

"Is there something special about Wednesday?"

"Yeah. It's church night."

"Greeley goes to church on Wednesday night?"

"Yeah. Half the town does."

"But you don't?"

"Not anymore."

"Disillusioned with religion?"

"Not exactly. I didn't have that many illusions to begin with. I just prefer other things."

"Such as?"

"Movies, books, art."

"Yes, I noticed you like books." Will pointed to the book Dale was holding in his hand, *All the King's Men*.

"I'm almost finished. Have you read it?"

"Yes, it's been called one of the best novels about American politics ever written."

Dale nodded. He couldn't make that claim because he didn't know much about politics. "So, if you're not doing anything tonight, why don't you come to dinner with me? We can talk more about other American political novels."

Will said fine and Dale suggested they drive their respective cars over to the Best Western and Will could leave his there. Then he'd take Will over to his place for a while before they went out to eat. Will agreed and five minutes later they were sitting in Dale's Chevy as he pulled into the driveway of Mrs. Kennicott's house.

"You live here?" asked Will.

"I just rent a room. The house belongs to an old lady who's in a nursing home."

They got out of the car and entered the house and Dale asked Will if he'd like anything to drink. Dale said he had milk, orange juice, and 7-Up. Will said he'd take a 7-Up so Dale poured two glasses of 7-Up and they walked into his bedroom. Will sat in the old easy chair while Dale sat on his bed.

"Sorry that I don't have beer or liquor."

"You don't drink?"

"Nope. I don't like how it tastes."

"I don't like the taste much either."

Will got up and walked around Dale's room, looking at the map of the United States and a National Geographic map of the American Southwest that were tacked to the wall. He examined the titles of the novels in the small bookcase. He noticed a stack of two-dozen albums on the floor next to the stereo.

"Mind if I take a look?"

Dale said he didn't mind and Will knelt down and flipped through the albums. Mostly groups from the '60s, including several Beach Boys albums. Also Bruce Springsteen, The Alan Parsons Project, and the Manhattan Transfer from the '70s.

"You have a lot of Beach Boys records."

"Yeah, that's corny, I know."

"I have a couple of The Manhattan Transfer records, too."

"Is that the kind of music you prefer?"

"I like all kinds of musical genres including jazz. I suppose The Manhattan Transfer qualifies. The group's name is taken from one of the novels in the Dos Passos *USA* trilogy."

"I've never read anything by him yet."

"He's interesting writer. His books could qualify as novels about American politics."

Dale asked Will about the *USA* trilogy and he gave an

incisive synopsis of the three novels and then they discussed a couple of other novels and got so engrossed in their conversation that they forgot the time. When Dale noticed it was almost seven, he asked if Will was ready to eat. Will was. Dale asked what he felt like eating. Will said he wasn't sure. What kind of restaurants did they have here?

"Guess."

"A lot of steakhouses."

"That's right."

"That's fine. I haven't had a steak since last night."

"I don't know any of the good restaurants in town," Dale said. "I don't eat out much."

"I remember seeing a pizza place when I drove into town. We could go there. I think I'd prefer a more casual dining atmosphere tonight. I know tomorrow will be more formal."

"That's right. Greeley will take you to the country club. I think they have international cuisine there like tamales and enchiladas."

Will grinned and the two of them drove to the pizza place, *Roy's*. When they arrived Will said, "Roy's pizza? That sounds very authentic."

They went in and sat at a booth and a waitress came over and took their order. They drank root beer while waiting for their pizza. The place wasn't very busy.

"So how did you get this *gig*?" Dale asked.

Will grinned at the word. "Greeley has a friend at the OU journalism department and he mentioned to this professor that he wished he had an extra hand for this week. The prof said since it was Spring Break he might be able to find someone. That someone was I."

"So the professor picked you?"

"He knew I wasn't a Spring Break animal. I'd be available."

"Yeah, but you're a good writer, too. Did you major in journalism as an undergraduate?"

"No, I majored in history. But after I started working at the school paper, I decided to minor in journalism."

"How do you like Buffalo City?"

Will narrowed his eyes as if he needed to concentrate on his answer. "Dusty, dry, brown, windy – "

"All apt adjectives. It also has a distinct aroma of cattle."

"Very distinct. The last time I smelled such an aroma was when I visited the Kansas City stockyards."

"You can't say that Buffalo City doesn't have it own peculiar sense of charm. Otherwise, why would President Carter return?"

"Maybe in some peculiar way it reminds him of Plains, Georgia."

Dale asked Will some biographical questions. Will told him he'd been born in Tulsa but his family moved to Oklahoma City when he was ten because his father accepted a promotion from Kerr-McGee to head the company's public relations department. He went to OU for college and when he started graduate school his parents moved to Minneapolis. He might attend the University of Minnesota next year because they have a doctoral program in journalism and mass communications. Dale asked if he was close to his parents and Will said it was more like they were close to him. He was an only child.

"You're in the right profession, Dale."

"Why is that?"

"You ask a lot of questions. I haven't had a chance to ask you any."

But before Will could their pizza arrived. While they ate, Will made some inquiries but their chowing down limited Dale's answers. He didn't like talking about himself much anyway, especially not about personal matters. He felt embarrassed by his family. His father had been a navy career man and retired after twenty years and now was the chief ranger of the lakes and parks of Oklahoma City. His mother had a history of mental illness, schizophrenia to be exact, and was living with his grandparents, who were hillbillies (he liked his grandparents in spite of their Arkansas origins). His parents had divorced when he was in high school. His father remarried last year only because he'd gotten his girlfriend pregnant. Dale had a six-month old half-brother named Marlon. He also had a sister, June, who was attending his old college, Galilee Nazarene, and was staying in the dorm, even though she'd once declared she couldn't go to GNC because her brother had disgraced the family name with his April Fool's Day parody when he was the college newspaper editor.

Since Dale gave such terse answers to his questions, Will didn't ask for any elaboration. Dale appreciated that Will respected his privacy. Maybe when they got to know each better – if they did, and already Dale was hoping that would happen – he'd talk more about his background.

After finishing their meal, they talked for another hour. Mostly about movies. Will had been vice-president of the OU film society and the group had shown films on campus several nights a week. Not only did they screen fairly recent Hollywood films, they also showed classics and foreign language films. Dale asked if his group had shown any Frank Capra films. Will said the film society featured a whole month of screwball comedies and they showed Capra films as well as movies by Howard Hawks and Preston Sturges.

Dale had seen some of the movies that Hawks had directed but he'd never seen any by Preston Sturges. Once while reading an almanac just for fun, he came across a list of the best one hundred movies of all time. He recognized almost all of them; in fact, since he was such a diligent viewer of the Late Show movie he'd seen quite a few of them on television. But he'd never seen a film directed by Preston Sturges and the almanac had listed *four* of them. He still remembered the titles: *The Lady Eve*; *The Palm Beach Story*; *The Miracle at Morgan's Creek*; and *Sullivan's Travels*. Dale asked which of those films the OU film society had shown.

"*The Lady Eve* and *The Palm Beach Story*," Will said.

"Were they good?"

"The audience enjoyed them immensely."

"They never show those movies on television."

"That's true. I wonder why."

Dale felt himself burning a little with envy. He almost wished he'd gone to OU instead of GNC then he could have seen classic films on campus.

Dale asked Will what films he liked best. He said he especially liked film noir for classic, Bergman for foreign, and Robert Altman and Woody Allen for contemporary cinema.

Dale recognized the names and had seen several of those directors' films, except for Bergman. He'd seen only one Bergman film, *The Seventh Seal*, which had showed on the PBS channel when he was in college. His mother and sister complained about him watching the film. They wanted to watch something they could understand like *Mork and Mindy*.

When they concluded their film conversation Dale paid the bill (he insisted; after all, he was the working man) and Will left the tip and they drove around town for half an hour talking about their upcoming assignments on the newspaper and the amazing fact that the President of the United States would actually be in little ol' Buffalo City in three days.

Will also talked about politics and current events and Dale, impressed with his knowledge, asked how he came to know all that stuff. Will said he'd taken several political science courses in college and he read newspapers and magazines like *Time*, *Newsweek*, *The New Republic*, and *The National Review*.

Dale had begun reading *Time* regularly at the Carnegie Library. He'd also seen copies of *The National Review* and *The New Republic* displayed on the shelves but he didn't know what they were. Were they magazines about politics?

"Yes, politics and culture. They're called magazines of opinion. That means they present the news from a more partisan political viewpoint than newspapers. The reporters write more subjectively about political and cultural matters. The writing is first-rate and the thinking is cogent. Their perspective isn't knee jerk liberal or conservative though. They make arguments

131

in a rational and analytical way. The writers aren't political hacks."

"You read both liberal and conservative magazines?"

"Certainly. I want to keep a balanced viewpoint."

Dale was impressed with that attitude. Millard Greeley didn't do that at the *Stampede*. His paper was obviously pro-Democrat, although of a conservative kind as far as Dale could tell.

"Maybe I should start reading those magazines, too," mused Dale.

"If you want to learn about politics and culture at a deeper level, you should."

They were back at the Best Western and Dale parked next to Will's Volvo but he didn't turn off the Chevy's motor. He figured Will was weary from a busy day and didn't want to presume that he'd ask him in. Besides, it seemed a little awkward for a guy to go into another guy's hotel room.

"How do you like working at the *Stampede*?" Will asked.

"I like it fine. I've learned a lot. But the work is getting more routine now."

"You like working in sports?"

"Yeah, for the most part. But I think I'd eventually like to write about the arts. The popular arts, that is. Especially movies and books. But I don't know enough yet. That's why I'm thinking about going to graduate school."

"That's not a bad idea. Any ideas where?"

"One school I applied to was the University of Missouri."

Dale knew a former GNC newspaper and yearbook editor who had gone there, a girl named Flora Eliot. She was four years ahead of him at school so he'd never met her. But he'd admired her writing. He knew she went to graduate school at Missouri and he thought he might follow in her footsteps.

He also was considering attending a graduate film program. He'd like to study cinema as an art and maybe make a student film. Unfortunately, the few film programs in the country were located in big cities. Since he was a small-town boy he didn't think he'd like living in a big city. But there was a grad program in film studies at the University of Wyoming. The college wasn't located in a big city. Dale had also once visited Wyoming when his grandparents and his mother took a trip to Cheyenne to visit one of his uncles. He'd been impressed with the rugged beauty of the Rocky Mountain region. Three months ago he had applied to Missouri and Wyoming, as well as the University of Texas in Austin. He hadn't received word yet if he'd been accepted by any of them.

"Going to Missouri would be a good idea," Will said. "They have one of the best journalism schools in the country."

Dale nodded. Both he and Will grew silent for a moment. The pause was a little awkward, not unlike one that occurs during a first date except Will wasn't a girl. Still, Dale wasn't sure how to conclude their outing.

"I enjoyed talking with you tonight," Will said.

"I enjoyed it, too. There aren't many people I can talk to about such things in Buffalo City." Actually, there wasn't anyone at present except Byron Mors and he was older and married and had one licentious non-intellectual interest that Dale didn't mention to Will.

"Well, I'll see you at work tomorrow," Will said as he opened the door and slipped out.

Dale said goodnight and he backed his Chevy out of the parking space while Will opened the door to his motel room and went inside. Dale drove away, still enjoying the pleasant glow of companionship.

But when he turned into the driveway of Mrs. Kennicott's home and saw the stony house with its dark windows and empty rooms, the glow faded and he felt that familiar loneliness spread inside him like a dense fog.

Chapter Four
Thursday

"Oh, Millard please quit moping," said Carol as she removed the breakfast dishes from the small table in the breakfast nook. There weren't many dishes to remove; Millard was on a diet.

Carol's words, although spoken in a semi-sympathetic way for Carol was almost always considerate of his feelings, nevertheless deepened Millard Greeley's despondency. His rotund body sat slumped in his chair, his pudgy hands lying palms up as if posed in supplication for more nourishment. His belly still felt half-empty. No eggs, no bacon! Not even a slim wedge of buttered toast. How could Buffalo City's leading political light sally forth on so meager a repast?

He wished Carol hadn't used the word "mopey." He remembered some of his classmates back in school using that adjective to tease him: Mopey Millard. He'd never been mopey, just sensitive and introspective. Greeley thought back to those painful days of grammar school. Without wishing it, he pictured the jeering face of Byron Mors, age ten, leading the insulting chorus.

"But *he's* trying to sabotage me," Greeley groused, using several ounces of his formidable self-will to keep his voice from slipping into a whine. "He's attempting to undermine my greatest political accomplishment!"

"You haven't accomplished anything yet," Carol cautioned. "And I think you're over-reacting to Byron's behavior."

Greeley glared at his wife, but only for a moment, because he truly admired, respected, and loved her. But he didn't like her mentioning *his* name.

"He blocked the college fine arts auditorium for the venue of the town hall meeting. I had to make a humiliating call to the White House to notify them of the change. From the splendor of the fine arts auditorium to the humble, if not spartan, accommodations of the high school gymnasium."

"Yes, that's unfortunate."

"Unfortunate? It's treachery!"

"Millard, you're acting as if you're Julius Caesar." She smiled and motioned for him to rise.

Greeley frowned but he rose. Using her allusion, there was no need to mention whom Brutus was.

They walked out of the breakfast nook through the dining room into a large and handsomely furnished living room. Greeley walked over to the cloakroom to fetch his overcoat while Carol went over to a dresser and picked up a suit brush.

"And he's obstructed in other, smaller ways," Greeley said. "His behavior at the Kiwanis meeting was absolutely offensive. I noticed several times his smirk as he sat across the room. He has nothing but contempt for my civic contributions. And do you know what he told me during –" Greeley paused not wanting to mention the setting for that exchange since it brought back unpleasant memories concerning his temporarily blocked bladder.

"Millard, you won't need your overcoat today."

Greeley shut the cloakroom door. He walked over to Carol who stood waiting at the dresser holding the brush.

"He said the word Kiwanis is an Indian word for "foolish." Or was it wanton? A phrase that means, 'making foolish and wanton noise.'"

"From what you've told me that certainly describes some of your meetings." Carol smiled and began brushing the shoulders and back of Greeley's blue pinstripe suit.

"Absolute nonsense! Our motto is *to build*. What disrespect!"

"Millard, you shouldn't let him get your goat. You know how Byron especially likes to tease you because you don't react well."

"And how am I supposed to react?"

"Coolly. With amused detachment."

Greeley thought: in other words as *he* would react. As she brushed his jacket, Greeley caught their reflection in the large mirror mounted on the opposite wall. He looked at his wife's image as she performed her ministrations. He was reminded again of her quiet, perhaps modest, good looks. Petite with a trim and shapely figure. Medium length brunette hair, worn in a becoming style with small curls in the back that gently pressed against her delicate neck. Her individual features weren't striking but they combined for a pleasant overall effect: a heart-shaped face, well-defined cheeks with dimples when she smiled, a smallish nose, a sweet mouth, and blue eyes that sparkled in the light.

Greeley's mood mellowed as he watched the reflection of his wife. They had grown up together in Buffalo City although they had never been a couple in their youth. It wasn't so much that Carol was two years behind Millard; it was more that she was simply out of his league. Carol Quigley had been a popular girl, admired by all for her sympathetic personality and subdued good looks. An excellent student, she won several academic honors and would graduate as her class valedictorian. She came from a prosperous, influential family. Her father, C. Nash Quigley, was the town's most respected banker. He was chairman of the Farmers and Ranchers Community Bank and Trust and was known to be a shrewd but resolutely honest businessman. Carol had an older brother, also with the bank, and a younger sister, who'd married three years ago to a lawyer and she'd moved with him to Stillwater where he had a practice.

Greeley had enjoyed casual social relations with Carol but throughout their growing up they had never dated, never held hands or kissed or even enjoyed a private conversation with each other. After high school she attended Oklahoma University but Greeley, two years ahead, saw her even less often at Norman than he had in their hometown. In fact, Carol, who never had a steady beau in high school in accord with her parent's wishes, began to date Byron Mors during her freshman year and it appeared that the two of them were going to become engaged. They dated steady for eight months until Byron inexplicably fled to California at the end of his junior year.

Greeley doubted he and Carol would have ever married if they both hadn't returned to Buffalo City at about the same time. Carol returned first. Near the end of her sophomore year her mother became seriously ill and Carol came home to help nurse her. A month later, Greeley graduated from OU and returned to Buffalo City to help his father run the newspaper. By that time, Mrs. Quigley's condition had worsened. Her breast cancer had spread, and Greeley's mother was a regular visitor to comfort and assist Carol with the care for her mother. The unfortunate illness brought he and Carol together since Greeley often drove his mother to the Quigley's residence. Greeley remembered taking walks with Carol in the spacious back yard while their mothers were together in the upstairs room. Carol and Millard didn't speak at much length during these walks but Greeley's sympathetic presence seemed to impress her and after a respectful three months wait after Mrs. Quigley's death, he asked Carol out and she accepted.

They continued to date for almost a year and when Greeley asked her to marry him to his utter amazement she accepted.

The whole town seemed amazed. Why would Carol Quigley, an attractive young woman of such character and *class*, marry Millard Greeley, Jr., a young man who appeared on the surface to be a corpulent, pompous fool? No one knew.

Greeley didn't know either, but sometimes during dark moods he suspected the timing might have to do with the return of Byron Mors to Buffalo City. That idea pained Greeley but when he thought about their courtship he remembered that Carol's attitude toward him noticeably changed when Byron Mors returned from

California. Byron's younger brother, Blake, had been killed in Vietnam. Byron returned for the funeral still looking like a hippie. He hadn't even bothered to cut his hair or shave his beard! Greeley, along with hundreds of Buffalonians including Carol and her family, had been at the funeral. He remembered how Byron had stared at Carol when the two families encountered each other leaving the church. As Carol gave her condolences to Mr. and Mrs. Mors, Byron gazed intently at her but she didn't look his way nor did she speak to him. Greeley remembered that because he was standing just a few feet away with his parents and he too was gazing at Carol, trying to discern her attitude toward Byron.

The next time he encountered her, in the town library because Carol had a part-time job there, an effort to keep busy after her mother's death, Greeley noticed she was unusually nice to him. Greeley had come into the library on the pretense of checking out a particular book; in fact, one of Carol's favorite novels, *Wuthering Heights*. Carol had been surprised to learn that Millard had an interest in that novel. Greeley really didn't; he just wanted an excuse for seeing Carol. They had a pleasant conversation and just before Greeley was to take his leave he blurted that he would be pleased to take her out that weekend if she wasn't otherwise engaged. Instead of seeing that polite but uncomfortable expression that he had observed over the years on other girls' faces when he asked for a date, Carol gave him an genuine smile and her acceptance. Greeley could hardly believe it! Carol Quigley consented to go on a date with him? Of course, he'd always suspected that Carol had unusual sensitivity and perception, especially when compared to the typical Buffalo City and OU female. Greeley felt gratified that Carol had the ability to look past a façade and see the real man. (He wished some of those OU sorority girls had that skill.) Their date went well and he asked her out again and they began to date steady. It wasn't a passionate affair but a respectful and friendly courtship. Their maturing relationship only had one brief hiatus and that occurred in mid-January of 1969. Why then? Greeley didn't know for certain. Carol just grew distant for a short time and she refused a couple of dates. Did her dissatisfaction with their relationship correspond with Byron Mors leaving for OU to finish his degree? Did it have to do with Byron no longer being around?

Greeley allowed Carol two weeks to come to her senses. Then he asked her out again and she agreed and they continued to date all spring and summer. Greeley's behavior during the dates was always impeccably respectful like a true gentleman. They attended musical concerts and viewed tasteful cinematic fare (no R-rated films) and dined at sensible, moderately priced restaurants. Greeley had to admit that he hadn't been an ardent suitor. Of course, he was naturally dignified. And Carol didn't seem the kind of young woman who went in for that kind of thing. But when Byron Mors returned in August of that year, 1969, with his degree in mortuary science, returned to settle down in Buffalo City, Greeley for the first time had the pleasure of encountering a more receptive Carol. During one date in that memorable late summer she even hinted that she expected something more from Millard than

141

casual companionship. That was all the prompting Greeley needed. He asked, she accepted and they became engaged

Greeley's parents were astonished. Carol's family members were incredulous. The whole blasted town was dumbfounded! A part of Greeley himself, that private, boyish part that still occasionally recalled the teasing and torments of his youth, was also amazed. At the time, almost ten years ago, Greeley refused to wonder if Carol's acceptance had anything to do with the permanent return of Byron Mors. But in the back of his mind he feared there was indeed a connection.

Whatever her complicated motives might be, the important fact was that Carol did marry him. Their union had endured and prospered for nine years. The only disappointment was that they had managed to produce only one child so far, Millard Greeley III, but they hadn't given up hope of adding a brother or sister or both for him in the future.

Thinking of their complicated history produced an unwelcome powerful emotion in Greeley and he bit his tongue to keep his emotions in check. Greeley winced at the pain and Carol, now finished with the grooming, noticed his pained expression and misinterpreted his reaction.

"Really, Millard, you have nothing to worry about. Everything will turn out fine."

Greeley nodded, determined to make it so. He took on his commanding persona, the attitude of the town's leader, and thought about his son, three years old, and already showing an independence and determination that reminded Greeley of his father. Thinking of this annoyed Greeley a little, because there were times when he thought that his father's impressive attributes had jumped a generation.

"Where is little Millard?"

"You know where he is, dear. He's upstairs being attended to by Maria while I am down here tending to you."

"Perhaps I should go upstairs and see the little rascal."

"He certainly is behaving like a rascal this morning. But you don't have time, dear. You have appointments to keep and you're already late!"

As Carol walked with him to the front door she quizzed him about today's schedule, reminding him about the his hectic day, the meetings, the telephone calls, the various plans and promises he had to keep. Greeley nodded to each of her reminders and as he walked out of the door, holding his briefcase, looking quite dapper in his pin-striped suit, he was reminded that what success he had enjoyed was almost entirely due to her and his father.

He turned and kissed her soft cheek in good-bye as Carol closed the door. Greeley slowly walked down the pathway then turned to face his handsome two-story Tudor house that his father-in-law had helped getting favorable financial terms for. At that moment, he had an unreasonable urge to storm back in and grab Carol and demand if she still felt anything for Byron Mors.

But if he did that impulsive thing he knew what she would say: "Of course not, dear. That was over a long time ago."

Greeley, not a man given to doubts, straightened

himself and forced a resolute look on his chubby face. He marched to his shiny white Cadillac, opened its heavy door, and deposited his bulky frame in the embrace of the leather seat. He started the motor and listened with satisfaction at the deep, confident hum of the engine. Then he backed out too far to the left and crashed into the garbage can.

-II-

With reluctance, Byron Mors entered the Preparation Room. Although not naturally squeamish, over the years his distaste for the more gross aspects of his profession had increased. He took the required embalming course for his mortuary science degree and during the first few years of assisting his father he routinely handled corpses. He'd undressed them, cleaned them, drained them, stitched them, embalmed them, dressed them, and even painted their faces and manicured their nails. But his increased sensitivity of dealing with the deceased intensified with his marriage. Like most people, Kate had an aversion for anything dead. She had been reluctant to marry him in the first place but when she finally consented she emphasized she didn't want him to have anything to do with the dead people except for what was absolutely necessary. Byron had assured her that he hardly ever came into contact with them anymore. His expertise was in administration, sales, service, and public relations. He'd hired a skilled and dedicated team of professionals to directly deal with the deceased. Indeed, the new head embalmer and restorative artist, Mr. Haros, was working out superbly. Byron's explanation had mollified his fiancé, but even now if Kate detected a whiff of formaldehyde on his person she would refuse his touch until he completely cleansed away that offensive odor.

As he expected, Mr. Haros was busily at work with the recently arrived decedent. Byron closed the door softly, although neither Haros nor the corpse would be disturbed if he'd slammed the door. Haros worked with utter concentration. Byron doubted anything short of an explosion would distract him.

The decedent was unusual in that he was not elderly. About three-quarters of Byron's business consisted of elderly people. This cadaver had once been a middle-age man and now as he lay on a shallow stainless steel tub in the middle of a well-lit, immaculate white tiled room Byron noticed that he resembled in age and general appearance the embalmer himself.

Haros was a man of fifty-two, average height, average build, brown hair, brown eyes, an undistinguished face except for a rather large nose, one shaped and pocked like a cucumber. His other salient feature was his over-sized hands featuring lean, strong fingers that he used to great effect on his charges.

Examining the cadaver, Byron again noted the resemblance to Haros: approximately same age and physical characteristics. The only significant difference was that the decedent, a Mr. Jones by name, was nude except for a conveniently placed towel around his middle that served as a non-artistic fig leaf. Haros, busy with his preparations, seemed completely unaware or unmoved by his uncanny resemblance to the corpse.

On the worktable lay the usual tools of the trade:

145

bowls, basins, scalpels, scissors, augers, forceps, pumps, clamps, needles and tubes. It appeared that Haros was almost finished with his labors. The deceased's blood had already been pumped out and the embalming fluid pumped in. A trocar, a long hollow needle, had already been used to pump out the contents of the entrails and chest area and cavity fluid had been pumped into the resulting void.

Byron pattered a few steps closer and looked more closely at Mr. Jones face. His mouth was closed and Haros held in his hand a needle with surgical thread. Ordinarily, Haros would have sewn shut the cadaver's mouth earlier, but the nature of his death necessitated that procedure come last.

"How goes it, Mr. Haros?"

"Well, Mr. Mors, well."

"I stopped by because I wanted to remind you that the family wished an open coffin and I was concerned that the wound would prevent that."

"Not at all, Mr. Mors. I simply applied plaster of Paris to the anterior part of the skull. The bruising inside the mouth I handled in the usual way. I removed enough tissue to produce normal appearing cheeks. I also removed the tongue. Now all I have to do is sew up the mouth and apply a few finishing touches and the loved one will be ready for Miss Henderson."

Byron disliked that euphemism, *loved one*. But Haros was sensitive about the cadavers he worked on. And in this difficult case he'd done exceptional work. Mr. Jones had committed suicide by putting a revolver in his mouth and blowing some of his brains out. Fortunately, it was a small caliber pistol. Consequently, the damage wasn't too extensive.

"Excellent work, Mr. Haros."

"Thank you, Mr. Mors. I do take pride in my work."

"And for good reason. Well, I'll be off. Oh, by the way, we have another – " Byron almost said cadaver but he amended his speech in deference to Haros – "loved one arriving in an hour from the hospital."

"An older loved one?"

"Yes."

"A piece of cake compared to this one."

Byron crept out of the morgue and walked down the hall to the Cosmetic and Costume room. He found Louise Henderson sitting before her desk deftly filing her nails. One of the drawbacks of working here, she'd once confided to him, was she had to keep her nails short. She loved wearing her nails long and liked painting them all kinds of colors. Now she had to wear false nails in public.

"Hello, Louise," Byron said.

"Oh, hello, Mr. Mors."

Byron noticed that underneath her white smock she wore a rather low cut scarlet blouse producing pleasing cleavage. He looked for only a moment then returned his eyes to her smiling face.

"Mr. Haros is almost finished."

"Okay."

Byron nodded and was about to take his leave when he paused.

"Louise, how long have you worked here?"

"Almost three years, Mr. Mors."

"You enjoy the work here, don't you?"

"Yes, I do. I used to work at Reba's Beauty Parlor

and you can't imagine how much the customers complained."

Byron saw no point in mentioning the obvious differences in her clientele now, so he only smiled his slightly ironic smile, one of several smile styles that he could employ. Suddenly, an image of a naked Louise popped into his mind, completely unbidden. He abruptly left the room and swiftly walked down the hall.

The fast-paced walk to his office didn't help. He remained in the throes of a lust attack. Louise's image faded only to be replaced by another big-busted blonde, this one the featured actress in *Boobs and Bombs*, last night's X-rated feature. In that film, a crew of big-breasted female bomb disposal officers is taxed to the max when a serial bomber terrorizes their curiously unpopulated neighborhood. The climatic scene is when they can't defuse the bomb in time, so they flee. The bomb explodes but fortunately they are far enough away that only their clothes are ripped off. Miraculously, their tender flesh isn't even scratched by the bomb's fragments. As the three-girl bomb disposal crew runs down the street naked, the mad bomber chases them and he ravishes them all. While he copulates with one female cop, the other two go at it. The film, needless to say, blew him away.

Striding by the receptionist's desk, Byron Mors instructed Amy Comer that he shouldn't be disturbed for ten minutes.

He closed and locked his office door. He went over to his desk, opened the lower drawer and pulled out a copy of *Modern Mortuary Management*. He sat in his chair and gazed at the cover of a middle-aged man staring almost wantonly at the latest innovation, the Kreiger Car Casket. Byron read the copy displayed at the bottom of the page:

Why deposit your loved one in an ordinary casket when he (or she) can be interred in a casket that looks like his (or her) favorite automobile? Did your loved one adore his '65 Mustang? What about a '54 Chevy coupe? Or maybe a '62 T-Bird. The Car Caskets don't correspond to the actual size of an automobile; they've been scaled down and they don't have any engines or moving tires. But otherwise, they are remarkably convincing as vehicles. Of course, such creative caskets are somewhat higher priced than the traditional kind.

But what really interested Byron were the images hidden underneath the *Modern Mortuary Management* cover. He turned to the middle of another magazine hidden underneath the MMM cover and saw the tangled but very much alive naked bodies of two women and a man as they cavorted on a sandy beach. Byron gazed at one photo after another. He preferred moving images but there was something stimulating about stills, too, that is, as long as he flipped the pages. So he used his thumb to fan the pages, his eager eyes taking in the obscene images with practiced ease.

While visually occupied, he reached down with his other hand and opened his fly and relieved his frenzied tension.

At his climax he made an utterance, really a series of restrained hisses and gasps, very much like the ones he'd expressed Monday night with Dale Smith in the guest bedroom.

149

Satisfied, he collapsed back into his chair and closed his eyes. Those intrusive images were out of his mind. He smiled wearily. This was the second time this morning he had to resort to this demeaning practice. And he was afraid it wouldn't be the last.

-III-

Dale walked out of Crenshaw's Drugstore where he and Will Whitaker had recently had lunch. His friend remained inside, buying some "sundries." The drugstore was across the street from the *Stampede*, which is why they'd chosen it. As expected, the reporters had to pick up the pace to fill the larger newspapers. The President's upcoming visit had apparently stimulated ad sales. Today the Thursday paper would be a three "sectioner," which was often the size of the Sunday paper.

Dale walked over to a bench but instead of sitting he propped one boot on the bench and leaned his weight on a braced forearm that rested against his raised thigh. In his imagination he thought his pose made him look like a scout or a sentry or some kind of watchman as he scanned the jejune landscape looking for trouble. All he saw, however, was downtown Buffalo City and all its familiar and boring characteristics: cars and pickups driving down the two-lane street that, although asphalt, had a dusty look to it; pedestrians, middle-aged or older, strolling down the sidewalks, most of them going to lunch.

"Hi there, mister photographer," a loud, feminine voice called.

Dale turned and saw Louise Henderson walking his way. She waved and he nodded in return.

"Are you hanging out looking at the pretty girls?" she asked, smiling.

She had okay teeth but Dale thought she looked better when she didn't smile. Her best facial feature was her nearly voluptuous lips and her broad smile thinned her lips. She'd done up her face with loads of make-up: Red lipstick, mascara, eye shadow, blush, the works.

"That's right," Dale said. "Like those two babes over there."

Dale nodded his head at two crones across the street as they walked down the sidewalk. One was Mrs. Milford, the sixty-nine year old office manager of the *Stampede*, the other he guessed was her sister, even older. Both women were scrawny and pale and wrinkled-faced and dressed in old-fashioned gingham frocks. They crept down the sidewalk, the older sister holding in her gnarled hand a white doggie bag.

Louise giggled. "Oh, you're terrible."

Dale glanced at the rest of her. She was dressed casually, blue jeans, a scarlet blouse, short-heeled open-toe shoes that showed her red painted toenails. He especially noticed that the blouse was low-cut and revealed quite a bit of her impressive cleavage.

"What're you doin' round these parts?" Dale said, affecting a country twang.

"Shoppin'." Louise held up a department store bag. Written in elegant script over the front was the name of the emporium she'd visited: *The Bon Ton*.

"You went shopping on your lunch break?"

"Sure. That's the best time. Want to see what I bought?"

"Okay."

Louise eagerly reached into her sack and retrieved a red polka dot bikini. The two small pieces of cloth still had the sales tags pinned on them. The bottom piece was stretched out on a small plastic hanger. The top was hanger-less and the thin shoulder straps were folded into the rather copious cups.

"You bought a swimming suit? It's only March."

"Gotta buy them early or else you get stuck with the ugly ones. Besides, it's not easy findin' a suit that will fit me."

Dale thought to himself: ain't that the truth.

Louise positioned the two small pieces of cloth in front of her, the bottom in front of her broad hips, the top in front of her ample bosom.

Dale nodded appreciatively. "It's an itsy bitsy teeny weeny polka dot bikini." He liked the deep red background color and the full moon white polka dots.

"What?"

"It's an early sixties song. About the girl who buys an itsy bitsy teeny weeny polka dot bikini and then is too shy to go out on the beach." Dale figured Louise wouldn't have that problem.

"Then why'd she buy it?"

"You got me," he said in a pseudo-perplexed way.

Louise laughed and then Dale noticed that Will was standing not too far away watching them. A small, knowing smile appeared on his lips.

Louise glanced over to Will and pretended to be embarrassed. "I guess I better get my butt in gear. Gotta get back to work."

She smiled in a half suggestive, half sincere way and immediately took off down the sidewalk, her long blonde hair swaying as she walked. Will joined Dale and they watched Louise getting her butt in gear. Dale wondered if she was exaggerating the swing of her hips for his benefit or if she always walked that way.

"I thought you said there weren't any bikinis in Buffalo City," said Will, with a thoughtful expression on his rather academic looking face. Dale knew he wasn't thinking about the first amendment.

"Fortunately, I was wrong."

-IV-

At a special noon meeting of the Buffalo City Chapter of the Elks Executive Committee, held in the Excelsior Hotel executive suite, Milton Greeley sat between his father-in-law, C. Nash Quigley, and Earl Hennessey, the town's leading oilman. The two men were nearly complete opposites: Quigley, thin, ascetic, with a full head of red hair; Hennessey, broad-chested, lusty, and completely bald. They were carrying on a heated conversation; that is, Hennessey, in his deep, rather hoarse voice, bellowed in the direction of Quigley, a man renown for his laconic speech, undemonstrative demeanor, and conveniently poor hearing. Greeley, caught in the middle, tried to not to show his displeasure.

"Damn it, Quigley! The interest rates on the loans for those lower lots are just too damn high! You got to let me renegotiate!"

Banker Quigley showed no sign that he'd heard.

Hennessey blared his protest a third time, at an even louder volume, and most of his booming words funneled into Greeley's right ear.

After a pause, Quigley turned to the oilman. "Three legs of the stool, Earl. Three legs."

Greeley had often heard that phrase from his father-in-law. He meant that the Buffalo City economy was balanced on three legs: farming, ranching, and oil. The banker didn't favor any of one of the legs over the other.

Greeley, anticipating another verbal fusillade from Hennessey, pushed his chair away from the table and rose as quickly as his corpulent form allowed. His departure was hardly noticed.

Greeley disliked these executive meetings because he was the lowest ranking officer. But he had to attend them even though his presence was often overlooked. All the senior officers were older and held powerful positions in the community. Most of them, like Hennessey, had loud, argumentative voices and thus Greeley's greatest attribute, his verbal fluency, proved to be less effective in this setting.

Greeley waddled over to the buffet lunch. He'd already sampled small portions of all the dishes but his lack of relevancy in the meeting not only had deflated his ego but it also had whetted his hunger. He speared a sizable hunk of beef roast and prepared to lift it to his plate when the Rev. Jeremiah Gentry appeared at his side.

"Catholics think gluttony is a mortal sin," said the reverend whose own physique was so thin that five fewer pounds would result in emaciation. "Of course, we Protestants reject that antiquated attitude."

Carol must have mentioned the diet to him. The Rev. Gentry was the senior minister of the First Methodist church. Greeley's family was Baptist; Carol's was Methodist. That might have been a serious obstacle for marriage but Carol had magnanimously consented to attend the First Baptist church with her husband except on rare occasions when she attended her old church with her father. Greeley was certain that Rev. Gentry resented, as much as a true Christian could, Greeley for taking one of his most valuable members away from his congregation.

Greeley jiggled his hand to free the impaled piece of beef. The hunk of meat clung tenaciously to his fork. Finally, Greeley gave up and just left the piece of meat with the fork still piercing it on the serving plate.

He left the silently disapproving minister and walked over to the table where a tall cylindrical container of coffee stood. He grabbed a Styrofoam cup and filled it with steaming Java. Dr. Arnold Smith, the town's only psychiatrist, joined him.

"I had a dream about you the other night, Mr. Mayor," said Dr. Smith.

Greeley turned to him and blinked his small eyes three times as if he himself were waking up from a dream. "I find that hard to believe."

"I dreamed that you were a target of an assassination," said the psychiatrist. Dr. Smith was fifty-one, balding, with piercing dark eyes under heavy brows. He was of average of height but with an almost rigid, erect bearing.

155

"Considering the upcoming presidential visit, doctor, that dream is in very bad taste."

"But the assassin wasn't a white man. He was a Comanche, bare-chested, wearing breeches. He shot you with an arrow. What do you think is the significance of that dream?"

"You're the psychiatrist!"

"I only interpret my patient's dreams. I have no clue about my own."

"Excuse me doctor."

Greeley eased away from the deranged doctor but Dr. Smith shouted after him, "Consider the irony. A Comanche shoots an arrow into the mayor of *Buffalo City!*"

Greeley gave Dr. Smith a feeble farewell wave and considered departing from the meeting. No business was being conducted. Then he recalled that he'd driven his father-in-law to this special, and so far, pointless meeting.

Clarence Fincher, the town's most successful lawyer, accosted Greeley.

"I want to issue a protest, Greeley," he said, pointing a finger at the mayor's paunch.

"Yes, and I can guess the nature of the protest."

"Why didn't the city set aside more honorary passes for the town hall? One hundred is hardly enough."

Greeley gazed at Fincher. The lawyer was a short but broad-shouldered man with thick, silver hair worn rather long for a man of fifty. "I recall that you received yours."

"Yes, but my wife, my secretary, and the three junior partners of my practice didn't."

"They will have to take their chances with the lottery."

"The odds that all of them will win a ticket to attend the town hall meeting are dishearteningly low."

"That can't be helped, Mr. Fincher. The high school gymnasium seats only one thousand and one hundred at maximum. Since half the people of this fine city wish to attend, not to mention hundreds more who live in the county, that fact requires we have a lottery."

"I understand that, Greeley. Of course, a lottery was a sensible decision."

Yes it was, Greeley thought, it was and Carol who was responsible. She thought of it Monday night at home when he told her the good news. Instead of chastising him for not confiding in her about the possibility of the President's arrival, she instead offered a pragmatic solution to the demand for seating for the event. Since the high school gym could accommodate more people than the junior college fine arts auditorium Greeley was glad that he had agreed to the change of venue. Of course, many more people wanted to attend the event in relation to the number of available seats. A lottery gave the public an equal chance of being selected.

"But my point, Greeley, is that you should have reserved more seats for dignitaries and important officials and VIPs."

Other people, especially the ones not given honorary passes, had made that complaint. Greeley told them all what he was about to tell Clarence Fincher:

"Can't be helped. There are simply not enough seats to accommodate every dignitary who desires one."

"But all my junior partners are Democrats!"

Greeley shrugged his sloping shoulders.

"As is my wife and my secretary! They both voted for the man!"

"It can't be helped," said Greeley with an apologetic smile.

The mayor left the lawyer grumbling over that unpleasant reality and sought some safe haven where he would not be accosted. By now, he'd circumnavigated the large room and had no place else to go. He stood by the smudgy window and gazed out at the verdant expanse of well-tended turf. He enjoyed the hotel grounds' greenery. Even though it was spring, much of Buffalo City was as brown and seedy as buffalo dung itself.

More people than he had anticipated were protesting being left off the list of honorary guests for the town hall meeting. Some were even accusing him of favoritism and nepotism (Greeley's wife and mother and father-in-law were all included). Greeley knew more people would be disgruntled when the lottery winners were announced noon Friday. Almost six thousand people had enrolled in the lottery so far. Only one thousand would be selected. That meant that, if the numbers didn't increase too much by the deadline tomorrow at 10:00 a.m., the citizens of his town and county would have a one in six chance of being selected. As Mr. Fincher had recently observed, dishearteningly low odds. Only a fifteen percent chance. Or was it more? Sixteen? Greeley tried to do those calculations in his head but he grew frustrated with his lack of mathematical precision. At any rate, a low percentage. And he knew that some important people would blame him if they didn't get a winning lottery pick.

What else could go wrong? The weather, of course. The forecast looked favorable. Clear and warm weather until Sunday evening. Of course, weather prognostications were not without flaws. What if a dust storm struck? It had been a dry spring. Or maybe just an excessively windy day. That often happened. What if Air Force One couldn't land because of high winds? Or worst of all, what if a tornado materialized?

His fears were unjustified. Greeley simply wouldn't let anything dreadful happen. When necessary he was capable of admirable grit and determination. He would simply *will* favorable results. After all, he, like the President, was a man of sincere faith. They both sought only good things for their fellow citizens. They both were noble beings, humbled only by God. Nothing wicked, nothing tragic, nothing calamitous could happen to them.

Or so Greeley prayed.

-V-

Harley Dee Grubbs stood outside the back of the newspaper office smoking a cigarette when he saw her. Louise Henderson sat on a bench outside Haggard's Bakery writing on a piece of notebook paper. Grubbs, the cigarette dangling from his mouth, crossed the street and in a few long strides stood before her.

Louise looked up. When she saw Grubbs she didn't smile.

"What do you want?"

"Hey, Louise," Grubbs said in a not entirely friendly way. "Who you writin' to?"

"None of your business." She folded the note in half before he could get a glimpse of the contents. She stuffed it in her small purse. She stood and picked up a shopping bag.

"Hey, bitch, don't hurry off."

"Don't call me that."

"Whattaya doin' tonight?"

"Nothin' with you."

"Pretty soon you're goin' change your mind about me. I'm goin' surprise you and everyone else in this bullshit town."

"Is that so?"

She started to leave when Grubbs reached out and grabbed her arm. She pulled her arm away and glared at him. "I told you to never touch me!"

"You might like it if you let me."

"I've told you time and time again to stop botherin' me. I don't want to go out with you Harley Dee Grubbs. You're not my type. You're … you're repulsive!"

Grubbs made his left hand into a fist.

"Better not try. I'll get my brother to beat the crap out of you. And when you're layin' there all smashed to a pulp I'll cut off your balls."

Louise stormed away and Grubbs glared at her retreating figure. He'd show the bitch. He'd show them all. After he performed his historical misdeed, he might take care of a few other people. Like that snobby bitch.

Dale stood at the layout desk in the composing room and pasted the last headline on the sports page. He glanced at the clock on the wall. Five minutes past two. He had almost an hour before deadline.

Will was out of the office on assignment. Dale was especially impressed with Will's diligence as a reporter. He didn't just settle for telephone interviews, he'd go out in the field to talk to sources, especially if the person was reluctant to talk. At this moment, Will was interviewing the Republican county chairman at the chairman's ranch because the man wouldn't talk to him on the telephone from his office. Apparently, the chairman had been accused of using county funds to stage a protest against Carter's Saturday visit. That was against the rules. County monies could not be used for partisan political protests and the chairman had been avoiding taking questions from the press. Will, along with Floyd Byrd who was going to try and get a photo, had decided to hunt him down.

Dale, in comparison to the news reporters, had it easy. There wasn't a lot going on in the sporting world, certainly not locally, in the third week of March. But Dale's workload was going to get heavier starting tomorrow. He'd be helping with the news coverage both Friday and Saturday.

Dale decided he'd see what Percy Pollack and Grubbs were up to. They had probably finished inking the press. They wouldn't really have any work to do until they started shooting the page negatives.

Dale walked into the camera-ready area but didn't

see either Pollack or Grubbs. He also noticed that Grubbs' chess set was absent. So, no more games, eh? Just when he was getting good, too.

Dale ambled into the press-room but still no press-men. They might be taking their breaks so Dale was about to go back to his desk when he heard the back door open. He turned and a streak of sunlight momentarily brightening the gloomy press-room. He shielded his eyes from the glare until it disappeared with the closing of the door. Then he saw Harley Dee Grubbs standing there, finishing his cigarette.

Smoking was forbidden in the back shop for obvious reasons: too much flammable material. In particular, oily rags, old newspapers, and combustible chemicals posed real danger. Dale started walking over to Grubbs to remind him of the hazardous violation of policy when Harley Dee opened the back door just enough to flick his stub of a cigarette outside.

That wasn't a particularly smart thing to do either, thought Dale. He marched over to Grubbs who waited for him with an insolent look on his face.

"You know how seriously Greeley takes the smoking policy," Dale said. "You could get fired for that."

"You boss now back here?"

"No, I 'm just giving you free advice."

"Don't need your advice, college boy."

Dale didn't understand why Grubbs was being so hostile. He'd never done anything to him. He'd always treated Grubbs and Pollack in a friendly way. In fact, he'd appreciated their willingness to teach him the workings of the back shop. He'd even told them so.

Rather than make the confrontation worse, Dale

shrugged and shook his head disgustedly. He turned to walk away.

"Hey, I want to ask you a question," Grubbs said.

"Yeah? What is it?"

"Is all that stuff in the paper about the President's visit right?"

"The itinerary and schedule?"

"Yeah, is it right?"

"You mean accurate?"

"Yeah, that's what I mean, college boy."

Dale was getting sick and tired of Grubbs' attitude. Talk about a sore loser. "Yes, it's accurate. Most of it is from the White House. They keep pretty tight schedules."

"So the President is going to be at the high school at 7 p.m. Saturday?"

"That's the schedule. Why is that so important to you?"

"Cause I want to avoid it." Grubbs gave an insincere smile, showing his yellowish teeth. "I guess there will be Secret Service guys."

"Of course."

"Local cops?"

"Yeah. Highway patrol too."

"Sounds like it's goin' be one big mess."

"Not if Mayor Greeley can help it."

Grubbs smiled a more genuine smile this time but it still had a glimmer of animosity in it. "So, you wanna play a match?"

They went into the camera-ready room and Grubbs brought out the chess set from inside the dark room. Dale didn't ask why he had hid it there. They played a quick, competitive game. It looked like the match was headed for a draw when Grubbs made one mistake and Dale took advantage. He'd now won for the third straight time.

Dale could tell that Grubbs didn't like losing but he didn't knock over the board or fling chess pieces like the last time. Dale stood up from the bench.

"That was a good match."

"I'll be winnin' a bigger match than this soon." Grubbs grinned and in the strange light of the camera-ready room his eyes looked yellowish again.

"Okay, good." Dale guessed he was going to play in some chess tournament. "It's deadline."

"It sure the hell is."

Dale left Grubbs and walked back to the newsroom. He wondered what was wrong with the guy. He thought Grubbs had always been strange but not this strange. Dale didn't like him much so he didn't really care to figure him out.

When he walked into the newsroom, Dwight called his name.

"Someone left a note for you." Dwight gave Dale a folded piece of notebook paper.

"Oh, yeah? Who?"

"She didn't give a name."

Dale tried to keep his face neutral. Dwight didn't look at him in a suspicious or curious way. Dale thought that was a little funny considering he was the managing editor.

"Okay, thanks."

Dale walked over to his desk and sat down before

he opened the note. Written in a kind of loopy scrawl was the message: *You can have me if you want me. My place 9 p.m.*

He jumped up from his seat. He peered out the long, vertical window. He scanned the sidewalks. He didn't see her. But he knew Louise had written the note.

He could hardly believe her gall. To write something like that, just fold the paper over, and walk into the newspaper office and give it to Dwight. What if he'd read it? He was amazed she would do something like that. Well, one thing about Louise: she wasn't shy.

Her place. He didn't know where her place was. But he was a reporter after all; well, a sports editor, but he had some investigative skills.

He reached for the Buffalo City telephone directory that lay next to the phone. For a moment, he couldn't recall her last name. Then he remembered her baseball playing brother, the guy who went hitless, fanning all three times, Larry Henderson. He flipped to the H's and found Louise Henderson's telephone number and address right off the bat: 2001 Garfield Street.

Dale thought that was a good omen.

-VII-

After work, Harley Dee Grubbs walked four blocks to *The Happy Hunter* and bought a night vision scope. He used to have one, but Doug had busted it. Grubbs bought a fairy inexpensive one but it was a good brand. The store's clerk, Sam Henderson (Louise's uncle), a stocky middle-aged man who resembled a boar, coughed harshly then he handed the boxed scope to Grubbs.

"Goin' to be huntin' some possum, I reckon," Sam Henderson said. He sneezed and casually wiped his nose with the sleeve of his red and white flannel shirt.

"Bigger than that."

"Ain't nothin' bigger in season."

Grubbs said nothing as he walked out of the store.

He walked west on First Street for two blocks then turned left on McKinley and walked two more blocks. He paused at the corner of McKinley and Third Street and looked at the Buffalo City High School gymnasium. According to the itinerary published today in the *Stampede,* the President's motorcade would enter town on Broadway Boulevard then turn south on Main Street then turn west on Third Street before arriving at the high school gym at McKinley Avenue. People who wanted to see the motorcade would be lining up on the streets on that route. Grubbs didn't care about that. He just wanted to scout out the route and find a good place to hide. The motorcade was scheduled to arrive at 7 p.m., a few minutes after dusk. Even with the streetlights, there wouldn't be much light. That's why he needed the night vision scope.

Grubbs walked down the opposite side of the street from the high school gym. The Target was supposed to enter the high school by the gym's east rear entrance. Across the street from the gym was a park. But there wasn't enough foliage yet on the trees to hide him. Perhaps he could conceal himself behind the hedges near the chain-link fence in the back of the park but that brought back the problem of the angle. The distance flattened out the shot. He needed some elevation.

Grubbs walked down the street and passed the park and noticed the modest houses that stood a block away from the gym. He could break into one of the two-story houses and use it for a sniper's nest. But that was taking a huge risk. Besides, the Target would probably exit his limo on the passenger's side and the car would partially block his shot. The Target wasn't tall.

Grubbs was beginning to feel that familiar tug of frustration in his gut. Maybe he'd have to chance using the pistol instead. He drew in a frustrated sigh and turned to his left and looked south down the street, his eyes not focusing on anything in particular as he thought. Then he saw the answer. It was right in front of him.

Three blocks away, standing tall and sturdy and perfect, was the grain elevator. The silos, five of them, didn't interest Grubbs. It was the headhouse that commanded his attention. All he needed was to get inside it, climb to the top, and wait. He remembered there was a small vent near the top of the head house. He could pry it open and he'd have a perfect view of the high school. He'd be so well concealed that no one, not even a sharp-eyed Secret Service man, would spy him.

Three blocks wasn't that far. Less than three hundred yards. He'd shot and killed game farther away than that. But it wouldn't be an easy shot.

His position would be far enough away and hidden so well that he might easily escape capture. By the time the confusion came to an end and the cops and Secret Service figured out what happened he'd be leaving the grain co-op. The Secret Service might not even immediately understand that the shot came from the head house.

Grubbs became jubilant. He wanted to jump and clap his hands and shout at the top of his lungs that Harley Dee Grubbs wasn't just another loser in this bullshit town! He wasn't a loser at all. He had more guts than anybody; more nerve, more determination. He had brains, too, just as much as any college kid. He'd show them, he'd show them all.

Then Grubbs realized that if he succeeded and got away no one would know it was him. That realization led to another thought: should he try and get away immediately, maybe head to Mexico, or should he play it cool? Go back to work even. He could be at the paper when everyone came bursting in, wailing and bemoaning, especially that fat bastard Greeley. He'd like to shoot him, too, but Grubbs didn't think he'd have time. He could probably squeeze off two, maybe three shots with his semi-automatic before they all scattered or hit the ground. Greeley might not be with him, anyway. But it might be better to hear the mayor bawlin' about the infamy brought to him and his town. Anyway, he could kill Greeley later.

Grubbs always thought he had a special destiny. He'd always been overlooked and underestimated. Instead of commanding respect he'd always been insulted. Like how Louise had treated him earlier this afternoon. She'd called him repulsive! What a stupid bitch. She couldn't even look below the surface and see the finer qualities that existed in him: the brains, the guts, the will power. But come Saturday everyone in town would know if he wanted them to. Maybe he'd go see Louise later that night and show her what he had inside himself. He knew where she lived. And maybe after he raped her, he'd cut off her nipples just to teach her a lesson for threatening him.

Even the people who should have known better had dismissed him. Those assholes in Chicago. He'd gotten to know a few almost by accident while hanging out in Hyde Park watching the old guys play chess. He guessed what they were by how they dressed, talked, and their attitude. He didn't know if they were connected to the Weathermen or some other radical group because they wouldn't say. He tried to hang out with them, to show them he was just as disgusted and hate-filled for this country, for this world, for this life as they were. But they didn't take him seriously. They didn't trust him enough to let him get into their organization. Once one of the leaders asked him to pull a job for them. Help out with a robbery. Grubbs said no. Not because he was afraid but because he didn't trust them either. Even if the job offer was legit, he reckoned he would be expendable. He thought it was just as likely the bank job was a way to get rid of him.

When he said no to the job that was it. They cold-shouldered him and Grubbs decided he didn't want to join their bullshit group anyway. They were too political, always speaking in this pseudo-intellectual bullshit way. All of 'em were college types. In the end that's why they didn't want him in their group. He wasn't a college guy. They might use him on the outside, use him like a pawn, but they didn't want him to really be with them.

But Harley Dee Grubbs wasn't a pawn of life. He was a knight, a black knight, who struck when his opponents weren't paying attention. If skillfully used, a knight could be a lethal chess piece, almost as lethal as a queen. That was because every player anticipated the moves of the queen. The bishop and rook were easy to see coming, too. It was the knight that fooled you.

After being rejected in Chicago, Grubbs, tired of bumming on the road, went back to Buffalo City. He came back even more depressed and angry than when he left. He was just going to cool it for a while, rejuvenate himself before goin' out on the road again, but Percy got him his job and that was good because he needed to save some money for when he hit the road again. But one year had turned into two and it looked like Grubbs didn't have a destiny after all.

But in the back of his mind Grubbs knew he had one. He just didn't know the opportunity would present itself so soon and in his hometown. But that was Destiny for you. Just when you stop looking for it, it comes and gets you.

Destiny had provided for the time and also the place. Grubbs should have thought about the place before. He'd worked at the grain elevator during high school. Like Doug, he'd been a bin sweeper. After a few months, they'd fired him. For a bad attitude. Talking back. Being late. But he'd worked at the grain elevator long enough to know how it operated, how it looked inside. He'd ridden the man-lift and had been to the top of the head house and had walked on the narrow, inside platform. He even remembered that vent.

It wasn't easy to get to, and it would be very dark in there and he couldn't turn on any lights. But it would make for a perfect sniper's nest.

This time of year they had a small crew working at the grain elevator. No one would be present at night, especially not this Saturday night. They didn't even have a full-time security guard. He could probably break in and not be caught. But there was a watchman that checked on the place once or twice during off hours so it would be better if he didn't break in.

But then he didn't have to. Grover was president of the co-op for this year. He had a key. All he had to do was lift Grover's key off his big key chain. His father wouldn't even notice it missing. He'd be out with the other AAM bastards protestin' with their tractorcade.

Protestin' with a tractorcade. What a bunch of pussies.

-VIII-

Their workday concluded, Dale and Will walked down the sidewalk toward Will's Volvo. Dale's car was parked across the street not too far from the Carnegie Library.

"So did Greeley inform you where you two are dining tonight?"

Will looked a little abashed. "The country club. But it's not just us two."

"Who else?"

"His wife, his mother, and his father-in-law."

"Quite a family affair."

Will didn't look too pleased.

171

"So, no one your age will be along?"

"Not unless Greeley married his wife when she was in junior high."

"She's younger than Greeley but not by much. She's a nice woman. She's bright. You'll at least have someone who can make intelligent conversation."

"You know her well?"

"Not well. I was introduced to her when I first came to work at the *Stampede*. She comes into the paper from time to time. She's friendly and unpretentious."

"You mean unlike her husband."

"Greeley's friendly enough."

"Sometimes too friendly."

"Well, look at it this way. You only have a few more days working here."

"You're right. He's not so bad. Do you know anything about his mother or father-in-law?"

"Never even met them but the father-in-law, Mr. Quigley, is the president of the town's biggest bank."

"He should provide stimulating conversation."

"Especially if you like talking about mortgages and interest rates and depreciation and inflation and –"

"Okay, okay," pleaded Will. "Actually, I know a few things about business. My father has worked for Kerr-McGee for twenty-five years."

"Does he make stimulating conversation?"

Will thought about it for a moment. "No."

"Well, then, make sure you sit next to Mrs. Greeley and I don't mean the mother."

"I got to get going. The publisher-mayor is going to pick me up at 7:30."

"Okay. Make sure you wear your tux."

It took Will a moment – but only a moment – to realize that Dale was jesting. Dale waved so long and Will did the same and Dale crossed the street to his car. When he got inside he glanced in his rear view mirror to see Will's no-longer dusty green Volvo tooling down the street.

Dale sat there for a moment trying to ignore the little pins of jealousy pricking his mind. Greeley had never invited him to the country club and he'd been working on the paper for ten months. On one hand, Dale didn't care. He didn't enjoy fancy places like that. He didn't like wearing a suit or behaving like a civilized, cultured person in a semi-formal social setting. But on the other hand, it did disturb him because it indicated that Greeley considered Will Whitaker a more sophisticated person than he. Of course, Will was more sophisticated than he was. Dale supposed his ego had been bruised a little because no one likes to be overlooked.

Then he thought about the note from Louise Henderson. He had been amazed at how frank and direct it had been: *If you want me you can have me.* Ordinarily, he'd have no interest in a tryst with her. She really wasn't his type. He didn't think they had anything in common. However, he found her full figure enticing. As he meditated on her ample dimensions, his semi-resentment for Greeley asking Will to the country club faded. For months he'd felt bored and restless and lonesome and, yes, he had to admit, sexually frustrated. He wasn't even sure if he wanted to have sex with Louise. He wasn't completely convinced that was her intention. But when he thought about her low cut blouse, remembered how her cleavage looked, the narrow cleft that divided those two soft spheres of silky flesh, he felt a surge of energy shoot through him like bullets of fire and their combustion obliterated any lingering doubts. The fact that he could, if he wished, venture out on a tryst that had an aura of illicitness to it excited him even more. Everything in Buffalo City had been so boring and mundane ever since he'd arrived. He was young and strong and alive. Now, this possibility of erotic intrigue seemed even more alluring and tempting than it really was.

He started his Chevy. He revved the motor making the engine growl. He was going to do it.

-IX-

Through the night vision scope, Harley Dee Grubbs aimed at the scarecrow with the Styrofoam head. The scope with its greenish glow illuminated the magnified target so that the mannequin head was clearly visible. So clear, in fact, that he could see the smooth, almost creamy texture of the Styrofoam.

He squeezed the trigger. A moment later, the skull of the Styrofoam head exploded. The rifle's retort echoed in the barn. Three hundred yards away, tattered flakes rained down like confetti around the still standing scarecrow. What was left of the head, the lower half and neck, somersaulted high in the air. Its return path to earth was eerily erratic.

Doug, who'd taken cover behind an obsolete old tractor, leapt up with his hands extended in triumph. "Whoa!" he shouted. "Woo-wee!"

When Doug's excited yells faded into silence, a hoot owl's protest came out of the small stand of trees by the creek.

Grubbs climbed down from the hayloft, left the barn, walked two hundred yards across the field to join Doug at the derelict tractor.

"That was a real good shot, Harley Dee," Doug said, almost panting in admiration. "It was fun seein' the head blow up."

Grubbs said nothing to as they tramped an additional hundred yards to the scarecrow. They had transplanted the straw man, minus the straw head, within the tree stumps and placed an old rusty trash bin and other objects around him. Grubbs wanted to see if the obstacles would distract him. Not at all.

Of course, the Target and the agents and cops and other people wouldn't be stationary. At least not for long. He might pause for a few seconds after getting out of the limo to wave to the crowd. That would be the best time to take his shot. Grubbs doubted there would be much open space around the Target. But Grubbs would only need a small gap.

They arrived at the crime scene. The top half of his mother's wig head had been blown away. Grubbs picked it up and examined it. The bottom half of the face – the jaw, chin, mouth – was still intact and attached to the slender neck. The feminine features didn't move him. In fact, he liked the idea that he had blown off the top of a female mannequin's head. He thought briefly of Louise.

Grubbs was surprised by how jagged the flaky edge looked. It looked like some tiger or other big-fanged beast had taken a huge hunk off the head and left the ragged edge.

"This is a lot more fun than shootin' bottles," said Doug.

Grubbs had planted the scarecrow so he'd stand as high as Grubbs (and the Target) was tall, around five ten. He hoisted his rifle to his shoulder, like a soldier would, and felt a satisfying sense of pride.

When they got back to the house they walked in through the kitchen door so Grubbs could look at his father's key chain hanging on a hook by the wall telephone. Grover had over a dozen keys on his big key chain. He wouldn't miss the one to the grain elevator's back door.

But Grubbs didn't want to take it then. He'd wait and come over Saturday morning before work.

The brothers walked through the kitchen to the living room. Their father, Grover, sat in the big easy chair still in his overalls. He was watching the syndicated re-run of *Gunsmoke*. The reception this far out of the city wasn't good. Squiggles and wavy bands interrupted Marshall Dillon's duties.

"What the hell was you shootin' at?" Grover asked without turning his head to look at his sons. "You better not be killin' any owls."

"Possum," said Grubbs. He glanced at Doug, his fierce look silencing his brother.

"There ain't any possum left in them trees." Grover turned to give his youngest son a scowl. "You only should kill what you eat."

Harley Dee had always killed more than game. He shot birds, feral cats, stray dogs, even a coyote once when it was fool enough to wander onto their farm.

"So, you goin' to town Saturday and see our tractor-cade protestin' the President?" Grover asked.

"I gotta work."

"What? You're workin' on that special day?"

"I always work on Saturdays."

"Yeah, I forgot. Well, too bad. You'll miss a show. We'll have a hun'ered tractors rollin' around town in protest. They ain't goin' to let us get within a square mile of the high school but he'll see us when he drives into Buffalo City!"

Before Harley Dee could think of a smart-ass retort, he heard his mother wailing in the other room. She ran into the living room holding her wig in her hands. She was a thin, unattractive woman with short gray hair almost as wispy as Harley Dee's goatee.

"Where's my head? Where's my head?"

She held out the raggedy wig for them all to inspect. Its dull brown hair and general shapelessness gave an unfortunate appearance of a deceased shaggy toy terrier rather than a wig.

"It's on top of your neck," Grover Grubbs said. "But there ain't nothin' in it."

-X-

At nine o'clock, the night full and moist, Dale drove down the street where Louise's house was located. He parked two houses away. He thought that was prudent. As he walked toward her home, he realized he'd often passed her place when he'd go on his evening runs to keep in shape.

177

He ambled up the walkway to the front door. The house was just an ordinary brick house, not very large, and a small tree stood in the middle of the yard and several large evergreen bushes lined the front of the house and gave a little cover for him to scoot up the front steps.

He didn't feel especially nervous, perhaps because he still didn't believe she meant what she'd written in her note. He wondered if he should have brought something with him. A small gift of some kind. But he realized this wasn't really a date. Besides, all she seemed to want him to bring was himself.

He knocked on her door. There wasn't a screen just a wooden door. He waited. He heard nothing. He was about to leave when the door cracked open and he saw her semi-smiling face. She said come in.

He did. She closed the door behind him. The light in the room was dim. Only a small lamp provided any light and it stood on a table next to a cloth couch.

Louise wore blue jeans and that same red jersey that he'd seen her in during the baseball game. Her feet were bare.

She asked if he'd like to take a seat and they sat on the couch. He asked how she was. She said fine. How was he? He said fine. Things were getting a little hectic at the newspaper. Because of the President coming? He said yeah. She asked if he wanted anything to drink. He said a 7-Up if she had it. She meant a real drink. He said he didn't drink booze. She got up and said she needed a drink. She went into the small kitchen and he heard her open the freezer, then the cabinet. Dale stood up and walked over and said, okay, he'd have what she was having.

She brought back two glasses of vodka. She handed one to Dale and he took a sip and tried not to wince. She smiled and took a longer drink than he did. They sat down on the couch again. She asked about his work at the paper. He didn't ask about her work. He knew she was a cosmetician at Byron Mors' funeral home and he didn't want to think about that right then.

After they finished their drinks, Dale just about forcing his down his gullet, she took their empty glasses and put them on the coffee table.

"You know, I've seen you around town," she said.

"I've seen you, too. I didn't know who you were though."

"I've also seen you running in the evening."

"Sometimes I go running. You know, to keep in shape."

Talking was making him more nervous. The vodka, which had turned his tongue bitter, now felt warm in his belly.

"Would you like to go into the bedroom?" she asked.

Right to the point, he thought. He'd only met one other girl like this one. "Okay."

She got up and he followed her into the dark bedroom. She turned on another small lamp and the weak light illuminated a room with a bed, a dresser with a large mirror, a bureau, and a small table with a portable radio on it. Louise turned on the radio but kept the volume moderately low. Dale recognized the station as KBUF. Some country tune emanated from the radio's small speaker.

"Do you like Tammy Wynette?"

179

At first, Dale thought she was referring to a friend. Then he made the connection. The country singer. One of her songs was playing on the radio.

"Sure, she's swell,"

"I think she has the best voice of all the women singers. A sincere, honest voice."

Dale listened to the song on the radio for a moment. Tammy repeated, in her plummy wail, "he loves me all the way" so he guessed that was the title of the song. She did have an expressive voice but there was a kind of baby-talk quality to it, too, which he found a little comical.

"I wish I could sing like that," Louise wistfully said.

"Do you sing?"

"I used to sing in church but that's a different kind of singing."

"Yeah. But you have a good speaking voice."

"You think so?"

He didn't really but he thought he ought to compliment her. "Sure."

His praise seemed to please her. She smiled at him in a more suggestive way than before.

"You can go ahead and get undressed and get under the sheet if you want. I'm going in the bathroom to get ready."

Dale nodded but he felt a little confused. Get under the sheet?

Louise slipped out of the room and he walked over to the bed. It wasn't very large. It only had a white sheet covering it. He thought that was strange. But the night was still warm after an unseasonably hot day.

He sat on the bed and considered what to do. He

didn't really want to get undressed at that moment. He was naturally shy. He also wanted to undress her. He'd been looking forward to that. He wondered what she was doing in the bathroom. Maybe she was taking the necessary precautions. He wasn't exactly sure what that meant. Women had different devices they could use besides the pill. He hadn't even thought about bringing anything with him. He didn't like using condoms anyway. The more he thought about these practical matters the less interested he was in doing it. At least mentally. His body still felt energized. In fact, he felt a frustrated arousal, almost as urgently as he had watching those X-rated films at Byron Mors'. If he could see something, then he'd be more certain.

"If you don't get ready then I won't," called Louise from the bathroom.

Dale took off his boots first, then his socks, then his shirt and jeans. All the while Tammy Wynette was softly crooning another song on the radio.

"Everything now," called Louise.

Good grief, he thought. He wondered how much she could see. The room was dimly lit but there was enough light to see some details. Still sitting on the bed, he shed his undershorts in one quick motion and quickly got under the sheet. Then it occurred to him that this all might be some strange trick.

That thought vanished when he saw Louise enter the room. She wasn't naked; she was wearing some small garment. At first, he thought it might be a negligee but as she got closer he realized it was a white smock. She swayed her hips when she walked and held her hands behind her back. The smock just fell past her broad hips and the smock's top buttons were undone so her large breasts were almost popping out of the garment. He didn't think she had on any panties underneath. His arousal grew.

The sheet was rather thin so he turned on his side so his erection shouldn't be so prominent. She sat down on the edge of the bed.

"You have a sexy body," she said.

"So do you."

"Why don't you lie completely flat on the bed?"

He hesitated and she unbuttoned one more button so that her breasts fell free. He gazed at them appreciatively, noticing with a little disappointment that she had rather small nipples.

He complied with her request and stretched out on his back on the bed, producing a tent effect with his erect penis underneath the sheet. The bed wasn't a very comfortable. Rather hard and unyielding.

She leaned over and stroked his face almost as if she were blind and needed to use her fingers to make out his features. He reached up and cupped her breasts and marveled at how soft and abundant they were.

"Close your eyes," she said.

He didn't want to but he did and then he felt her hand on the sheet over his erect phallus. But she didn't grasp it. Instead Louise lifted the sheet a couple of inches. He opened his eyes but she said in a soothing voice to keep them closed.

The weirdness of it all was starting to get to him. He didn't like keeping his eyes closed. He hadn't especially liked her touching his face. The only thing he'd liked so far was fondling her breasts.

Her other hand left his face and then he heard a familiar noise, like a lock opening, quickly followed by a sound of cloth tearing. Then he placed the noise. The sound of cutting scissors.

What the heck! He lifted his upper body and as he did she released the sheet and it fell against him, all of him except his erect phallus that poked out of the hole she'd just cut.

The next thing he knew Louise had climbed on the bed and straddled him. He felt his penis enter into this hot, moist cavern and his alarm diminished as he became inflamed with lust. She began pumping her hips against him. She moaned loudly, he grunted, she rocked her hips, his hands squeezed her breasts. She bucked, arched her back, bringing her breasts to his face. His lips caught one nipple while his hands reached behind her and cupped her ample buttocks. He thrust himself into her. Her vagina was incredibly wet and hot and demanding. She reared up. He tugged on her big ass to get leverage for one final thrust and he couldn't hold back any longer. He ejaculated. His penis throbbed and convulsed and he thought that sensation would never stop. But it did and he felt a little nauseous but he keep thrusting and Louise kept bucking and in a few minutes he heard her voice wail almost like Tammy Wynette's and then she shuddered and collapsed on top of him.

For the first time she offered her mouth and he kissed her but he didn't like the taste in her mouth or in his. He wanted to get off his back but she lay prostrate on him and he didn't think it would be gentlemanly to shove her off.

The radio was still playing Tammy Wynette. *Stand By Your Man*. Dale thought: more like *Sit On Your Man*.

Finally, Louise lifted her hips and Dale withdrew and she rolled over and sat on the edge of the bed. His pecker was still sticking out of the sheet and it was sticky. He sat up and pulled the sheet up and slipped his phallus out of the hole. He looked up and saw Louise smiling at him.

"Did you like that?"

"I don't know."

"Would you like something to drink?"

"Water. Just some water."

Louise got up, put her boobs back in her smock, then turned and walked away. Dale watched her big butt bounce and he felt himself getting aroused again but since he feared a return engagement would be even weirder, he sat up and quickly put on his shorts.

She came back with two glasses of water. He gulped his down. Louise sipped hers like she had with the vodka.

She sat down on the bed next to Dale. He looked at her face. She wore very little make-up now and her features were plainer. Her green eyes were rather small. Her nose was long and had sort of a bulbous end. Her lips were attractive, though. The lower one had a nice fullness that he'd always appreciated. Then he noticed something else. Her hair. It still had that poodle like puffiness in front but it was much shorter in the back.

"What happened to your hair?"

"Oh, that. I wear a fall."

"A fall?"

"A hair extension. I hook my hair into other hair to

make it longer."

"Other hair?"

"Hair you can buy."

Who would want to buy someone else's hair? He hoped the hair wasn't from any of the occupants in the Mors' Funeral Home and Peaceful Prairie Chapel.

"I better get going," Dale said, reaching for his Levi's.

"You can stay the night if you want."

Dale thought if he did he might not wake up in the morning.

"I better not. I got to get up early for work."

He tugged on his pants while Louise sipped her water. A commercial squawked on the radio. Something about Jimmy Dean's sausage.

"You know," Louise said, "you have really smooth skin."

Dale looked at her.

"I mean for a man. Not a lot of hair."

He pulled his polo shirt over his head. He looked on the floor for the scissors. Not there. She couldn't be hiding them on her person.

"What are you lookin' for?"

"Oh, nothing."

"Most of my male loved ones have rough skin. We have to apply all kinds of lotions and creams to make them look shiny and new."

For a moment, he thought she was talking about her other lovers. Then he realized she meant the dead people she worked on. Good grief. Things couldn't get much more macabre if Dracula walked in right now.

"Louise, you don't have any unusual interests in deceased people, do you?"

185

"What do you mean by unusual?"

"Forget it."

He finished putting on his boots. "Well, I better get going."

She got up and followed him as he walked into the living room. She was still wearing that damn smock but she'd buttoned it up most of the way.

He opened the door and said goodnight. She said goodnight in a singsong kind of way and closed the door.

As he walked to his car he thought he'd gotten what he'd deserved. You should never trust women who give you notes. Of course, the sex was rather energetic. But still, the whole scene was too weird for him. He preferred a little romance. This experience was the most bizarre experience since that X-rated film fest last Monday night. Dale was beginning to think that Byron Mors, in spite of his intelligence and sophistication, was a pervert.

Chapter Five
Friday

Dale, sitting on the padded chair before his desk, rubbed his eyes and yawned. He hadn't slept well last night. If he could tolerate the taste of coffee he would walk into the break room and drink ten cups of it.

All the editorial staff except Will Whitaker sat at their desks, busily preparing for that day's edition. Even Rosemary Rogers had arrived early. Today was a big day for her. That evening she would be covering the Miss Buffalo City Pageant.

Dale had been assigned to help her. He had protested to Greeley. He was the sports editor. Why couldn't Floyd Byrd help with coverage? After all, he sometimes served as the roving reporter.

Greeley had said that Floyd, the photographer, would be covering the arrival of the state delegation of Democrats. Greeley wanted to Floyd to accompany Will to the meeting; Will would interview the august group of state officials and Floyd would take several pictures. (Why several photos? Dale had wondered. They would only run one in the newspaper. Then he guessed that Greeley wanted several photos for his own purposes.) Floyd should make it back to the Miss Buffalo City Pageant in time to take photos of the winner. But just in case he didn't Dale's presence would be needed.

Dale now wished he hadn't told Greeley during his interview ten months ago that he had photography experience. Now he would have to take his camera with him to the pageant and if Floyd didn't get back in time he'd have to take photos. Since the event was being held in the high school auditorium he would have to shoot with a flash. He didn't have much experience using a flash. He grew worried that he wouldn't get the exposure right and the photographs would turn out even murkier than Floyd's often muddy prints. Since the Miss Buffalo City Pageant was one of the major town events, doing a poor job photographing the winner would bring him disfavor from Greeley and especially Rosemary.

Dale decided not to worry. The Bird would almost certainly make it to the pageant in time. If Floyd didn't and he had to shoot the winner then he'd ask for more light and not use a flash.

He also had to cover the high school baseball game that afternoon. Of course, Floyd would be too busy with his assignments to shoot any photos so Dale would have to handle the photography chores, too.

Dale was almost dreading covering the baseball game. He knew Louise would be in the stands watching her bellicose brother striking out. He wasn't looking forward to seeing Louise at the game. He'd dreamed about her last night. Dale rubbed his eyes then opened them, trying not to remember the horrific dreams, nightmares really, he had last night. Most of the nightmares had faded from his memory but he still remembered the last and most disturbing one. He'd dreamed that Louise had become pregnant. In the dream he and Louise are in bed, his bed, and he's wearing his usual sleeping attire, sweat pants, and she's wearing her itsy bitsy teensy weensy polka dot bikini. At first she's normal then suddenly her belly grows gravid in a matter of moments. It looks like her belly is about to pop. She doesn't seem bothered by her super fast pregnancy. As she starts to go into labor she says, "Quick, Mr. Photographer, the camera!" Dale grabs his camera from the table and rushes back to her. Louise is on her back, her legs spread (a position he hadn't seen and now definitely didn't want to see), her bikini bottom off, and something seems to be about to make its appearance.

Fortunately, he woke up before the something's birth. But right before he woke up, he felt a feeling of utter dread. A feeling so profoundly bad that he knew something was terribly wrong. Maybe she wasn't giving birth to a baby at all. Maybe it was something alien or subhuman or evil. The dream was scarier than *Rosemary's Baby*.

The glass door opened and Dale saw Will Whitaker walking past the swinging gate that led to the newsroom. Dale was glad to see Will. Maybe his arrival would dispel his gloomy mood.

Everyone exchanged greetings with Will. Dale rose from the padded office chair behind the desk in order to move to the nearby wooden chair. Will motioned for Dale to remain where he was.

"No," Dale said, "you use the desk. You have a story to write."

Will hesitated. Dale reminded him that he wrote his stories later when the typesetting machine was free.

Will took the seat before the desk and noticed that Dale did not look chipper. "A rough night?"

For a moment, Dale wondered if Will knew about

his tryst with Louise. But how would he know? Dale noticed that Will's expression looked completely normal. Will was just asking a general question prompted by Dale's grumpy condition. Dale considered telling Will about his bizarre night but the time and place was not right. Besides, he still felt somewhat ashamed of what he did. He didn't think Will had the same disdain for "middle-class morality" as Byron Mors did, but he imagined that Will would be either disappointed or amused by his behavior. Dale didn't want to see either reaction that morning.

"I didn't sleep well." Dale tried rousing himself. "How was your night with the Greeley clan?"

"Not bad. I did as you suggested and adroitly positioned myself next to Carol. You're right. She's a nice woman. Intelligent. Good-natured. I wonder why she married –"

Will noticed The Bird listening from his seat, which wasn't far away.

Dale leaned closer to his friend and said lowly, "Everybody wonders that."

-II-

Noon in the Buffalo City High School gymnasium. The lottery to select those lucky Buffalonians was about to be held. Millard Greeley approached the microphone, receiving polite applause, and addressed several hundred people sitting in the stands, giving a brief (for him) statement about how this part of the lottery would work.

Before today's grand finale, the ballots first had to

be distributed. The *Buffalo City Stampede*, beginning Tuesday, had printed a ballot on the back page of the first section. Townspeople could also have picked up ballots at KBUF, the WOCC student center, the Carnegie Library, city hall, the three supermarkets, and Bison bowling alley.

All a citizen then had to do was to fill out the ballot, writing his name, address, and phone number then return it to city hall or the *Stampede* before Friday at ten in the morning.

Greeley now said he would explain the simple process of ballot selection. He paused a moment, allowing what he thought was his resonant voice to fade. He pointed to a large hopper positioned behind him and standing next to a large table. In that hopper contained all the eligible ballots, estimated to number 6,293. One thousand ballots would be selected. The hopper would be churned after every ten selections. Once a ballot was selected, that person's name would be announced and then alphabetically recorded in a large, leather bound notebook. After the process was completed, the *Stampede* would print the names of all the fortunate one thousand in today's paper.

Greeley thought he'd explained the process in a concise, clear way. After all, he'd majored in journalism and knew how to organize his words. Now, he said smiling as broadly as he could which still only showed about half as many teeth as compared to his political paragon, he was going to turn over the proceedings to his wife, Carol.

At the mention of Carol's name, the crowd clapped enthusiastically. Greeley tried not to frown at how his wife had received a warmer reception than he had. He graciously kissed Carol on the cheek and left her to announce the names of the selectees.

As Greeley walked away from the center of attention, he glanced back at the three women who remained: his wife; Mrs. Swift, who would record the selectees; and the lovely Susan Smith, who would be reaching her slender hand into the hopper to make the selections.

Greeley wished he could remain and make sure everything went properly. He knew Carol would supervise it superbly (she thought of the idea first!), but still Greeley was reluctant to leave the spotlight, so to speak.

But he was a busy man with many important details to see to. Just imagine! It would all come to fruition tomorrow. Greeley would show them all that he was not one to trifle with. His under-appreciated talents would finally be duly recognized. Because of him, the President, the national press corp, and hundreds of visitors were coming to Buffalo City, a most welcome invasion, that would pump thousands of dollars into the local economy, that would –

Greeley had been so lost in his less than humble thoughts that he didn't see his nemesis standing before him at the rear gym entrance. Greeley actually bumped his belly against the obnoxious Byron Mors. Greeley felt his sizable stomach rebound from the collision and he took a step backwards. But Byron stood his ground, hardly registering the blow.

"As I once said before, Millard, we have to stop meeting like this."

Greeley tried to take Carol's advice: to act coolly during an assault of Byron's nasty wit. Greeley tried to compose his flabby face into a mask of indifference or better yet a façade of amused tolerance. He held that expression with great effort of will.

"Is there something wrong with your face?" Byron asked.

"Whatever do you mean?" Greeley asked, his lips hardly moving as he maintained his grin.

"You have an expression on your face that I've seen before."

"Oh, where?"

"In the embalming room."

Millard Greeley's perfectly composed mask of savoir-faire suddenly shattered into livid, red-faced indignation.

"Byron, I resent being compared to the grisly occupants of your necropolis! Your depraved humor is –" Greeley paused, trying to think of the proper word.

"Depraved?"

Greeley took in a deep breath, trying to keep from exploding.

"I must congratulate you, Millard, on one thing."

"And what may I ask is that?" Greeley's temper was beginning to cool.

"This lottery."

Greeley glanced at Byron's rather handsome face trying to decipher if he was being sincere.

"It's been handled with surprising competence."

"Yes, well."

"However, I have detected one slight flaw."

"And what, pray tell, is that?"

"You didn't take any precautions about ballot stuffing."

"What do you mean?" Greeley felt a drop of panic fall in his very dry brain.

"What is to prevent someone from returning more than one ballot?"

Another drop fell. Then another. Greeley could feel his brain growing damp with the fear of failure. A debacle in the making.

"The people of Buffalo City are honorable."

"No doubt. *Most* of them are."

Greeley's brain had turned from crust to mush. He was on the verge of screaming an obscenity.

"But what about the rare unethical fellow who returns not just one ballot but ten, twenty, or even a hundred? All it requires is the time filling out the ballot. In fact, he could fill out one ballot then photocopy dozens of them. His odds of being selected to this magnificent historical event would be dramatically increased."

Greeley bit his tongue to keep from denouncing Byron. The pain caused the panic to subside. He forced his brain to start working again in a calm, logical manner. (Why didn't Carol think of this flaw? Because she was a paragon of virtue, a woman of such pure motives, that she would never suspect anyone in our noble town of such base motives.)

"You're speaking nonsense, Byron."

"Think of the consternation if word got out that some people were gaming the system because you didn't take adequate precautions."

"Ridiculous. No one in Buffalo City would behave so – " Greeley paused, but when he saw Byron was again

194

to provide the word, he quickly added: "unethically."

"Are you sure of that?"

"Of course. I am confident of the sterling character of the citizens of Buffalo City."

"Well, you're wrong, Millard. I know of at least one citizen who did stuff, so to speak, the ballot."

"Who?" demanded Greeley.

"I."

"You?"

"That's right. I did. I returned dozens of them. In fact, I can't recall exactly how many."

"Byron, you are a cad!"

"Oh, don't worry, Millard. I might not be selected anyway. And if I am, I'm fairly certain I'll give my selection to some dim-witted Democrat who will appreciate what the peanut farmer has to say."

"I am nearly speechless."

"That takes some doing."

"Even I didn't imagine that you'd sink to such subterranean depths. To deliberately sabotage such an important, such a historic, such –"

"I got to go, Cicero."

Byron Mors began to walk away when the voice of Carol Quigley Greeley sweetly chimed over the microphone. Byron returned to the flabbergasted mayor. "You do have one outstanding attribute." Byron looked past Greeley, which was easy to do since he was five inches taller, to view the speaker at the mike.

Greeley turned and saw what Byron gazed at. Greeley was about to actually use physical force against the scoundrel. But when he turned, with hands clenched, he faced only space.

195

His nemesis, Byron Mors, was jauntily walking out of the gym.

-III-

Some of the national press had descended upon Buffalo City. While walking back to the newspaper after lunch, Dale, Will, and Dwight caught sight of a television truck with an ABC logo on the side and the call letters of the affiliate in Amarillo. They all recognized the Amarillo reporter who stood before the open side door talking to the cameraman and the soundman. That was interesting enough but when they crossed the street to the sidewalk, they spied the ABC White House correspondent sitting on the front bumper of the truck looking grumpy. Dale had seen him on television doing his spots; he had a bumptious, exasperating manner, often calling out questions in a braying voice to President Carter as he walked across the East Lawn or while boarding the helicopter to take him to Air Force One.

Dale wasn't too impressed to see a celebrity in the flesh but Will and Dwight were excited and talked about it on the way back to the paper. Dale supposed they reacted with more eagerness because both of them were actual reporters with journalistic ambitions. Dale, merely a sports editor, would have been more delighted if he'd seen Johnny Bench or Tom Seaver.

"Did you think he was wearing a toupee?" Will asked, meaning the national correspondent.

Neither Dale nor Dwight knew. They'd never to

196

their knowledge seen a man wearing a rug.

"The hair looked too perfect," observed Will.

"Every lock in place," said Dale.

"And it's a windy day," said Dwight.

"A lot more people than you'd expect wear them," Will said.

"Like who?" Dwight asked.

"William Shatner for one."

"You mean Captain Kirk?" asked Dale.

"Yes. And Sean Connery and Burt Reynolds."

"Not Clint Eastwood?"

"No, not Eastwood."

Dwight asked about politicians.

"Not that many politicians." Then he named three of the most prominent ones.

"How do you know so much about this hair piece business?" Dale asked Will.

"My father's bald."

"Does he wear a toupee?"

"No."

Dale and Will grinned about the non sequitur. Dwight didn't get it.

When they got to the newspaper office they noticed another big shot standing at the front desk. At least, they guessed he was a big shot. He was dressed in an expensive suit, had a pricey haircut, and displayed a peremptory attitude. He was demanding to know when he could use the paper's teletypewriter. He wanted to file a story for his paper back east.

Poor Mrs. Milford stood behind the long front desk, trying to understand what the man wanted. When she saw the three men enter she pointed to Dwight.

"He's the managing editor. You ask him."

The big shot turned to Dwight and explained the problem to him.

"You mean you're looking for a telegraph?"

"No," said the man, fairly tall with dark hair and haughty eyes, "I assumed you were a modern newspaper and had a teletype sender. I would write my copy here and send it back to D.C."

"D.C.?"

The man stared at Dwight as if he'd broken wind. "District of Columbia. As in Washington D.C."

"Why didn't you say that in the first place?"

"Well, do you?"

"Do we what?"

"Do you have a teletype sender on the premises?"

"Mister, we have a wire service. Is that what you mean?"

Will stepped over and gave Dwight a general idea that the big shot wanted to know if the newspaper had a teletypewriter. Dwight nodded but still looked at the easterner with a jaundiced eye.

"Nope, we don't have a teletypewriter."

The man gave a that's-what-I-thought kind of disdainful smile and was about to leave. "You don't by chance know where I could find one?"

"No, sir, I don't."

"Thanks a great deal," he said. "You've renewed my faith in the ignorance of small-town Americans."

The big shot departed.

Dwight, his mustache more droopy than ever, turned to Will and Dale. "Who was that guy?"

-IV-

Dale would have preferred watching the Friday edition press run but he had to cover the baseball game.
He drove to the Buffalo City Memorial Park and got
there just in time to see the first pitch.

The Buffs won, beating Quanah Parker High School,
5-3. Dale remembered playing baseball against Quanah Parker, an all-Indian school, back when he was in
high school. That had only been five years ago, but that
more simple time seemed like an epoch ago.

He watched most of the game from the press box
with the sports reporter from KBUF, a guy only two
years older than him named Jerry Dewberry. Dale
had known Dewberry back in their hometown of Galilee. They went to the same high school and they had
been as friendly as was permissible for a senior and a
sophomore. Dewberry hadn't gone to their hometown
college, Galilee Nazarene, instead he went to OU. He'd
majored in broadcast journalism and his first job was
with KBUF. When Dale found out that another Galilee
kid was working in sports here in Buffalo City he'd
been pleasantly surprised.

During the football and basketball seasons they
sometimes traveled together for road games. They
didn't have very interesting conversations, however. Dewberry, married to a girl he'd met at Norman,
seemed preoccupied with domestic and professional
concerns. His wife, Donna, who'd studied advertising
and public relations, didn't think she had a job befitting her educational level. She worked at the town's
hospital in the P.R. department, but she wasn't paid

well and her work was tedious, mostly writing public relations releases. She also complained about Jerry's long work hours, comparatively low pay, and how he spent too many evenings broadcasting Buffalo City sporting events. She also disliked living in such a small and boring town as Buffalo City. She wanted them to move back to her hometown of Tulsa or better yet relocate to Dallas.

Dale had tried to get Dewberry to talk about more interesting topics during their journeys. He'd asked Dewberry what books he read. "Who has time to read books?" he had responded. Dewberry and his wife sometimes went to see a movie. They'd seen *Grease* last summer when it showed at the Prairie Palace. They both had really enjoyed it. Dale didn't say anything in response to that because he thought he film had been ridiculous. Not only was it a rather banal parody of that time period, the early '60s, but the cast had been ten years too old for their characters. So, it appeared that they didn't share the same taste in movies.

Dewberry, during football season, had once invited Dale over to Sunday dinner and he'd met Donna. Mostly he remembered her for four things: first, her dark brown hair, curled in a stylish way; second, her fashionable eye glasses that seemed to enlarge her attractive hazel eyes; third, her slender figure that featured a narrow waist and a perky butt. He couldn't help but notice that last feature because she wore very tight fitting green women's slacks and she seemed to be scooting all over the house, going from the kitchen to the dining room to the living room back to the kitchen. Dale had tried not to look too directly at her retreating rear and he'd once glanced at Dewberry to make sure he hadn't seen him impolitely appraising his wife. Jerry, however, hadn't noticed. He hadn't been gazing at his wife. Instead, he'd been staring down at his mostly clean dinner plate, not in an appreciative way a man does after a good meal, because the roast hadn't been very appetizing, but in a pensive, moody way that suggested he had serious things on his mind. Things that didn't involved rump roasts or any other kind of rump.

The fourth quality that Dale remembered about Donna was her petulant, almost haughty personality. She hadn't been hospitable, hardly spoke during dinner, and only gave a few perfunctory, polite smiles. Dale didn't know if she was miffed with him or Jerry or both of them. Maybe that was just her usual temperament. Anyway, Dale had never been back to the Dewberry household. The last time he and Jerry Dewberry spoke privately, during the ride to the regional basketball tournament three months after the Sunday dinner, Jerry had confided to him, "Don't get married too young, Dale. There are too many expectations and then too many problems."

Dale had also seen Donna Dewberry a few of times around town: strolling down a supermarket aisle, walking into a bank, traipsing across a park's semi-verdant lawn with her poodle, and each time she wore tight fitting slacks of differing colors that showed off her shapely derrière. Such behavior by women puzzled him. If he had encountered her and complimented her for having callipygians he knew she would have reacted with shocked indignation. *How dare you!* And yet she must be aware of how her figure and attire would entice male viewers. Only twenty-one, Dale couldn't fathom this seeming feminine contradiction.

Now, with the baseball game in the fifth inning, Dale nodded at Dewberry, signaling his departure. Dale headed down the stairs to the diamond. He snuck out on the outskirts of the baseball field to take a couple of photos and when the game concluded he got a quote from the coach and checked the scorer's book to make sure he hadn't missed anything.

While in the press box, Dale hadn't noticed Louise Henderson sitting below in the stands. Now walking away from the field, he glanced again at the stands and the concession area and still didn't see her. He felt relieved. He wasn't relishing the idea of seeing Louise after the phantasmagoric evening they had spent together. However, she'd picked the wrong game to miss. Her brother, Larry Henderson, had struck out twice but he also hit a three-run homer in the bottom of the seventh to win the game.

Dale ambled over to his car, in a better mood than that morning, and was thinking about how Helen Brown would be arriving in Buffalo City for her Spring Break this evening. He was looking forward to talking to her. While walking he stared at the spring sky, enjoying how one billowy cloud looked like a blimp as it slowly sailed through the sparkling azure sky. And that's why he didn't see her until he was twenty feet away from his car.

Louise sat on the hood of his Chevy, waiting for him, smiling.

Dressed in blue jeans and a sweater (red, of course), with the same toe-less shoes and the same painted toenails, her legs where crossed at the ankle and she swung them a little from her perch upon his car. Dale immediately felt that contradictory, divided feeling: in his mind he felt wary but viscerally he felt a throb of excitement, especially at the sight of seeing her plump bottom sitting on the hood of his car.

"Did you see the game?" he asked, trying to sound jovial.

"I missed the first half," she said. "You know, work."

"Yeah," he said, his voice less jovial. He didn't like thinking about the work she did. At least she wasn't wearing her white smock.

"But I saw Larry hit his home run."

"Yeah, he really smashed it."

"Oh, he's *strong* all right."

Dale thought she said that in a peculiar way. Almost like she was reminding him she had a strong brother. A strong brother with a bad temper. A strong brother with a bad temper who loved his older sister.

"If he made more contact, he'd be a really good hitter," Dale said.

"Oh, I think he can make *contact* when he wants to."

Dale was growing tired of this conversation. What was really on her mind?

Louise pointed to the camera he carried. "Did you ever develop my picture?"

"I developed the film. I can make you a print if you'd like."

"That would be nice."

Dale waited for her to hop off his car. When she didn't he walked to the driver's side, hoping she'd get the hint.

"Do you know that I was once married?" she said in a strangely accusatory way as she turned only her head to look at him.

"You're not married now, are you?" Dale asked with concern. He'd once had a brief "affair" with a married woman. The daughter of the woman who'd married his father. At the time he hadn't known she was married but it had been a big mistake and thinking about it, which he rarely did, still embarrassed him.

"I said I used to be."

"You have the same last name as your brother."

"After my divorce, I changed my name back to Henderson. I sure didn't want to keep his name."

"Why? Did you dislike him that much?"

"No, he wasn't all bad. Sort of scrawny though. And he drank too much and couldn't keep a job. His name's Euple Pugh."

Euple Pugh? What kind of name was that? Actually, Dale knew. He had hillbilly relatives and some of them had odd first names like that. He thought about Mrs. Pugh's problems with Euple. He didn't know that many Tammy Wynette songs but Louise's marital experience sounded like good material for Tammy to wail about.

Louise shook her head. "I sure as heck didn't want to be Louise Pugh if I wasn't married to him."

"I can understand that."

An uneasy silence settled between them. Dale put his hand on the door's handle.

"Would you like to come over tonight?" Louise asked, still sitting on the car with her back to him.

"I got to work tonight. I have to help cover the Miss Buffalo City Pageant."

Louise slipped off his car; actually, she pushed her hips forward and slid off the hood. "Oh, *that*."

"Were you ever in the pageant?" Dale asked, trying to sound jovial again.

"That's for rich girls." Louise turned and faced him. "I mean, come by *afterwards*."

"I don't think so. I've had to work a lot this week. I'm pretty tired."

Louise stared at him. "I'm not into one night stands."

Dale was surprised by her offended tone. "I'm not either."

"Well, then?"

He thought he ought to be direct with her. He didn't want to hurt her feelings. He didn't want to make her mad or give her reason to make her brother mad.

"Look, Louise, I think I made a mistake. You're an attractive girl and I like you. But this wouldn't work out between us. So maybe we should stop before things get any –" he almost said "weirder" but he caught himself in time. "Any more complicated."

"You don't like me?"

"Of course, I do. I said I did."

"Is it my job?"

It was more than her job. It was the disturbing fact that she didn't leave her work at the workplace.

"Yeah, I think that's it."

"A lot of people don't understand what I do."

Maybe they understood all too well what she did. But he didn't really blame her for having that job. Somebody, he guessed, had to do it. Then again, maybe the living ought to leave dead people mostly undisturbed.

"That's because most people don't have your sensitivity," said Dale.

Louise's glum face brightened. "That's true, isn't it?"

"I got to get back to the newspaper, Louise. Do you need a lift?"

"No, I got my car back over there." She pointed to a red Volkswagen.

Dale was glad to see she drove a normal car. He opened his door. Before he got in he said, "I'll make a print of the picture I took of you and send it to you."

Louise gave a half-smile. "Okay." She took a step back. "Good-bye."

Dale returned the farewell and got in his Chevy. Before starting the engine, he watched her walk away. Her blonde fall didn't sway as gaily and she didn't swing her hips with the same suggestiveness as she had yesterday. But he guessed he'd always remember that day when she had.

He felt sort of guilty and he didn't know why. She'd initiated it. But he knew he was at fault too. He knew all along there wouldn't be anything of meaning between the two of them. Maybe Louise didn't understand that, but he did. So, as he now saw it, he was more responsible than she was. As he watched her get in her little red bug and drive away, he felt sorry for her.

-V-

Harley Dee Grubbs strode quickly to the Buffalo City Farmers and Ranchers Trust and Loan and got there with just a few minutes to spare. As soon as the press had spit out the last Friday paper, he'd taken off, not even asking Percy if he could go. The bank stayed open late on Friday, until 4:30, and he wanted to take his money out.

Grubbs walked into the handsome lobby of the FRT & L, as it was informally known, and tried to disguise his disgust for all the older people shuffling in and out of the bank. He hated banks to begin with, and would never have opened the account except that he was basically coerced by Greeley to do so as a condition of being hired. Grubbs especially despised this bank, with its big lobby and its gold and maroon furniture and the replicas of farming and ranching paraphernalia artistically displayed in corners and on the walls. If he wanted to rob a bank, this would be the one he'd pick.

Grubbs saw a middle-aged man, a farmer judging from his duds, leaving one of the five teller windows. Grubbs dashed over there and rudely brushed past a young woman who was a few steps away. He heard her say, "Excuse *me*," but he didn't look back at her. Instead he stared at the teller, a nearly elderly woman, who titled her head up to look at him through her granny glasses. She'd been working at the bank forever. Grubbs knew she was Mrs. Swift, the mother of the woman who worked at city hall.

"May I help you?"

"Yeah, I want my money."

Mrs. Swift looked momentarily alarmed. His assertive manner had slightly frightened her and at first she thought he'd said, "I want *your* money."

"Did you hear me?"

Mrs. Swift nodded but she still looked confused.

"Look, is there someone else I can talk to that's not hard of hearing?"

Grubbs heard murmurs behind and around him. Other customers were disturbed that he was acting so rudely to this fine old woman.

"I'm in a hurry!" Grubbs all but shouted. "I want to take all my money out of this here bank!"

Grubbs' loud, almost threatening voice, further pixilated the old lady. She began to tremble. One of the other tellers noticed and called for Mr. Quigley.

Mr. Quigley, the son of the bank's president, was essentially a younger replica of his father: ruddy, thin, ascetic but with even better styled red hair.

"May I help you?" he asked in a voice that suggested just the opposite.

"Yeah, I want to take my money out."

Mr. Quigley asked to see Grubbs' bankbook or a check. Grubbs gave him a withdrawal slip with his bank account information printed on it. The assistant bank manager quickly looked up the pertinent information.

"You want to withdraw all your funds?"

"That's what I said ten minutes ago."

"You wish to close your account?"

"That's right."

Grubbs suddenly sneezed. He wiped his nose on the sleeve of his work shirt keenly aware that his uncouth act had repulsed all the good people standing near him. He could almost feel the attractive young woman, Donna Dewberry – the one that he'd cut in front of to get to the teller's window and was now standing behind him – flinch.

"Very well," Mr. Quigley said with a grimace. The banker performed the necessary paperwork and handed Grubbs two hundred and thirty-six dollars and seventy-four cents.

Grubbs grabbed the money.

"I'd like to remind you to treat our personnel in a courteous –"

Grubbs turned away and ignored the offended faces of the people around him. He strode to the bank's glass front doors and almost bumped shoulders with a rancher, Buck McMurtry, who was also leaving. That would have been a serious mistake since McMurtry outweighed Grubbs by thirty pounds and would have reacted strongly if a hippie bumped into him. (Grubbs, in spite of moderately long hair, didn't consider himself a hippie. In fact, he had as much contempt for hippies as did the rancher.) However, Grubbs managed to evade the collision and marched out of the bank ahead of the tall and weathered man.

Grubbs sneezed again. Damn, he was getting a cold. Grubbs rarely got colds or the flu. He had an impressive constitution. Because of that he regarded other people who caught colds and other seasonal maladies as weaker willed individuals. When he encountered them he looked upon them with more disdain than usual. He recalled how the people in the bank had reacted to him when he'd sneezed and used his shirtsleeve to wipe his nose. He'd perversely enjoyed repulsing them. He wished he'd sneezed right into the face of the young woman that he'd cut in front of. The fact that she was good looking and had a great ass made him want to offend her all the more.

Grubbs stuffed the cash into his pocket. He'd been paid last Tuesday and thus he wouldn't be paid again for eleven more days. (Greeley kept his father's policy of paying employees on a Tuesday. Greeley senior had thought paying workers, especially young men, on a more typical Friday would encourage them to blow most of their paycheck on weekend revelry.) Taking his money out of the bank was just a precaution. He wasn't sure what he'd do after taking down the Target Saturday evening. If he thought he could get away with it, he'd return to the newspaper. If not, he would make his getaway and head to Mexico. He'd already stuffed his essentials into his car. The cash he now had would fund his way to Mexico.

He'd rather not flee. He'd rather return to the newsroom and witness the commotion. He still wasn't sure what he'd do with his rifle. He couldn't leave it at the grain elevator. They would dust it for fingerprints and he had a record. Not an adult one, just a juvenile record. But the authorities might match his fingerprints on the rifle with his juvie record.

Grubbs thought he could stash the rifle in the trunk of his beat-up Chrysler. Would the feds look in car trunks that night? Wouldn't the bastards need a warrant for that? There were times when he wished he had more education.

Grubbs walked back to the newspaper office. He still needed to help Percy clean the press. He had to act as normal as possible. Maybe he shouldn't have ruffled people's feathers at the bank. He wanted to do worse. He wanted to grab that old biddy and knock her head against the counter. And that smug sonofabitch Quigley. He'd wanted to punch his sour face.

Back there he'd controlled his temper, mostly. People didn't understand how hard it was for him to control his temper. That's what got him in trouble, those times when he flew off the handle. When he was sixteen he'd punched a kid two years younger and broke the kid's jaw. Since he'd been in a couple of fights already that school year, the judge sentenced him to two months at the juvenile work farm. Grubbs hadn't minded it so much. He'd learned from another kid how to pick locks.

He'd committed other juvenile crimes but he'd never been prosecuted until that assault and battery charge. He stole and shoplifted. But he was careful and good at it and the few times he'd been caught the store clerks let him go when he gave back the stuff. Maybe they were persuaded also by the hostile look in his eyes. He'd also committed arson. He'd burned down a shed in the back yard of the ninth grade English teacher he didn't like. He'd gotten away with it. He'd also molested two younger girls. He would have raped the second one but he'd heard Percy coming unexpectedly into the garage. Percy's little sister never told on him. A few years later, she dropped out of school. Last he heard she was living in Las Vegas. Since Percy and his family didn't like talking about her, he guessed she wasn't doing too hot.

After he turned eighteen he stopped doing that shit. There were times when he was tempted. But for some reason he knew he had to stop for a while. Maybe he knew he was preparing himself for something big. Even in Chicago, when he could have joined a gang to rob a bank, he refrained because in the back of his mind he knew there was something momentous, something bigger than life itself, that he was destined to do.

People would look at him and not suspect a thing. They'd just see some loser and not give him a second thought. Or like those bastards in that bank they'd see him and treat him with disrespect because he wasn't a college guy, didn't make a lot of money, didn't wear nice clothes, and had an ugly, sneering face.

What they didn't know was that he had a Destiny. He had the smarts, the guts, and the will. With those things he would make his mark.

Grubbs walked in the back door of the press room. He saw Percy cleaning the press and walked over to him.

"Where'd you run off to?" Percy asked.

"Nowhere special."

Grubbs tugged on his wispy goatee and smiled one of his rare genuine smiles. He knew it showed his bad teeth but he didn't care. In spite of the fact that Percy was hopelessly naïve, he sort of liked him. He had liked his little sister, too.

-VI-

Miss Buffalo City was not a beauty pageant. It was an achievement pageant. Young women participated (not competed) in five primary categories: the interview; the on-stage question; evening gown; fitness (bathing suit); and talent.

The interview portion of the pageant was conducted "off-stage." The participants provided the judges with letters of recommendation and information about their high school or college grades and activities. Judges then interviewed the participants, asking them questions about their grades, activities, and community involvement. The judges evaluated the girls on their poise, how articulate they were in giving answers, and their disposition and personality.

The other skills were evaluated on-stage. The participants demonstrated their poise and grace during the evening gown activity. They also were given an on-stage question to answer, usually an opportunity for the girl to express her interest in a particular "platform;" that is, her concern for a vexing social or political problem or debilitating disease. In the talent phase of the pageant the girls usually sang, danced, played a musical instrument, recited poetry, twirled the baton, or demonstrated some other skill befitting young ladies of good breeding. The swimsuit was the one part of the event that most obviously displayed the young ladies physical attributes but even that portion of the pageant was characterized as showing the girls' "fitness" rather than their beauty.

Besides gaining the admiration and respect of the townspeople, the young women who finished in the top three were awarded scholarships. The winner won $2,000, second $1,000, and third $500. The scholarship money could be converted to cash if the girl wasn't attending or going to attend college, which was a rare occurrence. Almost every year, at least two dozen girls participated. The winner advanced to the Miss Oklahoma Pageant held in Tulsa later that year.

The winner of the state pageant then would be off to Atlantic City to vie for the crown of Miss America.

The Miss Buffalo City Pageant was held on the Friday closest to the spring equinox. In the past there had been some controversy from the more conservative Christians in the community because they thought connecting the pageant to the vernal equinox gave the proceedings a slightly salacious, pagan quality: A reminder of The Rites of Spring and all that other heathen stuff. The more progressive thinkers in the community, of course, publicly dismissed such reactionary talk although informally they did nothing to discourage that notion. It helped attendance.

Carol Quigley Greeley knew all these things; she knew because she had been voted Miss Buffalo City herself back in 1966, the spring of her senior year in high school. Now, as she sat at with the other four judges in the front row of the high school auditorium she began to recollect those days of her youth.

With the title she won a scholarship. The money would help defray the cost of attending Radcliffe or Vassar. She'd been accepted to both as well as Oklahoma University and Southern Methodist. Part of her wanted to go to Radcliffe. She often daydreamed of living in Cambridge, going to coffee houses to listen to folk music, attending social mixers and meeting the young squires of Harvard. She thought she'd like living in a cosmopolitan city like Boston. All that history and literature! She imagined visiting the homes of some of her favorite writers: Emily Dickinson, Thoreau, and Emerson. She thought going to Radcliffe would help prepare her for a career as writer, or, using a word she liked even better for its antiquity, an *authoress*. She wanted to write poetry like Emily or novels like Harriet Beecher Stowe, Jane Austen, and the Bronte sisters.

She remembered standing in the wings of this very high school auditorium thirteen years ago so full of hope and promise and dreams. And also doubt. Because that dream of leaving dull Buffalo City and venturing to Boston and fitting in seemed hopelessly naïve to that more skeptical part of her mind. She'd always been a clever student. She always received the best marks in her class. She sang in the chorus and in the church choir. She participated in student activities, including being elected vice-president for student council. She edited the yearbook. She enthusiastically pursued all the necessary tasks available to a young woman at her prosaic if not backward high school. Outside of school, she volunteered for civic and charitable work. She scored high on her college admission test, although not as high as she had unrealistically expected. That was perhaps the first warning that maybe she wasn't as special as everyone – her teachers, her minister, her parents – said.

She remembered standing on that stage and being awarded Miss Buffalo City and feeling gratified, of course, as five hundred of her townspeople, men and women she'd known all he life, applauded her. She had accomplished yet another feat. Wearing her chiffon gown of blue, she almost felt beautiful that night. Ordinarily, she never felt beautiful; even her mother would characterize her as "attractive" or "nice-looking" or "sweet-looking" never using the word beautiful or even the less exalted word, pretty.

She didn't mind really. She'd always received attention from boys. Not the leering gazes or lascivious grins that some of the other girls received. She was glad of that. She'd always been taught to be a lady and to graciously accept attention from the opposite sex but never to shamelessly flirt, and never give any out-of-control boy the slightest provocation that she was less than a well mannered, properly brought up young lady. As a consequence, she thought the people who really approved of her were the parents of her friends. The boys respected her, the girls admired her, but the parents regarded her as a perfect role model for their impressionable children.

Carol snapped out of her reverie for a moment. Susan Smith, probably the most attractive girl in the pageant, was taking her turn in the evening gown competition. Susan strolled across stage, looking ravishing in her baby blue and crimson trim taffeta gown. She walked properly, not swaying her hips too much (but a little), and smiled becomingly at the appreciative audience. She *was* lovely. Susan stepped toward the microphone stand and listened as the Master of Ceremonies, Ed Reeves, asked her the on-stage question: What would she say was the most pressing health problem in our society today and how would she go about alleviating that problem? Susan, the daughter of the town's only psychiatrist, said she thought *mental* health was the most serious problem facing our society today. More and more people were suffering from various forms of *mental* illness. Some of the problems were quite *serious* like schizophrenia but many other people were afflicted with different kinds of *phobias* and *syndromes*. Thinking mental health was the most serious health concern today didn't mean that other more obvious health problems involving different *organs*, like the heart and liver, weren't important too. She just thought the *brain* was the most *important* organ in the body since it regulated all the other organs and controlled our thinking. As a consequence, Susan thought people should *practice* good mental health. That meant a healthy lifestyle, eating properly, including lots of *vegetables*, exercising regularly, having interesting conversations to *exercise* the brain, and keeping busy doing constructive things. Oh yes, a belief in a higher power, namely *God*, was very beneficial in keeping one mentally fit.

Susan beamed a beatific smile as she left the microphone stand and floated back across stage. Carol thought Susan had acquitted herself well. She gave a completely conventional answer but that was not a bad thing. Better to speak in platitudes that people approve of than say something too perceptive or unusual.

Carol thought Susan had good but not great off-stage qualifications. She had been the most ravishing participant during the fitness portion of the pageant. Her blonde hair and green eyes were highlighted by her turquoise one-piece (all the girls were required to wear one-piece bathing suits) but her suit was either cut a little more revealingly or perhaps Susan's full figure just couldn't be completely contained in the modest bathing suit. Susan looked more alluring than any of the other girls as she strolled across the stage. Carol had glanced at the only male judge, the attorney Clarence Fincher, and noticed his undisguised approval. If Susan didn't blow the talent part, she was a lock to win.

As the talent portion of the evening commenced, Carol's thoughts drifted back thirteen years to her night as a Miss Buffalo City participant. Her future was, as her high school English teacher had exclaimed the day before, "unlimited." And yet even as she won the title, as she stood on stage and smiled her characteristically modest smile, doubts lurked in the back of her mind.

There were three reasons, three doubts, as to why she wasn't sure about leaving for the East. First, she doubted she had the ability to succeed. She knew she was intelligent but she wasn't brilliant. She knew because she'd gotten to know a brilliant girl at Girls State. They were roommates but they never became friends. Naomi, her roomie, was from Tulsa. She came from a well-off family. Her father was a doctor but Naomi wanted to be a writer of some kind. They had enough initial conversations that Carol knew she didn't have as keen of an intellect as Naomi. And when Naomi realized this, they had fewer conversations. That was the first time that someone had deemed her inadequate in some way and it undermined Carol's confidence for a while even though she'd acquitted herself quite well at Girls State, winning the race for State Treasurer.

Naomi was the first Jewish person Carol had ever known. Naomi seemed to lack the more ostentatious forms of femininity. She didn't smile easily; she wasn't socially adept; she had disdain for most of the rituals at Girls State. Instead of attending some of the required meetings, she would stay in their dorm room

218

reading a formidable book. Naomi also didn't seem to care if she was attractive. She had fairly arresting good looks but she never did all the grooming and beautifying that the other girls did. As the days passed, Carol became uneasy around Naomi, and she had never felt that way before with anyone.

Carol thought there would be more Naomis at Radcliffe. And even more of the other kind of girl she'd encountered at Girls State that had also somewhat unnerved her: the beautiful, wealthy, confident, socially advanced girl.

Applause. Carol looked up and saw one of the participants, Laura Hennessey, giving a modest curtsy after concluding her dramatic recitation. Almost all the girls sang or played the piano or recited literature. (Carol had played the piano, the first movement of Beethoven's Moonlight Sonata.) Sometimes Carol wished a girl would do something unusual if not bizarre, perhaps demonstrating a ventriloquist talent or skill in archery.

The second reason that had given Carol doubt was the health of her mother. She was becoming a frail woman and Carol, even though she sometimes felt her mother withheld her full approval, nevertheless loved her. She didn't want to be too far from home.

But the most disturbing reason was the most obvious: a boy she had loved since adolescence was going to school at OU. He was two years older but ever since her sophomore year she'd had a crush (no, it was more than that) on him. He was tall and handsome with dark hair and striking blue eyes. She had never thought blue eyes could look warm, but his did when he smiled. And he had a variety of smiles, all attractive, especially his rakish one. But what interested her more than his good looks was his energy and confidence and irreverence. She found those attributes especially appealing because she felt she lacked them.

Byron had been attending college at OU for two years and she had heard that he was just as successful in college as he had been at Buffalo City High. In high school he had always been an accomplished student and a good athlete and a class leader and he had attained those accomplishments with a flair, an insouciance, that bordered on indifference. In his intellect, too, she saw the brilliance that she lacked.

When she entered high school they could have dated. In her sophomore year she did a little flirting. But he was a senior and he had a steady girlfriend for most of that year and he had a reputation for preferring flashier girls. The only thing they had ever done with each other was to have one dance. She'd played it cool but near the end of the waltz as he held her closer than he should for a first dance she had looked at his face and seen his almost mesmerizing blue eyes staring at her and she knew that he knew how she felt.

Nothing developed. She saw him around town that summer, cruising in his new red Mustang with his less appealing friends, the radio blaring the loudest rock 'n' roll he could find. Miffed by his seeming indifference, she ignored him and forced herself to try and forget him. But she didn't.

Her last two years of high school passed pleasantly. She excelled at all the things she should. She dated regularly, but she didn't have a steady beau. She even dated Byron's younger brother, Blake, who was in her class. Blake, however, wasn't like Byron although he desperately wanted to be. Blake wasn't as tall, wasn't as athletic, wasn't as bright, wasn't as charismatic. He didn't even look much like Byron. He had an ordinary face with basic brown hair and mild green eyes. Blake also had a very different personality. Byron took his success in stride whereas Blake always tried too hard. When she and Blake graduated from high school, Carol wasn't surprised when Blake enlisted in the marines during the build-up of the Vietnam War. Now maybe he could do something to better his older brother. But that didn't work out for poor Blake either.

The other boys Carol dated in high school were no more interesting to her. She dated because it was expected of her. She never went steady with anyone. People thought it was due to her parents' strictures, but the truth was that she didn't want to have a steady boyfriend.

Thirteen years ago she had smiled standing on that stage. She also discreetly cried. She shed just a few tears and those watching could easily imagine they were tears of happiness for receiving such a coveted honor. But her tears were due to something less cere-monial. At that moment of triumph she somehow knew at that her life was going to change and she feared that she would not attain any of her dreams. Later, after the pageant was over, her doubts turned into a foreboding, then into a fear that was almost as petrifying as getting a whiff of mortality.

Then summer arrived and her life returned to normal. That fear she had sensed hovering over her during the pageant faded. Her natural optimism and good cheer returned. She planned for college, thinking about what her major would be, what activities she would pursue, which sorority she would eventually pledge to. But a sense of foreboding remained, pushed into the back of her mind like an unwanted guest at a party.

Carol broke off her reverie once again, returning to the present to see another musical performance conclude with the sound of polite clapping. Carol tried not to reveal on her features a nagging feeling that the pageant was all nonsense. She had to attend these kind of events. She was expected to; it was required duty for a woman of her position. During the first few years of her return home and her subsequent marriage, she'd fairly enjoyed fulfilling her civic and social responsibilities. But now she increasingly sensed the hollowness in them, the polite desperation that lurked under the smiles and applause. But attending this ritual and all the others was part of her penance.

Thirteen years ago she turned down Radcliffe, Vassar, and SMU and went to where she knew she would go all along: Oklahoma University. After she arrived on campus she expected she would quickly run into Byron. But she didn't. During registration she scanned the long lines of students and never saw him. Since her class schedule consisted of mostly required courses and Byron was a philosophy major she didn't encounter him in the classroom. Of course, he didn't dine in any of the campus cafeterias. She foolishly thought she might bump into him when she attended the opening home football game. But if he was among the sixty thousand spectators she didn't know. When she traversed the campus grounds she expected – hoped – she'd run into him. But for the first month of her freshman year she never even got a glimpse of him. She lived in one of the women's freshman dormitories and Byron lived in the Sigma Chi fraternity. She considered strolling down fraternity row but she couldn't bring herself to be so brazen.

Then it happened. She attended a music concert on campus in late September. She went with her roommate to hear a soul singer, Percy Sledge, who had a hit single that summer. She hadn't really wanted to go. She preferred classical and folk music but somewhere in the back of her mind she thought she remembered that Byron liked soul music. She and her roommate arrived in the full concert hall and took their seats and because she felt hot sitting in her seat with the crowd of people she got up and walked back to the entrance where the doors were open to catch a cool breeze from the night air. She was about to return to her seat because the concert was beginning when saw him.

Byron was standing in the back of the auditorium with a young woman. Of course, she was very pretty, a sorority girl judging from her manner and stylish dress, but Carol thought Byron looked rather bored standing there with her. At that moment, Percy Sledge began crooning his hit song, "When a Man Loves a Woman" and Byron didn't look at his date but instead he looked past her and saw Carol. Their eyes met. Byron grinned just slightly, his dark blue eyes narrowing, and he continued staring at Carol. She averted her eyes for a moment, then she looked at him again and felt astonished to see that he was still staring. When the beautiful song ended, another young man appeared, spoke to Byron and the three of them began to walk down the aisle to find their seats. When they walked past, Carol noticed that Byron gave her an insinuating look.

After the concert concluded, she didn't see him or his friends again. Carol dawdled leaving the auditorium, but apparently he and his friends left by another exit. She felt so disappointed that she almost cried while walking back to her dorm room. But the next evening Byron asked for her at the dorm desk and she came down and they had a short, exciting talk in the common room and he asked her out for that weekend. On their first date he took her to a lecture of all things, a policy lecture on foreign affairs, but afterward they went to the campus coffee house and had a stimulating discussion then Byron walked her to her dorm. The night was warm and a little sultry and just when she thought he wasn't going to kiss her goodnight, he took her in his arms and kissed her rather passionately. They had grown up in the same town, went to the same schools, but that was the first time he had ever really touched her with feeling. His kiss surprised her and she keenly felt how his strong hands were holding her. That was all it took for her love for him to completely flower.

One month later they were going steady. He "pinned" her and she accepted it like a butterfly receives its own impaling. They both returned to Buffalo City during winter break and they continued their romance, but they downplayed it, because Byron thought their parents would make too much fuss about them being together.

Byron and his parents were already in conflict. They thought he was too impressionable and high-spirited. It didn't look proper for the eldest son of the town's most respected funeral home director to be cavorting like a wild man. His parents were very austere, respectable citizens. Like all the good people of Buffalo City they attended church regularly, participated in civic functions, and projected personae of complete propriety to the townspeople. But Byron, as they sat in his car in the dark after they had almost gone too far, would tell Carol about how his parents were hypocrites. His mother sometimes drank too much. His father had engaged in unethical business practices. A few years ago, he'd undermined a competitor and forced the man to leave town. His father had spread rumors that his competitor didn't take precautions in separating the races during preparation. As a result, that funeral home lost much of its white clientele. Byron told her that he'd never be like his father. He wouldn't take over the family business. That was for Blake. He'd achieve his own goals. He used to have notions about being a lawyer or a doctor but he thought his talents were best suited to the humanities. He'd been taking philosophy classes and reading the literature and he spoke avidly about it, how fascinating it was, how it had expanded his thinking, enlarged his mind. Maybe he'd become a professor. But he would be one who did more than give dry lectures. He'd be more of a mentor, even a guru, to those with bold, curious minds.

Their relationship became more intense during

spring semester. They did the usual college activities that couples did: frat parties, basketball games, concerts, movies. But with each date Byron became more insistent about making love. One night he tried to convince her to go to his fraternity room. She refused not because she didn't want greater intimacy but because of the banal setting. He told her that his sexual frustration coupled with the philosophical ideas he'd been grappling with was putting great pressure on his thinking. He thought he might be on the verge of a psychological breakdown. He was beginning to think that the world was utterly corrupt and worried that maybe life itself was meaningless. The only thing that could save him was her love. He then confessed his love for her. He said if she loved him the way he loved her then she should want to go to bed with him. She was willing but it wouldn't be in the frat house or a cheap motel or in the backseat of his Mustang.

Two weeks later, Carol told her parents that she was going to Padre Island with a couple of girlfriends for Spring Break. Instead, she and Byron drove north to a secluded cabin at Lake Hudson in Northeastern Oklahoma. She remembered thinking how beautiful this part of the state was, with the forests, hills, lakes, and rivers. Nothing like the flat, dry, hard prairie of Buffalo City. The edenic landscape seemed perfect for the culmination of their romance. They awkwardly consummated their love that first night but she could tell that he'd been disappointed. She was inexperienced and the lovemaking had proved to be more of an ordeal than a pleasure. She'd been fitted with a diaphragm before the trip but afterwards she brooded that she would get pregnant and disgrace herself. The situation didn't improve much the next night. Even in the cabin she felt exposed and licentious. Byron tried to understand her inhibitions but by the third night it was obvious that he was losing patience. Instead of enjoying the lake and the woods, he would go into terrible rants about the impermanence of life, the transitory nature of all things, and how our society had a Death Impulse. He quoted philosophers she had never heard of and whose ideas she thought disturbingly nihilistic. Then the weather turned dark and gloomy and the fourth day was full of rain, a sodden, bleak atmosphere that matched their moods. They didn't even try to make love that night. On the fifth day they left early in the morning and drove through the rain back to Norman.

Strangely enough, the situation improved once they returned to campus. Norman was drenched in sun, an invigorating contrast to the wet, dark woods. They still had four days of spring break and the campus was nearly depopulated. All of Byron's roommates were off in Padre Island or New Orleans. To make him happy, she consented to make love in his fraternity room. The lovemaking went well. She even achieved an orgasm and afterwards she felt profoundly in love with him. He seemed to feel the same way and they lay in bed wrapped in each other's arms, listening to the music of "California Dreaming" softly floating into their open window from a nearby frat house. She thought this was the true culmination of their love and nothing would ever be the same again.

They were going to try again the next day but a

couple of his buddies returned early from their spring break trip. They were noisy and drunk and she didn't feel comfortable going into Byron's room with them around. Byron seemed to understand. They returned to their usual pattern of dates with impassioned necking afterwards. But that didn't satisfy him and she felt responsible.

Classes resumed and as the days and weeks passed, she noticed that he'd gradually grown more distant from her. He became uncharacteristically silent. When he did speak it was in sudden outbursts, often ending with a kind of frustrated fury. He returned to his rants against the Vietnam War, against prejudice, against poverty, against the narrow-minded middle class morality that sucked the energy and imagination out of the more talented. Then he would hurl recriminations against himself, admitting that he was a fraud like his father. If he was against the war then he should have the integrity to oppose it. He thought about joining one of the more radical groups on campus. He attended one of the meetings but didn't care for their smug, chic radicalism. Increasingly, he thought it didn't matter anyway. We were all doomed. Life was without meaning. We live for a brief time and then we die. Why oppose the war? What did it matter if one fought in a war or fought against the fighting? Each option was equally absurd in a meaningless universe.

Then, as the semester neared its close, Byron grew calmer. He no longer ranted. He'd come to the conclusion that if life was meaningless in theory then it wasn't in practice. What mattered was enjoying one's self. Living for the moment. Carpe diem. He grew more energetic, more confident, almost like his old fun-loving, irreverent self. But Carol sensed he wasn't like his old self. He'd changed. Just as the zeitgeist was changing, so was Byron. Carol, who was deeply in love with him, maybe even more than in the beginning because his psychological turmoil had revealed a vulnerability that she'd never seen before, tried to become anything he wanted: the war protester, the intellectual, the hippie chick. She willingly submerged her personality into his. All she wanted was to make him happy.

Classes ended and she was certain that a summer together in Buffalo City would heal them completely. They were supposed to drive home together but the morning of their scheduled departure he said that a fraternity brother had gotten into trouble and he had to stay for a day or two and help him out. She wanted to stay too, but Byron took her to the bus station and said he'd be home in two or three days. She remembered sitting in the Greyhound as it pulled out of the station waving at him and how when he waved back he did so in an almost mechanical way and that indifference prompted a sharp fear that almost cut her in two.

Byron didn't return to Buffalo City for the summer. Instead he left campus the next day and drove straight to California, passing up the exit to Buffalo City on I-40. She received a letter from him one week into his stay in San Francisco. A letter full of enthusiasm and hyperbole and fantasy. He didn't ask her to come out to be with him. The next and last letter arrived two weeks later. Then nothing.

She wrote him a series of letters but she received

no response. She tried calling the rooming house listed on the envelopes. The girl who answered the phone said he'd moved into a commune. The commune didn't have a phone and she didn't know the address. The girl's attitude suggested that she knew Byron, probably had been intimate with him, and it was then that Carol realized for certain that Byron was no longer in love with her.

For the rest of the summer she was miserable. She put on a brave façade and told her sympathetic friends that she and Byron were never really serious. They just had a pleasant college romance and now it was over. She knew her best friend, Stella Moore, didn't believe her. Carol had been indiscreet with her, confiding how serious her romance had been with Byron, how desperately she loved him. But Stella kept her secret and the townsfolk of Buffalo City began to believe the fiction that Carol and Byron weren't lovers just dating partners.

Carol went back to school that fall. She expected Byron to show up any day. But he never did. Then she made another mistake, perhaps the worst of her life. She got involved with one of her instructors, a Ph.D. candidate in English literature. It wasn't much of an affair but it helped occupy her mind so she could pretend to forget about Byron. It lasted most of the school year but the last few months were a sad and dreary soap opera. When he grew tired of her, she grew more desperate. She even threatened to commit suicide if he tried to stop seeing her. She realized that it really wasn't this man she cared about. He was similar to Byron in superficial ways and in her confused mind she sometimes imagined that he was a diminished version of Byron. Before Spring Break when the doctoral student said it was over and that he was going back to his wife, she didn't protest. She had already collapsed into the pit of self-pity and self-loathing and now she was ready to make her slow ascent from out of that pit.

Then her mother became seriously ill and she returned to Buffalo City before the end of her sophomore year. She knew the townspeople were sympathetic to her. They already pitied her, aware of Byron's mistreatment, not knowing any of the salacious details. When she returned to Buffalo City, they admired her even more for sacrificing her education to take care of her mother. What they didn't know was the true reason for her return. She wasn't coming to care for her mother as much as fleeing the shambles of her collegiate life. She returned home because she was beloved in Buffalo City and she knew she would always be welcomed. The town and its people would always offer comfort and succor. It would always consider her a success when she wasn't; judge her as a young woman of sterling character when she wasn't; define her as an honest person when she really was a fraud.

That's when Millard entered her life. She'd grown up with him, gone to the same schools, even to the same college, but he'd always been that strange boy on the periphery of her life. She saw him at town functions and heard her friends making fun of him for his bombastic manner of speaking and his rather comical appearance. But she'd never felt like ridiculing him. She knew and liked both his mother and father. His father in particular she'd liked. He had a frank, almost brazen, independence and she admired that quality because she lacked it.

As her mother grew worse, Mrs. Greeley often came over to assist Carol with the care and nursing of her. During those frequent visits Millard would drive Mrs. Greeley over and he would wait until she had finished her ministrations. During those times Millard and Carol would have pleasant chats together. During these talks Carol, who'd never spoken much to Millard because he was two grades ahead of her, revealed a more appealing part of his personality. He could be attentive and sensitive and understanding when he tried. And he seemed truly smitten with her, which flattered her and made her feel better than she had in a year.

She knew she could never love Millard the way she loved Byron. In a way, she welcomed that reality. She didn't want to love another man like she had loved Byron. She didn't ever want to abandon herself to him and feel that what mattered most was his approval.

She also felt a strange sort of sympathy for Millard. His odd looks ceased to bother her. She knew she could be of help to him and at that time she intensely wanted to be of help to somebody.

Then during the fall of 1968, Byron came back and she feared she'd lose herself to him again so she accepted a date from Millard. Then Byron left Buffalo City, this time to finish his studies at OU, but not in philosophy but in mortuary science, and she grew more comfortable with Millard as they dated steady for another six months. When Byron came back for good to Buffalo City to help his father with the business, Carol, still wary of his presence, accepted Millard's proposal.

At first she refused to believe her acceptance of Millard's proposal had anything to do with Byron. She didn't allow herself fully understand why she agreed to marry Millard Greeley. Eventually she would admit the truth to herself: It was part of her penance.

Now, Carol realized that she had hardly been paying attention to the pageant for most of the evening. She couldn't even remember which songs the girls had sung for the last hour. She smiled to herself. Did it matter? Every year they were the same kind of songs sung in the same kind of wistful earnestness that she'd once felt.

She glanced down three seats where Kate Mors sat. Kate had won Miss Buffalo City in 1968. She did well in the Miss Oklahoma contest a few months later, finishing third. Carol scrutinized Kate's profile, a very flattering one at that, and wondered if Kate was dying her hair a lighter shade of blonde. She regarded Kate as being far more qualified for a beauty contest than an achievement pageant. She really didn't have any depth to her facile intelligence. Her charm was superficial. Her talent was minimal, a thin, almost reedy soprano. No, Kate's success was confined almost entirely to her blonde good looks, healthy teeth, and cool personality. In fact, Carol thought underneath that creamy exterior Kate really was something of a bitch.

The talent portion now over, the MC, Ed Reeves, the news announcer at KBUF, strolled to the microphone and smiled. He'd taken the vote tally from the judges (Carol, acknowledging she was being slightly unethical, had nevertheless voted even though she'd hardly paid attention) and announced that Miss Buffalo City

233

1979 was Susan Smith. The audience gave its ovation and Carol nodded in approval (she had heard enough of her perfectly adequate version of "You Light Up My Life" to vote for her). As Susan Smith beamed a smile and discreetly wept, Carol began to applaud as well. She knew that these ceremonies were overly romantic. But she remembered standing on that same stage thirteen years ago feeling that intoxicating idealism before that foreboding appeared. And as she remembered, tears filled her eyes, too.

-VII-

Dale had felt immense relief when Floyd Byrd showed up with Millard Greeley. Throughout the evening, Dale had sat in the farthest seat in the first row, hoping that The Bird would arrive in time to take photographs of the winners. Shy by temperament, Dale had been dreading the possibility that he'd have to go on stage and take the photos. Much of the audience would still be there and he'd feel foolish and conspicuous on stage.

The pageant now over, Dale scanned the audience to see if he could spot Helen Brown. So far, he hadn't seen her. But he was certain she was present. In her last letter, she'd written that she would meet him in the auditorium after the big event.

Dale stood apart from the convivial social interaction taking place. He often felt removed from social gatherings; he even felt that way in his hometown. But he especially felt that way in Buffalo City. Apart from the people he worked with, and a few other people, he didn't know many of the elite "Buffalonians." Right now, Dale looked over to a small crowd talking enthusiastically about the pageant. Rosemary was there; she stood next to a tall, gray-haired gentleman who Dale supposed was her husband, Judge Rogers. He wasn't a pageant judge but a real judge. Dale, fortunately, had never appeared in his court although he'd heard that Judge Rogers especially enjoyed handing out fines to traffic malefactors, in particular to speeders. Dale had a tendency to speed when he drove his '67 Chevy through town but so far he'd never been caught.

Standing next to the Rogers were the Greeleys. The mayor was talking in his voluble way to the other pageant judges and their spouses. His wife, as was often the case, stood next to him with a tolerant smile on her cute face as she listened to her husband pontificate.

Floyd Byrd, finished with taking the photos of the winner and the two runners-up, stamped down from the stage with his big feet. He was walking by when Dale accosted him.

"Hey, Floyd, did Will go to the newsroom?"

"I reckon he did. Least that's where he and his foreign car were headed."

Dale never knew The Bird disliked foreign-made cars. "You don't like Volvos?"

"Is that what they're called? All I know is I don't like German-made cars. Americans should buy American cars."

"Volvos are made in Sweden."

"Same difference."

"Not to the Swedes."

Floyd waved away Dale's comment and trudged off.

Dale wondered how he ever got to be a reporter-photographer, even on a small town newspaper.

Dale felt a tap on his shoulder and he expected Helen but when he turned around he saw the ironic smile of Byron Mors.

"You have a look of disappointment on your visage," said Byron.

"I thought you were someone else."

"Ah. No doubt a feminine someone."

Since Dale said nothing, Byron laughed. "You weren't expecting, perhaps, Louise Henderson?"

Dale tried not to show any reaction. He wondered if Byron knew about him and Louise. But how could he? He doubted Louise would tell him anything. No, Byron simply had those instincts. As for Louise, Dale hadn't seen her in the auditorium. Before the show began he even stood up and scanned the seats. He'd felt relief, and a little sadness, that she hadn't shown. He remembered her dismissing the event as being for "rich girls".

"Actually, I wasn't. We broke up today."

Byron chuckled. He didn't know that Dale wasn't being completely facetious. "So how did you like the highlight of the Buffalo City social season?"

"It was okay. But why didn't the girls wear bikinis?"

"Because this is not a beauty contest."

"Then what's the point?"

"The point is to honor our outstanding young women." Bryon gave a quick, but rather knowing, glance to the group of people standing in front of the stage; the group that included the Greeleys. "Do you know that your publisher's wife was crowned Miss Buffalo City in 1966?"

Dale quickly glanced over to the small crowd, too. He saw Carol Greeley now laughing. Dale thought she looked quite attractive when she laughed. She also had a pleasant laugh. Lilting and musical. Dale listened to it as it floated above Judge Rogers' deeper guffaw.

"Really? Carol Greeley?"

"Is that surprising?" Byron's voice had a light edge to it which surprised Dale.

"No, not at all. She's attractive. She's also a nice woman. I can understand why she won that title way back in 1966."

"For some of us, 1966 is not that long ago."

Dale nodded apologetically and Byron's expression returned to the usual slightly sardonic one that he used for Dale in the evenings. In the daytime when the two encountered each other in town or in the newsroom, Byron tended to have a much more dignified, wise elder look. Dale was beginning to think that Byron Mors had something of a Dr. Jekyll and Mr. Hyde quality about him.

"Do you want to know an interesting historical fact?" Byron raised a brow in a mischievous way.

"Sure. I'm always interested in historical facts."

"That song, "Buffalo Gals.""

"You mean the one they played ten times?"

"They only played it full-length twice. Before the pageant and afterwards. Do you know its origins?"

"No," said Dale. "I've never given it much thought."

"The song was composed by a black face minstrel named John Hodges back in 1844. Hodges would perform all around the country. He became quite popular. His nickname was Cool White."

"Cool White performed in black face? Isn't that sort of contradictory?"

"Interesting that our esteemed festival features a song that has racist origins, isn't it?"

"People don't know that. Only someone like you knows stuff like that. Everyone else thinks it's a song about werewolves. You know, Buffalo gals won't you come out and transform by the light of the moon?"

Byron chuckled and then acquired a sly look that Dale had seen on a few occasions, but only at night.

"The real reason I came over, besides wanting to engage in delightful banter, was to inform you about something before the festivities break up."

Dale had a feeling the Mr. Hyde was about to appear.

"My wife is going to be out of town again Monday. Her mother has the flu and she is going back home to nurse her. So, I'll have an open evening if you would like to indulge in a game of chess."

"Chess, eh?"

"We'll see what else we can indulge in afterwards."

Dale was debating whether he should accept. Not the chess. The other activity. But ever since he'd decided that Louise would no longer be available to him his libido had been anticipating enjoying those X-rated movies again. Sometimes his lustful ways surprised him.

Byron had been closely watching him, using his cool blue eyes to intuit Dale's libidinous ways.

"Okay," Dale said. "Same time?"

"Same time. And this time I'm going to beat you."

Dale hoped he was referring only to the chess match.

Byron Mors sallied off and Dale watched him encounter the small group of people who were still chatting. Byron greeted several people that Dale didn't know then spoke with Judge Rogers. After a moment, Byron moved over and spoke briefly with Greeley. Dale smiled at the mayor's reaction. He seemed to be making a concentrated effort to smile. Dale had seen Greeley straining for that smile before. It was his not very convincing I'm-not-bothered-by-you smile. Dale had seen Byron and Greeley together on a few occasions and they behaved in completely different ways toward one another. Byron seemed aggressively confident and stood at full height. Greeley stood more warily and tried to maintain a rather unconvincing smile on his pudgy face. Dale had never actually heard them converse. But he could tell from their postures and expressions that the two men didn't like each other.

Byron broke off his chat with Greeley and then spoke with the other members of the group. He briefly spoke to four of them. But Dale noticed he never spoke to Carol. He hadn't even said hello. Carol in fact, seemed to avoid Byron, not in an obvious way, but when Byron moved in her direction, she discreetly danced away. That was interesting. There was something between them or had been. Dale didn't think it was rancor as with her husband and Byron. For one thing, she didn't look angry. Instead she looked like she was trying to disguise her emotions. She smiled more broadly to the person she was talking to, but her smile didn't look genuine. But most of all, the look in her eyes seemed to show discomfort if not pain. And once she gave Byron a quick but meaningful glance. A glance that seemed to say she didn't want to look his way but she couldn't help herself at that moment.

Then Dale saw another interesting thing. A tall, slender, blonde woman appeared and encircled Byron's arm with her two hands. Dale concluded that she must be Kate Mors, Byron's wife. When she smiled, Dale thought she looked quite pretty. Dale had seen her sitting with the judges during the pageant so she must be one of them, too. But she hadn't been with the post-pageant group until now.

When the Morses took their leave of the group, Dale noticed another curious thing. Kate gave a quick glance behind her and Carol, almost at the same time, turned to quickly look at the Morses leaving. Or was it just Byron?

Dale gave a small shrug. There was certainly something going on with the Greeleys and the Morses but he didn't really know what it was. He was interested in finding out, though. Generally speaking, he thought people should mind their own business. But figuring out a mystery might be different.

Another tap on the shoulder. Dale this time knew it wasn't Byron. He turned around and saw Helen Brown smiling at him.

"What were you looking at so intently?" she asked.

"Byron and Kate Mors. Millard and Carol Greeley."

"Oh. And why?"

"Something is going on between the four of them. But I don't know what. Do you know anything about them?"

"You mean anything mysterious or diabolical?"

"I hope not diabolical. You've lived here all your life.

You must have heard a few things."

"You mean rumors? Really, Dale I thought you had disdain for gossips."

"Well, normally I do but ..."

Helen laughed. "Well, I don't know if there's much to tell. But then my family doesn't travel in the same social circles as those two couples. But there is one interesting fact."

"Well?"

"Byron Mors and Carol Quigley, that was her maiden name you know, used to go out. In fact, I think they were a serious couple."

"In high school?"

"No, I think it was at college."

Dale did some quick calculations. Byron, like Greeley, was two years older than Carol. He knew Byron had left OU after his junior year. That meant that he and Carol must have been dating steady during her freshman year because when Byron went back to OU Carol was already married to Greeley. At least, he thought so.

"What are you contemplating so seriously?"

"Do you know what year Greeley and Carol got married?"

"Yes, I do. Even though I was only nine at the time, I remember the wedding. It was November 1969. Why do you want to know?"

"Just curious." Actually, Dale now wondered if Byron's "existential crisis" had something less to do with philosophy and more to do with Carol.

"Well, you should be. You *are* a reporter."

"A sports *editor*."

"Well, you need to learn to edit a little better. I spotted a typo in one of your stories today."

"You read today's paper?"

"Of course. I am a devoted reader of the newspaper. I even have a subscription sent to college."

"Why is that?"

"I want to keep up with everything in Buffalo City."

"Yep. Keep up with all the Buffalonians."

"You like saying that word, don't you?"

"You bet. It's a sonorous word, don't you think? Buff-a-lon-ians."

"You shouldn't make fun of your adopted hometown. But then you have a tendency to make fun of a lot of things you shouldn't."

"What do you mean by that remark?"

"Like the college newspaper. The April Fool's Day satire you wrote. When I got there last fall, I was surprised to found out that there are still quite a few people upset with you at good old GNC."

"Still upset. It's almost been a year."

"Well, some people have long memories."

"And thin skins."

"That's right. That's why you shouldn't make fun of the wrong people."

"Yes, only the right people. The uncool, the unhip, the physically unattractive and the socially maladroit."

"I don't know about that. That would include almost everyone."

"Not the *right people*. And it's the right people who should really be the target of satire."

"I hope you haven't been making fun of the right people here."

242

"I am only the sports editor. And by the way, I need a proofreader. That's why there are typos in the sports pages."

"I remember when I heard about your football pick last fall. You didn't pick the Buffs to win their opening game!"

"I know. A profound mistake."

"I'll say. I'm surprised you weren't tarred and feathered."

"I learned my lesson. I'm determined to become a genuine Buff –"

"Buffalonian!"

They laughed.

"Well, I suppose you're going to be working tomorrow?"

"Yep. All the day and all the night. Just like the Kinks."

"Like who?"

Dale forgot that Carol didn't know much about sixties music. Fortunately, he didn't think she knew much about Tammy Wynette either.

"Someday, I'll educate you about the British Invasion."

"Okay. So no time to talk tomorrow. What about Sunday?"

"I thought your parents were leaving for their cabin tomorrow?"

"They are. But I thought I'd stay behind. I can always join them later this week."

"Okay, if you like."

"We haven't had a good talk since Christmas."

"That's true. Okay, Sunday sounds good."

"All right. Sunday it is."

"I'll come by around one thirty."

"Okay, that'll give me plenty of time to get ready after church."

"Me too."

Helen laughed. She knew he didn't attend church. But she didn't mind.

"Gotta go. My parents are probably waiting for me."

Dale watched Helen walk away. She wore a gray skirt, a blue blouse, a pinkish sweater, and flat-heeled black shoes. He noticed that her plain brown hair was a little longer, it hung to her shoulders. Before it had been shorter. The other quality he noticed was that she didn't have much of a figure. She wasn't fat or skinny but sort of undeveloped. Well, they were just platonic friends. He liked talking to her. She was bright and cheerful and they shared an interest in literature and movies. In her rather lengthy letters she told him about all the GNC social events she attended. He didn't really like hearing about it. It reminded him of attending those same annual festivities with his ex-girlfriend. Helen wrote about going to them with her female friends. She never mentioned going with any guys, although he knew she had male friends at GNC. After all, she was an affable kind of girl.

Most everyone had left the auditorium. If Dale gave a shout a lonely echo would resound through the large room. Instead, he walked out into the fresh, mild spring night. He looked at the stars and the half moon. He remembered how he used to visit a hill outside his hometown and contemplate his existence as he contemplated nature. He realized he ought to engage with nature more. He worked long hours and often didn't feel like taking walks or going for a drive in the country after he got home. He also had to cover sporting events on some evenings, too. But he missed communing with nature. Maybe he'd take Helen on a walk in the country Sunday.

During these past months, on a night like this when he was about to head to his lonely room, he'd feel a little despondent. That was because he usually didn't have anyone to talk to. Now, this week, it had changed. In addition to Byron Mors (who was more of a mentor than a friend) and Helen Brown, an old friend, there was Will Whitaker, a new friend. Now he had three people to have lively discussions with. He was having a cornucopia of conversation! Unfortunately, Dale hadn't been able to have any lengthy discussions with Will since Wednesday night. Both of them were so busy at work that they hadn't had time for any extended discussions. They wouldn't have tomorrow either. Then Will was scheduled to leave Sunday before noon to drive back to Norman. Dale wished he could stay longer; in fact, he wished he could be part of the regular staff.

As Dale drove down the street on his way back home, he considered going back to the newspaper to see if Will was still there working on his story about the big shot state Democrats. He wanted to, but Will probably had already gone back to his motel. He thought about showing up at his motel but that didn't seem right. Besides, Will was no doubt tired from his long, active day.

Dale didn't really want to go home to the dark,

empty house. He was momentarily tempted to drive to Louise's place. The weirdness of last night had sort of faded, and he now could focus more on Louise's sensual attributes. Maybe he could get her to be less abnormal in her sexual expression. Maybe she wasn't as semi-crazy as he had thought. Didn't Byron Mors advocate the life of the senses as well as the life of the intellect? Shouldn't someone with artistic aspirations sample all of life's flavors?

He was just about to convince himself to go to Louise's place when another part of him, perhaps his "super ego" or something more old fashioned like his conscience, reminded him that it was wrong to take advantage of people. Exploiting someone, whether it was emotionally, physically, sexually or financially, was wrong. Dale knew Byron didn't believe in the concept of "right and wrong," at least not for superior people. Maybe he was correct. But all Dale knew was that somewhere inside him he felt it would be wrong to go over to Louise's house again for sex. The problem with living the life of the senses was that it could lead to exploiting people. Hedonism was sort of "in" nowadays but the people who advocated it didn't seem to fully consider the consequences of what happened when you value personal pleasure more than other people's feelings. Dale knew if he saw Louise again the situation would become complicated and in the end it would hurt them both.

When he came to the street where she lived, he drove past it. Instead he drove to that dark, lonesome house where he had his room.

Chapter Six
Saturday

Dale woke up before the alarm went off. He jumped out of bed, quickly got ready, and motored in his Chevy to the *Stampede*. Even though he didn't really have any interest in politics, and had felt a sort of sardonic amusement about the excitement that had been building in town, he had to admit that now he was looking forward to today's historical event.

Everything was closed in downtown Buffalo City at 8 a.m. on a Saturday except the newspaper and The Duke's Diner a block away. As Dale arrived at the newspaper in his Chevy, he noticed Dwight's little blue Datsun, Floyd's rusty red Ford pick-up, Greeley's white Cadillac, Rosemary's pink '65 Mustang, and Will's green Volvo all parked in front of the newspaper. All the other parking spaces on the block were empty. Dale parked his Chevy beside Will's car and ambled inside the well-lit newspaper office.

The usual morning greetings took place, although with more energy. Even Floyd waved with more fervor than his usual phlegmatic flop of the hand. Dale went over to Will at their shared desk. Will sat in the padded chair and studied his notes from the interview he'd conducted last night.

"How'd it go last night?" Dale asked.

"Copacetic," Will said, using one of his favorite words. Dale, too embarrassed to ask what it meant when he first heard it, had to look it up in the dictionary. It meant "okay."

"Did you get some juicy quotes?"

"The story is oozing juice. How did your coverage go?"

"I wasn't even needed. But I got to hear "Buffalo Gals" played ten times."

"You covered a concert?"

"No, the Miss Buffalo City Pageant. They use that song as a theme song."

"You mean the one that goes: Buffalo gals won't you come out tonight?"

"And dance to the light of the moon."

"That's an old song."

"Yeah, you'd think they would at least update it to Buffalo chicks."

Will grinned and Dale thought they'd engaged in enough early morning repartee, said he had to run the wire. He'd leave Will to study his copacetic notes.

Dale took the AP story list from Dwight, went into the composing room and performed his task in record time: twenty-six minutes. The paper would be running on a tight schedule today. The classified section had been run last night; this afternoon at the usual 3 p.m. deadline they'd get the feature and women's section and sports section finished and go to press with them at the usual 4:30 p.m. time. They would also finish six of the eight news pages. The front page and back page would be kept open for tonight's stories after the town hall. That meant Dwight, Will, Dale, and Floyd would have to high-tail it back to the newsroom and write their copy (and develop the photos, that was Floyd's duty) under a little more pressure. The town hall was supposed to end at 8:30 but it was quite possible it could run pass that time. If all went well, they'd go to press at midnight and the paper would be printed and assembled by 2 a.m. The distributors would get it to the carriers at the usual Sunday morning delivery at 4 a.m. Then the delivery boys (and men, quite a few were adults earning a little extra cash) would toss the historic paper on about four thousand doorsteps. Another two thousand copies (an increase of a thousand) would be delivered to gas stations, convenience stores, groceries, restaurants, and over one hundred vending machines. Instead of the usual five thousand press run, this special historical issue's press run had been increased to seven thousand.

After running the wire, Dale got his three sports pages ready. The front page was open, no ads. Ads filled about half of the other two pages. When Will took a break, Dale took over the desk and made one phone call to the high school track coach and got the results from yesterday's Clinton Invitational meet and a not-so-juicy quote from the rather grumpy coach.

When the typesetter was free, Dale composed his story about yesterday's baseball game. He wrote the story in less than ten minutes. Then he dashed out a 20-inch column in which he made his fearless predictions about the upcoming major league baseball season that would start in one week (he picked Boston in the AL east; Kansas City in the AL west; Philadelphia in the NL east; and Cincinnati in the NL west).

For the second part of his column he added a topical twist by rating the best opening day presidential pitches of all time. That part of the column was something of a joke. He rated Nixon's last, LBJ's next to last, JFK's fifth, Truman's fourth, Eisenhower's third, and FDR's second. (He wrote that Ford, the never-elected ex-gridiron star, had mistakenly tossed out a football instead of a baseball and that had disqualified him.) Who had the best throw on opening day in baseball and presidential history? None other than Jimmy Carter.

Millard Greeley had appeared early in the morning looking a little anxious although it was ten hours before the President would arrive in town. He had stood in the middle of the newsroom and said, "I know every one of you will do a bang-up job, a real bang-up job" and that seemed to satisfy his need for a publisher's pep talk. He went into his office to write his editorial, emerged to briefly offer more rah-rah, then departed for city hall.

No one missed his absence. In fact, everyone preferred when Greeley was out of the office. Otherwise, he might find some minor fault and berate the offender or he might think of some impractical approach to a story or he might try and exert his authority in another confusing way.

An hour later when Dale was doing paste-up of the sports pages, Greeley bustled into the composing room and paused to read some of his copy. Dale tried to ignore his presence. It was possible that the publisher would make one or two pointless suggestions and he'd have to type a new paragraph or redo a headline.

"What may I ask is this story about?" Greeley pointed to Dale's column.

"It's my column."

"So I see. But what is the nature of it? I understand the first part, the predictions of which baseball teams will win this season, but I don't comprehend the second half of the article."

"You mean the ranking of the best presidential opening day pitches?"

"Precisely."

"I thought in honor of our current President's visit, I'd list the top seven pitches."

Greeley looked lost in thought. Dale, instead of waiting for him to apprehend the absurdity of his column (because what was the criteria for ranking a presidential pitch and how would he know about the quality of the toss anyway?), he simply pointed to the name listed as performing the best: Jimmy Carter.

Seeing that name pleased Greeley. A smile appeared on his chubby face and he nodded agreeably.

"I didn't know that President Carter had such a good arm."

"Oh, yeah, all the sportswriters at the Orioles game complimented the President on the accuracy and speed of his pitch."

"The Orioles? Aren't they located in Baltimore?" asked Greeley.

"Right. There isn't a baseball team in Washington D.C. anymore."

"No team in our nation's capitol?"

"Not since 1971. The team moved to Dallas."

"The Senators are in Dallas?"

"They changed the name to the Texas Rangers."

"I thought you said the team moved to Dallas."

"That's right." Dale thought in a few more exchanges this would turn into an Abbott and Costello routine.

"So, we don't have a baseball team in Washington D.C. anymore. Instead that team is in Dallas and we also have another team called the Texas Rangers?"

"Yeah, that's right." Dale thought there was no point in trying to clarify it all.

"Very interesting news, Dale. I have to admit that I don't follow baseball as closely as I did in my youth. I used to be a Milwaukee Braves fan."

"The Braves are in Atlanta."

"There's not a team in Milwaukee anymore?"

"Yes."

"I thought you said that team moved to Atlanta?"

"Right."

"I'm afraid I'm not following you. There used to be a baseball team in Milwaukee when I was a child."

"Yes, but that team moved to Atlanta."

"Did the previous team in Atlanta move to Milwaukee?"

"No, there wasn't a team in Atlanta."

"Then what team is now in Milwaukee?"

"The Braves moved to Atlanta in 1966 and then the Seattle Pilots became an expansion team in 1969 but that team folded and was replaced by a new team in 1970 but it moved to Milwaukee."

"So the team now in Milwaukee is the Pilots?"

"That's right," he said, knowing very well that the team was called the Brewers.

"Well, Dale, thank you very much for enlightening me about this baseball evolution." Greeley slid a pudgy finger over the copy that proclaimed that Carter was ranked first for presidential first pitches. "I think President Carter will be immensely pleased to see that he is ranked first."

Dale nodded and Greeley patted him on the shoulder and bustled out of the composing room. Dale glanced over to a second paste-up desk and saw Dwight Willard staring at him in consternation. Dwight knew baseball. In fact, Mike Hargrove, the major leaguer, had grown up with him in the Texas panhandle.

"If anything happens, be sure and tell Greeley I had nothing to do with your column."

Another odd things happened that afternoon. After Dale completed his three sports pages with time to spare, instead of moseying into the back shop as he usually did (he wasn't in the mood to play chess with Grubbs; maybe they'd resume their matches next week) he glanced at some of the other copy. He read Will's interview story and once again was impressed by how clean and concisely Will wrote. He was certainly a skilled journalist. He also read Rosemary Roger's story about the Miss Buffalo City Pageant, an article he otherwise wouldn't have any interest in. It was the only story on the front page at this point. Dale had expected it to run in the women's section of the features pages but then he remembered the pageant was one of the celebrated events in Buffalo City. Since he'd attended the soirée, he was curious to see how Rosemary would characterize it.

The story was as absurd as Dale assumed it would be. It described in tedious detail (to him) the finery of the girls' gowns, mentioned their performances (winner Susan Smith "warbled sweetly the inspirational tune "You Light Up My Life;" first runner up Laura Hennessey "gave a riveting dramatic reading from "Medea;" and second runner-up Anastasia Anderson "performed a scintillating modern jazz dance to music from "Cabaret") and then stated where the girls were going to high school or college, their majors, who their parents were, and where they lived in town.

But the strangest part of the story was that it quoted none other than Rosemary Rogers herself. Since Rosemary was the director of the pageant, Dale supposed her opinion was relevant; it just seemed a little journalistically inappropriate for the reporter to quote herself. ("Many hours of time, energy, and money goes into the annual production with the end results being the gaining of experience and the developing of potentials," stated Rosemary Rogers, the director of the pageant. And "The judges have picked a fine winer and our thoughts and effects are now centered on the Miss Oklahoma pageant," Mrs. Rogers continued.)

Oops. Dale spotted a typo. Rosemary meant to type "winner" but she'd left out the second n. He debated whether to mention that error to her. Once before he'd told her he saw an error in her copy and Rosemary, normally a jolly woman (ex-Buffs cheerleader and former winner of Miss Buffalo City 1957) had glared at him, looking at that moment a little like Medea herself.

Who knows, Dale thought, maybe Rosemary actually meant to write "winer." Maybe Susan Smith's real talent was viniculture.

The problem was that the *Stampede* didn't have a copy editor. All the reporters (except Floyd who was mostly a photographer) were also editors. They wrote and edited their own copy, which was a difficult thing to do. It helped to have another pair of eyes to scrutinize copy. But Greeley didn't want to pay for another position. So instead of having a copy editor on hand to check for typos, grammatical mistakes, AP style errors, and general incoherence (are energy and money quantified in hours?), the editors on the *Stampede* were left to their own devices.

Dale walked into the newsroom and glanced at Rosemary. She was bustling about, filing some papers, stuffing a few things in her tiny, chic purse, obviously in a hurry to get home to the Judge. Both Judge Rogers and pageant director and feature/women's page editor Rosemary had been selected as one of the favored one hundred to receive reserved seats for the town hall. Once again, Dale was reminded of the somewhat incestuous civic nature of the Buffalo City elite. Who knows, maybe Rosemary's husband doubled as bartender at the Blind Justice Saloon when he wasn't administering punishment to traffic malefactors.

"Bye-bye, honey," Rosemary said to Dale as she prepared to hustle off home. Dale started to speak, to warn her of the embarrassing mistake in her copy, but she'd buzzed out of the office already. Since he liked her, he'd tell Dwight and he could correct the simple typo.

As soon as Rosemary left, Greeley arrived. The mayor burst into the newsroom, looking dapper in his blue pin-stripped suit in spite of his shiny, sweaty face. He'd been scurrying to and fro, going from city hall to the *Stampede* and back and who knows where else. As he'd told Dale during his interview ten months ago, he was a busy man who wore "many hats."

"A Secret Service duo is driving to the airport and they have room for a passenger or two. Any interest?"

"Too busy," said Dwight.

Floyd Byrd, studying one of his murky contact sheets, said nothing.

Dale looked at Will. "Want to go?"

"Sure," he said. He rose from the desk and joined Dale.

"We'll go," Dale told Greeley.

"Excellent. We ought to have representatives from the *Stampede* on this trek. Follow me."

Dale and Will followed Greeley out the door, across the street, and they walked one block to city hall. They saw a dark sedan parked in a reserved parking space with two formidable men sitting in front and one attractive young woman sitting in the back.

The driver rolled down the window and stared at them through his sunglasses. Dale glanced at the bright blue sky. It was a sunny day but he thought the agent would wear sunglasses even on an overcast day. His square, rugged face looked genetically designed for sunglasses.

"We have two passengers for you," Greeley said in his rather unctuous voice that he used in the face of authority.

The driver nodded his head toward the backseat and Will opened the door first. Dale knew what he was doing: getting in first so he could sit next to the young woman. Dale didn't follow Will; instead he looped around the back of the sedan to enter on the other side. He noticed the second agent, a shorter man but with an even more impressive build, giving him a suspicious glance. Dale almost said, "I'm not trying any funny business, agent. I just want to sit next to the babe."

And she was a babe. The young woman, she didn't look any older than twenty-five, sat up straighter and smoothed her skirt when Dale climbed in. She glanced at him and Will with a prim look of discomfort as a female rider might regard a big, clumsy man who has just flopped down in the seat next to her.

"We're not crowding you, are we?" Dale asked.

"Of course not," she said but she didn't smile.

The sedan left the parking space and sped down the street. Dale glanced out the back window and saw Greeley gazing at them for a moment before he waddled into city hall.

The young men introduced themselves. The young woman said her name was Sondra Scofield. She spoke in a tony, sophisticated manner that Dale found both a little off-putting and intriguing.

"You're not part of the Secret Service, are you?" Dale asked.

"She's with the White House," said Will.

Dale wondered how he knew that but Sondra confirmed it with a demure, pleased smile. She was dressed in a tasteful beige skirt and lady's jacket with a pink, ruffled blouse underneath. She wore nylons and pinkish pumps. Her golden hair was rolled up and braided in the back and held together with a small wooden spike and a leather catch. Her skin gleamed with creamy perfection. None of her facial features were especially large but they all fit together with symmetrical precision. Her green eyes had another color emanating in a ring around the pupil, a sort of cornflower blue, and that additional hue enlivened the ordinary green eye color. When she turned her delicately shaped face slightly to the left more sunlight shown on her face and the color of her eyes transformed into a brilliant bluish green. Dale had never seen eyes like that before.

The rest of her face was almost as remarkable. A small, narrow nose with exquisitely shaped nostril wings. A rather small mouth, but her lips were finely formed, not especially full or pouty, but they were attractively kissable and highlighted with pinkish lipgloss. Dale kept waiting for her to open her mouth wide enough so he could see her teeth. But he was certain they were flawless.

A subtle, rosy scent emanated from her perfectly poised body. She smelled as if she'd been dipped in a delicate bath of rose petals and then left to dry in a warm, moist breeze. Sitting next to her, Dale had never been this close to feminine loveliness since his ex-girlfriend.

"What's your position with the advance team?" Will asked.

"Media relations."

"Hey, that's us."

She glanced at Dale with a polite look of dismissal. "The *national* media."

He thought she was rather haughty. He didn't expect otherwise. Her posture, her tone of voice, her dress, and her refined looks emphatically declared that she was made of finer stuff than he.

"You're not southern," Dale said.

"The White House staff employs the finest people from all around the country, Dale," Will said. "Not only from Georgia."

For the first time, Dale grew annoyed with Will. He was trying to impress her by showing him up.

Sondra, however, seemed to appreciate his indirect praise. "I grew up in White Plains, New York."

Dale had never heard of it. But he wasn't surprised to hear that she was a Yankee. "Did you go to high school there?"

Those green eyes turned blue green again as more sunlight poured into the car during a turn onto the interstate highway.

"No, I attended Choate."

Dale looked puzzled so Will clarified. "It's an exclusive private school in Connecticut. JFK went there."

At the mention of the martyred president's name, Sondra smiled broadly for the first time. Her teeth were as immaculate as the rest of her, like ivory keys on a grand piano.

Will turned his attention back to Sondra. "Did you attend college in New Haven?"

"No, I wanted a change in environment. I matriculated to Harvard."

Some change of environment. But Dale wasn't surprised. Yale, Harvard, Princeton. His only familiarity to those schools was the GE College Bowl that he used to watch on television. He remembered that almost all the contestants had been male. Most of them looked like dorks, too. Wearing suits and narrow ties and spectacles with thick black frames. He was recalling the show from fifteen years ago, of course. Those schools probably sent teams with members like Sondra now. Maybe all four team members were Sondras. Four cloned golden goddesses who beamed brilliant smiles when they correctly answered in unison the question of which American president attended Choate and was later assassinated.

Will and Sondra continued their conversation. Will asked her how she became involved with the Carter White House. Quite by accident, she said. She'd not even been interested in politics in college. She'd majored in art history. But her fiancée was from Minnesota and had served as an aid for Mr. Mondale during the summer before Neil, that's her fiancée's name, entered his final year at Harvard Law. After Mr. Carter and Mr. Mondale were elected, Neil accepted a position on the White House legal staff and one day while visiting his office she met Mr. Mondale. He was so taken with her that he offered her a job. She started off doing simple tasks. She didn't even have an official title! But she acquitted herself well and was promoted into the White House Press Office. She just got her present position a month ago.

Dale noticed when she mentioned her Harvard Law fiancée that a subtle look of disappointment momentarily crossed his friend's professorial features. Dale didn't know if Will had a girlfriend let alone a fiancée. But he'd certainly seemed interested in Sondra. And who could blame him?

Dale's interest had faded a little and not with just the mention of her big shot boyfriend. While Sondra spoke to Will he looked for flaws. She didn't have a curvy figure. She looked small breasted and had slender hips. Her figure wasn't bad, just the willowy kind he didn't prefer. He also definitely decided that her mouth was too small. And she had a slightly pointed chin. But still: those eyes.

While they continued chatting, now about more boring matters, her daily duties, how she liked living in D.C., etc., Dale examined the two Secret Service agents. It was uncanny how stereotypical they looked. They could be cast as agents in a Hollywood movie and perfectly fit that stock role. Both of them were clean-cut, clean-shaven, and cleanly attired in navy blue business suits, physically fit and strong, in their early thirties, and projected no-nonsense, almost grave demeanors. The taller one had precisely tonsured brown hair; the shorter one had tightly cropped curly black hair. The shorter one, wearing high quality sunglasses like the driver, somberly scanned the straight black asphalt highway and the surrounding dusty flat countryside as the dark sedan cruised down the road. He moved his head with such practiced regularity that he seemed more like a robot than a man.

Neither agent spoke. Dale thought about asking them some questions but they didn't seem in the mood to converse. Besides, it would be difficult talking to them while Will and Sondra were chatting.

The Clinton-Sherman Regional Airport, the closest airport equipped for an airliner like Air Force One, was forty miles away from Buffalo City. Since the sedan had settled in at a 55 mile speed and hadn't varied from that rate since its entry on I-40 (55 mph was the national speed limit imposed by the Carter administration to save energy and one of the executive decisions that infuriated some of the residents of Buffalo City who were used to traversing vast rural distances at high speed), Dale guessed it would take another twenty minutes to arrive at the airport.

His calculations proved correct. Twenty minutes later they arrived at the airport and the sedan drove to a security gate. The agent driving the car showed his security credential, the cop opened the gate, and they rolled in.

The sedan drove over to a group of mostly men standing next to two vans. Dale could tell by their disgruntled demeanor that they were reporters. Not the *national* press, though. They didn't have that well-groomed arrogance. No, they were guys from Oklahoma City, Amarillo, and other smaller, regional newspapers.

The sedan rolled to a stop. Sondra smiled at them, not an entirely pleasant smile, more like the one she used to confirm the comparatively low status of her suitors, journalistic and otherwise.

"This is your stop, boys."

Boys! She was only a few years older than they were.

Dale and Will got out and watched the sedan zip down the tarmac to a destination closer to the terminal. Then they walked over to the group of reporters who ignored them. Journalists were sure a bunch of friendly guys, Dale thought.

Ten minutes later they watched Air Force One sail to a landing on a far runway then taxi to a special disembarking area. Dale saw the two Secret Service agents from the car join a contingent of another dozen agents. They fanned out and took protective positions from inside the cordoned area.

As Dale and Will and the other reporters waited for the President and his team to emerge, another young woman, snazzily dressed, came over to them. She wasn't as attractive as Sondra, but she wasn't bad either. She told them that there would not be a press conference. She suggested they depart or risk being detained for ten minutes after the presidential motorcade left for Buffalo City.

No one wanted that. The reporters boarded one of the vans. Dale and Will joined them and found seats in the middle. They stared out the window hoping to get a glimpse of the President as he disembarked.

The press van drove out of the airport's gate and two minutes later it was cruising down the highway on its way to Buffalo City.

"Hey," Dale asked Will. "How do you know all that stuff?"

"What stuff?"

"Prep schools and Ivy league colleges. Did you go to one?"

"I attended Sundance Prep."

Sundance Prep was the most prestigious college preparatory school in Oklahoma City. Located in the Northwest part of the city it wasn't too far from Galilee, Dale's hometown. In fact, when Dale was in ninth grade his high school football team had played at Sundance Prep. They lost 72-0.

Dale was amazed that Will had gone there.

"You didn't play football, did you?"

Will grinned. "No, I wasn't an athlete. I was in the band."

Dale nodded, glad that his friend hadn't been on the football team that creamed his high school team. He still rankled at the memory. The elite school had deliberately run up the score.

"Why didn't you go to a fancy college, too?"

"I considered it. But my parents preferred that I stay in state. I received a scholarship from OU. That wouldn't have happened if I'd accepted the offer from Vanderbilt or Rice. It saved a lot of money."

Dale was becoming even more impressed with Will. For a guy with a rather prestigious background he wasn't pretentious at all.

"By the way," Will said, "I remember that game."

"What game?"

"When we beat your high school team 72-0."

-II-

Byron Mors didn't want to go the town hall meeting. He had meant it when he'd told Greeley that if he won a ticket in the lottery he would give it away. After he read his name and Kate's name in the newspaper, he'd offered his ticket to Bette who hadn't won a seat. But Kate wanted him to go with her. Since she'd been more approachable of late, (her improved moods seemed to coincide with their seeing the Greeleys) he agreed to escort her to the grand affair. Besides, Byron decided it would be good for business. After all, he buried both Republicans and Democrats.

Byron stood in the middle of their attractive bedroom with his hands in the pockets of his trousers. He'd been ready for five minutes. Kate, meanwhile, was still in the bathtub. What was she doing in there? Luxuriating in a bubble bath he supposed. He considered going in to the large lime green bathroom and asking if she'd like to have him wash her back. They used to do that when they were first married. But he was afraid she'd give him *that* look: her don't-be-silly semi-offended look.

He heard some delicate sloshing as she emerged from the bathtub. Just the sound itself sent a sexual *frisson* through him. Even though he'd abused himself just two hours ago in his study, he felt himself growing aroused. He tried to think of something tedious to dampen his ardor. He thought of the upcoming town hall. How all those thousand bodies would generate an unpleasant heat in the gymnasium and how the verbal hot air would further increase his discomfort.

He heard the patter of bare, wet feet on the bathroom tile. She was leaving the shower room and entering the area with the sinks and toilet.

"Byron, would you mind taking my red hair brush from the bureau table and putting it on my vanity?"

He did as requested. When he took hold of the hairbrush he noticed the long dressing mirror next to the bureau stood at an angle. From where he stood he could look at the mirror and see a reflection of his wife.

A large pink bath towel covered her from her chest to mid-thigh but looking at that image pleased him. Then Kate simply dropped the towel to the floor and Byron saw her nude image in the mirror. He hadn't seen her displayed so revealingly in quite some time. Her back was turned to him and he saw a plumpness to her buttocks that he liked. When they got married seven years ago, he used to think she was rather too slender. Then she turned around to reach for her bathrobe and he saw the front of her. She still had firm breasts (she had never nursed Joy), more than average in size, and her pink nipples were erect. His eyes scanned downward and he saw her navel, then her rather sparse blonde pubic hair, then her startling white thighs and lower legs.

Byron became aroused again but when he heard her leaving the bathroom he quickly walked over to the twin beds.

She gave him a brief smile and that confused him a little. She went over to her vanity and sat down. She began brushing her thick blonde hair. He noticed that she hadn't taken the red brush he'd fetched for her from the dresser bureau. Instead she had picked up the white one that had already been lying on the shelf of the vanity.

"Byron, I think we should have another child."

He put his hands into the pockets of his trousers and shook his head. "I thought you didn't want another child."

"I didn't." She began examining her face in the mirror and tweezed out a single stray hair from her one of her shapely eyebrows. "But I've changed my mind."

"Why is that?"

"Joy needs a brother."

"You're so certain the baby would be a boy?"

"I have a feeling it would be."

"And you really want another baby?"

"You don't?"

"No, I'd like to have a son."

"Then it's settled. We can start when I get back from Mama's Tuesday."

Just like her to think of it as a project. The last time she wanted to get pregnant she kept rather precise schedules for their copulations. It wasn't very romantic but then Kate wasn't a romantic woman. She was pragmatic. Still, Byron was surprised. Her pregnancy had been fairly difficult. She wasn't a very maternal woman. He didn't think she had a deep motherly devotion to Joy. Byron thought Kate was rather disappointed in their little girl. It was already apparent that Joy wouldn't grow up to be a beauty. Rather ironic. Joy had two attractive parents but it appeared she had inherited the wrong combination of genes.

Byron hoped Joy hadn't inherited Kate's manipulative gene. He knew that Kate had deliberately put her dressing mirror at an angle so he would see her naked in the bathroom. A normal sensual woman wouldn't need such a pretense. She'd welcome her husband's interest. But this approach, or strategy, had the benefit of having a touch of cruelty to it. She'd given him a glimpse of something he wanted and now she could enjoy the perverse satisfaction of denying him fulfillment of that pleasure.

"Byron, would you please stop gawking. I've told

you before I don't like being watched while I'm getting dressed."

He thought about striding over and slapping her face. He removed his hands from the pockets of his trousers.

"Dear, why don't you go and see about Joy and Bette?" Her voice no longer scolded. It now affected a warmth that she didn't really possess.

Byron put his hands back in his trousers and left the room.

-III-

"Do you wanna get some supper?" asked Percy Pollack.

He and Harley Dee Grubbs had just completed the initial press run. They would have to come back later tonight to run the first section with the stories about the President's visit and the town hall meeting.

"Nope, I got somethin' else to do."

"Somethin' better than eatin'?"

Grubbs didn't answer. He went over to the sink and scrubbed the oil and ink off his hands.

"The motorcade won't get here for almost another hour. We got time to eat then go see it, " Percy said.

Grubbs dried his hands. "Like I said, I got somethin' else to do."

"Like what?"

"Like none of your fuckin' business!"

"Okay, man, forget it!"

Grubbs tried to control his anger. He had a headache and didn't feel well and his cold made him even worse tempered than usual. But he needed to exert complete control over himself for at least an hour. He smiled an unconvincing, jagged smile at Percy.

"It's nothin' personal. I'm not hungry and I don't want to see the motorcade."

"Okay, but make sure you get back here by nine."

Grubbs nodded as he headed out the door. Once outside, he sneezed, then coughed. Damn this cold! Well, he'd just ignore it. Grubbs knew he had the will power to do that. He pulled the dark windbreaker closer against him. He wore black trousers and shoes and as he walked he pulled a navy blue stocking cap out of his jacket pocket and tugged it over his greasy hair.

Earlier that morning at dawn, he'd put the first part of his plan into effect. He drove to the grain elevator, parked his Chrysler a block away, then walked across the train tracks and placed his hunting rifle, already sheathed its flannel case, in an empty barrel that once contained machine parts. He was certain no one would find it. If someone did, then he'd be forced to use his back-up plan with the revolver. After hiding the rifle, he drove to his father's farm and stole the key to the back door of the grain elevator. On such a monumental day as this, Grubbs was confident that Grover wouldn't notice the missing key. His mind would be focused on the AAM tractorcade.

Now, he tramped down the block, walking a circuitous way to the grain elevator. He didn't walk too fast or too slow just in case a cop, out early, spotted him. He crossed the railroad tracks, went over to the small junkyard where the barrel was located, pried open the lid, and lifted out his rifle case.

The night vision scope jostled in his left jacket pocket. He'd have to attach it after he climbed the ladder. That would be tricky but he needed the scope to help him see as he walked through the dark head house, the part of the grain elevator where the business office was located and where machinery was stored.

Grubbs walked in a normal gait to the grain elevator door, used his key to unlock it, and entered the large work area that was blanketed in darkness. He thought he remembered the general layout from when he used to work here. He couldn't turn on the lights, not even a small one. That might attract attention. He couldn't use the man-lift to get to the upper reaches of the head house. He'd have to do it the hard way.

He took his rifle out of the case then put the case against the door so he could find it easily in his departure. He put the scope to his eye and the greenish illumination showed a path through the work area. Grubbs slowly walked forward, his rifle slung over his shoulder by its strap. Fifty feet later he spied the narrow ladder that led up to the highest reaches of the head house. He put a hand on one of the rungs, then a boot on a lower one. He stuffed the scope into the top of his sweater. He hoisted himself up, paused for a moment to get his balance, and took a breath, not too deep, slightly annoyed by the irritation in his throat.

He wasn't nervous. He wasn't even sweating. He felt utterly calm. He imagined this was how people with Destiny felt. His plan was unfolding perfectly. No watchman hanging around. He hadn't even seen a cop car on his jaunt over.

He slowly climbed the aluminum ladder. Grubbs grasped one rung completely, feeling its ridged metal in his hand, before he lifted one foot. He advanced methodically, going higher into the head house. The building was so black that he felt like he was crawling in a cave. He knew he was advancing higher, but the black space in front of him didn't change in appearance.

Then it did slightly. He squinted at a less deeply dark pocket of black. He was pretty sure that was the vent. Its grill was allowing in the lighter darkness of the dusk outside. He moved up two more rungs. Now, he was certain he was near the vent. He reached one hand above him and felt the narrow platform that was connected to the top of the ladder. Grubbs kept his head straight and still so he wouldn't bump it on the handrails. He climbed on the platform and paused. He suddenly sneezed and turned his head so none of the snot would get on his rifle. He cursed then wiped his nose with the sleeve of his jacket.

Now, he was sweating. He felt the perspiration on his forehead. He heard his own breathing. He wasn't really winded. It was more a result of a sharp stab of excitement. He'd made it up to platform. Now all he had to do was creep toward the vent.

But first he attached the night vision scope. Then he reached into the chest pocket of his jacket for the screwdriver. He'd need that to pry open the metal slats in the vent so that his rifle's muzzle could extend far enough out.

Now, he was ready to venture out on the platform. He tested the metallic floor of the platform with his boots, then the grasped the handrail. He took one tentative step forward. Everything felt fine. He crept three feet farther until he faced the vent. He peered out between the metal slats. After his eyes adjusted to the light, he looked down at the three blocks of streets, roughly three hundred yards in length, and saw the high school gymnasium looking big and reddish in the dusk. He noticed there were groups of people milling around the sidewalks. He saw three patrol cars and two unmarked dark sedans parked on the block where the school stood. Cops and feds.

Grubbs tried to relax. After a minute of semi-deep breathing, ignoring the tickling in his throat and the rawness in his sinuses, he grabbed the flat head screwdriver and carefully inserted it between the metal slats. He worked the end of the screwdriver up and down slowly and carefully until he'd widened the opening enough to accommodate the barrel of his rifle. Then he performed a similar operation on the slat above. That opening would allow him to have an unobstructed view with his scope. He didn't want to extend the barrel through the vent yet. Since it was black Grubbs was certain it wouldn't reflect any light but as a precaution he didn't want to stick the barrel out until it was just about time. He'd know when the presidential motorcade arrived by the reaction of the crowd.

He didn't know what time it was. He couldn't read his watch's face in the dark. The last time he had checked was when he left the press room and it had been 6:20. He estimated it had taken him ten minutes to get here and another ten minutes to climb the ladder. If so, that would make it 6:40. If the Target kept to the schedule, Grubbs would only have to wait another twenty minutes before he made history.

-IV-

Byron and Kate Mors left their home at 6:40 and walked four blocks to the high school gymnasium. Along the way, they passed dozens of people including Helen Brown and two of her female friends gathered on the sidewalk of Main Street waiting for the presidential motorcade to drive by. The night was pleasantly mild, not warm not cool. A half-moon scaled the darkening horizon. It took five minutes for the Morses to arrive at the gym. Both were handsomely dressed and greeted a group of friends. They joined them, standing in line, waiting to go through security before entering the gymnasium to find their seats. Kate chatted with two women in front of her. Her voice was airy with excitement. Byron listened to a couple behind him who were excitedly whispering to each other. Byron shook his head and thought to himself how easily swayed people are. More than half of the gathered spectators hadn't voted for the man but now they awaited his arrival with almost giddy anticipation. If people were this impressionable maybe he should sell the business once his father died and go into politics. He'd like to defeat Greeley for mayor. Of course, maybe by that time, Byron estimated five to ten years from now, Greeley would have attained an even higher office. Byron could imagine the buffoon making it to the state senate by then. They wouldn't be that old in ten years. Both only forty-three. Just spring chickens in the political world. Or in Greeley's case a middle-aged ham.

-V-

Millard Greeley waited with the high school principal and the school's superintendent in the holding room, the classroom closest to the back entrance of the gymnasium. The Secret Service had already checked the room an hour ago. Two of their agents were waiting with the three men. Greeley glanced at them. They looked as ruthlessly professional as the two who had driven his two reporters to the airport. One of the agents, the one who had frisked Greeley, saw Greeley looking at him. Greeley gave an apologetic smile because he'd giggled for just a moment during the frisking. Well, he'd always been ticklish.

Greeley wondered how his mother was holding up standing so long outside. Carol was there to assist. As soon as the President arrived and they formally met again (the first time the President had just been a candidate) he and the two others would leave the holding room. Greeley would then go outside and escort his wife and mother into their special seats in the gymnasium.

Greeley started to put his hands in his trousers but he remembered that the agents didn't like that. They preferred to see people's hands at all times. He gave another apologetic smile again, but both agents hadn't noticed his near faux pas.

He felt a pleasant kind of nervousness. In just twenty minutes he'd be meeting the President of the Unit-

274

ed States! Everything was going swimmingly. All day nothing disturbing had happened. All his worries and fretfulness was for nothing. That strange malaise he'd felt earlier in the week had just been overwork and nerves. Nothing dreadful was going to happen. Not at all. Greeley was confident that this would be not only a historic night for Buffalo City but also the first step to greater political achievement for both he and the President. What a team they made.

After the town hall the President would drive to his mother's home and stay the night. Could anyone appreciate how wonderful that was? Two decades from now Greeley would show a newcomer to Buffalo City the hallowed residence of where President Carter spent the night. Maybe by then it would be a National Historical Site. Maybe a museum. By that time Greeley should have attained his own high political position. After all, he was a young man at present. Perhaps this night would be the first fateful step of his political ascent. Not just local, not just state, but national success.

An almost beatific smile appeared on the flabby visage of Greeley. He imagined himself as Governor Greeley; Senator Greeley; President Greeley.

-VI-

The van from the airport containing the regional press pulled into a reserved spot in the high school parking lot. Dale and Will scrambled out of their seats and walked swiftly out of the parking lot. Instead of going into the school by the front entrance they decided to walk around the building. They didn't have much time. Their van had left the airport only ten minutes ahead of the President's motorcade.

"Did you see all those tractors lined up on the side of the street when we got to Highway 66?" Will asked.

"Farmers. They're members of the American Agricultural Movement," Dale said.

"Radicals!"

"They're protesting with a tractorcade."

"Like they did in Washington D.C. last month."

"That's right. One of the organizers lives right here in Buffalo City."

"Is he a radical?"

"Worse, he's a Republican!"

They picked up the pace to a jog. They turned the corner of the high school and encountered a throng of people walking toward the gymnasium.

"How much time do you think we got?" asked Will.

"Seven minutes and thirty-two seconds," said Dale.

"Are you always so precise?"

"Didn't someone once say that timing was the most important quality in life?"

"Yeah, Bob Hope."

They were on the grounds of the gym's rear entrance now, threading through the thickening crowd. They decided to wait and see the arrival of the President before going inside. Most of the audience was already seated inside the gymnasium having arrived an hour ago to endure the lengthy security checks. The people milling around the sidewalk outside of the high school gym were those unlucky ones who hadn't won a seat in the lottery. The crowds were kept away from the entrance by a rope line and wooden barriers prevented the crowd from getting too close to the street.

Dale and Will heard sirens wailing in the distance. The crowd around them murmured excitedly. Dale and Will turned and looked down the street. The ululating sound grew closer. They saw people down the block waving their hands and miniature American flags. A few people held up placards and signs welcoming the President.

The motorcade consisted of nine cars and one half dozen police motorcycles: two sedans carrying Secret Service personnel in front, one highway patrol car, then the presidential couch limousine, then two additional dark limousines conveying the members of the state Democratic delegation, followed in the rear by two more Secret Service vehicles and one Buffalo City police car. The headlights from the caravan of cars glowed in the deepening dusk. As the cars approached the reserved parking area on the curb at the rear entrance of the gymnasium, the blaring sirens ceased. The cars eased to a stop with the presidential limo stopping in the precise place required of it. The Secret Service agents first emerged from their cars and gathered around the presidential limo. Three seconds passed and then the door to that vehicle opened.

-VII-

Harley Dee Grubbs had heard the sirens in the distance. He'd been crouching for ten minutes and the haunches of his legs ached. Now he slowly rose and peered through the rectangle hole in the vent and saw the commotion in the crowd three blocks away. He smiled to himself. This was a perfect sniper's nest. He had a spectacular view. Even in the deepening darkness, he could see the individual forms of people huddling around the school building and hundreds of others standing on the sidewalks. The fools. He wished he should shoot some of them, too.

It was time. He raised the rifle and carefully extended the barrel through the gnarled opening in the vent. He peered through the night vision scope. The lens reflected a greenish illumination. He had a good angle. All he had to do was lower the rifle barrel twenty degrees.

Grubbs focused on a middle-aged man standing closest to the curb of the street. In the scope, the man's magnified image showed with impressive clarity. Grubbs could even see the outline of his beard. Grubbs grinned. If he had a free hand he would have tugged on his own wispy goatee for good luck.

Grubbs' keen eyes watched as the motorcade arrived at the high school gymnasium. First the Secret Service got out, followed by the cops. He adjusted the rifle barrel slightly, aiming it at whom he thought the lead agent was. Grubbs had a feeling that this man would lead him to the Target.

Grubbs felt that tickling in his throat. He felt an impulse to cough but he restrained himself. He concentrated on the big black limo. That's where the Target would emerge. He took a breath. Just as he expelled it, the door to the limo opened. Grubbs moved the rifle barrel a smidgen to the right. The lead agent turned and looked at an emerging figure. In the green glow of the scope Grubbs saw the Target leave the protection of his limo. Grubbs took another breath, his finger poised on the trigger, then felt irritation in his raw sinuses. He tried to stifle the sneeze. His finger twitched on the trigger but before he could press it, he sneezed violently. To keep his balance, Grubbs took one step backward. His boot came into contact with the small pool of mucus on the floor of the platform and it slipped on the gooey substance.

Grubbs felt himself toppling backward into the darkness. He tried to break his fall by grabbing the handrail of the platform but the slick metal slipped out of his grasping fingers. His other booted foot lost its hold and his arms flailed at the emptiness before him. He cried a loud, "No!" as he swooned off the platform and plummeted down toward the concrete floor. His mind was empty except for one thought of shocked disbelief: This was not his destiny! He heard himself howl in fear and frustration as his body picked up speed in its backward descent. Then, for the briefest of moments, he felt his torso impaled by the blunt shaft of a grain auger. A guttural gasp escaped his dry lips. He died before he could understand that his entrails had burst out of his split abdomen.

-VIII-

Dale and Will watched the President walking down the rope line, pausing to shake hands with a few of the bystanders who reached out to him. Ahead and behind were the Secret Service agents running skillful interference. A small group of men followed, all wearing expensive business suits. Dale recognized the governor, a Democrat, and he supposed the other half dozen men with him were other political luminaries.

"The Governor is here, too," said Dale.

"Everyone wants to get on the act," said Will.

After the politicians disappeared into the gymnasium, the crowd of spectators began to disperse. Dale and Will, however, advanced to the building's entrance and had to show their press passes to security. Once their credentials were verified, they walked inside and saw hundreds of people packing the gym.

Dale had been in the gym many times to cover Buffs' sporting events. He'd never seen it stuffed like this not even when the high school boys basketball team played in the decisive district game. The two sections of stands on either side of the basketball court were filled with people. The basketball court itself had been covered with old wrestling mats and chairs had been arranged in ten neat rows. Those were the seats reserved for the dignitaries and VIPs, including 100 of the most elite Buffalonians. Fifty feet away, not too far from the south end backboard and goal stood a twenty foot long wooden platform with five chairs, a table with a pitcher of ice water, two glasses, and a Bible on it. Dale thought the Bible was a nice touch; most of the people in attendance, including those with Republican sympathies, would approve of that.

A podium with the presidential seal on it stood to one side of the table. It featured a lectern and a silver microphone.

Dale and Will walked down the sideline and passed five chairs lined up on the visitor's side of the scorer's table. Another five chairs stood over on the home side. A microphone stand stood next in the last chair in the visitor's section.

"I wonder what these chairs are for?" mused Dale.

"For the questioners. You know, it's a town hall."

"Right. So how were they picked?"

"How else?"

"A lottery."

Will nodded and the two of them mounted the steps until they came to an area reserved for the press. They squeezed into a small space on the last row. Before sitting down, they noticed sitting behind them were a beefy middle-aged farmer and his much smaller wife. The man, dressed in his Sunday best suit, still sported a red, white, and blue baseball cap. Stitched on the front was AAM in bold block letters.

"I thought all those guys were at the tractorcade," whispered Will.

"Maybe he's on a recon assignment," Dale whispered lowly.

Dale and Will watched the gymnasium fill with a few more latecomers. A low hum filled the air. Dale scanned the section of seats on the basketball court, the VIP seats. He spied Millard Greeley, his wife Carol, and Greeley's mother sitting near the front. He also saw the Judge and Rosemary Rogers. (In his haste to catch the Secret Service ride to the airport, he'd forgotten to tell Dwight about Rosemary's typo!) As soon as Dale thought of that, he caught sight of Dwight Willard sitting near the back of the VIP section. His wife wasn't with him. Dwight was present to cover the speech.

Dale recognized some of the other elite Buffalonians. In a whisper he identified some of them to Will: Dr. Smith, a shrink; Earl Hennessey, the wealthy oilman; C. Nash Quigley, the banker (Dale said he'd heard some men sardonically refer to him as "Cash" Quigley because the banker was regarded as "tight-fisted"); Mr. Anderson, the hospital administrator; and Buck McMurtry, a tall, leathery, cantankerous rancher. Dale knew who they were because they were all members of the Buffs Boosters, a group of wealthy older men who had monthly meetings at the American Legion post. Dale had to attend those meetings in order to write a flattering story for the newspaper but once he arrived he was quickly forgotten and sat by himself in the corner of the room.

Looking across the gym to the other grandstand Dale saw Jerry Dewberry sitting at the top of the far left section, wedged into the worst seat in the building. Dale didn't see his wife, Donna. He guessed she didn't win a ticket. His eyes scanned several rows of people sitting in the bleachers and to his surprise he spied Byron Mors and his attractive blonde wife sitting smack in the middle of the middle section. Dale knew Byron had a rather low opinion of the President so he wondered why he had come. Well, Byron had an image to maintain. Still, Dale planned on teasing him about his attendance of the town hall come Monday chess night.

"Do you play chess?" Dale asked Will.

"I was a member of the OU chess club."

"Were you any good?"

"I could hold my own. Do you play?"

"Not very well."

Then he remembered that he'd won three matches

282

in a row, one against Byron and two against Grubbs. Thinking of that odd guy, Dale guessed Grubbs wouldn't be in attendance. He didn't seem to like the President. Of course, Grubbs didn't seem to like anyone much.

Will, looking at his wristwatch, noted it was about time. He got ready. He poised his pen above his notepad. He was going to write the lead story for tomorrow's paper. Most of the story would be about the administration's economic policies. He'd already interviewed some local sources and he'd researched the most recent data. All he needed was a few quotes about the economy. Dale, seeing his colleague readying himself, got his pen and notepad ready, too. His story, a sidebar about the townspeople's reaction to the President's visit, wouldn't focus much on the speech itself. Instead, he'd have go into the crowd and get individual reactions afterwards.

The beginning of "Hail to the Chief" signaled the President's entry into the gym. There wasn't room to have the Buffs' pep band perform so recorded music blared from the loud speakers in the gym's rafters. The crowd's murmuring immediately stopped. Everyone waited for the President to appear.

And there he was! Most of the crowd cheered and everyone applauded. The President waved and gave his famous toothy grin and climbed the short stairs to the platform. Dale glanced at Will who duplicated his small smile that said, "we're professional journalists, we don't get excited over seeing the President." But in spite of their semi-skeptical smirks, inside both of them were excited.

The President started his short speech by recalling how back in April 1976 he made a short campaign stop in Buffalo City. He said during that first campaign he had visited over one thousand towns and cities and had never visited a single place that gave him as warm and openhearted and exciting a welcome as Buffalo City.

The crowd liked that. It heartily applauded.

The President then made a reference to his recent foreign travels in an effort to bring about peace in the Middle East. He'd recently been to Jerusalem and Cairo. And now Buffalo City.

Another ovation.

Then the town hall part of the event started. Most of the questions were quite predictable: inflation, unemployment, his efforts to achieve a Middle East peace accord, the high costs of energy. A girl of ten asked for a kiss. The President cheerfully obliged. Then three middle-aged woman also requested kisses. The President smooched them, too. Then came the question that all the radical farmers were waiting for: what was the administration going to do about the farming crisis, especially the low grain prices?

The President, anticipating such a question since he undoubtedly saw the tractorcade as his entourage motored in, said he would agree to meet with AAM representatives in Washington to discuss the issue.

That prompted the loudest ovation of all.

A few more questions and then the historical evening was over. The President beamed his big grin, waved, and departed with the "Washington Post" march blaring from the speakers.

Before the President had made it back to the holding room, Dale and Will had scurried from the press section of the bleachers. Even though there wasn't a scheduled press conference, Will was going to follow some of the national reporters to the holding room. Maybe he could get a direct quote.

Dale said he'd see Will in the newsroom in thirty minutes. He headed out the gym door. On his way he gathered four quotes from people exiting the building. But he wanted to get one more additional quote, a special quote, one to balance the story. He headed for the tractorcade.

He dashed away from the high school toward the tractors parked three blocks away on Broadway. As he ran, he realized that his evening runs had been useful after all. When he saw the farmers standing around their tractors across Highway 66, he slowed to a jog. He crossed the highway and approached one farmer, a big man dressed in overalls, a VFW jacket, and a red, white, and blue baseball cap with AAM stitched across it. Judging from his positioning and attitude, he looked like the leader.

The middle-aged man saw him coming. Dale identified himself, paused to gulp down a couple of big breaths, then inquired if he could ask him a few questions about the President's visit.

"Sure thing, young fella," said the farmer. "I know you're out of breathe on account of being all excited at seein' the President!"

The other AAM members who'd gathered around gave scornful laughs.

"May I ask your name?" Dale asked.

"Grover Grubbs, president of the local chapter of the American Agriculture Movement."

Dale asked one question to verify what he thought was the group's political objections and objectives then he told Grover Grubbs that the President had agreed to meet with AAM representatives in Washington. What did Grubbs think about that?

"About damn time." Then Grubbs launched into a diatribe against the administration's agricultural policies. Dale cut him off with one more question: would he be willing to go?

Grubbs thought about it for a moment. "I reckon I would. I'd be willin' to meet with that peanut farmer if it would help matters."

Dale thanked Grubbs, nodded at the other farmers, and sprinted toward downtown. When he hit Main Street, he slowed to a brisk walk. He wasn't late.

But when he entered the newspaper he noticed that Will, Dwight, and even Floyd Byrd were already there. Dale waved at them all and took a seat at Rosemary's desk. Since the typesetter wouldn't be taking any breaks, Dale would have to compose his story on the typewriter like everyone else. He rolled the yellow news copy paper into the manual typewriter and began to hit the keys. He'd already thought of his lead while running back to the newspaper.

He knocked out the story in twenty minutes. He didn't feature Grover Grubbs' quotes but he included them in the middle of the story. The other four sources had given favorable quotes. Actually, Grubbs last comment was sort of positive, too. He didn't think Greeley would object to the AAM quotes since their inclusion in the article presented both sides to the story.

-IX-

Millard Greeley nervously paced in the living room of his mother's home. He checked his wristwatch for the fifth time in five minutes.

"Millard, the President is on schedule," said Carol. "He'll be here on time."

Greeley glanced at his wife who came into the room carrying a pewter tray with a teapot and five cups on it. He started to walk over to partake of the tea when Carol spoke.

"Just wait one more minute, Millard."

Greeley sighed and glanced over to a rocking chair where his mother sat peacefully rocking herself. She was a small, gray lady of sixty-five who wore her hair up in a bun and had a feminized version of her son's face, although older and not as fat. However, the plumpness of her cheeks and the same kind of brown button eyes made her appear somewhat younger than her years in spite of the gray-white hair.

Mrs. Greeley had given birth to Millard when she was in her early thirties. It had been a difficult pregnancy. She'd lost two other children while they were still in the womb but she never talked about that. Actually, the sweet older lady hardly spoke at all anymore. Ever since her husband died, she, never loquacious to begin with, had grown gradually more uncommunicative. But it wasn't a sullen silence. Instead it was a quietude that suggested a stoical acceptance of life's hardships.

287

They heard the sound of a large car approaching. The Secret Service agent already present walked over to the door. A few seconds later they heard a knock, the agent opened the door and another agent appeared, entered first, then the President strolled inside. He shook hands with Greeley once again. As the mayor introduced his wife and mother, the President first went over to Greeley's mother and presented himself. Mrs. Greeley smiled and asked about the President's mother, Miss Lillian. The President said she was doing well and thanked Mrs. Greeley for her interest. Then it was Carol's turn. Greeley noticed that the President seemed especially taken with Carol. Greeley understood why. Carol looked a little like a younger version of Rosalynn.

The only other person accompanying the President, besides the Secret Service agents, was his chief of staff. Greeley recognized him immediately. The man, surprisingly young, was polite but a little distant unlike the President who seemed quite at home in the Greeley abode. They all took seats and Carol offered the tray. The President declined initially not wanting to consume any caffeine before bed. Carol sweetly informed him that the hot drinks were decaffeinated tea. The President nodded approvingly. That would do very nicely.

They sat in the living room and chatted. Greeley hardly listened. He was almost in a daze being in the mesmerizing presence of the Great Man. In fact, Carol did most of conversing with the President. They spoke about general matters, nothing political: the President's impressions of Buffalo City and the southwest in general. What Rosalynn had been doing of late. How Amy was faring in school. A few questions about the President growing up in Plains, Georgia.

With the mention of Georgia, Greeley abruptly became alert. He blurted out that he was sorry to hear that Atlanta had lost its baseball team to Milwaukee a few years ago. The President gave the mayor a somewhat puzzled expression. Then Greeley realized it had been the other way around. What he'd meant to say was that he was probably pleased that Atlanta had acquired Milwaukee's team but fortunately Milwaukee now had the Pilots.

The President smiled broadly and said he enjoyed baseball, too.

At 10:45 the President excused himself. He was scheduled to call Rosalynn. He went into Greeley's boyhood bedroom, now the President's overnight bedroom, to place the call on a secure mobile line.

Greeley helped Carol carry the used teacups into the kitchen. Once there, he shook his head in despair.

"I made a fool of myself," he whispered to his wife.

"No you didn't, dear."

"I got Milwaukee and Atlanta mixed up. Their baseball teams, I mean. I'm sure I babbled like an idiot."

"I don't think you babbled at all. You expressed yourself very well and even if I didn't understand you, because as you know, Millard, I'm not a sports fan, I think the President appreciated your effort."

-X-

Back in the newsroom, there was a problem in the

back shop. Harley Dee Grubbs was missing.

Percy Pollack came in and told Dwight. Dale, finished with his story, walked over to Dwight's desk after Percy left.

"What's up?"

"Percy said Harley Dee wasn't back yet."

"Did he know where he went?"

"Nope. Just took off after the afternoon press run. Didn't say where he was going."

"That's strange."

"Worse than that, it's going to delay the run."

"What about Joe Jones?" Jones had been the assistant pressman before Grubbs. Jones had been fired because he drank. But he sometimes helped out in an emergency.

"Jones is dead," said Dwight.

"I didn't know that. When? How?" Dale was about to say what, where, and why (he already knew who) just to complete the six journalistic questions.

"He died a few days ago. I'll tell you about it later if you want. Right now we got to either find Harley Dee or someone else."

"Is there anyone else?"

"Percy tried calling a retired pressman living in Dalhart but there was no answer. But even if Percy reaches him it would still take an hour for him to get here."

Dale thought about the duties of a pressman. He'd watched Percy and Harley Dee doing their jobs. He knew how to operate the vertical stat camera, how to make negatives and plates. He wasn't as sure about running the press. But he could probably do enough to assist Percy.

Dale told Dwight he could help out.

"Really? You think you know enough?"

"I think so."

Dwight's mustache, which had been even droopier than usual, almost bristled with energy. "Then go do it, Dale."

Before going into the back shop, Dale told Will about the emergency. He asked Will what he planned to do.

"I'll hang around until you get finished. Besides, I'd like to see tomorrow's *Stampede* hot off the press."

"That's because you have the lead page one story."

"W-W-Well," stammered Will with characteristic modesty.

Dale said he'd see him in about an hour. As he strode off, he wondered where the heck Grubbs was. The guy had left them in a lurch. He'd been acting even stranger than usual all week. But wherever Grubbs was, he'd committed a cardinal sin. When Greeley found out, he'd fire the weird guy.

Chapter Seven
Sunday

At 10:30 a.m. Dale stood near the entrance of The Duke Diner. He was going to met Will for breakfast before Will headed back to Norman. A minute later Will's green Volvo rolled into a parking space and the two young men went inside and sat in a booth. For a Sunday morning when most of the townsfolk went to church the diner was fairly busy. Farmhands, cowhands, oil roughnecks, and other disreputable types were sitting in the booths and on the stools at the counter.

"Why is this place called The Duke Diner?" asked Will.

"It's named after The Duke," said Dale. "You know, John Wayne."

"You're joking."

"No, that's the story. Supposedly John Wayne stopped in here on his way to the West Coast back in the '50s. Over there is his autographed picture."

Several glass-encased photos were mounted on the wall next to the old Wurlitzer jukebox. One photo showed John Wayne in his classic Western get-up: beat-up Stetson, bandanna, leather vest, western jersey and denim trousers.

"I guess he's the most famous person to ever visit Buffalo City except for Jimmy Carter," Dale said.

"If Carter isn't re-elected then The Duke will still

have top billing," said Will.

"Think he won't be re-elected?"

"Mayor Greeley thinks he's a sure thing."

"But you don't?"

"I don't make predictions. I just report."

"I can't even do that. I still can't believe that Greeley censored my copy."

Last night after Dale had helped with the back shop duties he and Will grabbed a couple of freshly printed papers and went to the The Duke Diner to read the historic newspaper. Dale had read Will's story first and complimented his friend on a superbly written piece of journalism. Then he read the story he'd written. Halfway through he noticed that the quotes he'd gotten from Grover Grubbs were missing. In fact, two paragraphs referring to the AAM tractorcade protest had been excised out. He asked Will if he knew what had happened. Will said Greeley came into the newspaper office around eleven and went into the composing room. He came back out ten minutes later and said goodnight to him and that was it.

Dale and Will had rushed back to the *Stampede* and caught Dwight as he was getting into his car to go home. Dale asked him about the two missing paragraphs. Dwight said Greeley ordered him to take them out. Dale asked why? Greeley said it "reflected poorly on their honored guest." Dale said the *Stampede* was a newspaper not a public relations firm for the Carter administration. Dwight, weary from a long day, shrugged and said Greeley was the publisher. He had the authority to do that. Dale wanted to argue more about his copy being censored but he knew Dwight was tired. Besides, the paper had already been printed.

"It's against journalistic ethics to do what Greeley did," Will said. "Of course, decades ago it was common for newspapers to be partisan."

"I guess that's what I get for working for a newspaper with a mayor for a publisher."

"Look at the bright side. At least he didn't censor your sports column."

"Yeah, I should have put Carter last in the ranking of best opening day pitches."

"Then Greeley *would* have censored it."

"Yeah, he probably would have. Censored fiction."

"Better than censoring fact."

Dale nodded and their breakfast arrived and they focused on chowing down. Twenty minutes later they left the diner and went over to their cars. Down the street they could see the closed newspaper office. Dale gazed at it with dissatisfaction. He was still miffed that his copy had been compromised. He'd run six blocks to get those quotes, too.

Down another street north of them they heard the rush and flow of several cars. They turned to see the presidential motorcade rolling down Highway 66 making its way back to the regional airport. The black limo of the President appeared in their view for two seconds then flashed by, gone.

"There's goes the President," said Will. "Leaving without saying goodbye."

"The ingratitude. We turned our paper into a propaganda sheet for him and he doesn't even stop and say thank you." Dale looked at Will. "So, how did you like your experience working at the *Stampede*?"

"It was …" Will paused a moment, "educational."

"It was fun having you around."

"I had fun hanging around with you, too, even if you are a muckraker."

"Well, I think I'm the one who got mucked over." Will laughed and Dale shrugged. "So your off to Norman now?"

"Classes resume tomorrow. Back to the old grind of graduate work."

Dale told Will that Friday and yesterday he'd received word about his graduate school applications. Missouri, Texas, and Wyoming had accepted him. But he'd been offered a teaching assistantship only from Wyoming. Because he didn't want to take out loans for grad school, he probably would accept the offer from Wyoming. Will congratulated him.

"What are you going to do after you get your master's?" Dale asked.

"Either get a Ph.D. or go into the newspaper racket."

"You're a good reporter. You ought to work for a real paper. Make sure they toe the ethical line."

"We'll see."

Will went over to his car and Dale followed. They shook hands. Then Will got in and started it up. Will rolled his window down. Dale felt a strange melancholy seeing Will Whitaker depart. He'd only known him for five days but he knew he'd miss his wit and good nature.

"Hey, keep in touch," Dale said.

"Okay, I will." Will backed his Volvo out then leaned his head out of the window. "Hey, I don't have your address."

"Mail it to the *Buffalo City Stampede*. To the sports editor!"

Will grinned and waved as he drove off. Dale watched the green Volvo drive one block north then turn east on highway 66 and head in the same direction as the Presidential motorcade.

Dale walked slowly over to his car. He sort of wish he was leaving with Will Whitaker.

-II-

Millard Greeley started his Cadillac and backed out of the driveway. He'd just gotten home from attending the First Baptist Church with Carol, his mother, and the President's entourage ten minutes ago. A delightful and inspirational service. But now there was an emergency and, as to be expected, they needed Greeley.

Sheriff Johnson had called five minutes before and said something terrible had happened at the Buffalo City Grain Co-op. He needed to mayor to come as soon as possible. He didn't want to say any more than necessary on the telephone.

Greeley didn't feel too much alarm over the phone call. What terrible thing could possibly happen at the grain co-op? As he drove his Cadillac down Highway 66 he reflected on the last wonderful sixteen hours. He felt much better this morning than he had last night. After he had left his mother's home, left the President and the Secret Service agents, and returned to his own home with Carol he'd been a little mopey. He didn't think he'd impressed the President very much and he wanted the President to know how deeply he respected and admired him. After he dropped Carol off at home, he'd popped over to the *Stampede* just to check on his charges. Just as he feared, his staff couldn't function at a superior level without his leadership. He'd read the three front-page stories and fortunately he had discovered the highly critical and completely unnecessary criticism of the President! He'd ordered Dwight Willard to eliminate the two offensive paragraphs. The managing editor was reluctant to perform this command so Greeley, the editor and publisher of the *Buffalo City Stampede* had to insist. Imagine if the President had read that portion of the story. Being criticized by radical farmers! Greeley thought he'd have to have a talk with Dale Smith. He'd done a yeoman job helping out in the back shop but he'd showed poor judgment by including those irresponsible quotes in the news story. A reporter, after all, must show journalistic judgment!

And the other problem of last night: the disappearance of Harley Dee Grubbs. How could he have not shown up on the most important night in the newspaper's entire existence! The miscreant was no doubt boozing it up during his extended break. Probably got too drunk to go back to work. Just like that other reprobate (and drunk!), Joe Jones. Well, Greeley would get to the bottom of that mystery, too.

The mayor turned off Broadway onto McKinley Street. He thought of how just minutes before the presidential motorcade had tooled down Highway 66 trekking to the airport. Greeley gave a satisfied smile to himself in his rear-view mirror. He tried to broaden it to Carter-like proportions. His cheeks hurt. He'd have to work on developing a big grin.

What a wonderful morning it had been. The President attended not only the service at the First Baptist Church but also the men's Sunday school class. What a devout man! How could a man be so pious and yet have such political acumen? Greeley recalled with wonder how the President (or Jimmy – as he'd insisted everyone call him) had commented on the story of Jesus forbidding the stoning of the adulteress. The President, rather, Jimmy in this context, had said that even though the adulteress had sinned more than just in her heart, she was no more sinful than all those men who were trying to stone her. Many of them were just as guilty as she. Thus the moral of the story is not to stone anybody but to love everyone.

Of course, Jimmy didn't mean it sexually. That would be like adultery and that was wrong. But no more wrong than thinking lascivious thoughts, of course. He'd admitted in that courageous *Playboy* interview that even he had committed adultery in his heart many times. Greeley admired the President's candor. Greeley just last night had sinned in his heart when he had a brief chat with that White House press aide. What was her name? Sondra Scofield. Now that was an attractive young woman. No, he shouldn't think of her. He'd start lusting in his heart again.

Greeley drove three blocks and noticed several cars, including the sheriff's patrol car, parked at the grain co-op. Greeley got out of his Cadillac and walked to the back of the head house where he saw a parked ambulance. Rather odd. He saw one young man – Greeley thought his name was Pete McKenzie – sitting on a crate beside the open door. Pete looked ill. He hung his head and when Greeley walked by he looked up and showed a disturbed expression. Maybe the ambulance was for him thought Greeley, although why wasn't he in it then?

Greeley stepped into the head house and blinked his eyes trying to adjust them to the gloom after being in the brilliant sunshine. He heard the Sheriff Johnson's voice thanking him for coming over so fast. Another man, Dr. Petersen, the county coroner, stood next to the sheriff. Greeley was about to ask Dr. Petersen what he was doing here when the coroner glanced over to the far end of the building. Greeley's eyes followed and he saw a horrific sight: Two men lifting another man from off a large shaft of some kind. The shaft, part of a long, sharp tool, had impaled the man. As the two men, ambulance attendants, lifted the stiff body Greeley saw that something dangled from the puncture. He strained his eyes and realized that what was hanging from the hole in the middle of the dead man (for he surely must be dead) was his intestines. A glistening chain of guts extended from the dead man's belly to the floor below.

Greeley turned away and felt his body tremble. He staggered. For a moment he feared he might fall. Two hands reached out and steadied him. Greeley had stopped breathing for a moment. Now, he gulped down air. With the air came a deeply nauseous feeling. Two arms steered him to a chair and he sat down.

After a minute of regular breathing, he felt better. He looked up and saw Sheriff Johnson and coroner Petersen staring down at him.

"Are you okay, Mr. Mayor?"

"What is that hideous spectacle?"

"It's your employee, Harley Dee Grubbs."

Greeley jumped to his feet, tottered, then flopped down again. "Grubbs! Why is he here?"

"Well, Mr. Mayor, we don't know exactly."

"You don't know exactly? Amazing." Greeley stood up, his legs steady this time. "Grubbs went missing last night. He was supposed to be at work by nine to help run the press. Do you know when this happened?"

"Judging from the condition of the body," Petersen said, "some time last night."

"I suppose that explains Grubbs absence. But how did this happen? Why was he here at all?"

Sheriff Johnson and Dr. Petersen explained their theory. Grubbs must have been standing on the platform near the top of the head house. Why he was there they didn't know yet. But he must have slipped or fell or jumped. He dropped fifty feet and landed on an auxiliary grain auger. The shaft impaled him. No doubt immediately killed him.

Greeley glanced over to where the ambulance attendants had finally removed the corpse from the auger. They deposited the body on the gurney and covered it with a sheet. Greeley tried not to look at the puddle of intestines lying on the floor, but he saw enough to almost make him sick again.

The air was bad. Greeley walked over to the open door and breathed in the fresh air. He looked at Pete McKenzie sitting on the crate. The young man looked even worse than Greeley felt.

Greeley returned to the sheriff and the coroner.

300

"Did the young man sitting outside discover Grubbs?"

"Yep. Pete McKenzie came in this morning after church to check on things. Found Grubbs dangling. The feller's a little shook up."

From high above they heard a shout. It was deputy Scott. He had found a rifle with a scope. It was lying on the platform.

"Bring it down!" shouted Sheriff Johnson.

Three minutes later Deputy Scott walked over, holding the hunting rifle. He handed it by the strap to the sheriff. All three of them, Greeley, Johnson, and Petersen knew what it signified. The stood in silence for a moment contemplating something that ordinarily would have seemed inconceivable.

"We've called Grover Grubbs to come over," Sheriff Johnson finally said.

"Why? Can't he view the body later?"

"He's the president of the co-op. We want to know how his son got in here."

Greeley nodded. What a terrible event. Grubbs with a hunting rifle. Standing on some platform looking out of an opening. Looking? Aiming. If it had been someone else Greeley would not have believed it.

"Do you want the body to go to the coroner's office?" Sheriff Johnson asked.

"No need."

The sheriff and the coroner looked at each other.

"We have a reasonable idea of how he died," Greeley intoned lowly. "It was an accident."

"We should perform an autopsy," said Petersen.

"That will not be necessary."

"But this might be a crime scene."

"How is that? No one committed a crime. Grubbs' death is not a homicide."

"But he broke into ..." Sheriff Johnson's voice trailed off.

"We don't know that. It's quite possible that Grubbs borrowed his father's key."

"For what reason?" asked Dr. Petersen.

"And why did he bring a hunting rifle?" asked the sheriff.

"For all we know he came here to shoot rats. It doesn't matter. It was an accident. There's not been a crime committed. We're not going to bring any scandal to Buffalo City, certainly not after the President visiting our fine town just last night. Is that understood?"

The sheriff glanced at the coroner who was thinking over Greeley's assertions.

"What do you want to do with him, then?" asked Sheriff Johnson.

"Take him to a funeral home, of course."

"Which one?"

"Take him to Mr. Mors' establishment," the mayor grimly said.

-III-

In the upstairs den, Byron Mors stretched his legs out as he sat in his easy chair reading the Sunday *Stampede*. He only subscribed to the local paper to silently ridicule the banality he found within its pages. The three front-page news stories hadn't been too bad. But Rosemary Roger's article about the Miss Buffalo City Pageant proved to be as preposterous as he had expected. But the best source for comedy would no doubt be Millard Greeley's front-page editorial.

Byron first read the headline, *Thank You, Mr. President.* Then he read:

Thank you, Mr. President.

In Buffalo City and this surrounding area, we appreciate that you kept your noble promise to us and came back.

We thank you for your tireless efforts for peace and we thank you for your stalwart leadership for our country.

We thank you for listening to our problems and hope that your visit here may have contributed to your positive understanding of them.

Byron shook his head over the conventionality of Greeley's sentiments. He skimmed three more paragraphs until he came to the concluding paragraphs:

Mr. President, as you deal with enormous and weighty problems and diversity of interests, we want you to know that our thoughts, prayers and love go with you until we meet again.

God bless you.

Byron stared with disgust with that embarrassing display of sentimentalized verbal mush. Greeley had finally outdone himself.

He flipped to the next page and swiftly scanned the usual tedious news articles. On the third page, however, one article caught his attention. It concerned the opening of Dr. Arnold Smith's part-time private clinic. Dr. Arnold Smith, head of mental health and psychiatric studies at the Great Plains Regional Medical Center, had decided there was a need for private mental health counseling. The story quoted Dr. Smith stating that he planned on seeing a select number of patients during evening hours twice a week. Dr. Smith was doing this in response to several requests from Buffalonians. Dr. Smith had agreed since he believed that mental health was just as essential to one's well being as physical health.

Byron lowered the paper to his lap and stared out into the distance. Perhaps he should make some discreet inquires about Dr. Smith's services. Byron thought he might be suffering from erotomania. For several weeks he'd been obsessed with sex. His late night indulgence of X-rated films hadn't sated his lustful appetite as it had in the past. He woke thinking erotic thoughts; he conducted the day's business with obscene images running through his mind; even contact with his wife and child during the evening didn't result in the abatement of his obsession. He masturbated three times a day: In the morning shower, during his noon meal in his office downstairs, and before dinner in the bathroom. Actually, four times because he concluded his day with an exercise in onanism while watching the porn films.

He feared all this self-abuse was taking a toll on him physically and psychologically. He worried that he was becoming addicted to pornography and autoeroticism. And he was afraid he would increase his indulgence to more than four times because when he recuperated from one orgasm those powerful carnal feelings soon returned as insistent as ever. If he didn't slow down he was fearful that this burning lust would eventually immolate him.

He was feeling that urge at that moment. He tried to think of something else. He thought about the scheduled round of sexual congress with Kate for Tuesday evening when she returned from her mother's. That idea helped. He felt the surge of lust subsiding. Of course, thinking about his upcoming propagation duties produced another concern: what if he was unable to perform Tuesday night? What if he was simply too depleted? That had never happened before and if it did Kate would be suspicious. Or contemptuous. Now his arousal was completely doused.

Maybe he needed to get out of the mortuary business. That was part of the problem. Dealing with the dead was depressing and even if he no longer had much contact with the corpses those images of lifeless bodies lingered in his mind. He needed something to dispel those gruesome pictures from his psyche.

The peculiar family business had never adversely affected his father. Byron couldn't remember his father ever complaining about the business, not even the more gross aspects of it. His father had inherited the business from his father. Byron's grandfather had moved to Buffalo City from eastern Oklahoma after serving in World War I. Grandfather Mors had served in a burial detail during the war and realized that he, unlike most people, didn't shrink from dealings with the dead. When he returned to Oklahoma from overseas he decided to go into the funeral business. He left the prosperous family farm in eastern Oklahoma to his older brothers (his father had been Sooner not a

Boomer and had staked out prime land) and decided to head to the sparsely populated western part of the state where there was less competition in the funeral business. What his grandfather started, Byron's father perfected. Byron's father had excellent business acumen as well as a commercial ruthlessness and he made the family business into a very successful enterprise.

Byron had never wanted to take over the family funeral business. But Blake's death had compelled him to do so, not only to please his father, but also to expatiate some of his own guilt. Byron didn't believe in guilt, didn't believe in sin, but he nevertheless felt those dark feelings from time to time. He felt those irritating emotions most deeply when he thought of Blake and Carol. He now felt a twinge of guilt about Blake because he knew his younger brother had joined the marines to distinguish himself, to prove that he was just as worthy as his big brother. He and Blake had never been close. It was more than the two years difference between them and the usual big brother sense of superiority. Byron, in fact, had never lorded it over his younger brother. He never compared his accomplishments to his brother's mediocre academic and athletic record. But maybe that made it even worse for Blake. Maybe it caused Blake to feel that he wasn't even worth a comparison since he was so clearly inferior. And maybe that fueled his sense of competition even more and that was why Blake joined the Marines: to prove something to his older brother. Byron thought if he had been more communicative, more supportive, then maybe Blake wouldn't have felt the need to prove himself in such a high-risk way.

So it was feelings of guilt and responsibility that had kept Byron in Buffalo City. Even though in theory he rejected those feelings, he nevertheless at times felt them. He didn't want Blake's death to haunt him. But occasionally as the workday came to a close, that quiet time when he shuttered the funeral home and shuffled up the stairs in the gloom of a dying day, he thought of his younger brother and how he should be the one continuing the family business instead of him. But Blake had been killed in a travesty of a war. Now Byron had to shoulder the responsibility of the family business even though he didn't have the temperament for it. Unlike his father, Byron had never adjusted to the creepy craft of undertaking.

His father had simply viewed his business as a necessary one and he had the knack of forgetting the unpleasant nature of his trade once the workday was concluded. His father was on the surface religious. Byron didn't think his father really had any genuine religious feeling except for a generalized notion that there was a heaven where the dead would return to life and feel gratitude for the excellent service he'd provided for them. In almost all respects, his father was a conventional, down-to-earth, punctilious, shrewd man who excelled in the narrow world of business and small town life. Byron had been surprised when his father turned sixty and decided to hand over the business to him. Byron's father and mother moved out of the comfortable rooms above the funeral home to go live in their attractive vacation home near the Washita River. The old man still cheerfully assisted with the funeral home on a part-time basis, mostly to give Byron a break. But Byron had decided he needed a full-time assistant and he planned to hire some young OU graduate in mortuary science soon. Kate would appreciate that. He would have more free time and they could go on a more trips together.

Whatever quality his father and grandfather had, a certain pragmatic acceptance of death, Byron realized he lacked it. Simply put, he was in the wrong business.

He had been so lost in thought that he didn't hear the ringing of the business phone.

"Byron!" Kate called from the other room. "It's your business phone."

Byron Mors reluctantly rose. He had hoped that he would have a full day off. But it was not to be. The dead could not wait.

-IV-

Carol Greeley discreetly watched as little Millard toddled off to the playground. He didn't like her to be too attentive. The other kids might think he was a sissy. Even though he was only three, Carol could already detect something of his grandfather in him.

Carol, pretending to focus her eyes on the bright blue sky instead of her son, walked over to the park bench. She sat down without really looking about. Dressed casually for an outing in the park, she used her slender hands to smooth out the pink slacks.

"Hello, Carol."

Carol glanced to her right and saw Kate Mors smiling at her. The smile wasn't genuine. It was large enough, showing her fine teeth. But Kate's eyes had the usual calculating look in them.

"Hello, Kate."

Carol noted that Kate's attire was more refined than hers even though they sat in Custer Park on a sunny Sunday afternoon. Kate wore slacks, too, but they were light blue and made of a better material than hers. She wore an attractive light blue blouse, the top buttons undone, showing a little of her impressive bust and a red cashmere sweater.

"Did you bring Joy?"

"Oh, yes. She's over there."

Kate pointed to her little girl, also three years old, blonde as the mother, who sat in the sand pile shoving clumps of sand into a pink pail.

"Joy is a lovely little girl."

Carol noticed that Kate gave her a searching look as if wondering whether the compliment was genuine. But it was genuine. Joy might not be the cutest little girl in the park but she had a sweet personality.

"Well, your little Millard is a delight, too."

Carol smiled. Kate didn't really mean it, but it was true nonetheless. "Is it just the two of you?"

"Yes. The same for you?"

"Yes. Millard couldn't come with us. Some kind of emergency."

"That's funny. Byron couldn't come because of an urgent case at work."

Carol glanced at Kate who was looking back in an oblique kind of way. Carol wondered if the emergency had something to do with the urgent case.

"Did I hear that the President stayed at your mother-in-law's home overnight?" asked Kate.

"Yes, the President spent the night there. He and two Secret Service agents."

"That's interesting. I suppose you met the President at your mother-in-law's?"

"Yes. We all chatted for an hour. Then the President went into Millard's old room to call Rosalynn before retiring and Millard and I left. Mrs. Greeley, even though she is a very proper lady, said she didn't mind being alone in the same house with three strange men."

Carol glanced to see Kate's facial expression. She smiled that same kind of broad smile but her cold green eyes had a glint of jealousy in them.

"How interesting."

"This morning we all attended church together."

"The President went to church with you?"

"We meet him at First Baptist. He attended the men's Sunday school class with Millard."

"That must have been very pleasing for the mayor."

"Millard was ecstatic. He said the President made a wise observation at the Sunday school class. Everyone was impressed."

"I'm sure they were."

Carol, even though she didn't like Kate Mors, felt she'd gloated enough. She knew Kate would be jealous of her. In a way, it was only fair payback for all the times she'd showed off with Bryon in front of her. Kate knew about her and Byron's history together. Carol supposed almost everyone in town did. Kate had enjoyed hurting her in all the small ways that women enjoy hurting other women. But Carol had decided she wouldn't play that game anymore.

"It's a beautiful day, isn't it?" Carol looked at the infinite blue sky and the cotton candy clouds.

"Yes, it is."

Carol knew a part of her would always love Byron Mors. But the feeling was slowly fading. She no longer felt that fierce pang of passion when she saw him. It had been difficult being in the same town and seeing so much of him all these years. As she sat there now on the park bench with Kate she wondered how it would be if everything had happened differently. If she had married Byron would her life be any better, any happier? Byron eventually came back to Buffalo City and settled down. She had planned on that happening those many years ago but he didn't settle down with her.

But she had other things in her life. She had her family. She had Millard, who was becoming a better man. He'd always be a little foolish and bombastic. But under her guidance she thought he would eventually become what he always wanted to be: a leader of the community. And she had her hobbies and civic clubs and books and music. All those years ago she had imagined herself as a woman of letters living in London or Paris. Or she imagined herself as the wife of Byron Mors and the two of them living exciting, sophisticated lives before returning home and settling down and having three children. None of that had happened.

But she was going to continue to grow and develop and help her husband and child to do the same. There were books to read and people to help and fun to be had. Her life wasn't perfect, but what life was? After little Millard and maybe another little one got to high school she would finish her college degree. She'd already earned her associate bachelor's from the community college. Maybe she'd get an education degree and become an English teacher. That had been her practical dream. But whatever she did she wouldn't look back too often. Just enough to know where she'd been and where she was going.

"Look, Carol," said Kate, her voice genuinely interested. "Joy and little Millard are playing together."

Carol looked over at the playground. Her son was helping Joy build sand castles.

"Yes. They are playing together very well. They are both lovely children."

-V-

At 1:30 p.m. Dale drove to the Brown's residence, a white two story wooden structure, a farmhouse really, and parked in the gravel drive-way. He started to get out when Helen appeared at the front door.

"Right on time!" she called.

She got in the car and Dale drove down the rural road and turned onto Highway 66.

"How about movie?" he asked.

"Okay. Which one?"

"We'll decide when we get to the multiplex."

Almost all movie houses were now multiplexes. He didn't really like that. He had more choices once he arrived there but the theatres were narrow, utilitarian boxes and the small screens didn't have any of the majesty of the old, more ornate theatres with their big single screens. Well, he thought, that's progress for you.

As he drove they talked about the recent events,

the biggest one being, of course, the President's visit to Buffalo City.

"Tell me who you were with last night?" Helen asked.

"You saw me last night?"

"Yes, outside the gymnasium."

"It's funny how you're always seeing me and I don't see you." He was referring to the fact that Helen had attended Galilee Nazarene College last year as a freshman but Dale had never encountered her on campus. She had said she'd seen him several times.

"Well, who was he?"

She meant Will. So Dale told her about him, how he worked for the *Stampede* as a special assignment reporter for five days to help with coverage of the historic event. How he had been student newspaper editor at OU and was now a graduate student there.

"William F. Whitaker," Helen said. "A good name for a byline. Do you know what the initial stands for?"

"No, I never got around to asking him. He goes by Will. Maybe F stands for facts. He's a very fact-oriented guy."

"And you like that?"

"He's an excellent reporter. But I'm not as interested in fact-oriented journalism as he is. I like more subjective journalism. I like expressing my opinion."

"That's what gets you in trouble."

"I guess that's true," Dale said in his pseudo-philosophical tone of voice.

Helen laughed.

Dale followed Highway 66 until it connected to I-40. Helen noticed they were driving west.

"Why do you always drive to Amarillo instead of Oklahoma City? OKC is actually ten miles closer."

"I know Okie City already. Amarillo is still sort of new." Actually, he thought both cities were pretty much the same. Flat, dry, southwestern prairie towns. Cattle, oil, wheat. Not much sophistication or urbanity. Few aesthetic opportunities.

"Is that the only reason?"

"What do you mean?"

"You never seem very interested in what is going on in Galilee, for instance. And it's your hometown."

"It's not my home anymore."

Dale thought he didn't really have a home any more except for the temporary one in Mrs. Kennicott's house. He didn't like visiting his folks because their situations sadden him. His mother, fortunately, was still sane. Living with her parents had provided some stability. His father had bought a new home, a two-story job, in northwest Oklahoma City. He'd visited twice so far and both times he'd been restless and uncomfortable. He didn't like Blackie's new wife, Cleoma. He'd known her a little when she was still his father's girlfriend and even then he thought she was a phony. When she got pregnant, his father had to marry her. His half-brother, Marlon, was now six months old. When Dale heard they'd name him Marlon he didn't have to ask why. He knew Cleoma was crazy over Marlon Brando. When Dale saw his half-brother for the first time, when Marlon was three months old, he'd not felt any fraternal bond. Sometimes he wondered if there was something missing in him, some lack of family sentiment.

"Galilee will always be your home," said Helen.

Her observation irked him. But instead of responding in a curt way, he remained silent and concentrated on driving down the smooth, black highway.

"I see your sister sometimes on campus," Helen said. "I don't think you've ever asked about her in your letters."

"What about her?"

"She's a junior varsity cheerleader. She's cute. She's popular. She's social unlike you."

"That's sis, all right."

"Don't you ever see her?"

"Not often. You know I don't get back to Galilee much."

"Hardly ever."

Dale almost said, "what's that to you?" but he didn't. He was growing vexed, though. Helen ought to know from his letters and conversations that he wanted to get away from Galilee.

"Oh, did I tell you who won Heart-Pal Sweetheart last month?"

Heart-Pal was one of those curious GNC traditions. Five girls were nominated and the college held a banquet in their honor and selected the "sweetheart." The banquet was held during the week of Valentine's Day and one of the traditions was the announcement of engagements. Dale had attended two Heart-Pal banquets with his ex-girlfriend.

"No," he said without any enthusiasm.

"Your old girlfriend, Amanda Meeks."

Dale gritted his teeth and focused on the road.

"Actually, I had expected Amanda to win homecoming queen last November. She was in the court, of

315

course, but Abigail Van Brocklin won. You knew Abby, too, didn't you?"

"Yes."

"She's a wonderful girl. She has such a good character. Intelligent, affable, considerate, and she's attractive, too, not in a flashy way, of course. She's engaged to Robert Henshaw, you know, the student council president. He's trying for a Rhodes scholarship. You knew him, too, didn't you?"

"I knew them all."

"But I mean you knew them well. Just not casually."

Dale caught himself, in his annoyance, speeding. Damn the Carter administration for the stupid 55 mile per hour speed limit.

"That was a long time ago."

"Just last year."

"It seems like a long time ago. Besides, I'm really not interested."

"Oh, excuse me for making conversation."

He glanced at Helen who actually looked offended. She pursed her small mouth and her gray eyes stared at him.

Great, Dale, thought, we have eighty miles to go and we're already annoyed at each other.

"Look, I don't mean to be rude. I just don't like thinking about all of that," he said, trying to keep his voice mild and reasonable.

"Very well, I understand. We won't talk about it anymore."

Dale thought, good. Actually, Helen had written informing him about who won homecoming queen last November. He'd been astonished to hear that Amanda hadn't won. Then he had felt something like a kick in the belly thinking that the reason she hadn't won was because of her association with him. Even though she'd broken up with him in spring 1978, maybe the fact that she was once the girlfriend of the notorious newspaper editor and campus iconoclast had besmirched her reputation just a little. Enough to cost her homecoming queen the next fall.

So what? Those traditions were sort of silly anyway. But thinking that someone he still cared about might have been aversely affected by her connection to him nevertheless made him feel hollow and sick inside.

Dale and Helen drove in silence for several miles. He thought it was rather strange that this was their first real argument as friends.

He turned up the volume on the radio when he heard a song he liked, "Darkness on the Edge of Town."

"Oh, you like that song?" Helen asked. "It's not bad."

"Not bad? Sacrilege."

"Not bad for rock and roll. I should educate you about real music: Vivaldi and Bach and Handel."

Dale grinned a little. He often told her he was going to educate her about something. Didn't he just say that Friday about the British Invasion music of the '60s?

"I've listened to classical music. I like it. I even have some records. But for driving on the highway it's better to listen to rock."

"Not country?"

"Not Tammy Wynette at any rate."

He glanced at her and saw a puzzled smile on her face. Maybe he'd tell her the source of that joke sometime; then again, maybe never.

The tension broken, the two of them talked about music, movies, and books. Helen was an English major at GNC. She especially liked the novels of the Bronte sisters, Emily and Charlotte. Also the works of George Eliot.

"Her real name was Mary Ann Evans," Helen informed him.

"No kidding!" he said mockingly.

"I forget how you've read everything."

"Not everything. Not by a long shot." He told her that he'd just finished *All the King's Men*. He was now reading *A Handful of Dust*. He used to base his readings on a fairly strict chronological order. Lately, he'd been reading novels based more on what took his fancy: what he heard mentioned by someone or a reference to a novel in a movie or magazine article.

"Who wrote *A Handful of Dust*?" Helen asked.

"Some English guy named Evelyn Waugh."

"Evelyn? A guy?"

"Yeah he's a man. Just like George is a woman."

Helen laughed. She had a nice laugh, sort of lilting and unaffected. In fact, her laugh reminded him of Carol Greeley's.

"Several southern women writers have sort of masculine names. Flannery O'Connor, Carson McCullers, Harper Lee," he said.

"You've read their novels, too, I suppose?"

"Yeah. Well, only one novel each so far. Of course, that's it for Harper Lee unless she's going to publish another sometime. But it's been over eighteen years since *To Kill a Mockingbird* appeared."

"Didn't Margaret Mitchell only write one novel,

Gone With the Wind?"

"That's right. It won the Pulitzer, her novel was made into the most popular film of all time, and then she got hit by a bus."

"Not really!"

"Really. Killed her. That's a valid reason to have not written another novel."

They continued to discuss novels for a while then they changed the topic to movies. Helen liked them, too, but GNC still didn't show any regularly on campus. Many Nazarenes were still opposed to seeing movies, especially today's "indecent" films.

They drove into the Amarillo city limits and two miles later he turned north on Osage Street. He drove to the Panhandle Multiplex 12 but when he saw the marquee he didn't find any of the films interesting.

"Everybody is still going to see *Superman*," Helen said.

"There's a theatre for second run movies on the other side of town. Let's see what's playing there."

Helen said okay and he turned around and drove to The Bijou. *Midnight Express* was playing. He asked Helen if she'd seen it and she said no. He hadn't seen it either. It was supposed to be a good movie. It had been nominated for several Academy Awards just a month ago.

They went in and sat in seats near the back. The movie was about a young American guy who tries to smuggle hashish out of Turkey. He's caught and put in a hellish prison. In the end, the American kills a sadistic prison warden and escapes.

Afterward they went to a diner for dinner. He paid

even though this wasn't an official date, but he said he was a workingman. When she got a full-time job she could pay for the next dinner. They talked about the movie. Dale had liked it. Helen said she did, too, but she didn't say it very convincingly. He wondered if the violence bothered her. The film was R-rated. There were also a couple of nude scenes and some profanity.

They drove back to Buffalo City and mid-way during the drive the sun began to set. Unfortunately, they were driving east so they couldn't watch the magnificent melting of the sun on the shimmering purple horizon as he drove. But Helen turned around in her seat to watch and Dale often glanced into the rear-view mirror. One of the best things about living on the Great Plains was the glorious sunsets and sun rises.

They got back to Buffalo City at 7:30 p.m. He parked his Chevy on the curb of the street, forgetting that her parents were already off at their cabin. Helen had told him that her family had a cabin near the Black Kettle National Grasslands. That area was about fifty miles north of Buffalo City. There had been a famous Indian battle fought there, the Battle of the Washita. Actually, from what Dale had read, it was more of a massacre. Federal troops had slaughtered almost two hundred Kiowa. A young George Armstrong Custer had been involved in the battle.

The whole Brown clan was staying at the cabin: Helen's brother and sister and their spouses and kids. Dale asked if the cabin was large enough to accommodate them all.

"It's two story but it's really not that big. It gets sort of cramped with everyone there. Daddy has talked about building an addition."

Helen told him that her father first bought the land ten years ago. Over the years, he worked on building the cabin. It had taken him eight years. She also said that they used to have a ranch. But her father grew tired of ranching; a small outfit like his always had it rough. So when land prices got a little higher, he sold most of the land and used the profit to finish the cabin.

"We can walk over and see some of our old ranch, if you'd like," she said.

Dale said okay and they got out and walked down a worn path for two hundred yards until they came to a barbed wire fence. He leaned against one of the fence posts and stared out at the pasture. The waning half moon was scaling the horizon, headed for the center of the darkening deep blue sky.

"The people that bought the ranch have horses."

"Yeah, I can smell them," Dale said.

Helen laughed. "It's not that bad."

"No, it's not a bad smell. Maybe they're still in the corral."

Just then they heard one of horses give a whinny. Maybe they smelled them too.

"We better mosey on back," Dale said in his pseudo-rustic voice, "before we stir up them critters."

They walked back to Helen's house. When they got to the yard they came upon a large oak tree, gnarled but still alive in the semi-arid land. Helen noticed him looking at it.

"My brother built a tree house up there."

She pointed toward the middle of the tree and Dale looked up and saw part of a wooden structure within the limbs and leaves, fairly well concealed.

"Carpentry must run in the family. It looks like a well-built tree house."

"My brother is something of a handy man. He helped my dad build our cabin. Oh, there's a funny story about the tree house."

"Okay, please continue."

"You might notice that this tree is fairly close to the house. After he built the tree house, it was discovered a person could look right into my older sister's bedroom. She found that out one day when she came into her room after a shower. Before she shed the bath towel, she heard noises outside her window. Laughter, giggles, that sort of thing. She went over and fully parted the curtain and saw my brother and three of his friends staring back at her."

"The little devils."

"I'll say! The next day my father made him cover the space facing her room with three planks of wood."

"How old were your brother and sister?"

"At the time, Penelope was fourteen. My brother was eleven. I'm four years younger than my brother."

"Eleven. I guess that's old enough to start getting interested."

"How old were you when you started getting interested?"

"I was born interested."

Helen laughed but Dale wasn't being accurate. As a little boy he disliked girls. It was mostly an act but he didn't seem to develop any carnal curiosity until his early teens. At least, that's how he remembered it.

Helen glanced up at the partially hidden tree house.

"I bet a plank or two have fallen off. The old tree house is getting dilapidated."

They walked away toward the porch. Dale smelled the fresh evening air. The half moon hovered higher in the sky now. As Dale gazed at it he noticed that it was a little less than half full. He thought such moons were called gibbous waning. He noticed that on the western horizon a thick mass of clouds had formed.

"Your sister's name is Penelope?"

"Yes. But the family calls her Penny."

"Is your brother's name Ajax? Or maybe Hector?"

Helen smiled. "No, why?"

"Both you and your sister have classical names so I thought he might have one too."

"No, his name is Mark. After my father."

"Not spelled with a C?"

"Spelled the common way with a K."

"That's disappointing."

"Well, my parents weren't trying to impress any bibliophiles."

They went over to her porch and sat down. The Brown's house was rather secluded. They lived on the north side of town not quite out of the city limits. They had neighbors but their houses weren't close by. The Brown's house had an old fashioned kind of porch, with big steps and room enough on the porch for a swing. They didn't have one though.

He'd only been to their house twice. One time he picked up Helen to go to a movie in Amarillo. They didn't make it back in time for Sunday evening church and Dale got the impression that her parents didn't like that.

323

"You missed Sunday evening services again," he said.

"I know. I hope no one will tell my parents."

"Are they that strict?"

"No, but they like it when I go to church. Not only for religious reasons but for the social interaction."

"Why? Are you such a bookworm and an introvert?"

"They sometimes think so."

"They don't mind if you see movies, do they?"

"No, but then I don't always tell them what kind of films I see."

"Like today's film? You really didn't like it, did you?"

"There were times when I felt I would have rather seen *Superman* again."

"When?"

"During the violent scenes. Some of the other scenes made me a little uncomfortable, too."

"You mean the sex and nude scenes?"

"Well, certainly the sex scenes."

Dale had also felt uneasy watching the sex scene between the hero and his friend, too. Fortunately, it wasn't explicit. However, he liked the scene when his girlfriend takes off her shirt. He mused on that scene for a moment.

"The actor looked a little liked you," Helen said.

"You mean the lead actor?"

"Yes, didn't you notice that? The resemblance?"

"I didn't notice any resemblance." Actually, as he thought about it, maybe there were some similarities. Both he and the actor had dark hair, dark eyes, muscular builds, not tall. Suddenly, he didn't like thinking about that. He didn't like seeing himself from anoth-

324

er's perspective; how he looked in the eyes of someone else.

Dale glanced at Helen and he thought she was looking at him in a strange inquiring way. He felt a certain tension developing between them. It wasn't the kind of tension he'd felt earlier during the drive when they had a short argument. It was more like something was happening that might change their relationship.

In the distance, they heard the rumbling of thunder. They looked to the west and felt the turbulence in the night sky. Roiling clouds were mushrooming on the horizon, moving toward them.

At that moment, he keenly felt his physical existence. His senses were more acute. He felt the moisture increasing, adding electricity in the air. But more than that, he felt something inside himself. He felt his youth, his strength, his virility.

He looked at Helen. He'd never thought of her as being attractive. But sitting on the porch in the deepening evening, he thought her features looked more becoming. She didn't have large eyes; she didn't have large lips; her cheeks weren't especially full or dimpled. Her cheekbones weren't prominent, her jaw and chin didn't feature any generous curvature. Her nose was too large and her light brown hair didn't have any vibrant color to it. Sitting there in her blue jeans and turquoise blouse, her figure was rather ordinary. Not fat or thin but certainly not voluptuous. And yet there was something about her at that moment that piqued his interest.

Helen seemed to sense his mood. Her gray eyes looked directly at him for a moment, then she turned her eyes away from him.

"It's going to rain."

"Yeah, maybe a storm."

"We could go inside. My parents are away."

"We could."

Then he realized he hadn't really ever touched her. She'd playfully bumped into him once or twice, goofing around while walking. Once he'd hurt his finger while at work when he'd cut himself with an X-acto knife. He'd just washed the wound and forgot about it. But it became infected and when he came over to pick her up for an outing, Helen saw it and insisted that she clean it. He'd gone inside her house, the kitchen, and she'd put some disinfectant liquid on the finger then bandaged it. While she was tending to his wound he hadn't felt any erotic spark between them. Not even when their hands touched. And, of course, he had never kissed her. It had always been a strictly platonic friendship.

"Dale, I want to know something."

Her voice sounded different than before. No longer casually friendly.

"What?"

"You would never feel for me the way you felt for your ex-girlfriend, would you?"

He was glad she didn't say her name. Hearing her name spoken still wounded him a little.

"Probably not." Not even probably. He would never feel that intensely for Helen.

"Then what your feeling, what we're feeling at this moment, isn't ..." she searched for the word.

"Proper?"

"Healthy."

He knew what she meant. But he thought what they were feeling was almost the opposite. It was the call of the blood. The sultry night. Nature unbound. His loneliness. His sexual frustration. Wanting to be close to a girl. It was more than lust. He liked Helen. She had a pleasant personality, a good sense of humor, and other fine qualities. But he didn't love her. He didn't desire her. At least not before now. If they started things in that direction, it would turn out badly. He would hurt her and he didn't want to do that.

And yet, how he wanted to be close to a girl! Why did he have these potent feelings when they couldn't be fulfilled?

"I guess your right," he said. "It wouldn't be healthy."

"Not unless you have feelings for me."

"I have feelings for you."

"Feelings beyond the physical."

"I like you."

"It has to be more than that."

"So it can't just be physical and it can't be just friendly. I guess that means you want everything."

"Don't you?"

"No. Not right now."

They saw a flash of lightning burst inside a distant thunderhead followed by a crack of thunder.

"I better go in and you better leave before the storm gets here."

Dale stood up but he felt awkward and he didn't want to leave. He wanted to go inside and make love while hearing the thunder and rain. But he wasn't sure he wanted to do that with Helen. He knew if they went inside and did that then he would be held responsible for the emotional consequences.

He stood there; she sat there. He knew if he reached for her she'd agree to go inside with him. The animal part of him wanted to do it; his mind, his conscience, didn't.

"Yeah, I guess I better go. Anyway, I have to get up early for work." He took a step down from the porch.

Helen slowly stood up. She wouldn't look directly at him. She started for her front door.

"Good night Dale," she said, a note of disappointment clearly in her voice.

"Good night Helen. I'll see you later."

He jumped down from the last two steps of her porch and started walking to his car. He glanced back and saw her enter her house. He paused a moment and thought about returning. But it wouldn't do any good.

He didn't walk to his car. Instead he walked down the sidewalk trying to extinguish the fires of his frustration. The atmosphere of the night didn't help. The walk didn't either. The physical exertion only made it worse.

He turned to walk back to his car when he saw a bedroom light in Helen's house flicker on. Instead of opening the car door, he walked over to the oak tree. The tree still had wooden steps nailed into the tree's bark. His hand grabbed hold of one above his head while his booted foot stepped on the lower step.

He easily climbed up the tree and entered the tree house. It was sort of rickety, but he carefully moved to the boarded up window. One plank was loose and Dale pried it completely off. He peered through the gap at the light in the window. He could clearly see into the bedroom. The large window revealed the wooden floor, a red checkered carpet and a bed.

Then Helen, nude, entered the frame of his vision. She stood mostly in profile and he looked at her, momentarily excited at seeing her in the flesh. He'd been right about her figure. It was slender but not sinuous. He saw only her left breast, but it was small and not firm. It drooped a little, the nipple hardly visible. Her hips were too narrow, her thighs too slight. She turned slightly to her left and he saw her pubic region and the triangle of hair was the same dull brown as the hair on her head.

She walked over to her bed and simply laid face down on the mattress. Her rather skimpy buttocks and graceless legs did not arouse him. She laid there almost motionless, in the same passive way she had sat on the porch minutes before.

He looked away. He felt a terrible sadness seize him. His frustration and momentary lust had completely vanished. Her naked image had no erotic appeal. Instead, the image seemed sad and mundane and vulnerable. He hoped that image would fade from his mind before he saw her again.

Suddenly, it began to rain hard. No preliminaries. No sprinkle or drizzle. Just an abrupt release of heavy raindrops. It was as if a giant bucket of water had been upturned on the dry land.

Dale shielded his eyes from the rain and glanced through the gap again. He saw Helen still lying prone on her bed. Her arms were raised above her head and her small hands were pressed into fists. She appeared to be weeping. He said, "I'm sorry, Helen" but of course she couldn't hear him. He climbed down from the tree, feeling more like a fool than a voyeur for spying on poor Helen, still muttering his unheard apology.

He drove slowly back to town. The rain beat steadily on the windshield. The wipers cleared off a visible spot for only a second before the water obscured it. Lightening flashed overhead and thunder crashed. By the time he got to downtown the fast moving storm had passed. The rain halted almost as suddenly as it had started.

As Dale approached the *Stampede*, he noticed lights blazing in the newsroom. Ordinarily, no one came into the newspaper on a Sunday. Not even the ad people popped in.

Then he saw Millard Greeley, dressed in a dark overcoat, emerge from the building and climb into his Cadillac. Dale slowed to nearly a stop. He waited until Greeley's Caddy turned out of sight.

Dale parked his Chevy in a space next to Dwight Willard's blue Datsun. The glass doors to the newsroom were unlocked. Dale opened them and walked in. He saw Dwight sitting at his desk with a pensive look on his face.

"What's going on?" Dale asked.

Dwight had been so lost in thought that he hadn't even heard Dale come in. He stared at him for a moment almost as if he didn't know who he was then his eyes narrowed.

"Did you get caught in the rain?"

Dale glanced down at his still soggy clothes. They

had been almost soaked and the drive hadn't dried them. His denim shirt in particular felt clammy on his shoulders.

"Yeah. I got caught off-guard."

Dwight nodded then that pensive look reappeared in his eyes.

"Why are you here?" Dale asked. "Why was Greeley here?"

"Something strange happened this morning. Or last night."

"Like what?"

"Well, this morning they found Harley Dee Grubbs dead."

For some odd reason, the news didn't stun Dale. "Where?"

"In the head house of the co-op's grain elevator."

"What was doing there?"

"No one seems to know."

"How did he die?"

"He fell on a grain auger."

"What's a grain auger?"

"It's an aluminum tube that is used to suck up grain."

"You said he fell on it. How did he do that?"

"It seems that he fell from a high platform in the head house." Since Dale looked confused Dwight said the head house was the office and storage building connected to the actual grain elevators.

"Dwight, I don't get this. What was Grubbs doing standing on a platform up high in the head house? How did he fall? And is that the reason he didn't show for the press run last night?"

"That's why he didn't show. It's strange thinking that before the press run last night he might have already been dead. As for why, well, it seems that we officially will never know."

"Aren't the authorities investigating what happened?"

"They've already finished the investigation. If you can call it that."

"And what happened?"

"Look, Dale, I only found out about it all this evening. I got a call from a friend of mine who works at the grain elevator. He found him. Grubbs I mean. He walked into the head house this morning and found Grubbs stuck on the grain auger. I mean, Grubbs had been impaled by it. Went clean through him."

"Good grief. What a terrible way to die."

"So my friend called the sheriff and he and the coroner and an ambulance arrived. Then Greeley arrived. My friend was sitting outside but he heard their discussion. Seems that Grubbs went into the head house with a hunting rifle. He cut a hole in the vent near the top of the head house. Somehow he fell and landed on the grain auger."

"Did Grubbs break in?"

"Nope. Grover Grubbs, the co-op president, said he gave the key to his son. He said another odd thing. According to my source, when Grubbs saw his son he hardly reacted. He simply said he hadn't seen anyone that messed up since D-Day."

Dale in his one encounter with Grover Grubbs could believe he could be so cold-blooded.

"So, all this happened last night? Harley Dee at the

grain co-op with a hunting rifle." Dale paused, his mind arriving at a conclusion that astonished him. "I can't believe it. That crazy Grubbs was trying to –"

"We don't know that, Dale. Don't jump to conclusions."

"It's obvious, Dwight. Why else would Grubbs have a rifle with him? Didn't you say that the vent had a hole cut in it? A gap big enough to stick a rifle's barrel through, I bet."

Dwight said nothing.

"It's hard to believe. But since it's Grubbs somehow it makes sense." Dale thought about Greeley's departure. "And why was Greeley here talking to you?"

"After my friend called me, I called Greeley. He asked me to meet him here."

"Was it to plan tomorrow's story? What an amazing story it is! The man who tried to kill the President is himself killed."

"That's not the reason. In fact, there isn't going to be story. At least not that one."

"What do you mean, Dwight? It's a big story. A national story."

"The whole thing was an accident according to Greeley, the sheriff, and the coroner."

"That's ridiculous. I mean, Grubbs' death might be an accident, but what about what he was trying to do!"

"We don't know what he was trying to do."

"Of course we do. He had a rifle. He carved out a hole in the vent. Can't the coroner determine the time of Grubbs' death? I bet it's around 7 p.m."

"We don't have any facts to support that interpretation. We don't have any proof."

Dale took a step back to study Dwight. When he'd come into the newspaper office, Dwight was obviously bothered by something. It couldn't have been just Grubbs' untimely demise.

"So Greeley is going to kill the story."

Dwight shrugged.

"You don't agree with that, do you? I mean, Dwight, this is a big story. Maybe the most important story to ever come out of Buffalo City."

"I'm just the managing editor. Greeley decides such things. And I don't know; maybe he's right. What good will it do? Give us as reputation like it did Dallas? Publishing a story about a local would-be assassin would create a scandal."

"The scandal is not reporting the truth."

"We don't know the truth. Grubbs can't tell us why he was there or what he intended to do. Okay, so it looks suspicious. But unless the town leaders allow a thorough investigation then it remains just speculation."

Dale suddenly felt cold. His clammy clothes unpleasantly stuck to him. But he felt even worse inside. His felt that empty feeling in his belly. The feeling that things were going bad and he couldn't do anything about it.

"We're supposed to be a newspaper. We're supposed to print the news."

Dwight leaned back in his chair with a solemn expression. "Maybe there are some things you just can't print in the newspaper."

Chapter Eight
Monday

Aafter making his deadline, Dale went into the back shop and talked to Percy Pollack. Percy had heard about Harley Dee Grubbs' accidental death and he couldn't believe it. He said Harley Dee had been acting strange the whole week, more obnoxious than usual, but he'd chalked it up to personal problems with his family. Harley Dee didn't get along with his dad.

It was obvious that Percy had heard just the sanitized version of Grubbs' death: That Grubbs had experienced a strange and unfortunate accident at the grain elevator. The reason for Grubbs being there in the first place was never fully explained but the fact that his father was co-op president made it less suspicious.

"But I still can't figure out what Harley Dee was doin' in the grain elevator in the first place," Percy said. "He didn't want to go to supper with me. What was so important over there?"

Dale considered telling Percy a few more details but he decided not to. Why be a gossip-monger? Besides Percy would probably hear about it from other people. Right now the leaders in Buffalo City were suppressing the unsavory details pretty well but this was a small town. People would talk. Rumors would spread. But nothing official would happen and eventually the story would fade into a legend.

"I see you got another assistant already," Dale said, nodding his head at a tall, gangly kid who didn't look older than eighteen.

"Yeah. That's Bobby Joe Crenshaw. Greeley recruited him yesterday. He studied auto mechanics at the community college. But he's catching on pretty fast."

Dale nodded. He hoped Bobby Joe had better luck than the two previous departed assistant pressmen.

Dale said so long to Percy and was walking back to his desk when Dwight said Greeley wanted to see him. Dale studied Dwight's expression but it was a neutral one. Even his droopy mustache didn't rise or fall.

Dale walked over to the publisher's office door and knocked. Greeley said come in. Greeley sat behind his big oak desk without his suit jacket, showing his red suspenders. He'd also rolled up the sleeves of his white dress shirt. He always did that when he was in the newspaper office. A sign that he was hard at work. Greeley asked Dale to take a seat and he did.

"Greetings, Dale. How are we faring this afternoon?" Greeley said in his usual ebullient voice.

"I'm doing fine. Of course, I feel a little strange hearing about what happened yesterday."

"Oh, yes, that unfortunate accident."

Dale restrained an urge to shout "cover-up!" Instead, he remained silent but he didn't nod his head or show any sign of agreement either.

Greeley's corpulent body squirmed a little in his leather chair. He cleared his throat.

"I wanted to see you, Dale, to offer an assessment of your performance these past few days. First –"

"Why did you censor my copy?"

That word obviously offended Greeley. He leaned back as if the offensive word had struck a blow. His flabby face registered a momentary shock then it relaxed.

"As publisher and editor of the *Buffalo City Stampede* I obviously have the authority to excise offensive passages."

"What was offensive about those two paragraphs? They simply presented an opposing point of view. I thought we were supposed to present two sides to a story."

"Ordinarily yes. But we also have the duty to exercise good judgment, discretion even. Allowing critical comments and personal insults to appear in the newspaper during a historical presidential visit would not be journalistically responsible."

"What personal insults?"

"One quote contained the pejorative term, 'peanut farmer.'"

"How is that an insult? I mean Carter really is, or was, a peanut farmer."

"Yes, but the factual nature of the statement was biased by who the speaker was. It's common knowledge that Grover Grubbs is one of those radical AAM members and a virulent opponent of the President."

"Isn't that the very reason why we should have included his quote? To provide a little journalistic balance?"

Greeley held up a pudgy paw as if trying to deflect these arguments. "I understand your youthful exuberance. I also understand that covering hard news is something novel for you. I intend this meeting not as a reproach but as an opportunity to divulge some helpful advice."

Dale shook his head at Greeley's bombinating ways. How could he argue with a man who spoke so pompously?

"In fact, aside from those two questionable paragraphs your Sunday story was a competent piece of journalism. What's more, I wanted to commend you for your sports coverage and writing these last few weeks. I think you have consistently improved in your skills. In fact, I mentioned your Sunday sports column to the President upon the completion of the men's Sunday school class. Since he was probably too busy to read it, I briefly explained the column and congratulated him on his top ranking for Opening Day pitches. The President was so gratified that it rendered him speechless."

Dale almost burst out laughing. Instead he lowered his head as if overcome with modesty.

"So, to sum up, Dale, even though you demonstrated some questionable judgment in writing that news story, you've done yeoman work in regard to your sports duties. Also, I very much appreciate how you pitched in during a time of crisis to help with the production of the Sunday paper. Without your able efforts we would have been embarrassingly late on a monumental day in the history of the *Buffalo City Stampede*. So, as a token of my approbation, I have decided to raise your pay twenty dollars a week."

Greeley leaned back in his chair with a magnanimous smile on his face.

"Thanks, Mr. Greeley." What else could he say?

"And I think that you can look forward to additional

remunerative rewards as you continue to develop here as our sports editor."

Greeley, satisfied with his display of generosity and sage advice, stood up and waddled around his desk and offered his hand to Dale.

Dale thought for a moment about not shaking it. He could tell Greeley to take his job and shove it. But he needed his job, at least for a few more months. Quitting wouldn't change anything. He might feel a little noble for his principled stand but in the end it wouldn't have any practical effect. Last night, Dale had even considered writing a letter to the *New York Times* or the *Washington Post* to inform them of the shocking cover-up of a potential assassination until he realized that whoever read the story, maybe the ombudsman, would dismiss it as either a prank or a sign of mental illness.

But as Dale took Greeley's hand and shook it hard enough that the editor and publisher and mayor winced just a little, he resolved never to be a journalist like Greeley. He'd emulate William F. Whitaker instead.

As Dale walked back to his desk, Dwight said someone had left him a letter. It was on his desk.

"Who was it?"

"Some young lady."

Dale stared at Dwight. Unlike the previous time this had happened, Dwight revealed a small grin.

Dale said thanks and strode over to his desk, feeling an uneasy foreboding. A young lady? Dale doubted Dwight would use that description about Louise. But who else would leave a letter for him?

When he saw the note lying on his desk he knew for certain it wasn't from Louise. The letter was contained in a small, light blue envelope. He sat down, opened the letter, and read:

Dale,

I'm sorry about my behavior last night. I shouldn't have put you in such an awkward position. I suppose spending the day and evening with you affected me in ways I hadn't anticipated. I've decided to leave for my parents' cabin this afternoon. I won't be available this entire week. I think that's for the best. We probably should spend time apart from each other to think the situation through. Actually, I think we both know that we want different things and I don't see how we can reach common ground.

I'm not sure when I will write again.
Sincerely,
Helen

Dale dropped the baby blue note on his desk. She had attractive handwriting. He liked how her script gracefully flowed.

Well, he thought, looks like I've lost a friend.

He reflected on how difficult it was to find someone with all the requirements you want. It was difficult enough for ordinary people, but if you had additional demands then it was especially arduous. For example, he wanted someone who would have similar interests and habits. He couldn't get involved with a woman who smoked and drank or did drugs. He just didn't like those personal habits. She'd have to have some intelligence. Otherwise what would they talk about besides mundane topics that he found boring. He'd like for her to have a sweet personality. A feminine personality. Sympathetic and empathetic but not in a cloying or artificial way. She had to be physically attractive to him. Not necessarily a beauty (that was rare), perhaps not even pretty, but at least appealing to him. She had to inspire him to want to touch her, to make love to her. He didn't desire skinny women or really fat women. She had to practice good hygiene. He just threw that in because he knew his thoughts were sort of silly. But the point was that it was difficult to find someone that fit all of one's requirements. He thought it was even more difficult for him because of his personal habits and his intelligence. Not that he shared Byron Mors' philosophy. He didn't think he was superior or a person deserving special treatment. But he knew he was more intellectual than most people and he wanted a woman who wasn't too far below him (but not above). Helen met most of his requirements but not the physical one. She had a good personality, too. Good character. Was it so important that she be physically attractive to him? In ten years maybe not. But now, yes, it was important to him.

Finding a woman who met all his requirements would be difficult; finding one who also found him appealing further reduced the odds; and then meeting each other at the right time resulted in yet another lowering of the odds. It was a daunting prospect. Maybe he'd never find her.

Then he thought of his ex-girlfriend. She'd almost met all his requirements. She had intelligence although she wasn't an intellectual. Because of her religious views she closed her mind off to certain ideas and concepts. He could have accepted that but her devotion to her religion created further problems. She wanted him to become as devout of a Nazarene as she was. But he couldn't do that; if he tried he would turn into a hypocrite. Also, the timing wasn't right. He didn't really want to settle down at age twenty-one. But the problem had been solved when she broke up with him. Sometimes he wished he had conformed to her expectations. He could have become like her father, a successful businessman and Nazarene elder. But he couldn't imagine himself being happy doing that. Even his love for her wouldn't have been enough.

He decided to stop torturing himself about that. It was over.

Dale stared at the paperwork on his desk when he saw the print he'd promised to send to Louise. Oh, yes, his other "girlfriend." Or in her case, "girl*fiend*." He smiled to himself; she wasn't that bad. But an absurd thought appeared in his mind. If only he could combine the best qualities of both Louise and Helen then he'd have almost what we wanted. Too bad he wasn't a mad scientist.

Dale looked at the photo. It showed Louise in her vampish pose with her two less demonstrative friends. Dale studied Louise's zaftig figure. Best not to dwell too much on that.

He got a Manila envelope from his desk drawer and addressed it. He still remembered her address. He protected the print with two thin sheets of cardboard and put it inside the mailer. He sealed the envelope and walked over to Rosemary's desk where the mail bin was located and dropped it in. As he walked away, he realized that he hadn't written Louise a note.

-II-

Close to dinnertime at the Greeley household. Millard sat in his black leather Barcalounger watching the network news. The lead story was President Carter's historic peace agreement between Israel and Egypt. Greeley gazed with rapt attention as the television reporter, with the White House as a backdrop, intoned that this agreement might well lead to perpetual peace in the Middle East.

Carol entered the living room, wearing an apron over her attractive blue dress, and stood beside her husband.

"Amazing to think that just yesterday our President was here in Buffalo City," said Greeley. "Now he's back in our nation's capitol successfully negotiating for world peace."

"It's not quite world peace, dear."

"It's the first step, I believe. A magnificent achievement. This may well assure him of winning the Nobel Peace Prize. His re-election, needless to say, is an almost certainty."

"You've always told me that nothing is certain in politics. The political climate can change dramatically within the space of a few weeks."

"Yes, ordinarily that is the case. The fickle nature of the electorate. A chaotic world where Fortuna tips the scales at the last moment. But in this instance, I am

343

convinced that our President is guaranteed not only re-election but a victorious landslide in the nature of FDR, LBJ –"

"Richard Nixon?"

Greeley gave his wife a disapproving glance. "Really, Carol, to compare this ethically immaculate man to that scoundrel!"

"Didn't you vote for him in 1972?"

When did he reveal that shameful secret to her? He must have but he doesn't recall when. Perhaps after passionate conjugal relations when his mind wasn't as ordinarily sharp as a sabre.

"I need to check on the roast, dear. I'll pop back in a minute."

Greeley merely nodded just to suggest to his wife that he remained a little piqued over her display of wit with him as a target. He heard the tap tap of her footsteps as she left the room but the sweet aroma of her perfume remained. Or was that the roast?

Greeley leaned back into his chair with a serene sense of personal satisfaction. He'd done it. He'd organized the greatest political event in Buffalo City's history. His ill premonitions were unfounded. Well, not entirely unfounded. There was that nasty episode with that young Grubbs. As soon as he thought of his name, a horrific image of the impaled Grubbs leapt into his mind. Greeley frowned and forced it out with the exertion of his considerable will. He'd not told Carol the hideous truth behind Grubbs' demise. The *Stampede* had simply printed a terse newspaper account of the strange and unfortunate death of one of its employees and the son of a prominent Buffalonian. The basic details were present in the story but no elaboration. The article stated that Grubbs had died *Sunday* morning, a necessary inaccuracy to protect the good name of Buffalo City. No irresponsible speculation as to why Grubbs had perished in the grain elevator. No mention of his gaping wound or the rifle found in the sniper's nest, or rather, the upper corner of the head house. Greeley smiled a pleased smile, approving of his own self-censorship. In another year or two, he'd actually believe that the accident was as inconsequential as the official version pronounced.

Everybody concerned had agreed it was best for the town of Buffalo City to edit the facts just a little. Leaving out certain information wasn't unethical. It was showing prudence. Sheriff Johnson, Dr. Petersen, the two ambulance attendants, and the deputy, had agreed with him that an official version labeling Grubbs' death as an accident should be advanced. Even Harley Dee's father, Grover Grubbs, had surprisingly agreed. He didn't want any vile rumors about his family to be spread. Perhaps Greeley shouldn't have been surprised by the older man's good sense. After all, Grover was a patriot. A combat veteran and survivor of Normandy Beach in fact. It was truly unfortunate that the man lost his youngest son. Indeed, rather ironic because it appeared that the grain auger had been mistakenly been left in a dangerous position (shaft upwards) by the older Grubbs son, Doug. The only other potential problem was with the co-op employee who had found Grubbs and then later blabbed to Dwight Willard. Well, that problem had been taken care of. Pete McKenzie had been dismissed or rather told to take a long leave of absence for his own mental health. Grover Grubbs had seen the young man off via bus this morning. McKenzie had been given enough money to have a good time in Las Vegas where perhaps he could forget his discovery of the dreadful accident.

Perhaps Grover Grubbs wasn't such a bad fellow after all. If he could dispense with his involvement in the AAM, then perhaps Greeley could forge an alliance with him. Why should farmers be Republican anyway? Our President was a farmer and a Democrat. Of course, he grew up in the Deep South. Western farmers tend to be Republican. But maybe Greeley could lead a revolution that would convince the Southwestern farmer and rancher that joining the Democratic party would be in their best interest, not to mention the country's. Maybe Grubbs would assist in that project. After all, what was that rather risqué saying: politics makes for strange bedfellows?

Of course, there was one minor problem from preventing the Greeley plan from achieving perfection. He had to depend on Byron Mors. Greeley detested depending on anyone as Machiavellian as Byron. But if Byron leaked word about the specific nature of Grubbs' wound or voiced suspicion about the actual time of death then Greeley would advance the notion that Byron was an unprincipled undertaker who told all kinds of people intimate details of his ... not clients. Perhaps work materials. At any rate, Greeley and the other conspira – town leaders – would exert the necessary pressure for Byron to toe the line.

Yes, everything had turned out quite satisfactorily. Greeley had been up to snuff. He'd met the challenge.

He'd shown them all that he was a man of vision and leadership. He imagined his re-election was as guaranteed as the President's. Greeley recalled how he and the President had a delightful chat during his visit to the First Baptist Church. Greeley didn't want to ask any favors from the Great Man in that setting. A church should be reserved for questions of the spirit.

But Greeley did manage to buttonhole the President's chief of staff. He pointed out in a subtle manner that none other than Greeley had engineered the success of the visit, the well-oiled machine-like regularity of the whole enterprise. Greeley had masterminded the President's visit like a chess-master executing a perfect match. (Greeley had once tried to competitively play chess while in college and the results were dismal. In fact, his poor play had inspired another unpleasant nickname from his frat mates, the ironic moniker of Boris.) Then he suggested to the chief of staff – no nothing that direct – he *intimated* that Greeley would seriously consider a position of some importance in the next administration if the President and his wise advisers saw fit to reward the mayor in some tangible way.

Nothing too exalted. Perhaps a cabinet position. Agricultural Secretary? Greeley knew virtually nothing about farming or the attendant issues. Transportation? That position usually went to an urbanite. Attorney General? Greeley, alas, lacked a law degree. Health and human resources? No, too medical and specialized. Education? He'd never taught or been an administrator. That was the trouble with cabinet positions; they generally required experience in a particular field.

Perhaps he could join the team as an assistant in political strategy? He wasn't a pollster but he did possess an impressive political acumen, and dare he say it, intuition. How about a general political advisor? Or perhaps Greeley could work as a speech-writer. After all, the President had been impressed with his editorial. He said as much before the men's Sunday school class began. He said he had never read an editorial quite like it.

He noticed Carol strolling into the room.

"The news is over dear. And dinner is almost ready."

Greeley picked up the remote control and extinguished the television. The game show *Jeopardy* was on. He'd never done well playing trivia games.

"Carol, how would you like to move to Washington, D.C.?"

"Now, dear?"

"Of course not now. I mean in the future. Perhaps the near future."

"Where did you get that notion, Millard?"

"Just thinking."

"I'm very happy here in Buffalo City."

"But you would consider it? That is, if the opportunity presented itself?"

"What opportunity, Millard?"

"It's just a hypothetical, sweetheart. You would consider it if it advanced my career?"

"Yes, Millard I would consider it if it advanced your career. Now, it's time for dinner."

"Check," said Dale.

Byron Mors examined the remaining chess pieces then raised one brow. "It's your game in two more moves."

After Dale won, Byron went to over to an attractive serving table and poured wine into a crystal glass. "You sure you won't have any?"

"I have no taste for wine or any other alcohol."

"That's a pity. Maybe you should try and develop a taste for it."

"I've been told that before. But I don't want to."

"I suppose you would like your customary 7-Up." Byron said the brand name with a slight degree of disgust. He handed the glass with the soft drink to Dale. "You're getting to be a fair chess player. The first time you won I wasn't on my guard. But tonight I treated you like a genuine opponent."

"I think your mind wasn't completely on the match. You made a couple of uncharacteristic mistakes."

Byron reclined in his seat and nodded. "I have been having some trouble concentrating on certain matters of late."

"What matters?"

"Exactly. What matters?"

"Getting philosophical again."

"You're right. Shouldn't think of that stuff. But I noticed that you seem pensive tonight as well."

Dale told Byron about Greeley censoring his copy on Sunday's story. He didn't mention the worse transgression of not fully reporting on the true circumstances of Harley Dee Grubbs' death.

"You should know by now that Millard Greeley is a completely conventional man," Byron said. "Conventional in his politics, his journalism, his entire life."

"Is that bad?"

"No, just boring."

"Yeah, I guess you're right. But I was still bothered by what he did."

"Of course. But you shouldn't have too high of expectations for journalism. It's a grubby trade. It doesn't require much insight or talent."

Dale wasn't so sure about that. He thought Will had insight and talent and he might become a career journalist. But he didn't say anything.

"You ought to aspire to something higher than being a 'mere scribbler of words'."

"I'd like to someday. But for now all I can do is merely scribble words. And I have an editor who is taking away some of those words."

"You're still young. Still serving as an apprentice. But don't get to comfortable in that role."

"I'm not. In fact, I'm thinking about going to graduate school."

"Excellent idea. I once had those ambitions."

"Do you wish you had gone to graduate school?"

"Sometimes I do. I suppose as we get older we all imagine what we could be doing differently. I think about being a college teacher. A professor. Helping form young, inquisitive minds like yours."

"You'd be good at that."

Yes, I think I would be. But I have already told you about my existential crisis."

"Yeah. But I am curious about something else."

"Yes?"

"I don't mean to pry, but I was wondering what happened between you and Carol. Carol Quigley."

Byron's blue eyes narrowed. "Where did you hear about that? Not from Greeley."

"No. At the Miss Buffalo City Pageant I was looking at you when you went over that group of people that included the Greeleys. You spoke to everyone except Carol. And I got the impression that she was avoiding you. Later, I asked a friend of mine if she knew anything about you two. She didn't know much but she said you two used to be a serious couple."

"You're quite the reporter after all. Very observant."

"You don't have to talk about it if you don't want to. I was just curious."

Byron walked over to the table with the wine and poured another glass. He took a drink then returned to his seat.

"Your information is correct. Carol and I were involved for a while."

"During college. In your junior year and her freshman year."

"That's right."

"Was she part of your existential crisis, too?"

"I wouldn't have admitted it at the time. But as I reflected upon it, I suppose she played a role."

"How?"

Byron took another drink of wine then held the glass up and considered its contents. "You ought to learn to appreciate wine. It has many excellent properties. One being it relaxes you, makes you mellow. Of course, too much and it can lower your self-defenses. Makes you too uninhibited."

He drained the small pool of wine that remained. He looked at Dale in a thoughtful way. "Very well, I'll try and explain it concisely. We started dating at the beginning of my junior year. She fell in love with me. Actually, I think she had been in love with me for some time, probably back to when she was in junior high school. I wasn't in love with her, exactly. At least I didn't think so. At OU we grew more intimate as the year progressed. I also began to think too recklessly about what I was reading. And as Dylan sang, the times were a-changing. All that made a profound effect on me. As we became more intimate, I became afraid that I might fall in love with her. I thought she would deter me in my pursuit of living a free, unencumbered life. I wanted to be fully involved in the Zeitgeist. I wanted to fulfill my potential in every area of life. But I eventually realized that I didn't have the talent or the ability to achieve my lofty goals. Instead of accepting my mediocrity, I blamed life. I preferred to think it was meaningless and absurd. I grew depressed. I thought Carol's love could banish those nihilistic thoughts. When I began to feel love for her my depression lifted. I knew she wanted us to be a committed couple. But I wasn't ready for that. So, I fled. I went to San Francisco and became a flower child. I tried to forget about Carol. When I came home after my brother's death, I thought I might get back with her. Now, I was ready. But she began dating Millard Greeley. Ridiculous! I knew she did it just to spite me. I went back to OU and got the practical degree I needed to take over the family business.

I returned to Buffalo City and she did the unthinkable: she married Greeley. Thus the irony: In the end we both returned to Buffalo City as she had wanted but we were not together. We never would be."

"Why do you think Carol married Greeley?"

"I told you. To punish me."

"That was her only reason?"

"Of course there were other reasons. But that's the primary one. And it worked. She did punish me."

Byron stood up and walked over to the desk with the wine but he didn't pour another drink. Instead he put the empty glass on the silver tray.

"I think that's enough talk. Unless you want to confess something to me."

Dale considered telling Byron about Louise and Helen. But he didn't want to. Especially not Helen. If he told Byron about Louise he was sure Byron would laugh heartily at his reluctance to experience the wild side of life.

"No, I have nothing to confess."

Byron smiled ironically. "We all have something to confess. Or at least we should. Sometimes I think life is composed of three realities: the tragic, the absurd, and the boring. And most of it is boring."

"There are good things in life, too."

"And speaking of one of those pleasures, are you in the mood for some visual stimulation?"

Dale knew he would get around to that. Actually, he was hoping he would. Even though he thought it was wrong, he had been looking forward to it all day at work. Maybe just to divert himself from things that were bothering him.

"Okay."

Dale followed Byron out of his study down the hall and as they had last week they passed the Viewing Room. For some inexplicable reason, when Dale saw the coffin he slowed down. Almost against his will, he was drawn to it.

Byron came over. "That's our new guest. Arrived yesterday. Mr. Horus had to employ all the tricks of the trade to make him presentable."

Dale walked toward the black casket. His perspective broadened and he saw a young man lying in the crimson satin folds. To his amazement and shock he recognized Harley Dee Grubbs.

Dale took one step closer. He gazed at the strange waxen face. Grubbs had been spruced up. His hair cut and neatly combed. Even his wispy beard shaved off. His completely clean-shaven face had been oiled so much that it practically shined. His eyes were thankfully closed shut so Dale didn't have to look at those odd yellowish eyes in a state of death. But the one characteristic that truly appalled Dale, almost to the point of horror, was the strange, unnatural grin that had been forced upon Grubbs' artificially pink lips. It was an obscene parody of a smile.

"Good grief," Dale muttered.

He felt Byron standing near him, looking over his shoulder. "Yes, I know. Not one of Miss Henderson's better efforts."

Dale turned away in disgust.

Byron seeing Dale's reaction made the connection. "I suppose I should have realized that you knew him."

Dale glanced one more time at the deceased Grubbs.

"Yeah I knew him. But I didn't like him."

They left the viewing room and walked toward the circular staircase that led to the private residence upstairs. Dale, still stunned by the sight of the late Harley Dee Grubbs, felt like he was in the middle of a dream. Everything seemed real but surreally so.

They approached the stairs and Byron began to ascend, but Dale remained below. The idea of going upstairs and watching X-rated movies filled him with disgust bordering on despair. The reproductions of naked bodies engaged in obscene rituals seemed even more corrupt with the corpse of Grubbs displayed below. The whole experience was too weird, too lewd, too pernicious for Dale to accept.

Byron paused on the steps. "Aren't you coming?"

"I don't think so."

"Are you disturbed by seeing your friend in that condition?"

"He wasn't my friend. But yes, I'm disturbed."

"You shouldn't be. He's just an example of the natural phenomena of life and death. Here death is downstairs and life is upstairs."

"Is it really life?"

"People making love is about as alive as you can get."

"But they're not making love."

"All right. Fucking then."

"That's not enough."

"There can be more."

Dale looked at Byron. He was deliberately misinterpreting what he meant.

Byron took one step down. "You're disturbed by

what you've seen. I can understand that. When you feel that way you need an escape. Watching those movies is just an escape from the tragedy and absurdity and boredom that fills our lives. You shouldn't feel any moral prohibition about it. There isn't right or wrong. Not for people like us. We have curious minds. But we think too much. Sometimes we need a respite from all that thinking. We need to enter into the world of the senses."

"I don't know."

"Maybe the problem is that you need to get rid of the frustration that watching such films creates. If you want, you can relieve that tension."

Dale took one step back.

"If you want to fully enjoy the experience you really have to do that. There's nothing wrong with it. It's better than repressing your desires. I won't do anything. I'll just watch."

That's all it took. Dale turned and started walking. He heard Byron call his name. He started running, slowly at first. He passed the Viewing Room and began to sprint. He threw open the door that led outside. He continued to run all the way to his car.

Early next morning before work, Dale dropped a letter into the mail accepting the offer to attend graduate school at Wyoming. He planned to remain in Buffalo City for two more months before leaving. He thought he could do it. Maybe he'd even make a new friend.